WITHDRAWN

MUSIC CITY DREAMERS

What Reviewers Say About Robyn Nyx's Work

Never Enough

"Nyx's debut is a grim but entertaining thriller that makes up for some truly grisly moments of violence with two well-realized heroines. …But readers who can handle the gory content will find it well balanced by plenty of romance and copious amounts of sex, as well as a solid cast of supporting characters and some insightful handling of contemporary social issues."—*Publishers Weekly*

Escape in Time

"As an opening to the Extractor Trilogy, *Escape In Time* is the perfect introduction as it introduces main characters Landry and Delaney who have a complicated friendship, lifestyles and job. The perfect mix of sci-fi and history, the story is fascinating and will make you think!"—*LesBiReviewed*

Change in Time

"I didn't think it was possible to top the first in the Extractor Series by Robyn Nyx but I was wrong. *Change in Time* is exciting, tense, romantic and sexy."—*Kitty Kat's Book Review Blog*

Death in Time

"A seriously impressive end to this amazing trilogy! …The mission is full-on action that never lets up."—*Kitty Kat's Book Review Blog*

Visit us at www.boldstrokesbooks.com

By the Author

The Extractor Trilogy

Escape in Time

Change in Time

Death in Time

Never Enough

Music City Dreamers

MUSIC CITY DREAMERS

by

Robyn Nyx

2019

MUSIC CITY DREAMERS

ISBN 13: 978-1-63555-207-2

This Trade Paperback Original Is Published By
Bold Strokes Books, Inc.
P.O. Box 249
Valley Falls, NY 12185

First Edition: January 2019

CREDITS
Editor: Cindy Cresap
Production Design: Susan Ramundo
Cover Design By Robyn Nyx

Acknowledgments

My thanks, as always, go to Rad and Sandy for keeping Bold Strokes Books the best publisher in the world for lesfic authors. You keep the bar high, and I'm really proud to be part of your company.

This story began with the introduction of Louie in *Change in Time*. She demanded her own book, and this is it (without Landry's money because that just wouldn't make sense to anyone who *hadn't* read the Extractor trilogy). So, a heartfelt thanks to my editor, Cindy, for showing me the ropes of contemporary romance without resorting to strangling me with them.

Thanks to my parents for reading my books. I love that you enjoy them so much. Your support when I was a kid made this dream of being an author a possibility.

And thank you to my wonderful wife, Brey, who boots me up the ass every day to keep me writing.

Dedication

For my beautiful lady, Brey.
You're my fluffy romance novel personified.

Chapter One

Aaron Collins had been the vice-president of Rocky Top's A&R department for over ten years and was credited with saving the label from bankruptcy as the record industry floundered in the face of the digital revolution. Collins pioneered the music streaming business model, and shares in Rocky Top have continued to rise exponentially since.

Rocky Top president Donny Taylor refused to comment, but inside sources say Collins was fired because of his sexuality. Nashville hasn't had a scandal like this since Caren Wright came out as a—"

Louie Francis hit the mute button. She didn't want to hear about the homophobia on the Nashville music scene, especially since she'd finally scraped enough money together to pursue her own country dream. She pulled out her phone and checked her savings account. A little under five thousand dollars. It wasn't much to show for a year at the WoodBack Bar, doing unsavory things for even more unsavory people. But it was more than she'd ever have been able to save by working at the GrindStar coffee shop alone, like she had been doing when she and Mia were saving for their future together. *Damn you, Mia.* An image of the perfectly poised beauty Louie used to call her sweetheart forced its way, unannounced and unwanted, into her mind. It was closely followed by the memory of Louie finding their apartment and shared account cleaned out.

Louie looked at her watch: eleven a.m. She poured herself a quick shot of cheap bourbon anyway. After the solid burn made its way along her throat, the warm sensation snaked through her veins and tranquilized her thumping heart. It was time to stop making excuses and just go for it, time to get out of this place and get her life back on track.

Mia made another unsolicited showing in her mind, and Louie rubbed her forehead, trying to erase it. Had Mia made it to Music City? She was a talented woman. Louie had no doubt that if she *had* made it to Nashville, Mia would be doing just fine. But now it was Louie's time.

Louie smiled at her GrindStar manager and slipped past him to retrieve a small selection of her belongings from a temporary locker. His name was Deighton, or Dean, or something beginning with a D, but Louie couldn't bring it to mind. And it didn't help that he wouldn't wear a badge. She supposed he thought it was some sort of power play to remind the baristas who was in charge, but Louie believed it was to prevent the customers from complaining directly to him because they had no idea he worked there. GrindStar baristas across the nation had to present in a sharp pink polo shirt and navy chinos. His uniform was ill-fitting trousers that were way too long for his short stature and way too tight for his keg-sized beer belly, and he wore a button-down shirt that threatened to pop open and blind someone with projectile buttons.

"What are you doing, Francis? You're already ten minutes late for your shift."

Her smile broadened as she realized this was the last time she'd have to put up with his droning voice. "I'm not working my shift, this one or any other. It's time for me to leave this wonderful establishment."

Keg-belly's face reddened, and the vein in the middle of his forehead seemed to double in size.

"Get your coat off and get on the shop floor. Now."

Louie dropped her wallet and other possessions into the same beat-up leather satchel she'd had since high school and shook her head. "Sorry, boss. I'm out of here." She unpinned her name badge from her shirt and tossed it to him. She hated name badges; there was never a good place to position them that didn't give permission to pervy guys to stare at women's breasts. Not that that had ever been a problem for her. Unless it counted when guys were rude enough to ask where the hell her breasts were.

He fumbled the catch and yelled after her, "If you step out of that door, you'll never work in another GrindStar in this country."

"Let's hope not." Louie offered a wave as she opened the door and headed to the bank to withdraw enough money to buy a truck. It would be her transport *and* her home if necessary. But she couldn't spend a minute longer being tainted by this city. Failure be damned, she was taking one step closer to her dream.

CHAPTER TWO

Heather King raked her fingers through her hair in an attempt to finger-comb it into some semblance of acceptability. It needed a wash, but she'd been so desperate for the extra hour in bed after watching new talent at the Bluebird until two a.m. that she'd sprayed on some dry shampoo and hoped for the best. Mistake. Her boss, Donny, was meeting with the current Queen of Country, and he'd sprung it on her that Savana wanted Heather present. How Savana Hayes even knew Heather existed was beyond her comprehension, but the looming meeting had made her so paranoid about the state of her long hair that cutting it all off had crossed her mind. At least then it wouldn't take two hours to wash, dry, and straighten.

"You're the new A&R VP. I guess that's why she wants you there. You make damn sure you say all the right things, girl. And if it's just so she can look at your pretty face while we negotiate her contract, keep that sparkling smile plastered on it."

Donny's barked instruction knotted her insides tighter than they already were. His utter oafishness and lack of interpersonal skills were a particularly unfavorable concoction. She'd hoped that her new promotion might mean that he'd show her more respect, but it seemed his sexism was only suspended in the presence of the owner of Rocky Top, Lexi Turner. *This* hadn't been her dream when the hiss of the Greyhound bus doors opening announced her arrival in Nashville. She was supposed to *be* the next Savana Hayes, not sit around being her eye candy. Though that was a stupid thing for Donny to say. Savana wasn't interested in women. And even if she was, Heather was sure he wouldn't know it. After the way the country community abandoned Caren White when she came out a few years before, no one seemed in a big hurry to follow in her rhinestone-adorned footsteps.

Her thoughts drifted inevitably to her mentor, Aaron, and his recent dismissal from the company. He'd brought her into Rocky Top. He'd been her mentor for over five years, and he was the reason she was the new A&R veep. Heather didn't want to believe that Donny had only promoted her to Aaron's position to bolster his heterosexuality because he felt threatened by Aaron's sexuality, but she couldn't help it. And Aaron had always challenged Donny's lascivious comments to female staff. With Aaron out of the picture, he could be as much of a bigoted boar as he wanted to be, and what better way to prove his masculinity than lord his power over a new female vice-president?

Heather took a deep breath and followed Donny to the glass-walled boardroom to wait for Savana's arrival. The thirty-foot-long table was covered with a vast array of fresh fruit and around fifty chilled individual small bottles of water. Savana's management team had been very specific about her requirements for the meeting, including the condition that it could be no longer than seventy-five minutes in duration. If negotiations were to go on longer than that, the meeting would have to be adjourned for two and a half hours before Savana would return. Heather wondered what kind of country superstar she would've made if she hadn't given up on her dream. She was sure she wouldn't be that kind of diva.

Donny positioned himself at the head of the table, and Heather waited until he indicated where he wanted her. She sat to his left and smoothed her skirt over her knees. Though she preferred skirts generally, when she started at Rocky Top, the lecherous looks from male colleagues forced her to opt for trouser suits. And Aaron was fine with that. But after firing Aaron and promoting Heather, Donny had sent her home to change so she looked "like a woman," which he underlined by telling her that meant she should always wear a skirt to work. It wasn't like her suits were masculine in any way, and neither was Heather. Irony was she loved wearing skirts, but his demands were like reverse psychology and made her hate wearing skirts to work.

"Would you like your usual?"

The soft voice of Donny's assistant, Mandie, was a pleasant contrast to the sound of Donny on his phone. "Sure, that'd be great." Heather smiled and Mandie turned to make her a milky white drink that barely passed as coffee.

"Anything good at the gig last night?" Donny asked after tossing his cell phone onto the table with a muttered curse.

Heather shook her head. "Maybe. I made a recording of one guy I'd like you to listen to." She closed her eyes briefly and the deep, smooth sound of the artist filled her ears. He was an amazing singer and played the guitar beautifully, but he didn't exactly personify the archetypal country singer. He was black, and his buzz cut and tattoos gave him a look that would have been less incongruous at a stereotypical rap battle. But he definitely had the talent, and if Heather had her own label, she'd sign him in a heartbeat.

But she didn't. Not yet. Donny called the shots at Rocky Top Country Music, and beyond him, Nashville didn't have a penchant for embracing any kind of otherness. It'd been over a decade since Darius Rucker had entered country music, and despite his success, he had yet to be inducted to the Grand Ole Opry. It was still a heterosexual, white male bastion.

"Have you uploaded the recording to my cloud?"

She bit her lip, knowing Donny liked to hear them while they were fresh in Heather's head. With the late night and early morning meeting, she hadn't had the chance to fine-tune the recording to show the artists at their best. "Not yet. I'll do it first thing after this meeting."

"Great." Donny patted her on the shoulder. "You keep finding me the diamonds in this giant shit-pile of coal, and we'll make Rocky Top the number one studio on Music Row."

She smiled back at him and didn't react to his use of "we." Privately, Donny commended Heather for what he called her star whispering ability, but publicly, he enjoyed taking all the credit for her discoveries. Aaron had always given her the proper recognition for her work, and she had the Grammy-winning, platinum-selling artists on the wall of her office to prove it. "Sure thing, Donny."

Mandie placed a cup to Heather's side. "Warm milk with a hint of coffee bean."

"Thanks, Mandie." She picked up the drink and took a small sip. She was ready for the slight hit of caffeine that would take the edge off her lethargy. This meeting was a huge deal for Donny and Rocky Top, and though she couldn't fathom why Savana would want her here, Heather wanted to present her best side.

The elevator pinged its arrival, and two stocky men in tightly fitted gray suits held both of the doors as Savana Hayes and her manager, Joe Johnson, stepped out. Savana looked stunning in an unpretentious outfit of faded blue jeans and a stars and stripes tank top, and it made Heather question the validity of the meeting requests. Stars were expected to be high maintenance, so maybe all of that was just part of a persona her manager had dreamed up.

She swept through the corridor toward the boardroom, obviously knowing exactly where she was heading. Heather found herself admiring Savana's poise. She looked every inch the confident and composed country star. *How does she get her hair to bounce like that?* It was like Heather was watching a commercial, complete with a wind machine to make the most of Savana's long locks. She swallowed and stood, ready to greet her as Mandie opened the boardroom door.

"Savana, I'm so glad you could make it." Donny offered his hand.

Heather thought she saw a slight hesitation before Savana extended her own hand and shook Donny's.

"Thank you for the invitation, Donny." She let go of his hand and looked at Heather. "And it's a pleasure to get the opportunity to meet you, Heather King."

"The pleasure's all mine. I'm a huge fan of your music." Heather stopped herself from gushing further and telling her that Savana had been the reason she'd taken a chance and come to Nashville in the first place. Her confession would be even less flattering since her foray into the performance side of the music business had been an epic fail.

"And I'm a huge fan of your ear."

Heather frowned and self-consciously pulled at her hair to make sure it was covering her ears. "Thank you?"

Savana laughed. "Sorry, that sounded wrong. You have an impressive knack for finding new talent. You're responsible for over a quarter of this label's Grammy wins. It's one of the main reasons I'm taking this meeting."

Heather grinned. "Wow. Thank you." She deliberately didn't look at Donny but expected he would be scowling beneath his smile. He wouldn't be happy that anyone thought Heather was responsible for finding all of Rocky Top's major talent during his tenure, let alone the undisputed Queen of Country.

"To business, then." Savana directed her attention to Donny. "I'm looking for a new label to support the direction I want my music to take. You think you're that label, yes?"

Heather leaned back in her chair and continued to sip her coffee. Savana was as impressive in a meeting as she was on stage, and she felt her hero-worship step up a couple of notches. This would probably be the one and only time she'd get to be in the same room as her, so she wanted to savor it. Times like this that reminded her she'd made a good decision giving up her dream of becoming a country singer. She had a decent voice, but it didn't compare to Savana's or any of the other top recording artists in this city. Heather had realized what she was good at, and it was finding the next big thing. She was happy at Rocky Top. For now.

CHAPTER THREE

L ouie slipped her credit card into the Divvy machine and it unlocked the bike closest to her in the rack. She pulled it out and felt a moment of melancholy as she pushed her card back into her wallet and realized this would be her last ride in Chicago. She headed down West Roosevelt toward the bike station on East 29th and South Michigan Avenue. On the corner of 28th and Michigan was Rich's Autos, a place she'd visited plenty of times over the past two years, optimistically scanning the lot for the perfect Jeep Wrangler soft top that would take her to Nashville. She had dreams of entering the city in style instead of being one of fifty country wannabes hitting town daily on the clichéd Greyhound bus. That dream lost its color slightly when Mia skipped town with her hard-earned savings, and Louie hadn't been this way for over a year. Hitting her savings target had come at the right time, but a Jeep Wrangler was still way outside her budget.

She guided the bike into an empty dock and strode the block quickly. It was already seven p.m. Louie wanted to be packed and out of the city before midnight in case she lost her nerve, and her truck turned into a pumpkin. Louie rounded the corner and nearly took out a mom and her midsize kid.

"Oh, I'm so sorry." Louie scooped up the phone the kid had dropped and was pleased to see it was encased in a shock absorber box, unharmed. The kid snatched it from her grip and scowled before returning to the screen, fixated once more.

"Don't worry. I sometimes wish it would break just so I could have a normal conversation with my son again." Neglected mom smiled and walked on.

It reminded Louie she hadn't spoken to her mom that week. She'd be stoked that Louie had finally made enough to get her started in Nashville. Louie could never tell her mom *how* she'd made so much money so soon after Mia had cleared her out. But her mom would be proud that she'd done it by herself. They'd never had anything given to them without strings or a favor to call in. Hell, her mom's own family had only taken them in because they were desperate and homeless after her father dumped them both and disappeared into the ether. She gritted her teeth and squashed the rising tension into a metaphorical ball. She opened her palm and blew the imaginary sphere into the air before opening the showroom door.

Louie scanned the shiny tiled floor for the Jeep she'd dreamed about driving off the lot and into Nashville. But she could only afford something far less flashy. A seven-hour road trip would be a baptism of burning rubber so she prayed for a genuine salesperson to trade her something reliable.

"Evening, sir. Are you looking for a particular ride?"

Louie was used to being mistaken for a dude but never let it bother her. Long held social constructs were hard to demolish. She turned in the direction of the female voice and smiled at the sexy woman in the skirt suit, plunging V-neck blouse, and heels that Louie estimated at an impressive four inches. How she managed to navigate the showroom floor without breaking anything was anybody's guess. "Yeah. I need a good truck, four doors, no more than four thousand, and I need it to drive to Nashville tonight."

Whether or not she registered Louie wasn't a guy, Heel-lady didn't miss a beat. "Four thousand miles or four thousand dollars?"

One day she might be able to afford a truck with no miles on the clock, let alone four thousand. "Dollars." Louie pulled out her wallet and handed the sales woman her bankcard and driver's license.

"Then you'll need temporary registration and insurance."

Heel-lady smiled and licked her lips. Louie assumed her mild flirtation was just a sales technique. It was wasted on Louie since she'd already made it clear she wouldn't be leaving without wheels tonight. "And you can help me..." Louie finally took the time to read Heel-lady's name tag and was once again reminded why she hated them when she saw it was positioned just to the right of her cleavage. "Joni?"

"Oh, I can help you..." Joni raised Louie's license and traced her finger over it. "Louie Francis."

Louie couldn't decide if she appreciated Joni's undertones or if she wanted to grab her by the shoulders, shake her, and tell her to stop using her sex to sell cars. She settled on neither, opted for willful ignorance and gestured to the cars. "Can you show me what I need?" Louie mentally reprimanded herself. Anything she could say in this situation could be misconstrued and made sexual. She looked beyond Joni to see that every other salesperson was male and wished one of them had approached her instead. She felt damn sure *they* wouldn't try charming her into...ah, the penny dropped. Joni would want her to spend more than her budget. "I can't go any higher than four thousand, so please don't show me anything you can't sell me for that price or less."

"Relax. I'm not going to give you the hard sell. I can recognize a desperate woman when I see one." She put her hand on Louie's shoulder.

Louie resisted the temptation to make a smart-ass comment about her failing to recognize she was a woman at all, let alone a desperate one. She wanted this to run smooth and fast, and pissing Joni off wouldn't make that happen. So she smiled and simply said, "Great."

"Follow me."

Predictably, Joni headed out of the showroom, onto the main lot, and halfway around the back of the building. Louie dutifully followed, trying not to drool over the brand-new Wrangler Rubicon Recon in Granite Crystal that she'd walked past to enter Rich's. It was *only* ten times what she wanted to spend, and it was so pretty. It'd be hers one day. Her passion for cars was something she got from her mom, but every car her mom had ever had was a junker. And vital pieces were often held together with duct tape and Gun Gum.

Joni stopped in front of a Ford Ranger. "This is a 1996 XL, four-wheel drive, and a hundred and twenty thousand miles. Dark brown, or as I like to call it, dirty black." She paused, maybe waiting for Louie to laugh. "One drawback is the transmission—it's a manual."

"That's no drawback. That detail just made the deal." Louie opened the door, checked the interior, and grinned when she saw bucket seats front and rear. *Mom will love this.* It'd been detailed and looked more than presentable for its age. She popped the hood and took a cursory look. The engine had been steam cleaned so it was impossible to tell if it had any leaks. "How long has it been parked here?"

Joni looked to the sky as if to pull the details from her head. "Maybe six months. There's not much call for the gas guzzlers these days, aside from…"

The way Joni trailed off made Louie think she might've been about to say something offensive, but she had no clue what. "And you'll be able to sort the registration and insurance for me?" Louie knew she should at least test drive it, but it was likely that if there was anything wrong with it, the dealership's mechanics would've done a good enough job of covering it up to last three months. And she was pretty handy under the hood thanks to a childhood friendship with a kid whose family owned the local garage. All she needed it to do was get her out of this place and to the city of her dreams. Then she could give it all the love and attention it needed to keep it going.

Joni seemed to hesitate. "Sure. You're in a big hurry?"

Louie smiled. "Yeah, I am. My dream's waited long enough."

CHAPTER FOUR

As soon as the phone began to ring, Heather knew who it would be. She'd met Emma on the Greyhound ride into Nashville, and while Heather had diverted the path of her dream from singer to record label owner, Emma had persevered. Just like she was persevering tonight.

Heather accepted the video call with a sigh. "Hey, Em."

"You're standing me up again?"

Heather shook her head at Emma's clearly indignant tone and the look on her face that Heather knew meant she was actually upset, rather than playing the martyr. "I'm sorry, babe, I just can't face another night out." Talent scouting all week meant Heather hadn't seen her bed the right side of two a.m. for ten days straight. Coupled with regular six a.m. rises, she was whacked. "I'm exhausted."

"Why don't I get takeout and come to you?"

Heather tilted her head and considered Emma's offer. Honestly, she'd be glad of some company, and Emma was someone she could spend time with in easy silences. "What about Mia and Diane? You've been looking forward to seeing Easy A perform since Diane scored tickets for you." Mia and Diane were the other reasons Heather wasn't overly interested in going out this evening. They were a couple, a duet, and a general pain in her ass, always pushing for face time with Donny. They both had talent, but there was just something about Mia that didn't sit well. She seemed like the kind of woman who'd sell her soul for fifteen minutes of fame. Maybe her granny's soul, not her own. She was too self-serving for that. But Heather was sure Mia would do anything to make it in this town, and she didn't want any part of making *that* star shine bright.

"I've seen them plenty before, and I'd always rather spend quality time with you." She grinned, then frowned. "And they'll be all over each other just to remind me that I'm alone."

"They're pretty full-on. New love, I guess." It'd been a while since Heather had felt *that* way. She was too busy with her career to worry about love, and there was no rush since she was still shy of thirty by a year.

Emma rolled her eyes. "Whatever. I don't want to see it after the date I had last night. Thai, Chinese, or Italian?"

"Italian. I have wine, and you can tell me all about last night's date."

Emma had such little luck with guys, she often joked she should try the dark side, and that Heather would have to be the one to induct her.

"Excellent. See you in an hour."

"Sure thing." Heather ended the call and looked around. Her living room looked exactly as it should since she'd neglected to clean or tidy it for the best part of a month. Luckily, Emma wasn't the judgmental type. Shift a few items of clothes and dump the far-too-numerable takeout cartons, and she'd be good to go.

Heather uncorked the second bottle of wine, filled their glasses, and washed down the last of her cannelloni al forno. "And what was his response to you calling the president a conceited cock?"

Emma scoffed and took a quick sip of her wine. "He said I had no idea what I was talking about because I hadn't been to a proper school."

Heather narrowed her eyes. "Meaning?"

"Ivy League jerk-off." Emma gestured the universal sign with a shake of her half-closed hand. "I wasn't about to tell him I hadn't been to college at all. He was already up on his social elitist white horse."

"What did you say to that?" Emma's tale made Heather thankful she'd never had a political argument on a first date in the middle of a restaurant. She had to admit that most lesbians she'd come across were liberal and the possibility of such an argument was low.

"I called him a douche and asked for the check." Emma picked up the small bowls of tiramisu and handed one to Heather. "That's not even the worst of it."

"It gets worse?"

Emma spooned a mouthful of the dessert into her mouth, building the tension. Heather loved her penchant for drama.

"He went to the restroom and didn't come back."

"No! Surely not?"

Emma waved her spoon at Heather. "He did too. Cheapskate ass."

"Dare I ask what the bill came to?" Heather had heard Tanker was the most expensive restaurant in Midtown. She braced for a ridiculous price.

"Three hundred and fifty dollars…plus tip. Jesus."

Heather laughed. "I thought he was in the sandal business not restaurants."

"I know, right?" Emma shrugged. "Anyway, enough about me. Didn't you have that big meeting with the Queen of Country today?"

Heather put her glass down and scooted her legs under her butt. "I did, and she was as amazing as I thought she'd be."

Emma leaned in, her interest in the gossip obvious. "You've had a helluva week. A massive promotion *and* a meeting with a country legend. Did you find out why she wanted you there?"

"My track record. She knew that I was responsible for a good chunk of Rocky Top's Grammy wins."

"I bet Donny didn't like that one bit."

Heather giggled. The third glass of wine was kicking in, and she felt a little lightheaded. She was glad they hadn't gone out with Mia and Diane. There was no way she could've had this conversation with Emma in front of them because they didn't have the faintest idea what discretion meant. Donny was a powerful man; Aaron may have helped her get on the map, but Donny could easily send her tumbling off the Nashville radar. But for now, he'd given her a dream assignment she was about to share with her best friend. "He didn't say anything about it…but he *did* assign me to take care of her career with us."

"WHAT? You let me prattle on about my ridiculous date while you were holding this news?" Emma put her glass down and pulled Heather into a tight hug. "I'm so happy for you. This is huge."

It was huge. Heather sank gratefully into the embrace, glad of Emma's positive reaction. Some of her colleagues had been less than enthusiastic when Donny announced it via the company's e-bulletin. It'd been less than a week since her promotion to Aaron's recently vacated position, but she'd already felt the animosity from people who believed her loyalty to Aaron should've prevented her from taking the job at all. She'd even heard a foul rumor she'd slept with Donny to advance her career. They had no idea he had entirely the wrong equipment to interest her. This gig would make her even less popular. But Savana had insisted, and superstars always get what they want. "Thanks, Em."

Emma sat back slightly and put her hands on Heather's shoulders. "I sense some reservations…Spill." She relaxed back into the couch and retrieved her wine.

"We were in the meeting talking about who Savana wanted running her, and she asked that I be the one to do it."

Emma raised an eyebrow. "*She* asked for you."

Heather shrugged as she recalled how it happened. "More or less insisted, to be honest."

"So your hard work is paying off. For five years, you've said and done everything you've needed to do, and you've never said no to anything Aaron or Donny asked of you. Word must have gotten around. This is your big break, Feathers."

Heather smiled at Emma's nickname for her. "People are jealous. I feel like they're waiting for me to fail. I need the support of my team if I'm going to pull this off."

"Ooh, 'my team,' eh?"

Heather tapped Emma's shoulder. "This is serious. Up to now, I've just had myself to worry about. I know what I'm capable of, but other people…"

Emma pulled a notepad and pen from her handbag. "How many do you need on your team?"

How was she supposed to do this? Maybe there was a book—A&R Vice-President for Dummies. So far, she'd just found the talent and had it taken away from her once she'd paired them with songwriters. This would be the first time she'd go beyond that, and it was going to be with the Queen of Country. *Jesus.* "I'll work closely with maybe two people, and we'll have to liaise with every other department in the company."

Emma tapped the end of the pen on the first blank sheet she came to. "Is there anyone you trust who works with you?"

Heather chewed the inside of her cheek while she contemplated Emma's question. "I like Vetti."

"Like or trust?"

"Both."

Emma wrote her name down and looked up expectantly. "Who else?"

Heather hesitated. The next name that came to mind was the guy Emma had recently dumped because he'd started talking about children. "Tim. He's been scouting with me a few times." The extra detail wasn't necessary given that was how he and Emma had first met, but she said it anyway.

Heather watched the way Emma wrote more carefully, taking extra time as she almost caressed each stroke of his name. If Emma wanted to talk about it, she would. There'd never been a need for a crowbar to open each other's feelings trunk. Emma and Tim seemed very happy and good for each other. But Emma was headstrong and knew her own mind. Her career came first. Far be it from Heather to advise or comment when her love life had been nonexistent since she'd moved here. Two serious relationships didn't make her an expert.

The rest of the wine bottle disappeared as Heather talked and Emma made notes. Halfway through their third bottle, Emma yawned and Heather looked at the clock. It was past midnight, and she wanted an early start in the office. She'd never been one to stroll into the office at eleven regardless of how late a night she'd had, and she wasn't about to start now that she was looking after Savana. "Jeez, where did that evening go?"

"Time is no one's mistress, Feathers." Emma closed her notebook, handed it to Heather, and stood. "You're going to be the best A&R veep this town has ever known."

Heather appreciated Emma's belief. "Thanks, buddy." She walked her to the door.

"This time next year, I'll be the Queen of Country," Emma said as she stepped outside.

Heather smiled and straightened her shoulders. "This time next year, I'll have my own label."

"No glass ceiling…"

"For women with a strong enough kick." Heather completed her half of their now-traditional parting mantra. It was their grown-up version of a high five. She waited until Emma had driven away before she closed the door and leaned against it. *Savana Hayes asked for me.* This was the opportunity she'd been working toward, and it had come along sooner than she could've hoped. She'd expected to work beneath Aaron for another couple of years before being given the chance to prove herself with a top talent. And she'd anticipated running at least ten much smaller acts to earn her stripes and show her mettle. Sure, she had Grammy winners hanging on her wall, but she hadn't been instrumental in their artistic development. She'd just discovered them. And how exactly was she supposed to develop the top female artist in country music?

Heather pushed away from the door and headed upstairs for a quick shower before bed. "I'm ready for this." She said the words out loud in an effort to make them more believable. This *was* what she wanted, and she'd give it everything she had. Nothing, and no one, was going to stop her from fulfilling her dream.

CHAPTER FIVE

L ouie parked curbside at her apartment and grinned as she
locked her truck. *My truck.* She'd never owned a vehicle in
her life until now, and it felt as good as she thought it might. It might
not be a Jeep Wrangler, but she believed she'd be able to buy one
with her first six-figure royalty check. When she'd finally driven off
after the stupidly long two-hour registration process, Louie knew a
house would be that first purchase, not a Jeep. She wanted roots, a
home, a place she could finally call her own. And she wanted her
mom to join her—in her own place of course. They were close, but
sharing a house with her mom wouldn't exactly be a lady magnet.
Not that love was any kind of priority. Mia had been an experience
she wasn't rushing to repeat, and unless she made it big, Louie
expected that no one would be interested in poor white trash. Nope.
She knew she'd have to make her fortune before she had anything
to offer any woman of substance.

She unlocked the main entry door to her building and jogged
up to her second-floor apartment. Louie closed the door behind
her and looked around. She'd lived there for two years but almost
everything she owned would fit in the bright orange duffel bag her
mom had bought her four years ago in an effort to encourage her
to pack up and follow her dream. Louie had left it in its plastic
wrapping for nearly two years before Mia finally convinced her to
go to Nashville via Chicago.

Louie pulled the bag from her closet and quickly emptied her drawers and single closet into it. She had more than she'd come to this city with but not much more. Mia had taken everything they had of value other than the Les Paul ES 335 her mom had saved up for and bought from a pawnshop. And that hadn't been for lack of trying. Louie pushed away the invasive thoughts of Mia once more. Since she'd hit the magic five thousand dollar target and decided to head to Nashville, she'd been thinking about Mia way too much. She'd spent enough time in the six months after Mia had left her thinking about how she could've done things differently. Had she done something to push Mia away? Had Mia gotten herself into trouble and needed their money to get out of it? Why hadn't Mia just talked to her? Louie shook her head and slammed her last belt into the bag, skinning the top of her fingers on the sharp buckle edge. *Fuck.* Mia should've been the one coming back to her, not the other way around. *Let it go.* She thought she had. Louie was certain she didn't have any residual feelings for Mia other than resentment. She'd been a doormat and given her everything she ever asked for. Louie knew it was a possibility, but she hoped their paths wouldn't have to cross in Nashville.

Louie placed her prize possession in its hard case and locked the clips in place. The guitar would have a seat up front with her. She got to her hands and knees and pulled a battered shoe box from beneath the bed. Out of habit, she rolled the elastic band from it, flipped off the lid, and ran her fingers over its contents; the cardboard spines of nearly twenty journals with her songs in them. She was grateful Mia hadn't considered plagiarism as another acceptable action when she left with everything else that belonged to Louie.

She wasn't sure what it said about her that she was able to pack up the past two years of her life in less than an hour but decided not to analyze it. Sometimes ignorance could be a good thing. Louie dragged a plastic box from her now empty closet and placed the rest of her stuff in it. A few books, her bag of toiletries from the bathroom, her laptop, and various electric cables she wasn't sure she needed but felt like she should pack them just in case. She turned around to face the paltry bookcase she'd made from a couple of storage pallets she'd found in an alley. Louie didn't have a handsaw, but with a few nails and a hammer, she'd managed to pull something together that did the job. The few people she'd had over to visit applauded her re-purposing. Louie just wished she could've afforded to buy some decent shelves. She took the frame of her and her mom down and placed it on top of the rest of the things in the box, before closing and sealing it.

"I'm doing it, Mom. I'm finally doing it."

She swallowed the rising bubble of emotion and headed to the kitchen to pack up a small box of supplies. She ignored the not-so-quiet voice telling her this was a mistake and that she should stick to what she was good at in the WoodBack. *Once a gutter rat, always a gutter rat.* She rubbed her forehead hard before opening the fridge to discover it was void of anything useful other than a couple of sodas and an energy drink that would get her fifty miles before she'd have to stop to pee. One cupboard yielded a half-full box of almost out of date pumpkin cereal bars, and another gave up a bag of ridged chips, a pack of cherry Twizzlers, and some caramel M&Ms. Perfect road trip nibbles. She tossed them all into the box and glanced around. Everything she owned fit on the double bed in the center of the studio. She grinned and grabbed her duffel bag. "Let's do this."

It only took Louie two trips to pack her shiny new ride before she sank onto the bed and pulled out her phone to email the manager at the WoodBack. She'd often talked about her plans to Terry, and she'd encouraged them, telling Louie that one day, she'd make it. Terry would be the perfect person to pass the news on to Frankie and ensure there was no comeback.

Terry, I'm finally giving it a go. I'm packing up and heading to Nashville, just like I've always dreamed about. Thanks for your support and for giving me a job that's helped me save up to do this. I hope you'll forgive me for not working a notice period, but I just know that if I tried to do that, I'd end up not leaving. Take care. Louie.

Louie took a deep breath and a final look around the four walls she'd called home for the past two years. There was no residual sadness, and her heart wasn't heavy with dread. She smirked; her give-a-damn was busted. If it were possible, her heart was bouncing. The voice in her head telling her she'd be found out, that she was a fraud, and it would only be a matter of time before she headed home to her mom with her dreams splintered like wood on a lumberjack's chopping block—Louie was ignoring that voice. She wavered between this state and fully accepting what it had to say, but it had never kept her from trying, and Louie wasn't about to bow down to it now.

She locked the door behind her, took the steps two at a time, and climbed into her truck. She programmed the GPS for Nashville, settled on the simple I-65 route in case her truck turned out to be less reliable than promised, and called her mom. She needed a hit of her mom's enthusiasm to back her current level of optimism.

"Hey, Noodle Doodle."

Hearing her mom's voice raised Louie's spirits even higher than they already were. "Hey, Mom." She was bursting to reveal her news but tried to keep herself calm. "How are you?"

"Oh, you know. Same old, same old. Nothing changes in this little town except the color of the sky. Let's talk about how you are instead."

Louie's high took a hit when her mom delivered the same phrase she always used. She'd sacrificed so much to help Louie move closer to her dreams. It was time to start repaying that with some real action. "Okay. Guess what I'm doing?" She slowed and shifted into second to join the on ramp onto the US-41.

"It sounds like you're in a fish tank. Are you driving?"

Louie smiled. All the technology to send people to the moon, and it was still impossible to have a quality conversation in a car over the phone. "Yup."

"Noodle! You saved up enough to buy a car?"

Her mom's zeal had never wavered, even when Louie called her in tears to tell her all about what her mom had labeled "Mia's betrayal." Having a cheerleader as exuberant as her mom had been essential to get her through the bad times after Mia had left. "Better than that. A truck. Guess where I'm headed?"

Her mom's answering gasp was audible. "Nashville?"

Louie's heart melted at the wonderfully hopeful tone of her mom's voice. "Nashville."

"I knew you'd do it, Noodle. I knew it."

There was a pause, and Louie knew her mom had stopped herself from saying anything about Mia just in case the wound hadn't quite healed. "Thanks, Mom. I wouldn't have made it this far if it wasn't for you." Her support had been as steady and constant as the Colorado River. She'd always been, and continued to be, the lifeblood to Louie's aspirations, even sending her ten dollars by mail every week to keep her going.

"This is all you, Louie. You've always had this in you, and you're making it happen. Lesser people would've given it up."

Louie loved the depth of her mom's belief in her. Whenever her own faith faltered, she could always rely on her mom to renew her conviction. "When I make it, you'll still join me?" Fulfilling her dream would mean she'd be able to repay her mom for everything she'd ever done for her. They'd finally have the better life they'd dreamed of lying on hay bales beneath the moon when Louie was just a runty kid with a bold ambition.

"I'll be there with bells on when you can afford it, Noodle, but not until you're on your feet with your own roof over your head."

Louie shook her head at her mom's practicality. If she could've made a wish with a fairy grandmother, it would've been to ask for her first big royalty check to be big enough to buy them both a house. "I know, I know. But you will come, yeah?"

"If you want me there, I'll be there."

Louie grinned. She was heading to Nashville in her own truck, and she had a mom who believed she could do anything in the world. "I'll make it happen, Mom. I promise."

"I know you will. I've always known you were special."

"As in the glass tastes like strawberries when I lick it, kind of special?"

Her mom broke into her infectious raucous laugh. "That too, yes." She chuckled some more. "Concentrate on driving. It's late, and it'll be getting dark soon. Which way are you going?"

Louie shook her head, knowing a geography lesson was imminent. "The I-65 route, Mom. It's quickest and less hassle."

Her mom sighed. "The 150, 41, 24 route is less miles."

"I'll be fine." Louie shook her head and was glad her mom wasn't on FaceTime to see her rolling her eyes. "My route's more populated. If I get tired, there are more motels to stop at."

"Make sure you *do* stop, then. I'm assuming you're driving alone?"

She didn't need to ask. She knew there'd been no one since Mia had broken her heart, and Louie doubted there'd be anyone for a while. Not for longer than one night, anyway, and Louie didn't tell her mom *everything*. "I am. It'll be okay. I'll call you when I get there."

"Make sure you do. And send me lots of photographs."

"Will do. Speak soon, Mom."

"Drive safe, Noodle."

Louie ended the call as she passed the Navy Pier on her left. Chicago had been a good home for two years, and she'd miss that place most of all. She had bittersweet memories of skating the Winter WonderFest with Mia, whose lack of balance was comical. And it had been the place she'd gone for every firework display from the Fourth of July and Halloween to Memorial Day weekend and as many as she could in between. But now it was time for a new city and fireworks of a completely different kind.

Chapter Six

Heather slid open the door of the music pod, stepped inside, and closed it behind her. Plugging her H6 recorder into the audio set up, she recalled the excited look on Gabe Duke's face as he realized she was recording his two-song set at the Douglas Corner Café. Heather tried hard not to be noticed by the artists she was checking out, because she didn't want them getting their hopes up unnecessarily. But that night had become unusually quiet by eleven, and it was impossible to blend into a crowd of ten no matter how small her recording unit was. She hoped that it wasn't Gabe's appearance that had reduced the regularly vibrant audience, but she suspected it might well have been.

She uploaded his set onto the PC and copied it to Donny's folder after reducing the background noise. She'd promised to do it after the meeting with Savana yesterday, but her whole schedule had been shot to pieces when Savana requested that Heather be her direct exec. Savana's manager, Joe, had claimed Heather for the remainder of the day to get her "up to speed on *Brand Savana*." Five solid hours with him made Heather wonder if she'd be working with a person or a product and if he only saw *Brand Savana* as a way to increase his bank balance. Heather had even started to feel a little sorry for her until Joe proudly proclaimed she was currently worth a hundred and twenty million dollars. That kind of money had to be worth some self-sacrifice. And Heather figured that Joe would've earned nigh on twenty million riding Savana's coat tails.

For now, Heather wanted to forget the daunting challenge of looking after Savana and concentrate on what she loved doing: discovering raw talent. She pulled on her noise-canceling headphones and flipped her hair out of the way over her shoulder. She wanted to hear the way Gabe's voice wrapped around the haunting lyrics of one of her favorite Johnny Cash covers to make sure she wasn't willing him to be better than he was. Gabe was in his early twenties, and attempting a song with such depth and tragedy was either exceptionally brave and personal or a show of ridiculous bravado and arrogance. Heather had managed to hold it together at the café, but in the privacy of the music pod, she didn't make it to the second verse before tears tracked their way down her cheek and onto the glass desk. She wiped them away with the sleeve of her shirt before leaning back in the chair to let Gabe's voice envelop her in regret and sorrow.

A sharp knock on the pod door made Heather jump, and she knocked her knees on the edge of the table. She bit back the desire to swear, despite knowing that it had been scientifically proven that cursing made it feel better, and opened the door to Joe.

"Savana wants to talk to you about songwriters. She's in studio four." He tapped his watch with two fingers. "Don't keep her waiting."

"I have to finish this up for Donny and then I'll be with her."

He pursed his lips. "Savana is always your priority whenever she's in the building, Heather. You need to realize that or you won't be her exec for long."

"Of course. I'll be there soonest."

Joe raised an eyebrow, and Heather couldn't define the emotion his eyes were keeping silent. She wondered if he was another doubter. Perhaps he thought Savana would be better taken care of by someone senior in experience, or maybe he thought a man would be more suitable. Heather could definitely see merit in the first option but tried to ignore the second as paranoia. Country music was still predominantly male, for sure, but it didn't make every man a chauvinistic misogynist.

"You've got this gig because Savana wanted you. She can *unwant* you just as fast if you're not attentive to her needs."

"I understand," she said, remaining as polite as possible, and slid the door closed on him.

Heather knocked on the door and waited to be invited in. Savana and Joe were deep in a conversation that looked like it was irritating both of them. Savana glanced up and motioned for Heather to join them. Joe stood and left with only a cursory nod toward Heather. When he'd gone, she bit her lip to keep the question she wanted to ask quiet. It was way too presumptuous to expect Savana to trust her with any issues that didn't concern the label and her music, and she didn't know why she'd think it, but the short part of the exchange she'd witnessed somehow seemed more of a personal than professional nature.

Heather lowered herself into Joe's pre-warmed seat beside Savana and placed her mug on the table. As she sat, she wondered if she should've chosen the chair opposite Savana in case she wanted distance between them. *God, looking after a diva is complicated.* Heather chastised herself for the unkind thought. Thus far, Savana had come across as surprisingly straightforward. Heather was the one making it difficult for herself.

"What on earth is that? It smells like perfume." Savana pinched her nose before wafting the aroma away as though it offended her.

Heather laughed at Savana's reaction. "It's Earl Grey tea. The bergamot gives it that distinct fragrance." She pushed the mug closer to Savana. "Do you want to try it?"

Savana wrinkled her nose. "Oh God, no." She tapped her own mug on its side with the diamond ring on her middle finger. "I'm a strong coffee woman, or water when I'm trying to be good."

That explained the excess of Evian at yesterday's meeting. Heather suspected it to be the work of Joe trying to keep his meal ticket healthy. "I love the smell of strong coffee, but I can't drink it. And freshly brewed coffee burns my nostrils."

"Oh no, I would never have asked you to be my exec if I'd known you were coffee-intolerant."

Heather was relieved when Savana followed that sentence with a wink and a gentle nudge to Heather's shoulder.

"Glad I kept it quiet then."

"Shall we get down to business?" She waited for acknowledgment from Heather before continuing. "Do you have anything you want to ask me?"

It occurred to her to ask Savana why she wanted Heather as her exec, but she didn't want to seem too grateful or unworthy of the task. She didn't need Savana thinking she'd made a mistake and that Heather wasn't the woman for the job. Savana must have her reasons, and they were largely irrelevant as long as Heather lived up to her expectations. And those should be set now to make sure they were realistic. Emma had gotten it right last night—she'd never said no to anything Aaron or Donny had asked of her—but she hoped she wouldn't be tied to Savana twenty-four seven. Donny had already reallocated her scouting duties, but she didn't want to be suffocated.

"I want you to tell me what you want from me." Heather opened her leather portfolio and turned to a blank page.

"That's beautiful. Is it real leather?" Savana reached over and touched the inside of Heather's organizer. "Where did you get it?"

"It's real. I had it made for me and shipped over from Europe." Heather was suddenly aware of how pretentious she sounded and backpedaled. "It was a reward to myself for finally getting a paid job with a top label. I'd never usually pay that kind of money for…" She didn't want to sound cheap either. Savana probably used toilet paper that cost more than Heather's folder.

"Well, it looks like it's worth every cent."

Heather smiled at Savana's generous response and appreciated not being pushed. She felt like she was already making a fool of herself and they'd barely broken bread. "So." Heather tapped her pen on the pad between them. "How do you envisage this working?"

"I want you to be everything a perfect A&R exec is. *And* I need you to be everything an A&R exec is *not*."

Savana relaxed back into her chair as if her words were enough explanation. They weren't. "Is there something specific you're looking for?" Heather wanted Savana to come out with whatever it was she was talking about. She was awful at guessing games. They frustrated her and made no sense. Savana obviously wanted something very specific from Heather, so why not simply say it and save a whole heap of time?

"I'm sick of all this machismo. I'm tired of being the country singer that heterosexual white males want me to be." Savana leaned forward and placed her hand over Heather's. "I've been in this business a decade, but the woman you see on the records and on stage, the woman you hear on the radio, that's not the real me."

"You want me to curate your reality."

Savana smiled in a way Heather hadn't seen on magazines or on billboards or TV. It exuded an authenticity that went beyond her facial expression and deep into her soul.

"Exactly right." Savana released her grip and clasped her hands together in her lap.

The assignment just took an unscheduled detour. The country world had expectations of their heroes, male and female. Success came for those lucky enough to fit the standards and for those willing to conform. It was hard enough for female singers to get recognition for their work even when they were long-haired, slim, and sang of their adoration for men and God. Donny had signed Savana looking for more of what she'd become famous for. If she deviated from that path and failed, it would be viewed as Heather's mishandling.

Or it could be the start of a stratospheric appeal to a far wider audience, transcending the confines of country music. Either way, their careers were now inextricably linked for the foreseeable future, for better or for worse.

Why Savana wanted Heather as her intermediary between her and Rocky Top started to make sense, but Heather hoped it wasn't because she thought she could walk all over her and get every decision to go her way. "Are you talking about a completely different sound or image?"

Savana reached for her mug and sipped her coffee before answering. "Both. I'm tired of women not singing about the things that are important to us. I'm sick of singing about Jesus, cheating lovers, and the all-American dream." She slammed her mug down, and coffee slurped out onto Heather's folder. "Oh crap, I'm so sorry."

Savana pulled off her scarf to dab at the liquid, but it was too late and the cognac-colored calf leather was stained. Heather pulled the portfolio away to stop Savana from spreading it and making it worse. "It's fine. It'll add some character." She smiled and told herself it didn't matter. It could be cleaned.

"I really am sorry, Heather."

Heather shook her head. She could see Savana was mortified, perhaps more so because Heather had told her the embarrassing story about its origin. "Honestly, don't worry." She wondered if Savana had something that meant more to her than a material possession should. "Let's start with who you want to work with. Do you have anyone in mind to write your songs?" Savana's previous material had always been written for her, but she said she wanted a new direction... "Or are you thinking of writing your own?"

"I don't have any fixed ideas aside from not wanting to work with anyone I've already had songs from."

Heather nibbled at her top lip. That narrowed the field since Savana had worked with all of the big hitters on the songwriting scene over the past decade. The top artists tended to work with three or four favorite writers, and few opted to give the lesser known writers a chance. "You don't mind trying out some no-hit wonders?"

"If you think their writing is good enough for me, I'm willing to hear them out. But I get final say—always."

Heather recognized the signature determination that had made Savana the country royalty she was. Savana had been sweetness personified to that point. This was what Heather had signed up for: keeping Savana happy and making the record label money. And it was good practice for when she had her own label.

"Let's see what I can come up with."

Donny was going to have something to say about this, but if he wanted to keep his biggest ever signing happy, he'd have to be more flexible than he'd anticipated. If Savana was happy with Rocky Top, it would signal a new era in its history and could make it *the* destination label.

No pressure, then.

CHAPTER SEVEN

L ouie had been sitting in the breakfast café for ten minutes thanking the bean god and paying homage to a giant mug of coffee that the wall sign accurately proclaimed to be "Black as hell, strong as death, and sweet as love." And she'd watched all manner of amazingly presented breakfast dishes scoot past in the hands of deft serving staff before she decided to ask for their menu. As the morning rush ebbed to just a few laid-back customers, she scanned the laminated card for what she could afford to order. Her stomach growled impatiently at her time wasting so she motioned to the closest server to take her order.

"How's the coffee treating you?"

He looked barely out of his teens, but his voice was deep and mature and belied his apparent age. Louie wondered if the cliché were true and every waiter in the city was chasing their own Nashville dream. "Your sign does not exaggerate." He smiled, and Louie noticed how unusually rounded his top teeth were. And they were the kind of bright white that toothpaste commercial models had. Self-consciously, Louie closed her returning smile to hide her own less than perfect ivories.

"Are you new in town?"

The question stumped Louie. Did she look that green? What gave her away? And why did he care?

"Sorry. The boss keeps telling me I'm too familiar." He gestured around the café. "This place is off the beaten track for tourists. It's mostly a locals kind of joint. And you've got that same wide-eyed look I had when I hit town a few months ago."

He must have sensed her discomfort, but his easy nature made Louie relax. She'd been around criminals a little too long and had forgotten how regular people who didn't have anything to hide behaved. "It's fine. You just surprised me. I've come from a city where it's almost too much trouble to ask for your order, let alone take any interest in you." She let go of the mug she'd been gripping to white-knuckle status and offered her hand. "I'm Louie. Louie Francis."

The server dropped his order pad onto Louie's table and shook her hand with vigor. She'd always appreciated a firm handshake. Her mom had drilled it into her that it was the sign of a trustworthy person, someone reliable. And this kid seemed nice.

"I'm Gabrielle Duke, but everyone calls me Gabe."

"It's great to meet you, Gabe." Louie pushed her misgivings away and pulled back memories of living in a town where people were genuine and honestly curious about getting to know newcomers. In a city whose population she'd read was increasing by a hundred people a day, that was a lot of newcomers. But then, people always brought their stories with them, and stories made great country songs. It was in her interest to be more open to that experience and forget the insular city life she'd become used to. "What brought *you* to Nashville?"

"Do you want my story before or after you order something to eat?"

Louie laughed. She'd got so caught up with Gabe that she'd forgotten she'd had nothing substantial to eat since around the same time yesterday. The cereal bars and chips she'd munched on her road trip had minimal nutritional value and had failed to satiate her ever-demanding appetite. "I'm going to go with after because it feels like my gut is about to start eating itself."

Gabe retrieved his order pad. "Go."

Louie picked up her menu and found the dish she'd been coveting since she'd seen Gabe take it to a previous customer on the next table. "I'll take a chicken and biscuit sandwich with country potatoes, a half order of beignets, and two peach cobbler pancakes." She handed Gabe the menu and noticed he looked a little surprised when he'd finished scribing her order.

"Wow, you've got a helluvan appetite."

Louie pointed to her legs. "They're hollow. All I'll have to do is stand up and shake it down some."

Gabe chuckled and slapped her on the back. "I'm about to go on a break. You mind if I eat with you while I answer your question?"

Louie surprised herself when she said, "Sure thing." Gabe reminded her of her childhood buddy Jake. He had the same innocence and zest for life, the same openness and inquisitive nature. Louie wasn't a great believer in fate, but she was already glad she'd met him. Making friends in a new city had been difficult for Louie in Chicago once she started working at the WoodBack because she hadn't wanted to get anyone involved in that world. In the year since Mia had left, Louie had concentrated on her jobs and on earning the cash to get to Nashville, so she had no social life to speak of. She was glad she'd found it so easy to slip back into relatively normal conversation.

Gabe returned with their breakfasts twenty minutes later, and strangely, she'd missed him. She and Jake had been inseparable from age seven through to seventeen, and as weird as it was, Louie found herself feeling a similarly instant connection with Gabe.

He slipped into the booth seat opposite her. "Okay, first of all, you can't laugh."

Louie frowned and pointed her fork at him. "Why would I laugh? And if you already think I'm going to laugh, then it must be something funny, so you can't ask me to make a promise I've got no chance of keeping."

Gabe wrinkled his nose, seeming to ponder Louie's objection. "Fine."

He shoved both sleeves of his shirt up to reveal some serious ink. She'd already spotted tattoos behind his ears, on his neck and on his chest, and she wanted to know the story behind all of them. "And when you're done with your funny story, you can tell me all about those." Louie swept her hands through the air.

Gabe shook his head. "Not happening. I'll tell you my story, and then you can tell me yours…then I'll think about the tattoos." He touched the tombstone on his right forearm. "They're all very personal."

His voice had lowered when he spoke about his ink, and she wondered if she'd been too bold and assuming. "I'm sorry. I don't mean to pry."

Gabe's dazzling TV smile returned. "Nah, it's fine. I've got a good feeling about you and me. I don't expect it'll be too long before we're swapping tattoo and scar tales."

Louie relaxed, picked up the overflowing biscuit sandwich, and attempted a bite. The egg immediately broke and ran everywhere, along her hands, and onto her shirtsleeves. She placed it back on the plate, sucked some runny, hot yolk from her fingers, and shoved her sleeves out of the way.

Gabe pointed his fork at Louie's forearms. "Looks like we might be a while exchanging fables of our flesh."

"That's an awesome line. Mind if I steal it?" She pulled her writing journal from her satchel but waited for Gabe's permission before she opened it.

"You think?"

Louie nodded.

"Then sure. As long as you let me have first dibs on the finished song."

Louie tried to keep her surprise unnoticeable as she unfurled the leather strap and quickly scribbled the line on the top of a blank page. She closed it but left it on the table. "I'll leave it out in case you come up with more."

Gabe grinned before he tackled a mouthful of banana and pecan waffle. "That's not my strength, but you're welcome to my words if they're of any use. You just have to promise to write me some occasionally."

"You came to Nashville to sing?"

Gabe waved his fork at her again. "I thought I told you not to laugh?"

Louie held up her hands. "I'm not laughing." And she hoped her disbelief hadn't been that obvious. She cursed herself for being so quick to make assumptions based simply on how Gabe looked. Given how much she'd been subjected to judgment and expectation, she should've known better.

"But you *are* surprised." He swigged a mouthful of orange juice. "Don't worry. I'm used to it. Most people think I got lost on my way to Los Angeles."

Louie wasn't following. "LA?"

"Hip-hop. When you look like this—" He motioned from his head downward with a sweep of his hand. "You're only allowed to do hip-hop. If that's even the phrase. Sing hip-hop? Whatever. I'm supposed to be rapping, apparently. Or just waiting on tables with no ambition to be anything better."

His words were spoken with humor, but an unmissable swirl of dark pain hummed around them. Louie sensed that Gabe had experienced more than his fair share of malevolence in his twenty or so years. Maybe that's why she felt drawn to him. A kindred spirit, trying to stay unguarded and open in a world that was only interested in hardening and hurting them. Louie felt like she'd lost that battle when Mia broke her heart. She wouldn't be skipping down that path anytime soon. But cultivating a friendship certainly couldn't hurt.

"You still with me?"

"Sorry, sorry. I'm listening. What you said got me thinking." She wanted to say this right without causing offense or comparing their experiences. "We're both here against the odds, fighting to make our dreams come true. Maybe we met so we can keep each other going when it gets tough?" Louie heard herself say the words and couldn't quite believe she was allowing them voice. Her hardships were probably nothing compared to what Gabe had been through, but he clearly needed support just as she did. She looked at Gabe to try to see how he'd reacted to her weird destiny shit. A small part of her thought about backtracking in case he thought she was interested in him romantically, but she reasoned he was plenty worldly enough to know she was queer.

He looked contemplative, screwing up his mouth as if he were measuring his words because he didn't know how Louie might react.

"Okay. I'm gonna come straight out with it, because if I dance around it, it's probably going to sound stupid." He put his knife and fork down decisively. "We've just met, but I feel like we've hit it off in a way that seems totally natural and easy. I don't know about you, but that doesn't happen very often for me."

Louie shook her head but stayed silent to encourage him to continue, unsure of what he was about to say.

"I've got a place in East Nashville on Berry Street." He sighed. "I can't afford it. I had a buddy who moved here with me, but it wasn't for him and he bailed a month ago. I need a new roomie and I need one fast…What do you think?"

Louie ran her hand through her hair and pulled at her quiff. "You're asking me to move in with you?"

"Hey, whoa, I don't mean it like that."

Louie smiled at Gabe's worried look, reached over the table, and shoved his shoulder. "I'm kidding. Relax. What's the rent like? I'm kind of a broke cliché pursuing the dream." She hadn't thought about spending any more on housing. She'd expected to stay in her truck for a week or so before she found a job, but this meeting did seem…fated.

"They're looking for waiting staff here. I could introduce you to the boss when you've finished eating?"

"Wow, you can hook me up with a job and a place to stay?" Louie couldn't have been any luckier with this breakfast stop. "You're like an urban Rumpelstiltskin without the creepy, gnarled skin."

"Gross." He frowned and gave her shoulder a light shove. "It's twelve hundred a month between two. It's a three-bed, two-bath house with a garage and yard. Decent neighborhood. Friendly folk on either side. Lots of singles and couples in the area, not many families. It's a great district for creatives."

"You sound like a Realtor. Is it furnished?"

Gabe nodded then shook his head. "A little…it's got the basics, and there's some great thrift shops around. We could kit the place out pretty cheap, and I'm good with my hands. We could repurpose some pallets and make most of the furniture we need."

Gabe looked so hopeful and excited that it didn't occur to Louie to politely decline his offer. Perhaps this was her life now. Relax and just let it be. How could she not take up Gabe's offer of what seemed like the perfect base to launch her assault on Nashville? "It sounds great. How about you take me to see it when your shift ends?"

Gabe bounced in his chair like an excited kid being taken to see Santa for the first time.

"Awesome. You're going to love it. I can feel it."

Gabe tucked into the rest of his waffle and Louie picked up her gooey, lukewarm biscuit. Everything was falling into place nicely. The voice that was telling her this run of luck couldn't possibly last was bleating quietly. She closed her eyes, imagined it belonged to a person she could be face-to-face with, and squirted it with a hose. It tumbled backward down a long hill and into a dark, sticky pool at its base. *That'll keep you busy for a while.* She hoped it would be long enough for her to find her place in Nashville.

CHAPTER EIGHT

Heather sat on the edge of her tub and turned on the tap. She looked up at the many jars and bottles of foams, oils, and salts lining the shelves looking pretty and inviting, but her brain was too exhausted to begin to make any kind of choice. What was supposed to have been a couple of hours with Savana had turned into the rest of her day. Savana was impatient to launch her new image at Rocky Top; she wanted an album of number one songs, a slick new look, an album launch date, and a burst of tour dates in all the major cities. Oh, and she wanted it all yesterday. Almost immediately following the moment Heather's prized portfolio was stained with coffee, the ghost of what was to come fell upon her like a ravenous golden eagle on a deer. Savana's soft approach peeled away with each demand, and the person Heather had hoped Savana would be had faded much like the daylight hours.

Heather couldn't argue with what Savana was trying to achieve, and it wasn't that she was being unpleasant. What Savana wanted to do made perfect sense, and she was being brave to challenge expectations of the way she looked and the music she was giving to the world. But when Savana finally called an end to their meeting after eight hours, Heather felt like she'd been picked up by a tornado, thrown around two or three states, and tossed back to the ground from three hundred feet up. She hoped that the performance might just be Savana's uncontained enthusiasm at the opportunity to finally let loose from under the watchful eye of her manager, Joe.

Heather stepped into the bath, unwilling to wait longer for it to fill. She needed the warmth of the water to wrap around her body and comfort her. She would've preferred the company of a woman to do the same job, but she'd almost forgotten what a lover's embrace felt like. How long had it been? She wasn't sure she wanted to remember. She'd said good-bye to her partner in Tacoma when Alison confessed to cheating on her. Heather hadn't been angry. She'd needed a push to leave the relative safety of her hometown, and Alison provided it. Heather should probably write and thank her, but she couldn't bring herself to be quite that magnanimous.

She cupped the hot liquid in her hands and let it fall onto her body. Water was about the only thing she'd been in intimate contact with for five years. *Jesus, five years?* She'd put everything on hold when she'd come to Nashville. She felt a distance from her family that didn't sit well, but it was probably for the best. They were never supportive of her passion for music and brief visits with them always involved Heather waiting for the inevitable question of "When are you coming home?"

Heather sipped the red wine she'd poured herself, promising that it would just be the one. There were so many clichés in this town, and a reliance on alcohol was one she had no intention of falling into. As lonely as she was, there was no mileage for her in numbing it. And though it would be easy to drink every night when she scouted, she didn't want her senses anesthetized to the music. It was only through feeling every note that she could find the raw talent in the "shit pile of coal," as Donny so poetically phrased it. What did she have to show for her life? A job hundreds of people would love, and she was moving ever closer to her dream of starting her own label, where she'd have control over the talent she found. It would be a place for artists to truly develop and grow their own identity, not the one forced on them by label heads too chickenshit to push the boundaries.

She'd have a place that would be a haven for talent like Gabe Duke. What she'd do with a voice like his. And he was young enough to develop a career that could span decades with the right management. It would be a few days before her meeting with Donny on whether or not he might offer Gabe an audition, but Heather was trying to figure out just how much information she needed to give him beforehand. On the one hand, she didn't want to blindside him. Donny liked to have as much background on the talent as possible. He'd even come up with a form for her to fill in to help him make his decision. But as much data as that gave him, it didn't include ethnicity. Donny had never explained the reason for its exclusion, but Heather suspected it was to keep his vetting legal. Any discrimination he would practice, it'd be without documentation. On the other hand, if she did tell him what Gabe looked like and Donny still offered him an audition, Heather would be satisfied to know that her boss wasn't as racist as he was chauvinistic. She did know that if Gabe was a young white guy, he'd be through the door and entering the country processing farm faster than a squirrel running from a BB gun.

She took another small sip of wine before carefully placing it on the shelf beside her. She turned off the tap with her toe and tried to relax. She'd kind of forgotten how to do that too. Every waking and sleeping hour was all about Rocky Top Country Music. She was struck with the thought that *she* could be the one being racist. She should just prepare Gabe's talent paperwork precisely the same way she prepared everyone else's and see what happened. And if Donny turned him down, maybe Gabe would still be an unsigned gem when she finally pulled enough money together to start her own record label. She'd be proud for Gabe to be her first signing.

Her phone buzzed twice for her attention, and she knew it'd be her mom. They hadn't spoken since Memorial Day, always a tough day for her mom because Heather's grandfather had died in the early years of the Vietnam War. Heather made an effort to call her on that day without fail, but that conversation had ended with the usual question of when Heather was going to come home and give up on her "musical nonsense." She picked up the phone and debated whether or not to open the message. Her mom always used an app that showed when Heather had read messages, and it felt like another way to control her. She closed her eyes, deciding whether she had the emotional capacity to deal with her mother tonight. Maybe she'd seem less intense compared to her day with Savana.

Are you free to talk?

She was very rarely free, and the concept of spare time had become alien. As soon as the message indicated it was read, she could see her mother was typing again. She didn't wait for the second communication to come in.

I'd love to.

Barely three seconds passed before her phone was ringing.

"Hello, Heather."

"Hey, Mom."

"How are you?"

"I'm great, Mom. How are you doing?" The initial exchange didn't vary. Stilted and cold. A series of words said perfunctorily before the conversation could start in earnest about whatever topic was bothering her mom.

"I'm concerned. Your brother, Mason, is talking about giving up teaching."

She didn't need to be told his name. She was thankful to only have one brother, seven years her junior. A mini mistake but not treated as such. Rather, he was the golden boy of the family after Heather and her sister hadn't pursued the paths their parents wanted them to by following in their footsteps.

"How can he give up something he's not even doing yet?" Heather tried not to sound as disinterested as she was. Just once it'd be nice if her mom asked sincerely about her life before launching into her own woes.

"You know what I mean, there's no need to be pedantic. He's talking about quitting college. I need you to talk some sense into him."

What did that phrase even mean? Sense as in her mom's arrow-like trajectory for his life? She picked up her glass to have another sip of wine, liquid courage to continue the conversation, but stopped herself. Was she turning into her mom? A bubble bath and a bottle of wine every evening? She promptly replaced the glass but decided to stay enveloped in the clear, hot grip of the water. "What has he actually done?" Heather knew her mom's penchant for the theatrical. She was happiest when lamenting some problem or other to an attentive audience, but Heather's interest in her mother's perceived troubles inched closer to boredom.

"He's finished his classes for the year and says he might try something different when he goes back in the fall."

Heather closed her eyes and shook her head, thankful she wasn't on FaceTime—her mom would be sure to see her now total lack of concern in her plight. "At least he's not thinking of quitting."

"No child of mine has ever been a quitter, and I'm not about to let Mason start a new trend."

Heather felt no need to resist the obvious answer to her mom's grand statement. "I quit."

"That's not the same. You took a chance, and you were lucky it paid off. I would have hoped Mason learned from your silly-hearted action."

Heather swallowed the more aggressive retort that came to mind and tried to quell the unpleasant version of herself she became when in verbal combat with her mother. She had only ever supported the safe choices Heather had made in life, the options her mother approved of as intelligent and worthwhile. Quitting her job as business and strategy manager of a national music and bookstore franchise hadn't fit into that category. And when Heather exchanged her dream of *being* the talent to *discovering* the talent, her mother crowed about how right she was, and that Heather's little gamble with fame failed as swiftly as she'd predicted.

"Are you still there?"

Heather jumped at the sharp tone of her mother's voice in an irritatingly similar way to how she'd reacted as a child. "I am, but I'm tired, Mom. Maybe we can talk tomorrow?" It was a half-hearted gesture and her mom would read it as such.

"You say that, but you won't call me back. You never call home to see how your father and I are doing."

That's because you're not interested in anything I have to say. "I'm so busy, Mom." The rote excuse fell from her mouth so easily. She wondered if she'd ever have the courage to engage in an honest conversation and give her mom the chance to try the kind of mother-daughter relationship Heather had hoped for. But as the opportunities passed, that hope lessened. "And I often don't get home until after midnight." She would occasionally like to speak to her dad, too, more out of parental obligation than a real desire to converse. He may as well have been a stranger. He'd spent such a lot of her childhood working long hours that he was usually too tired to engage with her and her siblings when he was at home. The expected daughterly respect she had for him diminished as she'd grown older, and he hadn't earned any other kind because he was barely around to do so. Now he always seemed terribly unhappy, and she simply felt sorry for him. He'd missed out on raising his family while he was busy providing for it. Or maybe he was just staying out of her mom's way as much as he could get away with.

"I often stay up late reading, Heather, you know that."

"I can barely keep my eyes open, let alone hold a conversation." Heather put her hand on her forehead and tried to rub away the ache that had gripped her temples and was squeezing harder with every word from her mom's mouth.

"You could just listen to the news I have to share with you from home. It doesn't always have to revolve around you."

Heather's hand fell from her forehead to her mouth in order to stop a Tourette's-like tirade from escaping. This was such typical behavior. No doubt the next barb would be about her sexuality.

"Speaking of you though, Tom's just starting his teacher placement with our school."

Bingo. Tom was the son of her mom's best friend. Both mothers had wanted her and Tom to marry and live happily ever after with three rug rats, two chocolate Labradors, and a clever speaking parrot. Maybe the parrot was an exaggeration, but there were still expectations that Heather knew early on in her youth she could never live up to. Tom's sister, Meg, was a far more appealing prospect, but she'd never ponied up and made a move. It was an opportunity missed on Heather's part, because her mom had recently taken immense delight in telling her that Meg had disgraced the family by running off with Tom's fiancée. That night, her mom's sensitivity level had been particularly low. Heather had resisted the temptation to ask if her mom felt the same about her. Instead she checked out of the conversation by concentrating on what it might have felt like to be under the hand of the boyish Meg. It was an even more interesting fantasy since Heather had only ever slept with long hairs, like herself.

She tuned back into the exchange. "That's nice. I'm happy for him. His mom must be proud." Would her mom ever be proud of her? Heather acknowledged the unkind thoughts knocking on her frontal lobe, desperately seeking voice. *No more.* "I have to go, Mom. I have an early meeting with a new client." She laughed quietly. She was working with country royalty, and she hadn't told her mom the amazing news. That was the kind of relationship she craved to have with her mother. One where what she did and how well she was doing in her job mattered to her mom. A slew of self-pity sloped its way over her. She had one friend in the world, and the only thing keeping her warm at night was her ambition. It was beginning to feel like it might not be enough.

CHAPTER NINE

It was like the universe was breathing a sigh of relief that Louie was finally following her destiny, and that breath had blown in a handy helping of good luck. Okay, the universe being involved was maybe a step too far. Louie wanted to believe she had control of her fate. She was willing to accept a certain number of life's chips falling outside her control, but that was after she'd decided one way or another. Her mom had taught her that there was always a choice, but that knowledge was the proverbial double-edged sword; her father had chosen the easy path when he left them. He'd made a conscious decision never to come back. He'd taught Louie all about the power of choice without ever having met her.

Louie held her arms out in front of her and shook her hands out. She closed her eyes and visualized the distracting thoughts as mere letters falling from her fingertips. An abstract alphabet was far less painful than putting words to the memories. Or lack of them.

"Are you casting a spell? I don't think witchcraft will help you build a career in Nashville."

Louie turned to see Gabe smiling. "Aw, dammit. That's what I was counting on." She snapped an imaginary wand and let her hands fall to her side. "Useless piece of wood."

Gabe laughed then tipped his head to one side. "Seriously, though, what *were* you doing?"

"Are you worried you've invited a crazy person into your home?" Louie crossed her eyes and stuck out her tongue.

"I live for crazy. Bring it on."

Gabe flopped onto the sofa and didn't press further, but Louie sensed he still wanted a real answer. "It's a coping mechanism someone taught me. I got into a lot of fights at school so they sent me to see a psychologist. She showed me how to visualize the bad stuff in my head and let it go." Once again, Louie surprised herself with the personal information she was sharing so freely. Still, she didn't feel like telling Gabe the *why* of her fighting. "Sometimes I do that physically; other times I visualize the action. Depends where I am. If I acted out a lot of my visualization, people would think I'm crazy."

Gabe had been nodding as Louie explained herself. "Sounds cool. I like it. Maybe you can teach me one day?"

"You seem the kind of laid-back guy that doesn't let anything faze you enough to need something like this. But sure, let me know." The conversation had taken a more serious turn, and Louie felt the need to escape it. "It's my first night in Nashville. Where are you taking me?"

Gabe stood and draped his arm around Louie's shoulders. "There's only one place anyone should go on their first night in Music City, and I have reservations." He swept his arm theatrically through the air in an arc. "The Bluebird Café."

Louie slapped Gabe's chest. "Perfect. Give me five minutes to wash up, and we'll get going. We'll take my truck." She liked how that sounded, and it wasn't getting old anytime soon.

"Sure thing, LouLou."

Louie grabbed Gabe's shoulder as he moved to leave. "Unless you want me to call you GayGay, please never let that nickname pass your lips again."

"Too girly for you?"

He grinned and his eyes sparkled with mischief. Louie had never been at all curious for boys, but she could see the appeal in Gabe. "Too *everything* I'm not."

"No problem."

He closed the door behind him. Louie positioned her bag on the sofa in the deep dent Gabe had left. Tomorrow, she'd go and buy a half-decent bed. Maybe a California king-size would fit if she stuck to just a couple of dressers. Her height usually meant her toes poked out of the comforter if she snuggled down some.

Louie pulled out a simple black long-sleeve shirt and some fresh jeans before she went for a quick wash in the en-suite. It was another in her long list of things she thought she might never experience and made going to the bathroom in the middle of the night in a shared household a whole lot simpler. For her or anyone sharing her massive bed. *Who am I kidding?* Despite her work at the WoodBack, Louie wasn't interested in entertaining a stream of women whose names she would never learn. She longed for the real thing. The desire and search for true love fueled the content of her songs. If she ever did fall hard again, how might it affect her songwriting? Would she be able to write anything if she were happy and in love?

She dressed quickly, sprayed a little cologne on her neck and wrists, and fixed some beach spray in her hair. She grabbed her jacket as she left her new bedroom, then shoved her wallet into her back pocket and snapped the leather clasp on the wallet chain to a front belt loop. She stopped at the hallway mirror briefly to check that she was ready to make her first impression on Nashville's nightlife. She caught Gabe's reflection as he stood in the kitchen sucking on a long-neck beer.

"The ladies are going to *love* you."

"It's my words and music I want them to love," Louie replied, slightly self-conscious at being caught acting so blatantly vain. Then she smiled as she realized she and Gabe hadn't had to have the usual obligatory and terribly awkward coming out/gender talk: *Yes, I like girls. Yes, I'm comfortable with the way I look. No, I don't want to be a guy.*

"Whatever you need." He held up his bottle. "Want one?"

Louie shook her head. "I try not to drink and drive." Her grandmother had delighted in telling her all about her father's drinking habits. Louie didn't want to follow in those footsteps. She tapped her watch. "Time to show me your town."

Gabe chuckled. "Oh, it's not my town yet."

"Then we take it together." She picked up her keys and headed out to enjoy the beckoning beauty of her dream.

❖

Just the walk from her truck toward the Bluebird Café took Louie's breath. The scarlet red neon lighting made it feel dream-like as she and Gabe wandered past the long line of patiently waiting walk-ins, and she silently celebrated their fortuitous meeting.

Gabe spoke to a guy at the door, and he navigated them to a table fifteen feet from the stage. He scooped up the reservation sign and stuffed it in his back pocket.

"Are you eating or just drinking?"

"Both." Louie was starving. She hadn't eaten anything other than some chips and a pumpkin cereal bar since brunch at Gabe's café. All Gabe had in his fridge were day-old pizza, beer, and water, and when Louie ventured briefly outside, there was no sign of a convenience store. On the drive in, she'd seen a Kroger around two miles away and had decided that would be her first stop in the morning. After that, she'd find a mattress store. Fresh food and satisfying sleep were lifestyle necessities; Louie's level of grumpiness was directly correlated to a lack of either.

The server put two menus on the table. "Can I get you some drinks?"

"I'll have a Coke."

He looked at Gabe. "And for you?"

"Whatever you have on tap will be great, thanks."

"Sure thing."

Louie opened her menu and scanned it quickly for chicken fingers. Fancy food had never been her thing. Growing up with a bowl of peas and black pepper served as a main course made it hard to appreciate nouveau cuisine. She spotted her desired dish and dropped the card to the table. Gabe didn't seem to have looked at his menu. "You're such a regular that you already know what you're having?"

He scratched at the stubble on his face and shook his head. "I wasn't going to have anything."

"Is the food not as good as the music?"

"It's not that…"

The comic book light bulb flicked on over Louie's head. "You're strapped for cash?"

He shrugged and looked away. "Like I said, I couldn't afford my house until you came along this morning."

Louie reached over and lightly punched Gabe's shoulder. "This is my treat." It'd be the only one for a while. The few hundred she'd have left after buying a bed wouldn't last long, and she wouldn't get her first pay check for a month.

"You're sure?"

"Dude, if it wasn't for you, I'd be sleeping in my truck with only my guitar for company. It's the least I can do. Let's celebrate finding each other—together we're going to…" Louie didn't finish the corny sentiment. She'd been handed a serious case of slack jaw by the beautiful woman who'd just entered through the back door, her hair made angelically luminescent as it bounced in the glow of the stage lighting. Louie searched her memory banks of *Nash Country* magazine to place her. If she was performing tonight, the evening had ramped up to perfection already. Louie shamelessly followed her every move as she glided elegantly past them, circled around the center tables, and stopped at the soundboard.

"I'd call dibs, but that woman might hold the key to my future."

"She can be my future right now." It sounded soppy, but she didn't mean it seriously. The burn of Mia still tingled painfully in her heart, and now that she was finally in the city to work toward her dream, a relationship was the last thing on her mind. But boy, that woman had something special. The way she held herself, how her hair moved as if caressing her shoulders as she walked. She had an air of arrow-like focus. She was a woman to write a song about.

The lady finished her conversation with the sound engineer and began to walk back toward the stage door. Louie remained content to simply enjoy the floor show and barely registered Gabe's movement to stand and block her vision.

"Excuse me, miss, but I saw you record my session at the Douglas a few nights ago. Can I ask why?"

Heather recognized Gabe Duke. This was exactly the reason why Heather made sure she stayed hidden at gigs. She was here to support Emma, who was performing in the Spotlight session for the first time. This one meager hour was her downtime before she watched the Writers Night at Donny's behest, though she was sure there was no new talent to mine. Worse yet, Mia and Diane were performing, and Emma had told Heather they thought she was here to see them, certain they were on the verge of being signed by Rocky Top.

"Sorry, miss, did you hear me?"

Heather gave her best public smile. This guy was a special talent, but that didn't make it any less inconvenient that he was impeding her path back to Emma. "Sorry, I was focused on getting backstage to my friend." She extended her hand. "I'm Heather King. I work for RTCM." When Gabe looked puzzled, she added, "Rocky Top."

He shook her hand with enthusiasm.

"I'm sorry. I should've known that."

There were a lot of labels to remember, and she'd heard Gabe was relatively new in town. Added to the fact that Heather had no ego or personal investment in the label meant Gabe hadn't caused offense. She smiled to help put him at ease since he was almost vibrating on the spot. "It's fine. Honestly."

Gabe stepped to the side to make way for the sound engineer. Heather glanced at the other occupant of Gabe's table, and undiluted desire came over her like a cloak. The person stood and smiled knowingly, as if acutely aware of their universal appeal. Their eyes promised an explosive encounter, but there was a clear non-physical barrier that guarded their heart and would offer nothing more. Perhaps precisely what Heather needed after five years of career-controlled celibacy. The cool night breeze slipped through the open door and traversed her spine with the feather-like touch of a familiar lover. *Please, God, be a woman.*

"I'm Louie."

The moniker was inconclusive, but the soft tone of her voice made it clear Louie was a woman. The lack of an Adam's apple as

Louie lifted her chin to reveal a faintly tanned and slender neck was additional proof. Heather found herself wanting to trace her tongue along it and taste Louie's skin. She reluctantly pulled herself from her absorbing fantasy to acquiesce to social etiquette and held out her hand. Louie took it, far gentler than Gabe, and kissed her knuckles. Heather was struck by the chivalrous nature of the gesture and had to stop herself from giggling. Was this what she'd been missing out on by just dating high femmes?

Heather felt Gabe's presence as he moved back to her side when the sound engineer had passed by.

"Sorry about that, Ms. King."

He smiled and Heather could see an army of sixteen- to thirty-year-old women and men falling at his feet to worship him. Not classically attractive, but square-jawed, muscular, and handsome enough for posters, dolls, and T-shirts to fly from his tour shelves. If only Donny could see past his color. "I have to go." Louie was still standing and her eyes were fixed on Heather. She looked like she would've been happy to push Heather against the wall and devour her. Heather was seriously inclined to let her, but Emma was waiting backstage after sending her to speak to the sound tech.

"Could I just ask if Rocky Top is interested in me?"

Heather bit her lip, again acutely aware of why she stayed in the shadows when scoping for new talent. The hopeful look in his eyes made her wish she could give him the news he craved, but Donny was still undecided on whether or not to offer him an audition. "You're being considered for an audience with the label head, Gabe, but it's by no means a certainty." She should offer some advice. It's what she needed when she hit the town, expecting to burn brighter than the Dog Star. "Do you have any original material?" Her heart sank when he hesitated and his hungry fire seemed to extinguish. There was no way he'd get through the doors if all he did were Johnny Cash covers, no matter how amazing they were.

"He will."

Louie draped her arm over Gabe's shoulder, and Heather saw his spark reignite. Had she misread the situation and they were... together? They certainly made an interesting combination and subverted so many stereotypes they probably put a bug up the ass of right-wing die-hard country fans on a whole raft of counts.

"You'll write for me?"

Gabe grinned at Louie, who'd nodded but focused only on Heather. Struggling to get a handle on the two of them, Heather scuttled for a new angle of conversation. They seemed so naturally familiar and yet Gabe's surprise at Louie's offer indicated a new relationship. Perhaps they were just friends. Heather could hope. Instead, she decided Emma could wait a few more minutes to give her time to push for confirmation. "You're a writer?"

Louie nodded. "I am. Is your label looking for fresh talent there too?"

Louie was confident, bordering on cocky, and Heather tried hard to push away the kernel of unprofessional behavior that was pressing for her to trade on her position with Rocky Top to score a horizontal position with Louie. She scolded herself, pushed her hair over her ears, and smiled as blandly as she could manage given the impure thoughts tearing around her mind. "Rocky Top is always looking for the..." She repressed the obvious sexual metaphor. "Looking for the very best of writers and performers. Do you sing?" Heather wasn't sure why she asked that particular question. It was hard enough to get away from the bewildering blandness of a whitewashed country scene; she'd wager that convincing it to love a short-haired woman who could easily pass as a handsome man was some years away.

Louie laughed. "I can hold a tune, but I'm no Savana Hayes. I'm just a wordsmith."

A hint of cockiness mixed with humility. Louie's appeal was increasing with every sentence. "So you write and your boyfriend sings?" Subtle. Sledgehammer subtle. Louie's mouth curled into that exceptionally sexy knowing smile again. It was clear she knew Heather was fishing for their relationship status, and Heather cursed her lack of flirting finesse. She'd been out of the game too long, and she had no idea how to hook someone like this. Someone so different than her usual pool. Like she was any kind of Casanova with her two long-term lovers.

"We're friends and housemates."

It was time to get back to Emma and out of this wildly unfamiliar situation. Heather pulled herself from Louie's gaze and checked her watch. "I'm sorry. I have to see my friend before she goes on stage." *Don't say it.* "Perhaps we could have a drink after the show?" Heather began to move away, already too embarrassed with her candid come-on that she didn't want to wait for a refusal, or worse, an acceptance. Louie's hand wrapped around her wrist and paused her flight.

"I'd love to."

Heather pressed her lips together in a tight smile, willing herself to say nothing else stupid. "Later, then." She felt Louie's firm grip fall away and thought of Louie holding her in the same way while they had sex. In her rush to escape, she almost tripped over an errant chair. *Jesus, get a grip.*

CHAPTER TEN

Louie bit her bottom lip as she watched Heather swoosh from their presence in that oh-so-seductive way only a femme could carry off, then she broke into a grin when she appeared to have a falling out with a chair that jumped into her path. Heather didn't look back, and Louie sighed, disappointed that she hadn't made a good enough impact on her. She returned to her seat at the same time as their server brought drinks to the table and took their order.

"You're pretty smooth. You'll make a good wingwoman for me."

She thought she'd forgotten how to be that smooth. Heather seemed reluctant to bite at first, but her questions around Louie and Gabe's relationship indicated at least a passing interest. Louie knew she should've backed off when it became apparent that Heather might be able to help her career, but she'd been unable to resist. She wanted to make a better second impression on Heather. She didn't know if she was being overly optimistic or believing too much in the run of good luck she was having, but it felt like Heather could be influential for her future. And Gabe's. "Man, I'm sorry. I totally messed that up. I should've stayed in my seat."

"What're you talking about? I'd lost her, but you rescued me with your songwriting. Speaking of which..." He thumbed the condensation on his beer glass and looked up at her.

"Yeah?"

"How will that work? You writing me a song, I mean."

"What kind of song are you looking for? True love? Lost love? Unrequited love? Do you want to sing about your truck or patriotism? Or maybe your mom?"

"Funny. I want something deeper than that. Something that hits hard and stays with you for years."

Louie scoffed. "You're not asking for much, then." Gabe shrugged and didn't respond. She'd only known him a few hours, but he was so open and unguarded that reading him was relatively easy. He went quiet when he was unsure of himself. "I'm just kidding. I love deep and hard-hitting." She blinked away the nanosecond flash of going deep with Heather and refocused. "I'm happy to go down that road, Gabe, but for it to ring true, it's got to be your truth. Your experience. Something dark you've never shared." It wasn't like Louie had read the A-to-Z of writing country songs, but this was always how she'd felt it should be.

Gabe leaned back in his chair. He rubbed his thumb hard into the palm of his hand, and Louie wondered if it was a coping mechanism he'd learned much the same as hers. He clearly had the something she was talking about, but if he'd never told anyone about it, opening up for inspection here might not be such a great idea.

"I didn't mean to talk about it now, Gabe." She wanted to reach over to comfort him, but he was too far away, and he might not react kindly to such an overt show of emotion. Louie had to remind herself they'd only met that morning. Everything had been buddy-buddy so far, but whatever it was Gabe had been through probably wasn't up for disclosure yet.

Gabe moved closer again and drank half his glass of beer. They sat in silence for a while, leaving Louie to think she'd overstepped the mark and should've kept her smart mouth shut. Their server brought their food, and they both tucked in with neither speaking.

The MC welcomed Emma Eagan to the stage so Louie turned her chair to the wall to get a good view. Heather came out of the stage door holding hands with another good-looking woman. They parted at the steps up to the platform, confirming the other woman as tonight's first performer, and Heather joined three other people at the table maybe ten feet from her. Louie's confusion heightened. Heather had invited her for a drink after the show, but her familiarity with Emma gave her pause. Were they together? Talk about a lesbian power couple. Heather glanced over somewhat sheepishly, making Louie think she must be right. Then again, they could just be friends like her and Gabe. If Heather was out with her significant other, surely she wouldn't have been so interested in their relationship? It didn't matter anyway. Louie wasn't about to have a fling on her first night in Nashville.

Gabe's touch on her arm pulled her from her reverie.

"Do you think they're together?"

"It looks like it," Louie replied, grateful that Gabe had chosen to speak again even if he had completely changed the subject. She couldn't judge. Sharing her darkest secrets wasn't high on the agenda with a new friend despite having hit it off so well. Hell, she hadn't shared herself with anyone since Mia. She spun the spare coaster around to distract from the unwanted thoughts of her ex. Maybe a new relationship would be the only way to rid her of these constant invasions. She picked up a chicken finger, dipped it in the honey mustard dressing, and munched it with gusto. "How's your food?"

Gabe nodded around a mouthful of the biggest burger Louie had ever seen. Drips of cheese, pickle, and mustard were escaping at every opening, squeezing through Gabe's fingers and dropping onto the plate. Perfect timing for their server to return to ask the same question.

"It's great, thanks. We'll take another beer and Coke though, please."

"Coming up."

Gabe managed to put his thumbs up in response. Louie returned her attention back to the stage and tried to keep Heather in her peripheral vision. Emma was a great singer with a big and gritty voice that would have easily filled the room without electronic assistance. Louie thought about being surprised she hadn't heard of Emma before reality hit her and she grasped where she was. The Bluebird Café. Nashville. She'd actually made it. She shifted forward in her seat to concentrate purely on Emma. She listened intently to the lyrics and the way Emma's voice told the story of each one. When her set ended after just three songs, Louie got on her feet to show her appreciation. She became aware that everyone else was merely applauding, albeit enthusiastically, and a flush shot across her chest and up to her neck.

Gabe pulled her back down to her seat. "Steady, tiger."

But Louie didn't want to contain her excitement. She'd waited years for this. Sitting here, listening to great musicians perform amazing music and working on her chance to write music for them had been her dream from the moment she understood what a dream was. She tipped her head back and focused on the ceiling as the emotion of the moment became too much for her face to contain and her eyes threatened to leak some of it. She tried to keep her eyes wide open, knowing that if she blinked, the tears would track down her face. No one but her mom had seen her cry, and she didn't want to break that habit tonight. Even Mia hadn't managed to do that. Thinking about Mia dried everything up. She looked back to Gabe, who looked faintly amused at her reaction.

"Don't say a word." She accompanied the warning with a missile of sweet potato fries aimed at his face.

Gabe held up his hands. "I got nothing."

The MC returned to the stage and announced the next act. A ragtag bunch of guys took to the stage and started their set with a rambunctious country rock effort. Heather smiled at her friends' conversations, hoping she was doing it in all the right places, but her concentration was torn between Louie and Emma. Louie clearly lived and breathed country music. As soon as Emma began to sing, Louie looked zoned in on the stage to the apparent exclusion of all else, presumably allowing herself to be consumed by Emma's stunning vocals and personal lyrics. Why Donny hadn't signed her, Heather could only put down to a lack of courage. Emma's songs were edgy, and she never shied away from the controversial.

Louie's disappointment when Emma's set ended after just three songs was blatantly obvious, and Heather watched, fascinated, as she unleashed her appreciation with wild abandon. Louie looked at the ceiling, and Heather knew she was trying to stop herself from crying with the emotion of it all. Music moved her soul for sure. She wondered what kind of lyrics Louie wrote and what her process was. She'd presented as a street smart sex god, but there seemed to be a far gentler woman camouflaged in a foxhole behind her eyes.

The scraping of a chair across the wooden floor brought Heather back to the evening.

"How was I?"

Emma positioned her seat beside Heather and put her hand on her thigh. Conscious of Louie's potential interpretation of Emma's gesture, Heather took Emma's hand in her own. "Em, you were amazing." She released Emma's hand, mindful that wouldn't look much better. She looked beyond Emma to glance over at Louie and smiled. Louie nodded before turning her attention back to the stage. She hoped Louie didn't think they were together.

"Distracted much?" Emma moved her head and blocked Heather's view before turning to see the object of Heather's preoccupation. "I'm confused. Who are you looking at?"

"Nobody." Heather knew she'd given herself away when she followed her disclaimer with a nibble of her lip. An obvious tell.

Emma leaned in. "Feathers. Are you thinking of playing on my team? All I can see are pretty boys."

"Look again at the first table next to the bathrooms." Heather clamped her hand on Emma's forearm as she turned to look. "For goodness sake, Em, could you be less obvious?"

Em waved her hand toward a waiter, and Heather watched her sweep over Louie from her toes to the cute little quiff in her hair. After she'd ordered a drink, Emma swiveled back in her chair. "The tall, skinny one's a woman…she's handsome. Isn't she a little bit not your type at all? Like, not enough hair and boobs for you?"

Heather tilted her head. "Not usually, but maybe that's where I've been going wrong. She kissed my hand." This time, Heather yielded to the temptation to giggle and felt like a ninth grader ogling the swim team captain. "Would we call her skinny? I would've said athletic."

"Why don't we go ask her to take her shirt off and we'll measure her biceps?"

Emma moved to rise from her chair, and Heather caught hold of her to keep her seated. "Oh my God, don't you dare."

Emma laughed. "As if I was going to do that. How did her kissing your hand come to pass? Spill...*everything.*"

Heather recounted the tale quickly, regularly glancing across to Louie and Gabe, but they seemed engrossed in the current band. She thought she was in Louie's peripheral vision, but it was impossible to be sure.

"What are you waiting for, then? Let's go over there and have a drink. Gabe's a cutey. A little young for me, but I'll keep him entertained while you get to know Louie."

Heather shook her head at Emma's use of air quotes around "get to know." For some reason, Emma thought women hooking up on a first meeting was more acceptable than a guy and a woman. "I don't know, Em. I like to keep a distance from performers, especially when they live with the hot woman I'd like to...I don't want to give Gabe the wrong idea. I can't tell him any more about his chances at Rocky Top than I already have."

"I'm sure he accepted that, and if he tries to talk about it some more, I'll distract him." Emma took Heather's hand in hers and looked at her seriously. "Feathers, how long has it been since you relaxed a little and had some harmless fun?"

Heather shrugged. She couldn't say with any degree of certainty that she'd ever done that. And she'd never had the opportunity for a one-night stand. Not that she would have taken it had it ever been offered. It was presumptuous to think one was being offered now. But she did deserve some fun. She'd been working her ass off for five years and had landed a golden chance to prove herself worthy of a higher position with the label. The dream of running her own label was looking more like a reality she could achieve. Maybe she could relax and celebrate where she'd gotten to, especially working with Savana Hayes. It *would* be nice to speak to someone outside the business for a change. Someone new. Someone she could imagine taking home.

"Fine." Heather inhaled in an effort to soak up the courage she wanted to feel. "Let's wait until the band swaps out with the girls."

On cue, the band finished their set, and Heather clapped as Emma's friends took the stage. She stood, ready to head to Louie's table before she changed her mind again but noticed Louie grab her jacket, all but leap from her seat, and take the long way around the tables to the exit. Heather's hopes for the rest of the evening sank like a bad song to the bottom of the Billboard Hot 100. *What about that drink?*

CHAPTER ELEVEN

Louie swung the door open and gulped the warm night air as if she'd just come up from a deep-sea dive. She half-stumbled down the concrete ramp and held onto the metal rail for support. She heard the doorman call after her, but his words didn't register. She looked right and left along the strip mall, for what, she had no idea. All she could see was Mia getting up on stage. The room seemed to close in and become even smaller, and Louie had to get out of there. Her first day in Nashville had been so picture-perfect, such an idyllic fairy tale, that Louie should've know better. She'd gotten carried away on the wave of luck she was riding, but predictably, it had just wiped her out and crashed her into shore, bedraggled and breathing hard.

She spun around at the touch of a firm hand on her shoulder to find a concerned-looking Gabe.

"Are you okay, Louie?"

She didn't answer for a moment and leaned against the rail while she tried to gather herself. Louie closed her eyes and tried to conjure up a coping tool, an image of some sort to help her deal with seeing her ex-lover, but everything evaded her.

"Louie, what's wrong?"

"One of the women who just got up on stage is my ex." When she heard her own explanation, it sounded lame. Like she was some lovestruck kid mooning over a lost love. Gabe must've thought so too because he didn't answer. Louie imagined he was waiting for more detail that might explain her overreaction. "It's a long story. You should go back in. I'm going to head home."

Gabe looked over his shoulder. His indecision may as well have been a comic cloud above his head. She had no idea how much he'd paid for that reservation, and there were still plenty of performers to come. Given his current financial situation, she didn't want him missing out.

"Hey. Aren't you that black kid that thinks he can sing country?"

Louie looked toward a group of three guys bearing down on them from the parking lot. Between the little light on the sidewalk and the Bluebird's illuminations, Louie figured they were probably all in their mid-thirties. She saw Gabe straighten up, ready to stand his ground. Rounding off an already busted night with a fight didn't appeal. She hadn't had one since high school, and she intended to keep that record.

"That depends—"

"Yeah, you are. I was down at the Douglas the other night, having myself a good time with the wife when you came on."

The guy in the middle spoke again, and Louie quickly scoped his two friends to get a feel for their intentions. Their eyes were already half-glazed; obviously their night had begun much earlier than Louie and Gabe's. If they were looking for trouble, Louie decided she and Gabe would easily evade their clumsily swinging fists, get to her truck, and be out of there with minimum fuss.

"And what did you think, sir?" Louie asked the pale paunchy one as she reached behind Gabe and tugged the back of his jacket to keep him from making any stupid moves.

Paunchy guy looked up at Louie. "The wife liked him. Pissed me off."

Louie spotted his battered Titans ball cap. "You're local, right?"

He tugged on its peak. "Born and bred, kid. What about you?"

"Wish I was. I just got in from Chicago, but I'm already in love with the place. I bet you could give us a tip or two about this business, huh?"

Paunchy guy tapped Gabe on the shoulder firmly. "I sure could. *You're* going to have a tough time trying to crack this town, looking like a gangbanger."

Louie kept Gabe's jacket balled up in her fist. He might have a short fuse, so she was hoping her physical contact with him would keep him grounded. "But does he sound like one, sir?"

He shrugged. "Not a bit. I closed my eyes and it was like listening to a regular white guy."

Louie didn't miss Gabe's jaw twitching, like he was clenching and unclenching his teeth to stop himself from knocking the guy out. Paunchy guy's friends had grown a little twitchy too. She needed to distract them with one of the other things men like this treasured—ogling women. And if they heckled Mia, Louie traded it off as karma. "Are you guys going to the Bluebird now?" Her question pulled the attention of all three back to her, and they nodded or mumbled yes. "There's a fantastic couple of girls singing right now. They've only just come on, but you should get in there or you'll miss their whole set."

Paunchy guy's buddies clapped him on the back. "That's who we've come for, the two blond long-haired hotties Ted told us about. Let's go."

Louie pulled Gabe backward to the metal railing to give space for the trio to pass. "Have a great night, guys," she called after them and saw Heather standing a few feet away, looking good backlit by the Bluebird's neon. She lifted her hand to acknowledge her, but her focus drew back to Gabe. "Are you okay?"

"Yeah. No. No, I'm fine."

Louie moved to follow his gaze, which was falling anywhere but on her. "There are always going to be assholes like that wherever you go." Contentment that she'd managed to avoid an ugly confrontation didn't mask the steady shake at her core. Assholes like that *were* everywhere, and she'd half expected them to take offense against the way she looked. She'd had plenty of that experience. Maybe the amount of alcohol they'd consumed had blinded their senses some, and she was glad of that, especially with Heather in the background. Who knew how long she'd been standing there, and Louie didn't want her thinking that she was a street thug. Louie accepted she was white trash in the eyes of someone as classy as Heather, but that didn't mean she had to act like the worst stereotype. Her mom had raised her better than that.

"I know. It doesn't make it hurt any less, you know?"

The look in his eyes suggested he knew Louie had probably had her share of altercations based on her non-traditional presentation, but she'd never compare what she'd been through to the racism Gabe had no doubt suffered. More words seemed patronizing so she just hung her arm over his shoulder. She snuck a glance back to see if Heather was still outside. Her heart jumped when she saw not only was she still there, but she'd begun to walk toward them.

Louie snapped her keys from her jeans and shoved them at Gabe's chest. "Any chance you could wait in the truck?"

Gabe looked up to see Heather's approach. "Sure, stud." He took Louie's keys but closed his hand over hers and sighed. "Could we talk though, y'know, when we get back home?"

Back home, not back to the house. Gabe's word choice spoke of both of their need to belong. Louie nodded and slapped him on the back as he left. The night had been so promising, but now she was heading home with her straight housemate rather than the sexy label exec. Gabe's need to talk trumped her need to get laid. She'd pushed him on getting to his truth for a song, then they'd had a run-in with some rednecks. And as much as she wanted to see where that drink with Heather might lead, there was also the presence of Mia to contend with, and there was no way Louie wanted to go back into the Bluebird to hear her ex and her new floozy sing.

"That looked like it could've gotten nasty if you hadn't stepped in."

Heather had obviously watched enough of the incident to make an interpretation. Louie shoved her hands into her jeans and leaned back against the rail. Her instinct was to reach out and pull Heather closer. "Guys like that can usually be talked down from doing anything stupid."

"Still, you were brave."

Heather touched Louie's forearm and smiled, but she seemed hesitant. Louie kept her hands deep in her pockets and resisted the urge to wrap her hand around the back of Heather's neck and lean down to kiss her. Heather seemed interested, but it was mixed with an uncertainty Louie couldn't miss. If Heather wanted something from her, she would have to make her need blatant.

"You ducked out of the show in a hurry."

Louie rolled her neck. Talking about an ex wasn't the kind of conversation Louie envisaged having with Heather. "It was hot. Had to get some fresh air." Smooth. If Heather *was* interested, she'd soon be put off by Louie's impression of a monosyllabic moron.

Heather took a tentative step forward and rested her fingers on Louie's belt. "Anything in particular making you hot?"

Louie swallowed down what felt like a bowling ball of cotton wool. Most of her body hummed gently; a particular place, not so gently. "You…" It wasn't a lie. Mia had been the reason Louie had vacated her seat as if her ass was on fire and the only remedy was outside the Bluebird's door. But Heather was definitely the one making her hot in *this* moment. The thought of her new housemate needing support intruded, as unwelcome as a priest in a whorehouse. "I have to go."

Heather moved in so her breasts pressed against Louie's ribs. "To support your friend?" Louie nodded. "That's sweet."

She pushed up on her tiptoes and kissed Louie lightly on the cheek before retreating to create an unwanted distance between them. Louie held fast, her fists balled in her pockets, furiously playing with change. "I'll see you around?"

"It's a small town," Heather said as she strutted back up the ramp and into the Bluebird.

Louie watched, her desire inflamed by Heather's sassiness. Her cockiness had hastily withdrawn and left her vulnerable and… genuine. She pushed away from the rail and sauntered toward her truck. Nashville already promised to fulfill *all* her dreams.

CHAPTER TWELVE

*O*h *my God. Where the hell did that vamp act come from?*
Heather returned to her seat, feeling a little buzzed and blaming that for her brazen bravery. Another table had been added, and Mia and Diane had joined them. Heather shook her head in Emma's direction, warning her that she'd be saying nothing in front of those two. She hadn't sat down before it was clear Mia had already taken control of the conversation.

"I can't believe it. After what she did to me, I hoped I'd never see her again."

Heather tried to tune her out. She didn't know what Mia was talking about, and she didn't want to know. Emma had naughtily refilled Heather's glass, a ploy she always used to ensure Heather stayed out that little bit longer than she intended. Get through this drink and she'd be able to leave. Emma would understand. She knew well enough that Heather's patience for Mia's and Diane's constant dramatization of their lives irritated her beyond words.

Mia's words drifted back into her awareness.

"She was violent when she drank, and I couldn't take it anymore. I had to leave. I had no choice."

Diane wrapped her arms around Mia and pulled her into a hug. "It's okay, baby. I know you did."

Emma tapped Heather's thigh and motioned toward the bathroom with a nod. Heather waited until Emma was halfway there before she joined her. Emma said nothing until the stalls were empty and they were alone.

"She's talking about your Louie."

Heather shook her head. "She's not my Lou—what do you mean?" Louie was a violent drunk? Surely not.

"Mia says they used to live together. Apparently, they moved from Wisconsin to Chicago to earn enough money to make it to Nashville. The way Mia is telling it, your girl has a dark past, Feathers. She's making her sound like Jekyll and Hyde."

Heather sighed and looked at herself in the mirror. The sexual confidence she'd just sprayed all over Louie faded like an old photograph exposed to bright light. All she saw in her reflection was a lost opportunity. "Do you believe her?"

Emma took Heather's hands in her own. "Whether Mia's tale is true or not doesn't matter." Emma smiled. "You haven't been interested in anyone like this in all the time I've known you. You owe it to yourself to hear the story straight from Louie's mouth." Emma let go of Heather's hands, took a step back, and winked. "I've heard all about you lesbians. You can be evil about each other when you've been scorned. It's the only reason I don't let you flip me like a pancake."

Heather laughed and swatted at her but missed. Emma had a natural propensity to paint a coat of fun onto a serious conversation. She would've been Heather's type before...before Heather found herself seriously attracted to Louie. "How do you ask someone if they like beating up their girlfriend when they get drunk? How would that friendly chat go? And where's the best place to talk that through? A coffee shop? Over dinner at a fancy restaur—"

"In bed?" Emma wiggled her eyebrows and smirked.

"What if it *isn't* true? Mia isn't the most discreet person in the world. It'll be all over Nashville within a week. What about Louie's career?" *I'm getting ahead of myself.* She could tell from Emma's amused expression she needed to dial down the crazy. "If Louie was a guy, how would you handle it?" Though only three years older than Heather, Emma seemed to have packed her thirty-two spins around the earth with a lot more experience, particularly the sexual kind.

Emma tilted her head back and looked at the ceiling of the restroom. "I'd make a date, get settled in, and then broach the subject of Mia. Easy." She turned both hands palm up and shrugged. "Louie knows you were backstage with me and is probably thinking you know each other. I'll wager she's already worrying about what Mia might be saying about her. If you bring Mia up, it gives Louie the opportunity to tell you her version of events, and you can ask the questions you need to ask."

Heather nodded and began to contemplate a plan of action. If Louie did have violent tendencies, it'd certainly put an abrupt end to her hard crush. It wasn't for her to judge before she knew all the facts, but she did have her own career to consider too. Working with Savana was the start of bigger things for her, and Donny wouldn't tolerate even a sniff of a scandal. She sighed, realizing that again she was jumping the gun. The attraction between them was undeniable, sure, but maybe they had nothing else in common. She could easily be worrying about things that would never come to pass. She *did* know that she definitely wanted that date to find out. As long as Louie was okay with being discreet. Heather hadn't let her libido get in the way of her ambition for the past five years. She didn't want to start now. And she'd already sailed a little too close to that wind with her performance outside.

"Earth to Feathers. Come in, Feathers."

Heather pushed away from the sink and draped her arm around Emma's shoulders. "It's a plan." She let her go and opened the door.

"You're going for it?"

Heather smiled at Emma's obvious surprise. She'd never been in the dating game or learned how to play. Her two previous partners were friends who developed into something more. She suspected that might be the reason they didn't last, but she had nothing to compare it to. It looked like now might be the time to suit up and get off the bench.

"Batter up," Heather replied with a grin.

❖

Louie handed Gabe a beer and flopped onto the couch beside him. She hadn't expected her evening to end up like this, but Gabe needed to talk, and Heather seemed to appreciate her sensitivity to that. Louie could only hope she hadn't blown it. She sipped her beer, waiting for Gabe to break the silence in his own time.

"Sorry I ruined your night."

"Didn't I ruin yours first? You followed *me* out of the Bluebird. You wouldn't have run into those guys otherwise."

Gabe shook his head and traced the etching on his bottle with his finger. "Nah, they would've seen me in there too." He tugged at his cheek. "It's not like I blend in."

Louie tilted her head in acknowledgement and said nothing. Prompting conversation with people she hardly knew wasn't her strong suit unless she was flirting. Her thoughts drifted to Heather again, but she pulled her focus back to Gabe. Jake had been her one true friend, and they'd shared everything, especially their fears and feelings. Thinking back, it had taken a while to get there. It felt like she and Gabe were on a similar path, but maybe it would take her sharing something with him to get him talking. The other side of the seesaw was that she didn't want to hog the conversation and make the night all about her woes either.

"Thanks for taking care of it. It's not like I can't handle myself. I just don't want to have to, you know?" Gabe took a long draw on his beer and shifted so he was in the corner of the sofa, looking at Louie.

She couldn't begin to imagine the life Gabe had left behind, but there was a subtext to his words that indicated his Georgia years hadn't been all peaches and pecans. "I'm glad they were easily distracted. I wouldn't have been much help. I'm no fighter." She pointed at Gabe's bicep, the cotton of his short-sleeved T-shirt strained to contain it. "It's probably good for them that you didn't fight."

He flexed and smiled. "I got these working in sanitation. Throwing those metal bins around for a couple of years built me up."

"Did you always want to be a country singer?" The change of topic felt clunky, but Louie figured Gabe would simply shut it down if he wasn't ready to talk.

"I always wanted to sing, I remember that much. I spent a lot of time in church on Sundays, and my mom forced me to join the choir."

Louie caught Gabe's jaw twitch when he mentioned his mom. She didn't miss his word choice, either. When Gabe didn't continue, Louie pressed gently. "Forced you?"

He nodded but didn't make eye contact. "It was the one thing she forced me to do that I actually enjoyed."

Louie swallowed another mouthful of beer. The truth she needed to write Gabe's song for him was seeping out. She suspected writing it would be far easier than the effort it would take Gabe to perform it publicly. "How did you get from church to country?"

His eyes brightened. "Darius Rucker." He swept his hand across the air before him as if he could see what he was saying. "I was fourteen when he made number one on the country charts in 2008...the first African-American to take that spot for twenty years. It also happened to be the year my dad found me and took me away from Mom."

"Bombshell much?" Unsure whether trying to lighten the mood was the right way to go or not, Louie did it anyway and was rewarded with Gabe's goofy laugh and a big show of his rounded, snow-white teeth.

"You'd have preferred me to build up to that?"

"Maybe a little." Louie finished her beer and stood. "Another one?" Gabe handed over his empty bottle, and Louie made a quick trip to the kitchen for replacements. She settled back into the sofa, scooched her feet beneath her, and faced Gabe. "Rewind a little. Did your dad leave you and your mom?" It seemed like this could be another thing they shared.

Gabe scrunched up his mouth and shook his head. "Dad didn't know about me. It was only when he happened to come back to Blakely that he found us. He was a traveling salesman, and he'd hooked up with mom briefly while he was in town selling bronzed baby shoes."

Louie held up her hand. "Wait. What? Bronzed what, now?"

"You heard me—bronzed baby shoes or anything else you wanted bronzed. Teeth, footballs, guns. If it was important to you,

Dad could bronze it for you. Pretty cool, actually." Gabe climbed over the back of the couch, took something from the sideboard, and handed it to Louie. "That's the stick shift from the car he taught me to drive in."

Louie hefted it and slapped it in the palm of her hand. "You could do some damage with this."

"Maybe I should carry it around with me for when I run into idiots like those guys tonight."

Louie raised her eyebrows. "Or…"

Gabe held up his hands. "I'm kidding. Someone like me takes to a white guy's head with something like that, and I wouldn't see another sunrise."

Louie placed the gear stick on the table and turned to Gabe. "Back to your story. Why did your dad take you away, and did he get thrown in jail for kidnapping?" Gabe was opening up, but Louie felt it was only because they were talking so lightheartedly. The dark shadows had been fleeting, but Louie didn't miss them because hers were similar. Gabe had clearly become adept at dismissing them as swiftly as they arose, just as Louie had.

Gabe took a long draw from his beer. He picked up his bronzed stick shift and fiddled with the ball of it in much the same way that Catholics turn over their Rosary beads.

"Mom wasn't the maternal type, and I was the product of a drunken one-night stand with Pops. I got in the way of the life she wanted to lead so she found ways around that. Sometimes…a lot of times, her anger would get the better of her, and I got my share of the devil inside her."

A track of tears traced a lonely path down Gabe's cheek. He wiped it away with the back of his hand before running his hand through his hair as if to disguise the real reason for his movement. Louie didn't draw attention to it. He'd bared his experience to her, someone he'd just met, and the significance of his revelation humbled her. She'd asked for his truth and he'd given it willingly, though the past still clearly burned hot.

"I'm getting my guitar. Let's write that song for your Rocky Top audition."

CHAPTER THIRTEEN

Louie's new boss, Clare, was a big improvement on Keg-belly back at the GrindStar. For starters, her clothes fit properly and she didn't act like she was better than her staff. Her induction had been mercifully brief—brewing coffee and taking money weren't a big drain on Louie's brain—before she'd returned to the kitchen and left her to staff the counter with a cute brunette called Hayley. In the spirit of proving that she was over Mia, Louie had wanted to be a little bit more than friendly and possibly even work up to asking her out. But meeting Heather King had put her game off kilter, and in the brief moments between orders, Louie drifted to their exchange outside the Bluebird. In every one of the twenty or so versions she'd imagined so far, none of them involved leaving alone.

"How're you finding it?"

Louie turned to Clare and smiled. "It's really good. The customers are great, a lot friendlier than the city types I'm used to."

Clare patted her on the shoulder and nodded. "That's the beauty of a place for the locals, Louie. You get to know everybody and they get to know you. It's nice to be part of something. Y'know?"

Louie grinned at Clare's coffeehouse philosophy, especially since almost all of her staff were wannabe singers from all over the country, but she wasn't wrong. She'd been searching for somewhere like this before she even left home. Her mom's family had made them feel like they didn't belong with them. "I sure do, Clare. Thanks again for this opportunity. I really appreciate it."

"Not a problem, Louie. You get through the rest of this shift like you've worked the morning, and you've got yourself a job." She tapped her watch. "Time for you to take a break before the lunch rush."

Louie looked up at the wall clock, surprised how quickly the morning had passed. "Am I okay to grab a coffee and sit by the bar?"

"Sure. Just take off your apron and cover your shirt so you don't get bothered for orders." Clare tapped her nose and turned back to the kitchen.

Louie slipped into the back area and did as she was told. She pulled on a hoody to cover her uniform, grabbed her lyric book, and took up a station at the bar where Hayley had already placed a coffee for her. "Thanks, H." She took a sip and closed her eyes as the strong, hot liquid coursed down her throat and the caffeine headed straight for her brain.

"Are you asleep or meditating?"

Louie opened her eyes to see Heather King standing in front of her. "Would you believe me if I said both?"

Heather smiled and Louie tried hard to stop her brain from making some romantic comparison to the light of heaven. That kind of gushiness was best utilized in song lyrics. She had to maintain some level of cool, even though the briefest glimpse of Heather had roused a bevy of butterflies in her stomach. But damn, Louie wanted to continue exactly where they'd left off at the Bluebird a few nights ago.

"You're an empty vessel, then? You've achieved some level of higher enlightenment that the rest of us could only dream about?"

Louie grinned, patted the stool beside her, and withheld the filthy pun about being happy for Heather to fill her empty vessel. She didn't want Heather to think of her as crass. "So I'm told. Take a seat, and I'll give you some tips."

"I only have ten minutes."

"Me too." Louie didn't miss the way Heather swiftly scoped the café before she sat beside her. Had Louie missed something? Heather hadn't seemed too worried about who saw her outside the

Bluebird when she snuggled her breasts to Louie's chest. Maybe she wasn't so open when she was sober. Louie pushed the thought to the deeper recesses of her mind. She didn't want to deal with a closet case right now. "You've obviously got great taste in coffee. This place serves the strongest you'll find in this town."

"Ah, you would've put me off with that line if I hadn't been in here hundreds of times before. They know exactly how I like my coffee." Heather pulled the takeout cup Hayley passed to her across the counter. "Thanks, Hayley. Perfect as usual."

"Only the best for the talent whisperer," said Hayley and winked.

Louie clenched her jaw. It was probably an innocent enough wink, one that had come from familiarity and one that wasn't steeped in lustful intent. Still…

Heather popped the lid on her coffee to add sweetener, and Louie noted that it looked more like steaming milk than any cup of beans she'd ever seen. "I don't know if I can trust someone who has their coffee that weak."

Heather tapped the side of Louie's mug with her manicured nail, and Louie wanted to be the mug.

"I don't know if *I* can trust someone who drinks coffee that looks like hot mud."

Heather flashed her show-stopping smile, and Louie wondered if everyone other than her had perfectly white teeth.

"Where does that leave us?" Louie didn't see the point in playing coy. There was no denying the attraction, and she hadn't misread Heather's interest when she hooked her finger in Louie's belt and moved in close enough to kiss her. Heather quickly surveyed the café again, and Louie raised her eyebrow. "Are you looking to see if someone else is more interesting before you say yes to a date with me?"

"Are you asking me on a date?" she whispered.

She'd avoided the question. Alarm bells sounded in Louie's head. She recalled the news piece about the VP at Rocky Top and the penny dropped. Heather was fearful of her sexuality being discovered. Her brazen behavior at the Bluebird had been a slip, possibly fueled by a little too much wine. "I suppose that depends on whether or not you'd consider going on a date with someone like me."

Heather looked beyond Louie and smiled at Hayley. "What do you mean, 'someone like me'?"

There were a few reasons Louie thought Heather wouldn't have entertained a relationship with her, but she hadn't considered this one. Maybe she was being naïve, thinking everyone could simply be who they were. Rocky Top's VP being fired should've been Louie's first clue. "I don't exactly blend into the crowd," Louie offered, not wanting to be too confrontational.

Heather's smile disappeared, and she bit her lip. She didn't answer immediately, and Louie thought she'd blown it. Dating someone like Heather was a nice dream while she had it, but she was already floating away from her like Aladdin on his flying carpet.

"I like you, Louie. And I'd like to get to know you. Dating *anyone* is hard for me; it doesn't matter what they look like." Heather sipped her coffee and again looked everywhere else in the café other than directly at Louie.

Louie wanted to take Heather's face in her hands. She needed to see that the look in Heather's eyes matched the words that were coming from her mouth. She had a drink of her own coffee and let the bitter taste fill her mouth for a moment before she swallowed. How hard could it be to date someone who wanted to be discreet? Wasn't it worth trying rather than always wondering what might've happened if she *didn't* try? "But you want to try?"

Heather nodded. "I do."

It was all Louie needed to know…for now. "Good enough."

After a short silence, Heather tapped Louie's lyric book. "Anything in there about me?" she asked quietly.

Louie grinned. She'd been close to writing some words for Heather but had been distracted by Gabe. "Not yet. I've been writing with Gabe. The story behind his songs should blow you away… hopefully." Louie added the last word to save herself from sounding over confident. No woman she'd ever met had found arrogance attractive.

"Can I see them?"

Heather's hand remained on the edge of the book, and Louie allowed herself a second to fantasize about how Heather's hand would feel on her neck as they kissed for the first time. She placed her hand on the other edge of the book and slowly pulled it from beneath Heather's hand, careful not to touch her though she was desperate to. Louie opened the book, thumbed through it to "Bronzed Baby Shoes," and passed it to Heather. "If you're not at least teary-eyed when you've finished reading that one, your heart is a cold, dead husk."

Heather laughed. "*Steel Magnolias* is the only thing that makes me cry ugly." She ran her fingers over the inked page. "Is it a deal breaker if there's only a slightly discernible lip wobble?"

Louie shook her head. "Total breakdown, ugly crying, complete devastation. I'm talking mascara running down your cheeks and banshee caterwauling…or no first date."

"Wow. That's a strong reaction you're looking for."

Louie pushed her book closer to Heather. "It's all in. Go on. I dare you not to cry."

"With so much at stake, how can I not?" Heather glanced up at Louie before beginning to read.

Heather's smile made Louie's stomach flip. She tried hard not to stare and looked at her coffee instead, but it was impossible not to. Louie thought about Heather's words—"Dating *anyone* is hard for me"—and what she might be getting herself into. After Mia, Louie had promised herself she'd be more careful with her choices, with her affections. But her attraction to Heather didn't seem to be under her control. It wasn't like she was already falling head over heels, can't live without you, let's U-Haul, in love, but she wanted more…more Heather. That much she knew. It looked like the die on that game had already been thrown.

Louie returned to concentrate on the song Heather was reading. She would've been far less confident if it was one of her other songs. With Heather's position, it would have felt too much like an audition, and more than that, it really mattered that Heather liked her words. But she *was* sure of Gabe's story and the emotion the song evoked.

Heather looked up, her eyes glassy with tears, and Louie grinned widely.

"Why are you smiling? Do you like making women cry?" Heather asked as she closed the book and pushed it back toward Louie.

"Only with my words, and only in joy." Or in the throes of mind-busting sex, Louie wanted to add but didn't. She imagined comments like that wouldn't fit into the "being discreet" box.

"That's really amazing, Louie. You're very talented." Heather dabbed at the corner of her eyes with a napkin. "Do you have music for it or do you write that separately?"

"We have it. I always write the music at the same time as the words, and Gabe is a great guitar player. But you already knew that."

Heather nodded. "Yeah, he's a real talent. If I owned the label, I would've signed him the first night I heard him sing…one day."

The wistful tone in Heather's voice was unmissable. "One day?" Louie asked.

Heather glanced at her watch and gasped. "Oh, crap." She stood abruptly and grabbed her coffee. "I'm sorry, Louie. I have to go." She opened her handbag.

"It's okay. I've got this."

Heather pulled out money and placed it on the counter. "I can't be…it's fine." She pushed the ten dollars toward Hayley.

"Thanks, Heather."

"We'll talk soon," Heather said over her shoulder as she walked out of the café.

Louie waved and smiled but didn't feel the emotion she showed. "I can't be" what? Seen to have a dyke buying her coffee? Louie clenched her jaw and tried to swallow the unpleasant feelings that bubbled up in her throat like bile. Is this what being discreet would mean? She picked up her song journal and headed into the back. Louie wanted to get to know Heather, but how much of Louie was Heather prepared for? She hadn't been in the closet for nearly two decades. The thought of returning to it, to not being who she was, and not being proud of who she'd become, was unthinkable. Would dating Heather ask that of her?

❖

Seeing Louie on her coffee run brightened Heather's day, but she'd left in a hurry and no doubt offended Louie when she wouldn't accept her kind offer to buy her coffee. She'd been skittish—Emma would be mortified by her reaction. God, why did she need dating lessons from her straight friend? Maybe because she had no idea what she was doing. Why had she even agreed to try dating in the first place? Her life had been on hold for five years while she chased her dream of owning a record label. Why couldn't she just wait another couple of years? Or choose a more suitable partner? Heather mentally slapped herself for judging how Louie presented herself. She was more comfortable in her own skin than Heather could dream of being. No, that wasn't altogether true. Heather was perfectly happy with who she was. She had no self-loathing over her sexuality. It was Nashville's problem, and Aaron being fired had proven that once again.

But in the three days since they'd met at the Bluebird, and between long and mentally draining sessions with Savana and her manager, Joe, Heather had thought about Louie a lot. When she wasn't entirely caught up in all things Savana, Heather had allowed her mind to flow toward Louie like a river to the ocean. She wouldn't admit to a fascination, that would be too strong a word, but Louie's lure *did* have her distracted from her work in ways no other woman ever had. Heather's previous relationships hadn't fulfilled her the way the lesbian fiction novels she'd read had led her to believe they would. Of course there'd been sex, and it was okay. Good, even. But it wasn't "ladies, start your engines" kind of hot. And it definitely wasn't the "I can't breathe without you near me" sort of romantic fiction love.

Still, her thoughts of Louie were different. How did she kiss? What would her skin feel like beneath Heather's fingers? Where did she come from? How long had she wanted to be a songwriter? Heather was thankful her lustful questions were partially tempered with an interest in who Louie was as a person. After the way she'd acted outside the Bluebird, she worried that exposure to Louie had caused an instant personality transplant resulting in her sex making the decisions instead of her head. Seeing Louie again had only intensified her need to know everything about her...including the truth about Mia's accusations of Louie being a violent drunk. They'd spent fifteen minutes together and they were drinking coffee not alcohol, so Heather had learned nothing of use in that department. Her subtle question about making women cry was met with a simple response, and Heather saw nothing lurking behind Louie's eyes that contradicted the sweet sentiment. Emma's advice to ask Louie about her relationship with Mia didn't seem like the way to go. If what Mia said *was* true, what was to stop Louie from simply lying about it?

A message chimed and appeared in the top corner of her screen: Donny wanted her in his office immediately. She checked the clock and quickly ran through the events of the morning. She couldn't recall any issues. Joe seemed his usual disgruntled self, but Heather had become used to expecting that after Savana had explained he wasn't yet on board with her change of direction. Savana was busy with auditioning the musicians Heather had gathered for her, and though she hadn't narrowed them down to a long list, never mind a short list, she seemed happy enough. While Joe was in a hurry to get Savana back on the radio stations, Savana was determined to take her time making sure everything aligned with her new vision.

Heather made her way to Donny's top floor office and ignored the numerous glances thrown her way by colleagues still sore from her promotion in the wake of Aaron being fired. Mandie greeted her with a broad smile and a cup of milky coffee, their code to let her know she'd be in with him for a while.

"Thanks, Mandie." She raised her cup toward Donny's closed door. "Anything I should be concerned about?" Longevity and certainty didn't exist in this business for the execs as much as the talent. Donny had put her in the VP position, and he could push her right back down again if he wished it. That knowledge made Heather even more determined to run her own label one day, and she'd do things differently.

"Of course not. He's just booking his auditions in for tonight."

"Ah, I forgot it's Wednesday."

Donny set aside the last Wednesday of every other month for a whirlwind of audition madness. With Savana, Joe, and Louie, she'd lost track of time, and this ritual had slipped her mind completely. She wished Donny would do it differently, but he seemed to like the power that holding the dreams of others in his hand gave him. Pick the talent, give them two hours' notice to be at Rocky Top, put them all in the same room, and make them wait while he gave them his ear for a maximum of three songs.

"Best get in there before he starts yelling," Mandie said before going back to the pile of paperwork on her desk.

Heather knocked, waited for an invitation, and entered Donny's office. She was glad she'd grabbed her iPad because he'd expect her to remember every band, duo, and solo artist she'd presented to him over the past eight weeks. In that time, Heather had seen almost one hundred and fifty acts, but she hadn't found anyone other than Gabe Duke that she sincerely believed in. He trusted her to narrow the field down to at least half that but always asked for thirty percent of what she'd listened to. Her final recommendations would usually number around ten. She had no idea whether or not he listened to the others. He'd certainly never offered up anyone from the discard pile in the years she'd worked for him as an exec, but she guessed it justified his claim to discovering the talent Heather found for the label.

"Talk to me about Purple Fire," he said as Heather settled into her seat.

She carefully placed her coffee on a coaster on his glass desk, opened her iPad portfolio, and tapped on her auditions folder. "A guy and a girl. Great harmonies. Interesting hooks and lyrics. Think Tucker Nails high on lithium."

Donny laughed. "Do we need another duo on our books?"

Heather shrugged and flicked over her photos of the pair on stage. "I think they're worth a listen. They're already well polished with a clean image. They know who they are, and they'd be a good fit with the label."

"Do they excite you?"

Heather knew what he was actually asking, and there was no point hiding it. "Honestly, it's not been a great two months, Donny.

There's only one guy who got me twisted up. The other nine were top quality, but in this town, there's a *lot* of top quality, isn't there?"

Nodding, Donny popped a handful of M&Ms into his mouth and leaned back in his chair. "Who's your guy?" He looked at his notes. "Bridge, Duke, or Moore?"

At least they were on the same stage. Donny had been responsible for finding all of Rocky Top's talent until he was promoted to label head. Heather was relieved he still had the ear for it even though he now relied solely on her. Other execs gave him recordings, but this was her gig, and she knew she was lucky to have it. "Gabe Duke. Huge voice. A depth and maturity that reverberate your soul. Young and rough but moldable. He's hungry for it."

Donny dragged his finger down the page headed by Gabe's name. "His set was covers. Nothing original?"

His tone was slightly accusatory: originality was make-or-break for Donny, and he was basically asking why she'd bring someone to him who was simply exceptional at karaoke. She suspected Gabe might already need all the help he could get. "I spoke to him after his set to ask him that exact question." *Technically not a lie.* "He writes songs with his housemate." His very sexy housemate. "And the lyrics are amazing."

"You already sound invested. Do you have a soft spot for him?"

Heather sipped at her coffee while she quelled the indignation at his question. Donny had no idea she was gay, but even so, that he was questioning her professionalism stung. Playing the game was getting old. Didn't her track record of seven Grammy winners garner her any respect? "Too young for me, but he's offering something fresh that country doesn't have in abundance." Time to discover if Donny's long list of character defects included racism.

"Go on."

Heather flicked her notes to the photos she'd taken of his performance, laid her iPad on his desk, and leaned back in her chair. His eyes widened and his eyebrows raised, remaining there as if glued. He wiped his fingers over his mouth and chin before he grasped his jaw, the palm of his hand keeping his mouth closed. It wasn't a good sign. Heather looked out the window and across the city, wondering where Gabe was right now. She hoped he was practicing his songs just in case she'd misread Donny's body language, and he surprised her by inviting Gabe for a short-notice audition.

She sighed and turned her attention back to Donny. Heather knew her place enough to know she couldn't voice the directive to give Gabe a shot, but she could hope.

He relaxed his hand and pushed Heather's tablet back toward her. "The voice sure doesn't match the face."

Heather tried to read his eyes to see if there was anything positive beyond his statement, but he stood and walked to the window, giving her nothing. She held onto the sarcastic retort that would probably result in her dismissal, gave him the benefit of the doubt instead, and waited for more.

"If you were in my position, would you give him an audition?" he asked, still facing the window.

Being in Donny's position and being head of her own label were two entirely different things. Rocky Top was a big player, aimed at becoming the biggest on Music Row. The label Heather wanted to run would be indie and small-scale, at least to begin with. The artists she'd sign would always be different. She uncrossed her legs and smoothed out her skirt as she realized, perhaps for the first time, that the decision of who to audition and who to discard wasn't quite as clear-cut as she'd thought it to be. Gabe was only the third black artist she'd come across in her time at Rocky Top, and she'd been quick to think it'd be a no-brainer on signing him. Faced with the hypothetical reality of being a big label head illustrated that sticking to the high moral ground perhaps wasn't that easy. The country audience wanted a certain product. Hell, there were only two women in the top twenty artists in last year's Billboard charts. What chance did non-white folk truly have? And what label head would be prepared to make such a huge financial investment on something their loyal customers might not even have the hunger for?

"I would." Heather wanted to believe that country music listeners were simply looking for top quality artists, regardless of ethnicity. Those artists just needed the exposure and faith, and Heather believed in Gabe.

Donny returned to his desk without response. Heather closed her eyes and staved off the desire to grab him by the shirt collar and shake words from his mouth. She had to be patient. This wasn't her label.

He ran his hand through his thinning hair. "An audition at Rocky Top is a big deal, girl. It speaks of our intentions and future direction even if we don't sign him."

She acknowledged his point with a nod. "Is that such a bad thing?" She so wanted Donny to be the good guy. If he signed Gabe, she could justify giving the less appealing aspects of his personality more leeway.

"Let's put a pin in Gabe Duke for now. Talk me through the rest of your list."

Heather pinched the bridge of her nose before reaching for her iPad and scanning through to the next prospect. It wasn't a definite no. But if Donny didn't take a chance on Gabe, she felt a responsibility to let him know. He was counting on this chance, and it seemed like a no might break his heart. Gabe was clearly a gentle soul, and Heather didn't want to see this town toss his dreams in its mouth and spit them out like chewing tobacco. Having to deal with a situation like this was exactly why she made a point not to be spotted by the performers she was reviewing. She nibbled on the inside of her cheek and tried to put a positive spin on it. If she hadn't spoken to Gabe, she would never have met Louie. And *that* would have been tragic.

CHAPTER FOURTEEN

L OUIE!"
Even over the sounds of Carrie Underwood at full volume, Louie heard Gabe shout her name. She peeled herself away from the California king-size bed reluctantly. Since its delivery yesterday, Louie had decided she would be orchestrating her run on Nashville from this amazingly comfortable mattress, and the only thing that might tempt her away from it would be to answer the door if Heather King came calling.

She swung open the door to find Gabe jumping manically on the sofa with his phone in hand. Either he'd gone mad or...

"Heather called?" Funny that one woman held both their attentions right now. Gabe's head was like a nodding dog on a dirt buggy dashboard.

"I have to be at Rocky Top in two hours." He stopped, jumped down, and ran toward her. "Crap. I've got a shift to work in an hour."

She tilted her head and wrinkled her nose. "Not anymore. I could cover it for you."

"No way." He grabbed her shoulders. "I need you with me. All three of your songs have two guitar parts, and I need your harmonies." He released her and smacked his forehead. "I can't do this. I should call her back and say I can't do it."

Louie caught hold of Gabe's upper arms. The size and solidity of his biceps made her want to find some gym time, and she wondered if Heather preferred a strong woman. Probably not. Lesbians with big muscles didn't tend to pass well as straight girls. Louie pushed the unkind thought away. "No way, buddy. You're doing this." She motioned to his phone on the sideboard. "Call Clare and explain. She knows you've been waiting for this opportunity. I'm sure she'll understand. You can tell her I'll work for her free for a week to make up for it." She smacked his arm playfully and released her grip. "Go. Call now. I'll get my guitar ready."

He gave her a huge smile and went to do as he was told. Louie could almost reach out and touch his excitement, and she smiled in return. This wasn't just the break Gabe had been hoping for, it was a chance for Louie to see Heather again. Their brief meeting at the coffee shop had been both exciting and worrying. It had reinforced Louie's attraction, that much was certain, but Heather's concerns about dating discreetly rang alarm bells. Couldn't it just be as simple as a romantic meet cute in the movies? Louie could've visited a home store to furnish her bedroom. They'd both reach for a two-pack of mixed pillows: Louie would want the down feather one, and Heather would want the memory foam one. They'd split the pack, and lunch, and then get to trying the pillows out on Louie's new cloud bed. Everyone lives happy ever after. No homophobia. Louie had seen too many rom-com movies to lose her deeply buried romantic side, regardless of Mia, and maybe her guard was slipping. It wasn't much of a guard since it was already failing.

Louie picked up her guitar to take her mind off Heather and sat on the edge of her bed. She closed her eyes and strummed the bottom E-string. She turned its peg a quarter turn to the left to tighten it, before fretting an A on the same string and picking the open fifth string. It was already in harmony so she moved on to the remaining four to complete the tuning process. She played the opening bars of the first song they'd written together, "Bronzed Baby Shoes," and heard Gabe join in from the living room. He came to the door and Louie stopped when she saw Gabe's chin tremble slightly. There'd been plenty of tears as they'd composed all three songs. They were all set in raw emotion and some distressing experiences. She wondered if Gabe would be strong enough to get through his audition without breaking down.

She didn't put words to her concern because she wanted him to feel she believed in him. Asking if he was up for it was the same as telling him that she thought he wasn't. "You're changing, yeah?" She pointed at the tomato stain on his T-shirt from the leftover enchiladas they'd eaten for lunch. She hadn't told him that when she was warming them up, she'd accidentally tipped the tray onto the floor and had to spatula them up from the kitchen linoleum and pretty it up with some spinach leaves. That was one of the best things about enchiladas: they were such a messy meal that presentation wasn't a key issue. She'd only found one hair in hers, and Gabe had barely taken a breath between bites so the floor time hadn't affected the taste.

Gabe pulled his T-shirt away from his chest and inspected it. "Damn. This is my lucky shirt."

"You want to show up to meet Donny Taylor, the potential future of your recording career, with enchilada sauce all over your chest just because it's your lucky shirt?"

"No?"

Louie raised an eyebrow. "No."

He laughed. "I was kidding." He pushed away from the doorframe and walked away whistling the final song they'd worked on, "Music City Dreamers." While the other two were personal to Gabe, this one was both of their stories and could be applicable to any performer or writer who wanted to burn bright in Nashville's sky.

Louie placed her guitar on the bed, opened its case, and laid it in as carefully as she might lay Heather on the bed if she got the chance. She clicked the metal catches closed and went to the dresser. She retrieved a couple of picks and shoved them into her pocket. She closed her eyes and saw the music for their songs scribed on the sunset orange backdrop of her eyelids. It wasn't a trick she'd affected. Whatever it was and however it had come about, she liked it. It made sheet music redundant...or at least it did until someone else wanted to perform her songs. She bit her lip and looked in the mirror. Could she be this lucky? She'd been in town less than a week and tonight, she'd be in front of one of the biggest studios on the Row. This was Gabe's audition and she respected that, but if it meant a little exposure for her too, it was a win-win for both of them.

Figuring she needed to look her best, she opened the drawer and pulled out her favorite shirt. She'd found it in a custom boutique in Boystown, and it featured the head of a woman through a ship's wheel with waves crashing around her. She was smoking a pipe, had neck tattoos, and wore a beanie. Maybe it was too much. She was about to choose something else when she realized what she was doing. Compromising and hiding herself, something she promised her mom she wouldn't do, no matter the opportunity. No matter the woman? How much compromise would Heather need from her?

Louie recited her mom's mantra to herself in the mirror. "Be who you are, all of who you are."

She stripped off her tank and pulled on a bralette and her original choice shirt. Louie was a behind-the-scenes writer and had no desire to be on stage. She was under no illusion that the average God-fearing country music fan was ready to see someone like her leading the band for Gabe. She picked up her hair product, popped the lid, and squeezed some fiber cream onto her fingers before working it through her hair to sculpt her standard two-inch quiff. It took three times the regular amount to fix, and she held back curses. It'd been a while since her last visit to the barber, and now all of it was too long and out of control. She used more to work some shine into the high fades on the sides and back of her head, and as she replaced the lid, she decided she'd ask Gabe where he had his hair done. His textured crop and sharp fade lines had made her jealous of his hair since they'd met.

Louie wiped her hands on a washcloth and applied a fine black pencil to the inner lash line of both eyes. It had been her only concession to makeup since Mia had told her it made her eyes pop. The phrase sounded pretty gross at the time, but enough people had commented on her eyes that evening that Louie believed her, and a new habit was born. *But* only for special occasions, and this was one. She didn't know if Heather would be there tonight. She could only hope that she would and that her preparation wouldn't go to waste. She thought about Mia on stage at the Bluebird, looking like she belonged, like she'd found her place in the world. *Without me.* Seeing Mia again had dredged up so many unwanted emotions, things she thought she'd cremated so they might never rise again.

Five years together clearly hadn't been obliterated in the year since Mia had left. Whatever was happening, Louie knew she'd need to find a way to deal with it. She thought she'd moved on and she *wanted* to move on. Louie wanted to be emotionally available to someone new, someone like Heather. And while deep down, she believed that Heather wouldn't be interested in the gutter rat she was right now, maybe if she could become the songwriter she wanted to be, Heather just might stick around. Mia had destroyed her heart a year ago, but Louie needed to believe in love again. Sometimes things had to be destroyed to rebuild them stronger.

She selected her favorite scent from the collection of bottles on the dresser top and sprayed it on her neck and wrists, before pulling up her shirt and applying a quick burst to her stomach. She tucked the front of her shirt into her jeans and pulled the rest of the hem over her belt.

"You didn't need to make such an effort on *my* account," Gabe said after whistling his approval.

"It's not for you, asshole. And why are you creeping around like some silent spy guy?"

Gabe did a little pirouette before stumbling back into the door. "It's not my fault I'm light on my feet."

"Yeah, well, maybe you should've gone into ballet instead of becoming a kick-ass country superstar."

Gabe grinned and once again, his pure light illuminated the room. "You really think I can make it?"

Louie nodded, feeling simultaneously proud and protective, neither of which she could genuinely claim since they'd known each other less than a week. But Gabe was fast becoming the little brother she'd never had. "You'll be in the top ten Billboard year-end charts in the next twelve months. I can feel it." A light burning sensation behind her eyes surprised her, and she went to her bed to pick up her guitar before Gabe saw anything.

He tapped her on the shoulder. "Would it be weird if I asked for a hug?"

Louie turned around, and the look of absolute innocence on Gabe's face would've warmed the coldest of hearts. "Sure, but don't *make* it weird by staying in too long." They negotiated an awkward dance of whose arms would go on top before Louie won out and wrapped hers around Gabe's shoulders while he draped his arms around her waist. "I'm taller. If we're going to hug often, it has to be like this."

He pulled away and buddy-clapped her on the back. "Thanks, Louie...for believing in me."

Louie's hands had rested on his shoulders, but she moved slightly and pinched his cheek. "It's easy to believe in someone with so much talent."

Gabe looked at the floor and swallowed hard enough for Louie to hear. When he returned her gaze, a thin film of moisture covered his dark brown eyes, and he wiped his cheek clear of a tear. Louie squeezed his shoulder firmly before letting him go. "Come on, Gabe. Let's get city-side and secure your recording contract."

CHAPTER FIFTEEN

Heather glanced at the time on her screen as she completed her notes from Donny's meeting. She liked to keep a record of all the singers and groups she recommended in some semblance of an order that reflected Donny's tastes. Each file contained photos, a set list, and details of the performer along with the exact words Donny had responded with when referring to them. She hoped that doing so would help her stop wasting her time and choose acts that actually stood a chance of getting an audition.

Someone knocked on her office door and Savana strolled in and closed the door behind her without waiting for Heather's permission to enter.

"You're still here?" It was nearly seven, and Heather had expected Savana to be long gone. She'd seen Joe leave when she'd gone to get water from the kitchen an hour ago. He'd given her a curt nod before getting in the elevator, and then she'd heard a bang as if someone was striking its metal wall. He seemed nothing but tense and irritated every time she saw him. She thought Savana had left midafternoon because she hadn't been called in to see her since her meeting with Donny.

Savana came around Heather's desk and sat on the edge beside her. "Not pleased to see me?"

She affected a flirtatious tone Heather had no doubt worked miracles with the men in her life. Heather figured she used it so much that the gender of the recipient barely registered. Or she knew Heather was gay. Panic wrapped around her throat like a boa constrictor and made it impossible to respond. She already had colleagues who were disgruntled with her speedy promotions through the Rocky Top ranks. Gossip about her sexuality would give them a weapon she had no defense against and undoubtedly derail her career.

"Heather, are you okay?"

Heather focused on Savana again, realizing she'd been staring through her. "Uh, yeah. I'm fine. Sorry, I thought you'd have gone home by now. It's getting late."

Savana shook her head. "Haven't you learned how seriously I'm taking this change of direction yet?"

She put her hand on Heather's shoulder, and it felt searing hot through the thin material of her blouse. A thousand ants marched up from the arch of her back and she shuddered hard. Savana removed her hand and laughed.

"That's not the reaction I usually get when I touch someone."

What the hell was going on? Heather pushed her chair away from the desk and stood, desperately aware that the door was closed and needing fresh air. It seemed like Savana was toying with her, and she didn't like it one bit. Heather hated it when straight women played this kind of game for some weird validation.

She picked up her iPad and pencil. "I have to go. Donny and I have auditions at seven in the studio."

"Really? How exciting." Savana picked up Heather's office phone and dialed a number. "It's Savana, is Donny there?"

Heather bit the inside of her lip, and her mouth felt dry. What was Savana doing?

"Hey, Donny…yes, that's correct. She's with me now. It's okay if I sit in on the auditions, isn't it? …Perfect. See you in a few minutes." Savana replaced the receiver and smiled at Heather. "Now I get to see the magic happen."

Heather nodded, slightly relieved, and remembered that Savana had said she'd come to Rocky Top partly because of Heather's "talent whispering." She'd overreacted and seen things that weren't there to be seen. *Paranoia. This is what happens when I hide myself.*

She wouldn't be hiding when she owned her own label, that was for certain. She hoped Louie would stick around long enough for that to happen. Heather needed to tell Louie her plans. She didn't want to stay in the closet forever. She knew that being an out lesbian might mean less commercial success, but that wasn't what she wanted her label to be about anyway. She wanted it to be a haven for the different. "That'll be lovely," Heather said as she opened the door. Why had Savana called Donny about being present for the auditions though? Why hadn't she just asked Heather directly? She pushed the questions away, thinking that Donny made the decisions and Savana knew that. It was folly of Heather to expect Savana to ask her permission for anything. Suitably self-chastised, Heather motioned for Savana to leave her office.

Heather attempted small talk, but Savana seemed more interested in the talent she was about to see in the studio.

"What do you see in the people you bring to Donny's attention?" Savana asked.

Heather smiled. "That's a strange question coming from you."

They got in the elevator and Savana pressed for the basement. She leaned against the mirrored wall and looked at Heather seriously. "Why do you say that?"

Heather shrugged. "Because you embody what I'm looking for. Lots of people have talent. They can sing, they can write, or they can perform. But not everybody has the *triple threat*, or even the *deadly duo* like you. Bizarre terms when they're great things, I know, but that's what I'm seeking." A little melancholy knocked at the door of her consciousness, and she allowed it entry. "I'm looking for what I didn't have." She'd spoken the words without thinking. Only Emma knew of her original ambition and the reason she came to Nashville. She'd been careful to keep it to herself lest Donny would think she didn't have the commitment he needed. Given what had just happened, she didn't want Savana telling Donny anything.

"You came to Nashville to be a singer?"

Lie. Say no. "Briefly, yes." *Idiot.* She couldn't bring herself to be untruthful. "But I quickly realized I had a talent for finding the next big thing instead of *being* the next big thing."

Savana reached out and touched Heather's forearm. "Maybe you could be a backing singer on my record when I finally find a writer I want to work with."

They reached the basement, and Heather was glad to step out into the small reception area. The longer she spent in the elevator, the smaller it seemed to become and the less air seemed to be available. Heather wasn't necessarily attracted to Savana, it was more that she was uncomfortable with the new territory Savana had begun to lay out. There was no denying she was a beautiful woman, but she was straight and Heather barely played with card-carrying lesbians, let alone dallying straight girls. Then there was the rather large issue of professionalism. Heather had no intention of wrecking her career at Rocky Top by falling for their number one star. Lastly, there was Louie. She was managing to drag Heather's attention toward her after just one meeting, and they hadn't even slept together.

And there Louie stood like a lighthouse on a foggy night. She was dressed in jeans that were baggy everywhere but around her perfectly formed ass and a baseball shirt with a crazy design of a female sailor on it. There were barely bumps where Heather would normally appraise a woman's breasts, and it suited Louie. Heather decided she'd look weird with breasts anything other than the tiny little handful she seemed to have. Her hair looked precisely coiffed, and Heather imagined grabbing a handful of it as Louie made love to her. She swallowed and ran her tongue over her lips, wishing she hadn't been interrupted by Savana. She'd planned to reapply her makeup and rock that killer black cherry lipstick Emma promised her would bring Louie to her knees.

Heather's gaze finally rested on Louie. She felt her face flush as she realized Louie was staring right back at her. The cocky little grin that greeted her guilt raced straight to the part of Heather's body that definitely shouldn't be awake at work.

"Hi, Ms. King."

Louie held out her hand, and the welcome seemed terribly formal considering how close they'd been in front of the Bluebird.

But no one here knew that. Louie had obviously listened to what Heather had said at the café and was being discreet.

"Hi...Louie, isn't it?" Heather instantly regretted the faux-forgetfulness and hoped Louie would see it as a cover-up and nothing more. She didn't want Louie thinking she hadn't made an impression because, by God, she had. Heather accepted Louie's gesture and tried not to react as her long fingers wrapped around Heather's hand. The strength and warmth of Louie's handshake had Heather's thoughts traveling to places they shouldn't.

"That's right." She motioned to Gabe, who'd stood as Heather approached. "You remember Gabe?"

Heather was grateful there was no sarcasm in Louie's words, and she reluctantly released Louie's hand to shake Gabe's. "Of course. How are you?" Before Gabe could answer, Savana coughed not-so-gently beside her. Heather had forgotten her current company in the haze of seeing Louie again. She stepped sideways to welcome Savana into the intimate circle they'd inadvertently formed. "I'm sure no introduction is needed here."

Louie smiled, but Heather convinced herself it wasn't the kind of smile she'd thrown Heather's way.

"The great Savana Hayes. It's an absolute pleasure."

Louie held out her hand once more, and Heather noted how her grip seemed gentler. She quashed the flare of irritation that Louie might find Savana attractive. "Gabe is here to sing, and Louie writes songs."

"Really? Even more reason for me to watch the auditions tonight."

Heather's stomach tightened in response to Gabe's face, which moved from awe to terror as he processed Savana's words. The pressure of a studio audition was great enough without having country royalty sitting in on it.

"You're...you'll be..."

Gabe's stuttering was painful to watch.

"You'll be glad you did," Louie said and squeezed Gabe's shoulder. "This guy is amazing."

Heather smiled at Louie's interruption and kicked herself for thinking that Louie and Gabe were anything more than friends. The way Louie looked after Gabe, Heather wouldn't have been surprised if they were family.

"And what about you?" Savana asked.

Heather stopped herself from clenching her jaw. Savana's interest in Louie was completely unwelcome, for Heather at least. She sighed, realizing her imagination was running away with her, and she dialed down the crazy. Savana had a huge army of fans, and she had to be charming to everyone. It had nothing to do with her sexuality.

Louie looked at Savana, and Heather swore she could see vague amusement in her eyes. She was probably used to straight girls swooning all over her. Visually, she was the perfect mix of gender, and Heather was becoming increasingly more intrigued to know if Louie's inner workings matched her outer visage. Heather envied Louie's apparent comfort around women. She figured Louie was so smooth because she'd had a lot more experience than Heather. But boy, did she want to learn from her.

"I'm not performing, Ms. Hayes," Louie said.

Her deep, husky voice vibrated through Heather's soul, and there was something about the way Louie said "performing" that indicated she knew exactly what Savana was up to.

Savana laughed. "Everyone is *always* performing."

She stepped around Louie to get to Donny, who'd just come down the stairs behind them.

Louie tipped her head in Savana's direction. "She's something."

Heather smiled, relieved that Louie didn't seem overly impressed with Savana. She was unable to respond with a similarly dismissive riposte and just nodded. Gabe still appeared somewhat lost, so she leaned in toward him. "You're going to be fine. Just focus on your music and ignore everyone but Donny." She gestured over to her boss. "*He's* the one you need to impress, not Savana." Heather pulled back, suddenly aware there were three other acts auditioning for Donny tonight, and her conversation with Gabe and Louie might be interpreted as favoritism. She reached out and touched them both briefly on their heavily tattooed arms. She longed to trace her fingers over Louie's ink and learn the story behind each one, sure they meant something and weren't simply off the book. "I have to go. Good luck." She couldn't resist one last sweeping look over Louie before she went to join Donny and Savana, already deep in conversation. She felt the pulsing of her body in response to Louie's returned interest. There was no running away from whatever this was going to be.

CHAPTER SIXTEEN

As Louie watched Heather walk away, her entire body felt like it was surrounded by an electric force field, ignited from Heather's light touch. Letting her go after having her so close again didn't seem right. After their short connection at the café, she'd hoped their next meeting would last longer.

Louie glanced at the others waiting for their audition and didn't miss the various looks of jealousy and curiosity thrown their way. When they'd walked in, a few eyebrows had raised, and Louie knew she and Gabe weren't exactly poster material for an all-American country label like Rocky Top. Now though, the looks were related to their interaction with Heather, or the talent whisperer, as Louie had learned was her nickname. Louie wondered if Heather realized the power she had. She'd calculated Heather must be in her late twenties and she'd already carved herself a respectable reputation in a town drowning in talent. She was impressive in so many ways, and Louie wanted to know more. Much more.

Gabe tugged at her arm. "Louie, I'm a mess. Can I do this?"

Louie turned to face him and whispered, "Of course you can."

He gestured behind him to where Savana Hayes, Donny, and Heather stood. "But Savana Hayes is going to be watching."

"That shouldn't worry you." She punched him lightly in the stomach. "You love performing for the ladies." She watched the power trio enter what she assumed was the audition space and smiled when Heather glanced back and nodded to her. She hadn't mentioned getting a drink after this was over, but maybe she knew Gabe was all but signed up, and she'd have plenty of opportunity to see Louie again. Still, Louie was eager to know when their first date might be. How were they ever supposed to get together if Heather wasn't comfortable talking to her in a public space? She wished she had a business card she could've given to Heather in the guise of looking for work. At least then Heather could make the first move.

"You're not worried?"

Louie shook her head and squeezed Gabe's shoulder. It was an action she seemed to be doing a lot with him, and she realized that despite what assumptions others might make based on his appearance, Gabe lacked confidence in himself. He needed repeated assurances that he was good enough. After what he'd told her about his mother and how she'd treated him, it wasn't surprising. Their third song, "Take It Like a Man," had made both of them a weeping muddle of tears and tissues. He was young, and it would take a while and perhaps even therapy to cast the shadow of his mother into the dark depths where it belonged. As Louie had learned more about Gabe's past, she had to wonder if his mother would show her face once Gabe became famous, which, one way or another, Louie was sure would happen.

"No. You deserve to be here, and you're an awesome performer. You were born for greatness, and you're going to own that stage, and every stage after it."

"Gabe Duke?"

A skinny guy dressed in a suit that looked like it cost more than Louie's truck emerged from the same room Heather had disappeared into.

Gabe raised his hand. "That's me."

Louie picked up her guitar and gently pushed him forward. "Let's go, superstar. Your destiny's waiting for you."

They followed the suit guy into a small room with an even smaller stage. Louie swiftly pulled her guitar from its case, plugged into the amp, and set the volume low enough not to overpower Gabe's voice. She tried to concentrate solely on what she was there to do, but she couldn't resist sneaky looks at Heather. Each time

Heather met her glance, Louie felt more assurance that she was still interested. Gabe checked the mic, and the sound woman at the back of the studio adjusted it slightly.

"My name's Donny. You've met Heather, and I'm sure you know Savana Hayes. Tell us your name and a little bit about yourself, son."

Gabe smiled at Louie, and she noticed how much more confident he appeared now that he was on stage. The vulnerable young man melted away, and the performer beside her held himself like a seasoned pro.

"My name's Gabe Duke. I'm originally from Hinesville, Georgia, but I spent most of my teenage years on the road. I got my love of singing from a lot of Sundays in the church choir, and I've wanted to be a country singer since my dad introduced it to me when I was fourteen and we started traveling for his work." Gabe gestured to Louie. "This is Louie, and we wrote these three songs together."

Gabe stepped back from the mic and nodded for Louie to begin. She closed her eyes and disappeared into the opening chords of "Bronzed Baby Shoes." If she was auditioning, she would've worked the small audience, but she wasn't so she didn't need to worry. Instead, she could simply play their music and be carried away on the wings of the story. This one didn't just tug on the heartstrings, it hung on them with fifty-pound lead weights. Louie heard Gabe as clearly as if he were inside her head, and God, he was pulling it off. His voice didn't waver even as the lyrics told the tale of the moment he reconnected with the father he'd thought had abandoned him. She'd loved Heather's reaction to these lyrics and hoped that the music and Gabe's voice would blow her away.

Gabe completed the song, and a brash whistle brought Louie back into the room. She opened her eyes to see the exuberant praise was coming from Savana Hayes. Gabe smiled widely, and Louie felt sure that would be enough to charm the country superstar. If she had any sway with Heather's boss, Gabe was practically signed already.

"Thank you. This next song is called 'Take It Like a Man.' It's a little dark, but I promise my final song will bring you right back up."

This was the real test, and Louie hoped with everything she had that Gabe wouldn't break down. On the night they met Heather, he'd shared the physical abuse he'd suffered from his mom and had revealed that some of his tattoos were covering up the visible scars she'd left him with. The giant lion on his back whose paw reached around his left shoulder was Louie's favorite. Its brightly hued mane of blues, greens, and oranges reminded her of a striking sunset over an ocean, with the sun fighting to stay afloat. Gabe's explanation of its significance and importance to him had inspired her to write the lyrics for this song in less than an hour. It had also resulted in an entire pocket pack of tissues loaded up with her liquid anger and sorrow.

When they'd finished and Louie looked toward their small audience again, she could see it'd had the same effect on them. Gabe had done the hard part, but it wasn't relief on his face; the kid was glowing. Donny and Savana looked as impressed as they damn well should, and Heather…she seemed even more beautiful with her eyes full of tears again. Louie wanted to hold her and share the moment, ecstatic that she'd been touched so deeply by Gabe's experience through Louie's lyrics.

She waited for Gabe's signal to begin his final song, and they launched into "Music City Dreamers." It caught hold of their audience from the pit of empathy Gabe's song had dropped them into and yanked them up in a joyful celebration of youthful ambition and daydreams. His performance was perfect, and Louie saw Donny raise his eyebrows and look distinctly impressed when Gabe hit the high notes.

When they completed his short set, Heather stood and gestured to the empty chair beside Donny. "Could you come on down, Gabe?"

Gabe quickly came over to Louie on his way down from the stage. "Man, that was awesome."

"You were fantastic. They'd be stupid not to sign you after that. Now go and get your record deal." They clasped their hand to each other's forearms and buddy-hugged before Louie turned to pack her guitar up.

"That was something special, Louie."

She looked up just as Savana shifted the hair from her eyes in that very special way that only women with long hair could achieve. It was a gesture that could easily be taken as seductive, and Louie smiled. This was a game she'd gotten particularly good at in Chicago, and it turned out that being outwardly charming while her guts were churning all sorts of anxious dread came somewhat naturally. She and Savana had something in common: they used their natural gifts to entertain. And even though Savana was a singer, Louie knew she had to use the rest of her body as part of the package. She shoved away the dark thoughts. She figured very few people lived their lives without having to do things they regretted, things for money and for people they didn't want to. But that was her past. Louie was here now, living her dream, and she was in a studio audition talking to Savana Fucking Hayes.

"That's very kind of you. Gabe is an amazing talent." Louie looked across to Gabe and wished they could swap the people they were talking to. Heather was smiling and laughing, and a thumb prick of unwarranted jealousy prodded at her.

"Are you and Gabe together?"

She asked the question just as Louie took a swallow of water. She spluttered some of it out but managed to cover her mouth in time not to shower Savana with her amusement. Louie wiped her hand on her jeans and shook her head, trying to control her astonishment into a tight smile instead of laughing out loud. She wasn't one for stereotypes or labels, but she was well aware her appearance screamed all kinds of queer to even the most open-minded of people. And she welcomed that. Hell, her mom would kick her ass if she considered hiding her true self for even a moment. "No. We're just housemates and good friends." Their fast friendship had taken Louie by surprise. But it was a pleasant and timely one. Both of them were going to need someone they could trust and rely on whether their journey got tough or they became successful. She had a feeling that authenticity might be in short supply around here.

"Was that a funny question?"

Louie shrugged. "A little. It's the same question Heather asked though, so maybe it's just me being oversensitive." Louie realized her words could be construed as Heather being interested in her. She scrambled to cover her tracks. "I think Gabe appeals to a wide range of people."

Savana tilted her head to the side and wiggled her eyebrows. "Maybe. But that wasn't why I was asking. Who wrote the lyrics to the songs you performed tonight?"

"I did."

"I thought so. And the music?"

Louie wished once again that she could swap conversation partners with Gabe. This was beginning to feel like an inquisition, and she had no idea what answers Savana wanted to hear that would help Gabe get signed to this label. "Gabe. He's a great musician." Surely it didn't matter whether or not he wrote his own songs. It was his ability to tell those stories to, and connect with, an audience that was important, and they were *his* stories.

"I get the feeling you're being overly modest. What are you in this town for, Louie? Is it a pit stop on your way to another life or is this the life you're after?" She gestured at the walls covered with platinum-selling records.

Louie rolled her shoulders, becoming increasingly uncomfortable with where this conversation seemed to be heading. This *was* the life she craved, but this was also Gabe's audition, and she didn't want to mess it up for him. Louie paused to consider the situation before she answered. It wasn't as though she and Gabe were competing for the same deal, and as far as she knew, Savana was just one of their artists and made no signing decisions. "I want this." She glanced over at Heather again. *And I want her.* "You're not afraid of asking the deep questions, are you?" She didn't know why Savana was even talking to her, and a small part of her recognized that it might make Heather a little crazy. She hadn't seemed overly fond of her when they'd met in the lobby area, and Louie had picked up on a little jealousy, though that could have been wishful thinking.

"Small talk doesn't interest me, especially when I think I might have found the missing piece of my current puzzle. Tell me about your writing process. How do you write such personal songs for other people?"

"It's a collaborative process. I need the singer to be honest with me, to sit and tell me about their experience, their truth. Everybody has stories to tell, some people just need help making them stories other people want to hear." The inquisition seemed to have taken a turn toward interview territory. Barely a week in town and she could be writing for the biggest name in country. This streak of luck was showing no sign of slowing down. "Are you looking for a new writer, Ms. Hayes?"

She smiled. "Do you believe in fate, Louie? In some higher power conspiring to bring the right people across your path at the right time?"

Louie laughed. A week ago, she didn't believe in much at all. "If you'd asked me that question while I was in Chicago, my answer would've been a definite 'no.' But with everything that's happened over the past few days, I'm beginning to believe in *something*."

"Well, I have enough faith for the both of us." She put her arm around Louie's shoulders. "And I think God wanted me to listen in on this audition so I could meet you. I've been at Rocky Top for four days trying to find the right person to write *my* truth. Almost everything else has fallen into place apart from finding that elusive writer. Then you show up."

Louie wasn't sure she could attribute their meeting to God, but if this was leading to a songwriting gig with the great Savana Hayes, she'd happily get on her knees and thank the Lord. "And you think I'm the writer you've been looking for?"

"I think it's a strong possibility. How about you show up here tomorrow at eleven a.m. and we'll take a shot at finding out?"

Louie nodded. "I'd be honored." She glanced back at Heather and saw Gabe was no longer with her. Heather motioned to the door, and Louie figured they needed to get the next act in to audition. "It looks like I better get going." Louie offered her hand. "Thank you for this opportunity, Ms. Hayes. I'm looking forward to seeing if we can work together."

Savana shook Louie's hand. "I'll see you tomorrow."

Louie picked up her guitar, nodded toward Heather, and headed out. Now she'd definitely get to see Heather again and she only had to wait until the morning.

Chapter Seventeen

Heather smiled at Louie as she left, disappointed that she didn't come over to say good-bye. She'd hoped to further the plot and perhaps even invite Louie to dinner if she could've grabbed her alone and away from prying ears. Unless she wasn't the one who was supposed to do the inviting. Louie's mix of gender on the outside made it difficult for Heather to know whether it would be welcome if she took the lead. Heather was far from well versed in labels and roles. She'd virtually stumbled into both of her previous relationships and she'd never learned to be a lesbian on the scene. Was there protocol? Were gender stereotypes in play? She cursed herself for being so naïve. Emma would know. She glanced at the time on her tablet. They had three more acts to audition, and Donny liked to analyze each one with her immediately after their performance. It was likely they'd be here until ten so it would be too late to go out for drinks, but she could at least call Emma to get advice.

"I believe I've found the writer for my new album," Savana said as she retook her seat, sandwiching Donny between them.

"What?" Heather realized her tone was way too harsh, but the words were out before she'd had time to run them past her thought police.

Savana raised her eyebrow and looked at Heather like she'd just demanded the blood of her firstborn.

"Excuse me?"

Savana seemed confused at Heather's outburst. "That's such great news. A writer was the only thing holding you back." Heather placed the emphasis on Savana's control to deflect the attention from her reaction to the thought of Savana working with Louie, which would mean Louie working with Heather. She could never date a co-worker, no matter how sexy they were. Heather was simultaneously glad and distressed she and Louie hadn't done anything about their attraction yet. It would've complicated everything, but now she might never find out if Louie could have been someone special to her. But at least they'd get to be friends this way without anyone being suspicious.

She nodded. "That's right, and it could be that Louie Francis is the answer."

Donny coughed loudly. "I have to ask, because although I tried to figure it out for myself, I couldn't. Is Louie a feminine-looking guy or a dyke?"

Heather stretched out her toes in the slightly uncomfortable heels she'd worn to impress Louie, though she felt sure she hadn't given them a second glance. Donny's incendiary insult struck deep, and as much as she wanted to, she couldn't respond defensively. Being discreet about her sexuality gave assholes like Donny carte blanche to speak their tiny little minds without fear of her ripping their tongues out. Not for the first time in the past five years, Heather hated the fact that she wasn't being true to herself for the sake of her career.

"Louie appears to be female, though I can't speak to their gender identity. There's such a spectrum these days, it's hard to keep up."

Savana's informed response saved Heather the possible trouble of saying anything at all.

"And that doesn't worry you?" Donny pulled a cigar from his jacket pocket and chewed on its end. "What happened to the days when girls wore heels and a skirt and guys wore jeans and a tee? I liked that. Things were less complicated."

Savana glanced at Heather and rolled her eyes. "I can handle anyone who hits on me, Donny, if that's what you're worried about." She ran her hand through her hair and sighed. "I learned the hard way that women can be just as much of an occupational hazard as horny guys."

Savana's statement sounded loaded, as though she'd had an unsafe situation with a woman. She also seemed sad and still affected by it. Heather wasn't surprised by her admission. Sexual violence wasn't limited to male perpetrators.

"Well, as long as *she* stays behind the scenes. Rocky Top can't be seen to be promoting unnatural states of being."

Heather tensed her whole body and tried to remain visibly unaffected by Donny's outrageous statement. Savana flashed her a look she couldn't decipher, and it was gone before she could decode it.

"They're auditioning tomorrow. I'll let you know how it goes, but it's *my* decision, Donny."

Savana's repeated and deliberate use of they instead of a female pronoun impressed Heather further, but it also made her think she might need to reassess her own position. Heather identified purely and simply as a femme lesbian, and she was attracted to women and the female form in all of its different manifestations. If Louie labeled herself as something different from that, what might that mean for Heather's attraction?

Donny mumbled something, but Heather didn't catch it, and either Savana didn't or she simply chose not to react. Conscious of the time and her now overwhelming desire to consult with Emma about all things gender, Heather held up her iPad. "So, thoughts about Gabe?"

Donny nodded. "I can't deny he's a great singer, and his performance was flawless."

Heather felt a "but" was imminent and chose to head it off. "It was. He's a natural on stage. He's charming and cute. I think his appeal cuts across all ages of women." Heather saw Savana raise and drop her eyebrows. Didn't she agree? "If he joins us now, he'd be young enough to carve out a long-term career, and I think he'd be loyal when everything he sings goes platinum."

"You seem to have a lot of faith in him, Heather. Why?" Savana asked.

Heather felt her forehead wrinkle at her question. She swept her hand across her face to move her bangs and disguise her surprise. Savana shouldn't even be here, let alone be asking questions.

Donny pulled the cigar from his mouth and re-pocketed it. "That's a good point, Savana. Why are you backing this horse so strongly, girl?"

Heather swallowed and composed herself, unsure as to why Donny was suddenly following Savana's lead. "He's got that something extra that goes beyond a few hit songs. I think he's got staying power, and he'll work twice as hard as anyone else given this opportunity. It's a win-win situation for the label." Heather couldn't explain why she was so sure Gabe would do any of what she'd said, but she felt strongly that his drive and desire backed her belief. She glanced across at Savana. She smiled and looked innocent enough, but Heather couldn't help but think she was somehow manipulating the situation to push her own agenda. If that was the case, Heather wanted to know. It seemed like a conflict of interest could be imminent, and Heather wasn't sure which position meant most to her and where her own agenda should lie. She *did* know she wanted all the information to make that decision, and she hated being kept in the dark.

"I have to think of the label's reputation, Heather. Consumers look to us when they're looking for new artists to follow. We have to be careful about who we're pushing on them," Donny said after a long pause.

Pushing? Gabe wasn't cocaine. "What are you saying, Donny? Are you afraid of something?" Heather leaned forward in her chair. When Donny's eyes fell to her breasts, she reclined so they were away from his lecherous scrutiny. For once, it'd be nice to have a professional discussion with her boss without his gaze falling south of her eyes.

"I'm not afraid of anything. I'm just not as sure as you are that the boy suits who we are." He scratched his cheek. "Sticking a cowboy hat on his head and a checked shirt on his back wouldn't make him country. This isn't just music. It's a way of life. And I don't think your boy is genuine."

The way Donny repeated "boy" several times scratched at Heather's racism radar like metal claws on a blackboard. He wouldn't say it outright. Donny was obviously too clever for that, but Heather knew what he was saying. Perhaps he hadn't been sure if Gabe's color could be whitewashed just enough to make him more palatable for narrow-minded rednecks, and he needed to see him in the flesh to decide.

"What do you think, Savana?" Donny turned his attention away from Heather.

Savana shook her head. "This isn't my label, Donny, it's yours."

Heather ran her hand through her hair and sighed. She hadn't wanted Savana to be here, but if she spoke up in favor of Gabe, Heather would appreciate it. She'd been in so many of these auditions with Donny and he'd never asked for anyone else's opinion. Why was he starting now? Did he think that Savana wouldn't stay with the label if he signed acts she didn't approve? If this was the way labels worked, it was yet another thing she wouldn't be doing when she had her own.

"Humor me. What if it *were* your label?"

She smiled broadly and shook her head again. "Not my call, Donny. I'm a performer. This kind of decision isn't for me."

Savana's avoidance of an opinion one way or the other was expert, and Heather supposed it was a necessary evil adopted during years of deflecting awkward and potentially inflammatory questions from the media. Having a strong opinion on anything might endanger an artist's popularity with factions of their fans. Watching Savana do it, however, made Heather lose a little respect for her.

Donny grumbled and swiveled back to face Heather. "It's a no."

Heather felt the dismissal like Donny had thrown a leaded weight at her heart. She was always saddened when Donny didn't give contracts to her find, but she felt this particular one more deeply. It was as if Gabe were her own brother. And his connection with the oh-so-enigmatic Louie had possibly secured his place in her heart. But his hope, his pure desire to achieve his ambition, had put lighter fuel on her own goal of creating her label, a haven for talent who were wickedly overlooked by the bigoted giants of this industry. Donny's excuse of being careful what he was "pushing" on their consumers was a pitiful excuse, and it didn't credit the American people with the musical intelligence to know good music when they saw it, whether it came out of a black, white, or bright green mouth.

"Edwards," Donny half-yelled. "Bring in the next act."

"Yes, sir."

Heather watched as Edwards reacted to Donny's barked instruction, indicating their discussion was over. He straightened the jacket of his one and only Brioni suit and strutted toward the door. She knew it was worth the equivalent of six months' salary and had often wondered why he'd waste so much money on a suit that he couldn't rightly afford. His sycophantic toadying to Donny had gotten him this gig, and depending on her mood, it amused or sickened her. With Donny's rejection of Gabe, Heather leaned toward the latter today.

The realization that she would have to let Gabe down was slowly taking root. Usually, Heather called the unsuccessful acts to tell them they weren't joining Rocky Top, but she knew she'd have to do this one in person. She wanted Gabe to succeed, and she didn't want this setback to floor him. She decided to visit him early tomorrow morning before she got into work, and before Louie came in to see Savana. Heather was looking forward to seeing Louie again but had hoped it would be under celebratory circumstances. Still, it gave Heather the chance to be close to her, and she'd take that no matter what the context.

Chapter Eighteen

Louie scrubbed at her face with both hands and squinted at the time on her phone: nine a.m. "Who the hell is coming by this early?" She pushed the thin blanket away and reluctantly climbed out of the bed she now called the cloud. Her sleep had been fitful with her dreams swinging between hot sex with Heather and intense songwriting sessions with Savana. The two of them had kept her restless most of the night, irrespective of the most amazingly comfortable bed in the world. The bell had sounded twice before their early morning caller had gotten impatient and started knocking on the glass through the screen door. Gabe was obviously a heavy sleeper, although Louie suspected he might still be unconscious after the number of tequila shots he'd had in celebration following his audition. He was one hundred percent sure he'd be getting the yes call sometime today.

She popped a mint and made her way to the door, stubbing her toe on the solid wood couch foot on the way. She was about to curse, but she caught a glimpse of their visitor and saw it was Heather. Louie considered ducking out of the way and zipping back to her room to freshen up, but Heather spotted her and waved through the window. Louie raised her hand then ran it through her hair to tame it a little. She'd used so much product yesterday to get it into some sort of style that now it stuck out at all angles, and it felt like a lion's mane after a raunchy night with a hellion lioness. She was also wearing last night's shirt. "Fuck," she whispered. Her plans to dress to impress Heather later this morning would now be colored by her seeing Louie in yesterday's clothes. She adjusted the waistband of her workout shorts to make sure she wouldn't embarrass herself further and reached for the door handle.

"You're doing house calls for contracts?" Louie's smile faded when she saw Heather's reaction to her joke. She raised her hands— one held a paper bag and the other a tray of coffees—and looked apologetic. It obviously wasn't good news.

"Can I come in?"

This wasn't how Louie had imagined Heather's first visit to her place. She'd wanted to be freshly showered, in her best outfit, and ready to sweep her off her feet with her charm. In a stinky shirt with no jeans and bed hair, Louie felt anything but sexy.

"Sure." Louie opened the door. "Excuse the mess. We weren't expecting any important guests." She closed it quietly behind Heather, not wanting to wake Gabe. This didn't look like the news he was convinced he'd receive today.

Heather placed the bag and coffee on the wooden table and looked around as if needing permission to park herself somewhere.

"Please," Louie gestured to the couch, "take a seat."

Heather did just that, and Louie sat opposite her on the armchair, as far from her as might be considered polite. She hadn't checked her armpit situation, and she didn't want to add anything else to the possible list of negatives she was sure Heather was now compiling.

"Is Gabe in?"

"He's sleeping." Louie gripped the arms of her chair and made to get up. "Would you like me to get him?"

Heather nodded. "You'll stay though, won't you?"

Louie sank back into the chair. "What's going on, Heather?" Louie didn't need to ask. She knew the answer but didn't want to verbalize it. She wanted Heather to tell her she'd jumped to an unwarranted conclusion.

Heather sighed and sipped at her coffee. "I've got bad news, and I wanted to tell Gabe personally."

Louie remained fixed in her chair. Movement failed her. As did her words. Heather raised her eyebrows and looked expectant but didn't speak. Moments passed until Louie finally jumped up from her chair. "Let's get this over with." She knew it sounded harsher than she'd intended, and she also knew it wouldn't have been Heather's decision not to sign Gabe. Her belief in him had gotten him the audition in the first place. But Louie didn't know how hard this was going to hit him. They were both convinced he'd done enough to get a contract, and they'd partied like it was a done deal. Big mistake. She walked up the corridor trying to figure out how much she should say when Gabe emerged from his room, rubbing his eyes and yawning.

"Is someone here?" he asked.

Louie pulled back and waved her hand in front of her nose. "That's some morning breath you've got there, champ." He grinned and blew air her way but waited for an answer. "It's Heather King." Louie's heart broke a little when Gabe's grin turned into the widest smile.

"Yes!" He punched Louie lightly on the shoulder. "I told you, buddy. I told you! Tell her I'll be right with her," he shouted over his shoulder as he jogged down to the bathroom.

Louie turned and trudged back to the living room. Heather looked up at her and for a moment made Louie forget why she was there. She was something special. A little younger than Louie usually liked, but Heather had an intoxicating maturity about her. This was their fourth meeting, and it was under some pretty rough circumstances, but Louie figured she might as well make use of it before Gabe came in and Heather destroyed his dreams.

"Are we destined never to have that drink?" She said it jokingly, but something swept through Heather's eyes that partly answered Louie's question. She wished she hadn't asked. This morning was getting worse by the second.

"You're going for an interview today, aren't you?"

"Is that a change of subject or is your inquiry relevant to mine?" Louie asked.

Heather smiled. "It's relevant."

Louie dropped back into the armchair, opened the paper bag, and pulled out a sticky Danish pastry. "You have good taste in breakfast food."

"Now who's changing the subject?"

Heather sipped her coffee again, and Louie couldn't help but focus on the way her lips caressed the cup lid. "Not so. Just delaying the anticipation." Louie took a quick bite of the Danish. She was glad she was blessed with a physique that meant a little running kept her in relatively decent shape. Subconsciously, she touched her stomach and felt a little too much softness. Maybe she needed to get back to running. "Savana told you?"

"Of course she did. I'm her exec. I'm helping her ease into Rocky Top and navigate her change of direction."

Louie bit her lip before responding. Heather's professional tone was quite the turn-on, and she certainly looked the part in her pencil skirt suit and killer high heels. "Is that a problem?"

"Sorry to keep you waiting, Ms. King. Louie and I had a late night after the audition," Gabe said as he flopped onto the couch beside Heather.

Louie ran her hand through her hair in exasperation at Gabe's intrusion. Heather smiled and inclined her head slightly. Louie had no idea what she was communicating, but it made her want to know all her little signs and tells. Louie wanted all manner of private conversations with Heather.

"It's not a problem, Gabe. Louie kept me entertained in your absence."

Oh, I'd love to entertain you. Louie leaned back into the soft give of the ancient armchair and waited for Heather to drop the nuke.

"I'll bet she did." Gabe threw Louie a look.

He knew all too well what Louie's intentions toward Heather were. They'd discussed them at great length last night over the tequila.

"I'm truly sorry..." Heather said then stopped speaking as though that were enough of an explanation.

Gabe's smile disappeared, and he looked as though he might collapse and meld into the couch.

"Sorry?" he said. "I didn't...you're not here..."

Louie swallowed down her sudden desire to pull Gabe into a buddy hug. "I should leave you to it."

"No." Gabe grabbed at Louie's wrist. "Please. Don't go."

His look of absolute desolation wrapped around her throat and squeezed, but Louie was already working on an alternative plan to help his career. She'd remembered a few years ago some snot-nosed kid launching his career on YouTube, and now he had Grammys, American Music, and Billboard Music awards. Facebook was the most popular social media platform now. All they needed to do was make some decent quality videos, and Gabe's talent would do the rest, Louie was sure of that.

"I thought you liked me." Gabe's lip trembled. "I thought you liked my voice."

Heather reached over and put her hand on Gabe's knee. "I do, and your audition was fantastic, Gabe. You couldn't have done any more, but Donny..."

Louie shook her head as Heather didn't utter the unspeakable, and the look on her face conveyed all Louie needed to know. Donny was a racist prick. It clearly put Heather in a difficult position. Maybe she wanted to say more but knew she couldn't in case it got back to her boss. Gabe smiled, but there was a sadness that overwhelmed his usually bright eyes. He'd been pinning his hopes on getting this contract, but it wasn't to be.

Gabe stood and offered his hand. "Thanks for coming over, Ms. King. I appreciate you taking the time to do this in person rather than over the phone."

Heather took his hand in hers. "I'm so sorry you're not joining us. There are lots of other options for someone as talented as you are, Gabe."

He nodded, looking disconsolate, and made his way back to his bedroom. Louie waited until she heard his door click softly closed, but Heather was already out of her chair and smoothing her skirt down.

"I have to get to work."

There was an urgency in her voice Louie hadn't caught before Gabe interrupted their conversation about the potential of her working with Savana. "I take it that you think me working with your top artist *will* be a problem for this." Louie motioned her finger between the two of them to indicate the attraction they both felt.

Heather offered a tight-lipped smile and walked to the door. She opened it before turning back. "I won't act on anything that might affect my position at Rocky Top. It's probably for the best."

She closed the door behind her, and Louie sighed at her abrupt departure. She tried to take it at face value. Heather wasn't out and proud, and she had to protect herself from potential embarrassment. It was understandable, especially in country music. They were no readier for lesbians than they were for black guys with incredible talent. Louie rested her head on the back of the armchair and closed her eyes. Getting the girl and the dream job in one week was obviously too much to ask.

She pushed herself upright and grabbed the coffee Heather had brought. It was time to freshen up. If she did get the songwriting gig with Savana, Louie figured it would probably only take a few weeks, a month at most. The songs she wrote would garner the attention of publishers, and Louie would work for someone other than Rocky Top, leaving the path clear to pursue Heather again. Heather was definitely a woman worth waiting for...if Louie was willing to negotiate a relationship behind closed doors.

CHAPTER NINETEEN

Heather leaned her head on the steering wheel. She'd handled that terribly. Seeing Louie in not very many clothes had scrambled her usually right-thinking mind. She'd had every intention of addressing their attraction and talking about putting it on the back burner while Louie wrote Savana's album. Instead she'd made herself sound like a career woman and callously dismissed Louie as a potential bump on her road to success. *I need Emma's advice.* She speed-dialed her and pulled away from the curb.

"Hey, Feathers, I'm glad you called back. Sorry I couldn't speak to you last night when you rang."

"No problem. I can't expect my romance guru to be on call twenty-four seven." Heather had a feeling there was more to it than Emma was spilling, but she'd wait for their next dinner together to get the probably lurid details.

"Sounds juicy. Now I wish I *had* answered the phone. What's the problem?" Emma asked.

Heather slowed down to take the left onto Dickerson Pike and started to move before she saw a moped. She jammed on her brakes, and the rider nodded their thanks for not taking them out. "Damn it. Concentrate."

"I'm going to assume you're driving and not talking to me."

Heather triple-checked before moving out this time and tried to steady the solid thudding of her heart. "Sorry, Em. I nearly wiped out a moped."

"Shame you missed. Would've been worth fifty points."

Heather laughed. "Are there prizes when I collect enough points?"

"Sure, whatever you want. Now cut to the chase. I'm at the studio, and I'm paying by the hour."

"Last night I was calling for advice on gender stuff, but I think I've just messed everything up so it probably doesn't matter."

"Okay, break it down for me, and start with last night."

Heather gave a quick rundown of the audition, Louie being in attendance, and Savana's use of pronouns. "I'd wanted to know if it'd be all right if I asked Louie out or if that would be stepping on her—their toes. I wanted to know if there were roles and expectations, but I think I've just blown it anyway."

Emma laughed. "You're being serious?"

"Of course, why?" Heather slowed for an elderly lady and her decrepit dog who were struggling to make the distance on the diagonal crossing. "Am I being stupid?"

"Naïve, not stupid. This isn't the fifties. You can damn well ask out anyone you want to. I can't believe you're nearly thirty and don't know these things."

"I've been a little busy with my career. I haven't had time to keep up with…" This wasn't the time for excuses. Heather simply wasn't *au fait* with anything to do with lesbians and labels. Coming from a small town and only having two femme girlfriends wasn't a justifiable reason for ignorance now that she was in a big city. It was time to get up to speed. "You've got to help me."

"I will, but it means you have to ask Louie some personal questions. We can talk about it more tonight when I bring takeout to your place. Now, how do you think you've messed everything up and won't need all the information I'm going to bestow upon you this evening?"

Heather took the second exit off from the rotary onto Music Square carefully. She hated the game of chance these weird circles initiated. "I went to Gabe's house to tell him Donny wasn't going to sign him—"

"No way. Why the hell not?"

"Because apparently I work for a racist asshole." Heather didn't want to believe it. She wanted to see the best in Donny, and she'd partly reasoned that he had no choice because the higher-ups might have fired him if he *had* signed Gabe. But didn't his professional integrity kick in at some point? Shouldn't he stand for something? She closed the door on the irritating part of her mind that accused her of the same thing around her sexuality. That was different... wasn't it?

"Wow. He didn't sign him because he's black?"

"He said Gabe wasn't country enough, that my 'boy isn't genuine,' which is code for not white enough."

"Guess that explains why Darius Rucker is still the only black country star in the past decade," Emma said. "But you digress. How have you messed everything up?"

Heather smiled, glad she had a true friend who saw beyond the veiled pretense of small talk, drove straight to the core of a conversation, and didn't sugar-coat her words. "The quick version is Savana wants Louie to write her next album for her. If Louie does that, she'll be working at Rocky Top for the next month or so. That means we can't do anything about..." Heather briefly contemplated how she was about to categorize the thing that existed between her and Louie. "About the heat between the two of us until we stop working together. And even then only if Louie's prepared to have a quiet relationship."

"Sounds dull, but I understand. You're in the closet, and you don't want to endanger your career. You have a 'plan,' and you're sticking to it."

Heather smarted at the statement, but Emma's observation was on the nose. They'd discussed her plans for her own label over many bottles of wine. "It sounds particularly callous when you say it like that."

"On the clock, babe. No time to play nice. You were telling me how you've managed to mess everything up."

"Fine." Heather pulled up in her spot at the Rocky Top lot and cut the engine. "I had every intention of having a reasonable discussion with Louie and telling her exactly that, but instead I said

I wouldn't act on anything that may damage my career. I must've sounded like an absolute bitch." She pulled her keys from the ignition and shoved them in her handbag. "Then I walked out."

"Without saying anything else?"

"Exactly."

"I can see why you called me. Tonight at nine. We'll figure this out over Thai and some Tiger beer. Don't worry, Feathers. Louie seems pretty astute, and I bet she's already got you worked out. No need to make some false conflict out of this, okay?"

Heather snorted. She didn't want Louie to have already worked her out. Straightforward was boring and surely wouldn't keep someone as worldly as Louie interested for long. "Am I that transparent?"

"Yes. At least, you are for anyone who's really interested in seeing you."

Heather bit her lip and smiled. "You think Louie wants to see me?"

"From what you've told me about her, I do. Obviously, I'm going to have to meet Louie officially to make sure her intentions toward my Feathers are noble and to give my permission and approval."

"You're hilarious, *Mom.*" Heather got out of the car and closed the door. "Thanks for that. As always, your counsel is appreciated."

"Your humble servant, miss," Emma said. "Will you see Louie again before tonight?"

"Probably. She's coming in to see Savana at eleven."

"Right. Be enchanting and glamorous. And take Louie's lead on pronouns. Look for any reactions to the use of 'she,' okay?"

"Enchanting. Glamorous. Pronouns. Got it." Heather shouldered her oversized handbag that held her life within it and started toward the office. "And when we're done with my crap tonight, you can tell me about your secret rendezvous with your mystery man." She ended the call before Emma could respond. She was certain there was more to last night than one of Emma's regular dalliances and wanted all the details. First though, she had to make amends with Louie. Tall, handsome Louie. She owed it to herself to explore their attraction. She was so different from her previous girlfriends, and Heather had no doubt that was *definitely* a good thing.

❖

"Did you sleep in?"

"Huh, I wish," Heather said, trying to act nonchalant instead of showing her surprise at Savana sitting in her office as she arrived. "I had to stop by Gabe Duke's house to let him know Donny's decision."

Savana inclined her head slightly. "Had to or wanted to?"

Heather shrugged her handbag onto her desk and collapsed into her chair. It wasn't as comfortable as Louie and Gabe's sofa, and she already wished she was back there, making out with Louie. *I wonder how she kisses.* "Both. I wasn't sure he was going to take the rejection well. He's young and seems quite vulnerable. If I were in his position, I would've appreciated someone coming to me personally rather than texting or emailing to turn me down. Wouldn't you?"

Savana pushed a coffee cup Heather's way and sighed. "It's been a long time since someone turned me down. For anything. And you might say I was lucky, because I was discovered when I was sixteen. I didn't have to jump through hoops like a lot of artists have to. It was sweet of you to see him personally though. I admire that, and you were brave. It could've gotten nasty."

Heather shook her head. "No way. Gabe is such a gentle soul. And Louie was there so I wasn't alone with him. Not that I was worried." Savana's concerns for Heather's safety resonated slightly. Maybe personal visits to people the label turned down weren't such a good idea.

"Was Louie ready for our meeting?"

Heather smiled as she recalled the scruffy state Louie was in. She'd clearly just gotten out of bed and though she was quite adorable, she certainly wasn't dressed for a career-launching meeting with Savana. "I interrupted her getting ready."

Savana raised her eyebrows. "Did you see something you liked?"

"What? No. What do you mean?" Heather panicked at Savana's question. How could she possibly know Heather was gay?

"Sorry. You had a wistful look in your eyes as if you were remembering what Louie looked like this morning. Am I wrong?"

"I'm not—"

"I know you're not out at work. I thought it might help our working relationship if you knew I was sympathetic, that's all. But if you're not comfortable talking about it, that's fine, too."

Heather forced a smile. That was shaky ground. She couldn't deny that being best buddies with the great Savana Hayes appealed, but a few alarm bells were ringing with her behavior around Donny. When Savana had first arrived, Heather was beyond excited. How had things changed? She couldn't see why Savana would have a questionable agenda, and it wasn't like Heather to be so suspicious. She liked to take people at face value, and Savana had been nothing but nice since she'd arrived. *And* she'd personally asked for Heather to be her exec. She dismissed her paranoia and decided to trust her. "I'm sorry. I just have to be careful. How did you know?"

Savana smiled as she reached over the desk and placed her hand on Heather's. "I believe it's called 'gaydar,' isn't it? There's no need to worry. If there's anything I'm good at, it's keeping a secret."

The warmth of Savana's hand flooded heat through Heather's body and muddled...*everything*. Savana had been one of Heather's greatest idols for over a decade. It was Savana's music that fueled Heather's fire to come to Nashville, and while it hadn't worked out quite as planned, this place still felt like home. She quelled the rising panic at her body's hair-trigger reaction to Savana's touch. *She's my artist.* And *she's straight.* Resisting the near-overpowering urge to pull her hand away from Savana's, Heather said, "I'd appreciate that. It's hard balancing ambition against personal freedom."

Savana removed her hand and sat in the chair opposite Heather. "I'm sure. And Louie?"

Heather looked at her hand that remained frozen and uncooperative. "There's nothing between Louie and me." Heather felt the need to keep that part secret but wasn't sure why. It wasn't like Savana needed to be protected from the truth or that she might be jealous of Heather's feelings for Louie. Heather just didn't want idle gossip about her sexuality going around the office any more than it might already be, and she didn't want *anyone* knowing she *was* attracted to Louie. Above everything, Heather was determined to keep her career plan on track.

Savana leaned back and crossed her legs. "Good."

Good, why? "You're worried about my professionalism?"

Savana got up from the chair. "Absolutely not. Remember that I asked for you to be my exec, and I wouldn't have joined this label if Donny hadn't given you the position."

She walked to the door, and Heather blinked and shook her head as she realized she was watching Savana's ass as she glided across the floor. "And I'll be eternally grateful for this opportunity, Savana. I promise not to let you down."

Savana smiled, showing her teeth in an almost predatory fashion.

"I know you won't. Bring Louie to the studio at eleven. I'd like you to stay with us for the meeting if you don't mind."

"Of course," Heather replied as Savana closed the door. She began to wonder about the nature of Savana's request. Was she worried Louie would hit on her? *Would* Louie hit on her, especially now that Heather had made such an ass of herself and acted like an ice queen? She resolved to speak to Louie before taking her down to meet with Savana. She'd invite her out for a drink and explain herself. And maybe Louie could dig out the bad seeds Mia had planted about Louie's past.

CHAPTER TWENTY

Nailing the job with Savana was easier than Louie had thought it would be. The hardest part was trying to concentrate on Savana instead of being distracted by Heather's presence, especially after she'd asked Louie to go for coffee once the meeting concluded. Louie ran her hand through her hair again, reminded that she should hit Gabe's barber.

"I've never been in here before. I love the restroom; all the fixtures are exposed copper piping," Heather said as she slid into the booth to sit opposite Louie.

"It's a cute place, isn't it? I discovered it a couple of days ago. The freak shakes are amazing." Louie took a breath, aware that she got terribly talkative when her nerves kicked in. The waitress approached with their drinks, and time seemed to stretch on while Louie added brown sugar to her tea, and Heather added sweetener to her coffee. "Did you know that sweeteners were originally developed as rat poison?"

"So I hear. Lucky I'm not a rat."

Louie laughed. "As long as you're not a love rat, I'm fine with whatever you are."

Heather folded the little packets and placed them neatly beside her cup. "Can I ask you something personal?"

"Fire away. It seems to be the day for it." Louie's meeting with Savana had seemed more like a personal fact-finding exercise than any sort of audition to be her songwriter.

Heather stirred her coffee and looked thoughtful. "That's kind of what I wanted to ask you about. Did it bother you when Savana asked about what pronouns you use?"

Louie shook her head. "I like it, even though it doesn't apply to me because I'm just your regular lesbian who doesn't fit into society's view of what a woman *should* look like. It shows a level of consideration I appreciate. I don't mind that people might think I'm gender fluid, or trans, or a guy. None of those things are an insult, not in my eyes anyway."

"If only everyone in the world thought that way."

The sadness in Heather's voice hinted at personal experience of prejudice. Louie considered withholding any questions about it but decided to run with it. "It must be hard for you, not being out at work?"

"It's not just that. It's all the discrimination—race, gender, sexuality." She paused as if to measure her response. "I don't want to hide, Louie. But I have to. For now, at least."

Heather moved her hand across the table as if reaching for Louie, but she pulled it back and picked up her mug instead. Louie gripped her own cup harder, struggling to control the urge to touch her. Heather had made it clear that morning that getting the gig with Savana meant staying away from a romantic entanglement. "Is no one at Rocky Top out?"

Heather shook her head. "No. And even if anyone was thinking about it, after what happened to Aaron, I'm pretty sure they would've changed their minds. It's not a progressive label in that respect, or in any respect for that matter. Why else would we have turned down a talent like Gabe? I just need to stay there long enough to build a reputation and get the means to finance my own label. Then I can be…me."

"And that's why you blew me off this morning?" Louie grinned and hoped Heather knew she was teasing her. The mood needed to be lightened despite the bombshell that Gabe hadn't been signed because of the color of his skin. If Rocky Top was indicative of Nashville's intolerance, they needed a plan to take Gabe to the top without the backing of a big label.

"Oh, God, I knew I'd made an ass of myself. I didn't mean to be so dismissive..."

Heather trailed off, and while Louie felt she knew what Heather seemed unable to say, she wanted to hear it directly from her lips. Louie needed to know she wasn't making something out of nothing. She had to know that Heather coming on to her at the Bluebird wasn't a one-time thing and she'd never get another opportunity. "Dismissive of what?"

Heather looked hard at Louie before she answered. "Of what might be between us. You bring some, some...need out of me that I've never heeded before. The way I acted at the Bluebird—I've *never* been that way before. I was out of control and so...vampy."

Louie laughed so hard she almost spluttered her tea all over the table. "It definitely felt like you were a pro at getting what you want."

Heather's eyes, which had been full of light, seemed to darken slightly, and her smile disappeared.

Louie wanted to reach over the table and rest her hand over Heather's, but instead she pressed her thumb into her palm as if rubbing a pain away. "Did I say something wrong?"

"No, not really. You've just got to the other personal question I needed to ask you." Heather took a sip of her coffee and placed the cup down carefully.

"Sounds ominous," Louie said, filling the silence with what felt like an expected response. She had no idea what subject Heather was about to broach.

"Do you know someone called Mia?"

The mention of Mia's name felt like a gut punch, and Louie rocked back on her seat. A week of such good fortune had to be equalized with something totally unpleasant to keep the universe in balance. She'd gotten so carried away with how great everything was going that, for a long moment, she'd forgotten Mia inhabited the same town. But why would an ex worry Heather? "I do. We used to be partners, in bed and in music." Louie didn't see the point in disguising the truth. She had nothing to hide, and Heather had nothing to worry about. She and Mia were finished. Mia had made it quite clear when she left with everything that her fascination with Louie was over. She'd used Louie to get one step closer to her dreams and decided she was no longer useful. Louie chose not to listen to the voice that was trying to convince her that Mia *did* actually love her once.

"Did you part as friends?"

Louie huffed. If she were a dog, her hackles would've raised. "She took all my savings, tried to sell the guitar my mom had scrimped and saved to buy, and left me with a heap of debt." She looked down at her hands, white-knuckled and gripping the table. She stretched them out and tried to relax. "I don't think the term 'friends' applies." She smiled but was aware it probably looked as false as it felt. "I'm sorry. It's still kind of raw."

"Then what I'm about to say will be more like dragging sandpaper over your wound than ointment."

"What do you mean?"

"She told me that you…that you got violent when you were drunk."

Louie's eyes widened. She couldn't believe what she'd heard. And the way Heather said it battered her heart like a piñata with a thick chunk of timber. They didn't know each other too well yet, but surely she couldn't think that Louie was capable of something like that? "It was nothing like that. I could never hurt anyone, let alone the woman I loved." Beneath the abject panic, Louie tried to reason that Heather was asking the question because she was interested in getting to know her better. She wanted the slate clean and everything out in the open. That was fair. It was honest. But she needed to take care of Mia running her mouth off. She looked up at Heather and tried to read her expression, but she was giving nothing away. "I know it's just my word against hers, but that's all I have. I can only hope you believe me."

"I'm sorry, Louie. I had to ask, and you should know what Mia's saying about you."

Louie nodded. "I understand."

"You need to have a conversation with Mia to stop her from spreading any more vile rumors," Heather said. "You've just secured a lucrative contract with one of the biggest stars in this city, but Savana will drop you like a hot coal if there's even a whiff of a scandal. And Donny might even blackball you with every publishing house in Nashville."

Louie sighed and shook her head. "I don't know why she'd say those things. Unless she's just trying to cover her own back. Maybe she thinks I'll tell everyone what *she* did to *me*."

Heather shrugged. "You're probably right. She does like to be the center of attention. Plus, everyone always wants to hear salacious gossip. They don't care if it's the truth."

"Do you know where I can find her?" This wasn't a conversation she wanted to have over the phone where Mia could end the call at any moment. Louie didn't want to see her, but it was clear their meeting was unavoidable. She began to feel anxiety grip her gut. If she didn't relax, she'd soon be doubled over in pain and have to blame the food. She closed her eyes briefly, tried to imagine the discomfort as the enchanted branches of a tree, and slowly unpicked the grip of the tendrils around her stomach. She pulled the pain away, tossed it to the ground, and watched it dissipate into silver smoke. She opened her eyes to find Heather looking at her intensely.

"She usually goes to see the Song Suffragettes every week at the Bluebird. The next one is tomorrow, and I expect she'll be there. I can ask my friend Emma if she could find out for sure. I could probably get you her number, too, if you want it?"

Louie smiled, thankful that Heather clearly wasn't the kind of person to believe trash talk. "I've got her number...and her cell." She didn't have Louie's contact any more. She'd changed her number as part of the process of getting over her when Mia had left. Louie reminded herself that Heather had asked her out for coffee and decided to park the Mia issue until later. It was talk of Mia that had distracted Heather a few minutes ago. And right now, Louie wanted to savor this, the first time she finally had Heather to herself. "Do you want to give me your number while you have your phone out?"

Heather flicked her hair back and dug into her handbag. "I'll give you my business card because we're going to be working together, and Savana likes to work beyond regular office hours so we might need to contact each other about that."

Heather placed the card on the table and pushed it toward Louie. She picked it up, entered the number into her cell, and began to tap out the message, *I want to kiss u right now.* Heather glanced at her phone when it vibrated to let her know she received a message. Louie could see her own number, but the content was hidden.

"Is that you?" Heather asked and raised her eyebrow.

Louie shrugged. "Just giving you my number the easy way."

"And I suppose it says 'test' or something similarly professional?"

"Of course." Louie sipped her tea and waited to see if Heather would give in and read it. She didn't. "Change of subject then. You were saying that you'd made an ass of yourself?"

"Is that what I said?"

Heather looked coy, making Louie think she'd probably let Heather get away with anything if they ever got around to dating. "Something like that. But I get the pressure you're under, Heather. And I understand that you have to be careful at Rocky Top. Did you know the VP who was fired well?"

"He was my mentor. Aaron brought me into Rocky Top and taught me everything he knew. He was preparing me to be his successor, but it was never supposed to be under these circumstances."

Heather's sadness emanated so strongly Louie could almost feel it. "It must be hard for you, staying there in that position."

Heather tilted her head and offered a tight-lipped smile. "I'm paying my dues and building my reputation so I can start my own label." Her eyes brightened. "I want to be able to sign a talent like Gabe and get his voice out there." She leaned back in the booth and looked upward. "And I want to stop hiding who I am."

Louie couldn't imagine how hard it was for Heather. Looking the way she did, Louie had never had the option to hide. And she faced people's reactions to that every day. But would she have been so quick to come out if she could pass as straight and her career had depended on it? Louie's mom had drilled it into her to accept herself from the first moment she'd been bullied at elementary school for being different, but how much less confidence would she have in her sexuality if she had been what society proclaimed as typically feminine and almost everyone around her detested lesbianism? "Is Nashville ready for a label like that?"

"It wouldn't be mainstream, and it wouldn't have to be. I don't see myself earning millions of dollars and being the biggest label on Music Row. But it's a couple of years away yet, and who knows how things will have changed by then."

Heather sounded optimistic, and Louie wanted to believe things would be better for everyone in Nashville, but change happened very slowly. And it could so easily be rewound with the wrong people in power. What if things didn't pan out the way Heather envisioned them? "What if it doesn't change? Would you stay in the closet forever for the sake of your career?" Louie felt sure she couldn't handle *that*, even for someone as wonderful as Heather seemed to be.

Heather straightened in her chair. "Haven't you ever wanted something so bad that you'd do almost anything to make it happen?"

"I've wanted *someone* so bad that I'd do anything for them," Louie replied, her voice tinged with the melancholy she couldn't shake when she thought of Mia's betrayal.

"So when you've finished this gig with Savana, you'd be prepared to have a closeted relationship with me?" Heather didn't wait for an answer. "I don't know what the future holds, Louie. I just know what I want from it in terms of a career and a label. That's all I've been focused on for the past five years. I wasn't expecting… you." Heather inched away when their legs touched beneath the table. "I have to go."

A waitress came to their table. "Can I top up your coffee?" she asked.

Heather stood and pulled her handbag close. "No, thank you. I have to get back to the office."

Louie held her hand over her own cup of tea and shook her head. She had no words. She couldn't figure out what was going on between her and Heather. One moment it looked like they were going to give it a go, and the next moment, Heather was categorically saying there was no possibility of them dating. Louie hadn't been in the closet since…well, ever. She felt like she might be prepared to date Heather behind closed doors. For a while perhaps.

"I'll see you at the office, then," Louie said as Heather began to walk away.

Heather turned and smiled, but it didn't seem like the emotion behind her eyes backed up her expression. "Of course. I'll let you know when Savana wants you to start."

Louie didn't reply. Savana had already said she wanted her in the next day. She wanted to start work on her new material as soon as possible. Heather was all business in a click of her patent black heels. Louie sighed and slugged back the rest of her tea. Black, like the mood Heather had managed to put her in.

CHAPTER TWENTY-ONE

D amn it," Heather said as a drop of green curry sauce landed on her light gray sweats. "That'll never come out."

Emma chuckled. "Like you, then?"

Heather picked up the nearest cushion and tossed it at Emma. "That's not fair. But I could very nearly have outed myself today." A romanticized blurry-edged picture of Louie's face came into Heather's mind. She'd wanted so bad to lean in and almost kiss her, and according to Louie's text, she'd wanted the same.

Emma was guiding a forkful of noodles into her mouth but dropped it noisily onto her plate. "What? Tell all. Right now."

"I was in a tiny café in East Nashville, so I guess I was relatively safe. But Louie was close, and I could smell her perfume—"

"Cologne."

"Whatever. She smelled great, and her eyes were so soft and gentle, like I could hide from the world and be safe in them. I was saying to her how I didn't want to hide forever, and then I found myself wanting to move in for a kiss."

"Whoa! What happened?"

"Nothing. I did nothing. I somehow managed to go from talking about my dreams of owning a label to flouncing off saying I wouldn't let Louie get in the way of what I'd been working toward for five years. She must think I'm either crazy or a complete bitch with how I keep blowing hot and cold."

"You've got it bad for this one, don't ya, Feathers?" Emma scooped her discarded fork back up and shoveled the noodles into her mouth.

Heather nodded slowly. "I'm attracted to her, yes. But I don't know what to do about it. One minute I think that we could date behind closed doors and the next I think it's too risky. And now Louie's going to be working with me for maybe the next month, and I can't do anything about it."

"Because of your plan." Emma stated it matter-of-factly.

"Partly. But some of me doesn't want to wait *that* long. There's something between us, and that part of me wants to see where it goes before I hit my thirties. I might not get financing for my record label for another couple of years."

"As soon as I hit the big time, Feathers, I'll finance the shit out of your plan. I suppose the other part of you is being overly cautious and wants to keep Louie as far away as possible to prevent temptation. Like you're Eve, and Louie's your snake." Emma sucked in a noodle, but some sauce escaped and smeared her chin. She wiped it with the back of her hand and kept eating.

"And you wonder why you're single," Heather said and laughed.

Emma raised her eyebrows and brandished her fork in Heather's direction. "I'll have you know that I *choose* to be single."

"Really? So about last night…" Heather was sure there was something Emma wasn't telling her, and when she chewed on her lip, Heather knew she was on to something. And she wanted to talk about something other than her indecisiveness and lack of courage.

"What about it?" Emma washed down a mouthful of food with a hefty gulp of white wine.

"I get the feeling you're hiding something from me. I've told you a hundred times I'm not the jealous type."

Emma placed her plate on the table and sighed. She leaned back on the sofa, pulled her legs beneath her ass, and turned to Heather. "I think I'm having a midlife crisis."

"Aren't you a bit young to have one of those?"

"I'm serious. I suddenly feel a little bit more…mortal."

"Any idea what's brought this on?" Emma was only thirty-two, but Heather wondered if she'd be hit with the same melancholy when she ventured into her fourth decade.

"I guess I thought I'd have achieved my dream by now." She held up her hands as if to stop Heather from interrupting. "I know you're going to say that you'll sign me as soon as you have your label, and that you can't believe Rocky Top wouldn't sign me. But it's not just the music."

Emma being this serious was such a rarity, Heather began to worry. "Is it a health thing? Are you okay?" Tens of different scenarios and health scares rushed into Heather's consciousness. She couldn't lose her only real friend.

Emma grasped Heather's forearm and squeezed lightly. "Wow, calm down. Don't put dirt on my grave just yet."

Heather put her hand over Emma's. "I'm sorry. You're being cryptic, and it's freaking me out. What happened last night?"

"I was with Tim."

Heather relaxed back into the couch, not realizing how tense she'd become. "And how is he an indication of a midlife crisis?"

"Because I was gripped by loneliness and ended up dialing a booty call." She put her head in her hands and groaned.

"You know you can always call me."

"I know, Feathers, but this wasn't your average, woe is me standard loneliness. This was bone-deep loneliness. This was 'Oh my God, I'm going to spend the rest of my life alone' loneliness." She blew an errant hair from her face and her shoulders sank.

Heather put her food down, draped her arm around Emma, and pulled her in for a hug. "You're not on your own feeling that way, Em. It gets me some nights when I go to bed alone and when I wake with no one beside me. I guess you and I aren't built to be single." Heather rested her head against Emma's. "And I don't *want* to be that way. I've got an awesome best friend, I'm developing the career I really want, and I've got a kick-ass little house that I love. It pisses me off that something inside of me feels incomplete, like I can't be happy without a woman in my heart."

Emma unfurled herself from Heather's hug and retrieved her wine glass. "Were you content when you *had* a woman—if you can remember that far back?"

Heather punched Emma's shoulder lightly. "Hey, that's mean. True, but mean." Heather rubbed her forehead and considered how she'd felt in those relationships. She'd been there in body, sure. And she thought she'd been there in mind and heart, too, but maybe she hadn't. Maybe that was why they'd failed. "I suppose I wasn't, otherwise I'd still be with someone, wouldn't I?"

"And are you happier or about the same without them?"

Heather shrugged, picked up her glass, and swirled the wine around the base. "I hadn't really thought about it. I think I'm happier. I like being independent and not having to run my plans past anyone but myself. No one's ever supported my dreams and ambitions before, you know? Not even my family."

"Then it's not just any woman you need. It's the right one."

"How did this become about me? I thought we were working out your midlife crisis."

Emma smiled and wiggled her eyebrows. "Talking about me makes me uncomfortable...Maybe *we* should try sharing a house. We could become old spinsters together and know we'd never be alone."

"Run that plan by me when we're fifty, and I'll think about it. There's way too much man-traffic in your life for me to consider sharing with you. Men are stinky, *but* Tim might be the exception. How did he react to your late-night booty call?"

"Well, he didn't turn it down, which I hadn't considered until I'd already dialed his number."

"I sense there's a 'but' coming."

Emma nodded. "We had sex—and it was as amazing as it always was—but then he wanted to *talk*." She gestured air quotes around the word talk. "Why? I mean, most men would have just turned over and fallen asleep exhausted after the workout we had."

"Tim isn't 'most men' though, is he? You've always known he was something special." Heather wondered if Emma was finally ready to hear her thoughts on their breakup. "Do you think that's why you broke it off?"

Emma snorted. "He was talking about having kids, and it was too soon. He already saw the white picket fence, gas grill, and riding mower."

"And you didn't?" Heather knew her love life gave her no authority to speak of these things, but it didn't stop her from *knowing* what love looked like in other couples. Something about Emma and Tim, how they reacted when they met each other and the energy around them when they were together, felt right. And in those lonely moments she experienced far more often than she liked, they'd given Heather hope that love wasn't just a fairy tale pedaled in Hollywood movies.

Emma fell silent, and her lack of immediate response indicated Heather's supposition was close to the truth.

"What did he want to talk about?" Heather asked, moving the conversation away from her challenging question.

Emma swirled the wine in her glass as if it were tealeaves and she was looking for guidance. "The future. The past. All of it was deeper than I wanted to go."

"But you went there anyway?" She asked the question more in hope than in expectation. Tim made Emma happy, and she liked seeing her best friend that way.

She nodded. "A little. And you're right, smart-ass, I did see a version of forever with him, and it scared me. My dad gave up his music career to raise a family, and that's a history I have no intention of repeating."

"Have you ever told Tim that?"

Emma rolled her eyes. "Obviously not until last night, I hadn't. And yes, I'm sure if I'd told him that the first go-round, we wouldn't have broken up at all because he's so super understanding and I'm a self-sabotaging idiot. Does that about cover it?"

Heather squeezed Emma's knee. "A little bit harsh, but yeah, you've covered the main points. And…"

"And he says he's happy to go slower, so I guess we're going to give it another go and see how things work out."

Heather raised her glass and clinked it to Emma's. "Here's to second chances."

"And first ones. Don't think we're done talking about your relationship status. What happened with the Savana audition? And let's talk about this morning's panicked telephone call since that's the reason I came over."

"Fine. But first, we need more wine." Heather quickly cleared their food to the kitchen and returned with a fresh bottle. She topped up both of their glasses and recapped on the mess she'd made of talking to Louie in the morning, how Louie had been tremendously understanding even when they talked about Mia's rumors, Louie's cute text about a kiss, and finally, how Heather had been a complete bitch and rushed out of the café. They were halfway down the bottle by the time Heather had finished.

Emma put her glass down. "Let me see the text."

Heather became conscious of her phone sitting on the table and used her toe to push it further away from Emma. "I deleted it."

"I don't believe you." Emma jumped up and grabbed the phone before Heather could stop her. "Here it is." She remained out of Heather's reach while she read the text.

"What are you doing?" Heather asked when Emma began to tap on the screen.

"Stirring the pot." Emma tossed the phone into Heather's lap, picked up her glass, and returned to her seat.

Heather scanned through her phone. *I wanted 2 kiss U 2. I'm sorry I'm such an ass. I promise I'll b worth it.* "Oh my God, Emma." Heather switched it off and shoved it down the side of the sofa.

"I'm just helping you out. So, Louie is just a good old-fashioned, boyish lesbian, then?"

Heather sighed. She couldn't retract the text, and it was hard to stay mad at Emma for long. "Looks like it." Heather smiled and thought of Louie's ass in her oversized jeans, her sexy short hair, and her small breasts. *Just enough of a handful.*

"Would your attraction have changed if she was...more complicated?"

Heather hesitated before she answered. To anyone else, she would have responded with an immediate "God, no," but she felt safe with Emma to be more truthful. "I don't know. I'm a lesbian, and I love women, apparently not just femme ones." She recalled the brief research into gender fluidity and trans guys she'd done before Louie had turned up for her audition with Savana. "I don't think I could be politically correct and say that I wouldn't have changed my mind if she'd turned out to be a trans guy. I really don't like men that way. I've never felt any inkling of arousal from the male...bits. Does that make sense?"

Emma nodded. "Sure it does. We like what we like. And it leaves more for us girls who *do* appreciate the male in all his glory, perfectly honed or a little softer around the edges."

Heather was sure Emma was referring to the slight paunch Tim had cultivated since their breakup. She also knew it was a result of the beer he drowned his sorrows in and expected it would soon recede now that he had Emma back. "Except now she probably wants nothing to do with me because I swing from one pole to the other about us dating."

"Nah, she'll just figure that you're a little high maintenance. What self-respecting femme lesbian isn't?"

Heather swiped Emma's shoulder gently. "Stereotyping much?"

"Just saying it like I see it, Feathers. Seriously though, do you know if you *want* to date Louie?"

Heather rubbed at her forehead. All this deliberating was beginning to make her head ache. "I do. Not now, not until the record's done, but maybe after. If Louie can handle a private relationship."

"By private, you mean never seen out together. Do you think Louie can handle that?"

"She said she was willing to try. But that was a few conversations ago. God knows what she's thinking now."

"If she realizes what an amazing woman you are, Feathers, she'll still be willing," Emma said, tapping her nose like an old crone. "How long will the album take?"

"Louie thinks she'll have it done in a month, and then she's hoping to get an exclusive writing deal with one of the publishers. I gave her the name of a few contacts."

She laughed and poked Heather's cheek. "Look at you, all proud of what she's doing already."

Heather smiled as she realized that Louie's ambition *had* impressed her. She wondered if it was because it seemed to match her own. Previous relationships had no interest in furthering their careers, or even having a career at all, and that was fine. For them. But they'd wanted Heather to be the same way, and that stifled her and clipped her wings. It'd be nice to spend some time with someone who shared a similar drive. "I like that she has a plan, too."

"Of course you do. And you two working closely together—you're going to be able to handle that?"

"It's been five years since I've been in a relationship, Em. I can control myself." Heather said the words. She heard them out loud. But she wasn't sure she believed them.

CHAPTER TWENTY-TWO

I can't believe I'd convinced myself that I was going to make it so easy." Gabe sank into the rocking chair on their back deck and chugged on his third beer. "What was I thinking? Darius Rucker was the last guy like me to make it in Nashville and that was eight years ago." He threw his arm out dramatically and spilled his drink on his jeans. "Look at me. I'm all kinds of wrong for this music scene."

Louie listened as Gabe continued his angry assault on the state of Nashville and the lack of diversity in its music. She could only agree. In the past five years, she could only think of one other person of color hitting it big in country, and that was Melanie Goodrich. She came in all guns blazing, signed to Capitol, and then all but disappeared after one hit. And it wasn't an unacknowledged phenomenon. She'd read that country music was the redneck soundtrack of the racist South. But Louie was certain that if he was given the right exposure, Gabe could add some interesting flavor to the vanilla sundae that was currently country music.

When he finally took a breath and actually looked as though he might like some input from Louie, she passed his laptop to him. "This is what we're going to do."

Gabe took the computer from her, stared at the screen for a while, and then gave it back. "Zuckerberg has a record label in Nashville?"

Louie smiled, not surprised at Gabe's quick dismissal. "No. And you don't need a record label just yet. Let's get you discovered by the people who really matter—the ones who'll want to buy your music."

Gabe put his bottle on the table and scooched up in his chair. She'd got his attention.

"What do you mean?"

"You've got four thousand friends on Facebook. What if..." Louie leaned closer to Gabe, already pumped about the project. "What if we start posting videos of you singing covers of some massive country hits?"

Gabe's eyes brightened. "You think that would work? How would that work? Won't we need a studio? And someone to video and edit everything? What—"

"Whoa!" Louie held up her hands. "Slow down, cowboy. The answer to almost all of those questions is no. We don't need high tech soundproofing; that would only sanitize your sound. We want to promote your raw and unmastered talent and blow people away with your voice, not some overproduced stylized tracks that might only appeal to certain labels." She put the laptop down, jumped up, and pulled Gabe to his feet. "I'll video you on your iPhone. We'll upload them to your page, do some sharing, and watch you take off." Louie motioned out into the garden as if Gabe's whole future were playing on a giant movie screen. "You'll get picked up by one of the major labels, and with some hard work, you'll be making history by topping all five country music Billboard charts."

Louie turned back to Gabe. He was as wide-eyed as she felt, but then his eyes softened and he looked at her with a seriousness she didn't expect.

"You see all of that for me?" he asked and Louie nodded. "And you want to help me do it?" He put his hand on her shoulder.

"Damn right, I do."

Gabe pulled her into a huge hug and held her tight enough to make her gasp just a little. He released her, and she felt the wetness of his tears through her shirt.

"You're like the big sister I never had, Louie. I don't know how I got so lucky that we crossed paths, but I'm damn glad we did."

Louie looked upward in a futile attempt to stop the burning tears from escaping. "Me, too." She wanted to say more but didn't for fear of choking on her words. He was the little brother she never knew she needed, someone to look after and protect the way her mom had done for her.

Gabe bounced on his heels like a kid ready to start an Easter egg hunt. "When do we start?"

"How about right now? I need to call my mom, but then I've got the rest of the evening free." Louie had kept her mom in touch with everything that was going on by text. Well, almost everything. She hadn't mentioned Heather yet. Not that she knew what there was to say about her or them. There was no them, and she didn't know how to handle the way Heather blew her off after coffee. It was clear Heather was conflicted, especially from the way she'd said, "I wasn't expecting...you." But the course of true love never did run smooth, and Heather was someone Louie could potentially see a future in. She was witty, classy, ambitious, beautiful, and kind...if only Heather would get out of her own way.

Gabe rubbed his hand back and forth over the fade lines in his hair, then moved to his chin. "Should I shave? Where are we going to do it?" He tugged at the front of his faded and holey white T-shirt. "What should I wear? Should I dress up?"

Louie shook her head and laughed. "So many questions, big guy. We can do it exactly as you are. You look great. We don't want you to look coiffed, preened, and staged. We want you looking real. Just you and your guitar, full screen coverage."

"Okay. Right. I'll go make sure my guitar's tuned and think about what cover I should do."

"Go, go, go," Louie said as Gabe loped off back into the house. She relaxed back into her lounger, picked up her phone, and dialed her mom.

"Noodle Doodle! I was just thinking about you. I'm glad you called."

As usual, her mom's enthusiasm made her smile a little wider. "Hey, Mom. How are you?"

"All the better for hearing your voice, Noodle. How are things in the Athens of the South?"

Louie laughed. "Check you out with all your Nashville knowledge. I haven't gotten around to visiting the Parthenon yet."

"Make sure you send me pictures when you do. You've only sent me a few since you got there."

Louie shook her head at her mom's teasing. Louie had sent plenty of photos, including every room in the house, a selfie of her with Savana, and pictures of her and Gabe goofing around the place. "You're going to run out of room for them."

"No, I won't. You know I only get them printed out three-by-five size. One shoebox fits three hundred so you better keep 'em coming. The Savana Hayes one was amazing. How did it go this morning?"

"It went great. She wants me to write the whole album with her. We're getting started in the morning."

"That's fabulous, baby," her mom said. "I'm so proud of you."

"I can't believe everything's fallen into place the way it has." Louie looked at the garden and felt a certain peace wash over her. "I found an awesome friend, a house, a writing job…"

"And?" Her mom clearly heard what Louie didn't say. "There's a girl?"

Louie grinned and was glad no one was around to see it. The thought of Heather made her feel giddy despite the situation. "Nope, there's a beautiful woman."

"What's her name? How did you meet? Give me all the details. Well, obviously not *all*."

Louie wrinkled her nose at the thought of sharing her sexual exploits with her mom. As close as they were, there were still limits. "It's complicated," Louie said and then ran through the tale of how they'd met, that Heather was a talent scout and had put Gabe forward to audition for Rocky Top. As she was telling her the rest of the story, Mia came unbidden into her mind. "Mia's here, Mom."

Her mom, who'd been making all the appropriate oohs and aahs in all the right places, harrumphed loudly. "Have you spoken to her about all of your stuff she stole or have you gone to the police?"

"Neither—yet." Louie had no intention of telling her mom that Mia was already causing trouble for her by spreading rumors. She'd go berserk if she found about the lies coming from Mia. "This is a smaller town than you think, and it looks like we're both here to stay. I'm going to talk to her. Hopefully, it can be amicable. It's possible we might even end up working together one day, so I need to be professional about this, Mom." Her mom made the grumbling sound that meant she'd accept Louie's decision but wasn't at all happy about it.

"You'll be careful though, won't you, Louie? She's a renegade runaway, that one."

Louie smiled, solaced by her mom's protective nature even though she was supposed to be all grown up and able to take care of herself. "I know, Mom. There's no way I'll be letting her in to hurt me again. You don't need to worry about that." Louie was fast becoming aware her feelings for Mia weren't completely dealt with, but she felt sure she could make that promise to her mom.

Her mom grumbled again, clearly not fully convinced. "Well, don't let her anywhere near your new girl."

"I arrived too late to stop that. They're already distant friends through a mutual friend." *And Mia told her I was a violent drunk.* The thought kicked at her soul, but her spirit lifted at the recollection of how calm Heather had been when she'd confronted Louie with that gem. Most people would simply have steered clear and not even given her an opportunity to tell her side of the story. She wondered if Mia knew what she was doing when she opened her mouth. Heather had confirmed Mia would be at the Bluebird after their conversation at the café earlier today. She closed her eyes and drifted to the time they'd shared, before thudding back to reality with the knowledge she had to face Mia and find a way to move forward.

"Keep me posted, Noodle. If I have to come down there and sort that girl out myself, I will."

Louie laughed. When she'd told her mom Mia had left and cleaned her out, she was prepared to do things she'd have to serve time for. "You said that before, and I almost wish I'd taken you up on your offer."

"Just say the word, and I'll have her buried in the farm faster than green grass through a goose."

"How is the farm?" Since Louie had left, her grandmother had died, and it wasn't a moment too soon for Louie's mom. She'd always been an oppressive, judgmental woman, and both she and her mom had suffered for it. Her grandpa deteriorated and stopped working, leaving all the hard graft to her mom. It was another reason Louie was determined to make enough of a success here to finally get her mom away from the ugly memories.

"Same old. It's taking a while to get the last stock off our hands. I'm tempted to let them roam the farm and keep the grass under control."

Her mom's response was typically casual, but Louie could hear the tired undertones coming through clear enough. She sounded weary of the life she'd been forced to be a part of just because Louie's dad had gone AWOL as soon as Louie's heart began to beat. "You will be able to pack up and join me when I can get you a place, won't you?" Louie couldn't bear the thought of her mom having to stay there a moment longer than was absolutely necessary. A familiar metaphorical hand took hold of her throat and squeezed a little harder than it ever had before. She *had* to get her mom out of there. Louie closed her eyes and pictured herself jamming a finger beneath the thick, glutinous grip of guilt. She pulled it away and swished it into the trash can through a basketball hoop.

"I want you to concentrate on getting yourself straight before you even begin to think about me."

Louie didn't like the sound of her mom's evasive answer. "You still believe I can do this, don't you?"

"I haven't a doubt in the world, Noodle. But I need you to do this for yourself, not me. I've put up with my lot this long; a few more years won't make a lick of difference."

"Mom, give me a straight answer. Will you join me when the time comes?" Louie wondered if her mom's misplaced sense of loyalty to a father who never showed any emotion other than disappointment would pull her to stay until he died. "We can find a retirement home for grandpa. You don't owe him anything more than that." Putting a roof over their heads was about all he'd ever done for them.

Her mom sighed deeply. "I'll be there, I promise. For now, focus on writing the best songs you can for Savana Hayes. It's so exciting that you're working with one of the greats."

Louie swallowed the other questions and doubts she had for now and allowed the sledgehammer-subtle subject change. "I can't believe I've hit so lucky, Mom. She had the pick of every writer in Nashville and she went for me, an untested novice."

"She obviously knows talent when she sees it. Those songs you wrote for Gabe are fabulous. They made me want to take him home and mother him for the rest of his life."

"Ha. Wait till you meet him, Mom. You'll love him." She stopped herself from saying he was like the brother she'd never had. Her mom had suffered a miscarriage only a year before she had Louie, one week after she'd discovered she was having a boy. Louie often wondered if her father had left because he couldn't face losing another child. She was probably cutting him way too much slack, but in the darkest moments when she thought about him and why he'd abandoned them, she found a little comfort in that excuse.

"I'm sure. He sounds adorable. Hey, is Savana still seeing Chip Jackson? I've always wondered why they don't get married."

Louie picked at a fleck of peeling paint on her chair. "I have no idea, and there's no way I'm asking. If she tells me anything without prompting, I'll let you know."

"You're no fun."

Louie smiled at the sound of laughter in her mom's voice. It'd been too long since they'd seen each other, and she longed for the kind of hug only her mom gave. "And you're a gossip."

Gabe appeared at the patio door with a massive smile and his guitar in hand. Louie nodded and held up a finger to indicate he should wait.

"Mom, I've got to go. I'm going to record Gabe singing a cover for his Facebook page. I'll let you know when it's up, and you can take a look, okay?"

"Sure, Noodle. Have fun, and don't forget to keep sending me plenty of photos."

"Will do, Mom. I love you."

"I love you, Noodle."

Louie clicked off, feeling slightly awkward about Gabe being present to witness the loving exchange with her mom. He didn't seem to react though, so she stood and gestured inside the house. "Let's find the perfect place to make your first video."

Gabe grinned. "I've got the perfect song. 'There Goes My Everything.' What do you think?"

"The seventies song that Jack Greene and Elvis Presley covered?"

"Yeah, but with my take on it. Do you think it'll work?"

Louie clapped Gabe on the shoulder and hurt her hand a little in the process. His physique was enviable and made her wonder what kind of body Heather appreciated most. "You're right. It's perfect. You're tipping your hat to the greats. I love it." As Louie followed Gabe back into the house to find the best uncluttered space, she found herself thinking about what Heather might be doing right now. She checked her phone to discover a text from Heather had come in while she was on the phone to her mom; *I wanted 2 kiss U 2. I'm sorry I'm such an ass. I promise I'll b worth it.* She tried to temper the soaring feeling in her heart, but thumbed a quick response. *I was just thinking about u x I know things are complicated. Sometimes the right people come into your life when u think it's the wrong time. I know u'll be worth waiting for.* It didn't deliver and Louie's disappointment tugged at her initial optimism, but it didn't quell it completely. There was a ray of hope, and that's all Louie needed.

CHAPTER TWENTY-THREE

Heather paced the office space nervously. Savana had specifically requested a top floor corner writing room for her and Louie to work, and that had resulted in the head of business affairs being "asked" to move to a different office. When he stomped in at nine a.m. to find everything had been moved, he'd termed the new space a "closet" and was further disgruntled when Heather explained that he'd have to put up with it for a month, possibly more. Closet was an inaccurate comparison since his new office was nearly two hundred square feet. It did lack the enviable floor-to-ceiling windows, but Heather had little sympathy for him otherwise. Her own office was big enough to fit her desk and two chairs for visitors, and if she were vulgar enough to try, she could probably spit and hit the wall opposite her desk.

In order to meet the requirements of the detailed list Joe had emailed her at one a.m., she'd been in the building since six and was on her third coffee by ten. She surveyed her hurried hard work and sipped on the milky drink, wishing she liked it stronger because she could use a more intense caffeine hit. She'd had to move practically all of the furniture herself, and her energy was running low since she'd only managed around three hours of sleep.

The sandman's call had been muted by Heather thinking about making love with Louie. She'd given in to the temptation around two a.m., put fresh batteries in one of her trusty vibrators, and settled under the comforter to imagine Louie making love to her. She'd been soft and gentle, taking her time to discover *everything* that turned Heather on. When Heather's silicone bullet finally gave her release, imaginary Louie had already exhausted her with five consecutive orgasms.

Her cell buzzed and drew her back into reality.

"Heather, I feel terrible. I think I ate some bad shrimp last night, and I'm paying for it. I've been up sick since three a.m., and I just can't face coming in today."

Heather fell back into one of the overstuffed suede sofas that had been top of Joe's list, closed her eyes, and forced out a carefree tone. "That's no problem, Savana. Do you need anything sent over?"

"Joe's taking care of everything on this end, thanks. I hope you haven't worked too hard on his list for the writing studio?"

Heather looked around the office. "Don't worry. It was no trouble."

"I've jerked a knot in his tail for emailing you so late. You're not his personal assistant, and I'm sorry he did that. He swears he won't do it, or anything like it, again."

Heather smiled, grateful that the list wasn't at her behest and for the promise of it not happening again. "I sure would appreciate that. Would you like me to let Louie know she shouldn't come in?" Heather couldn't suppress her disappointment that she wouldn't be seeing her today but tried to keep it from tingeing her voice.

"I'd still like her to come in. Joe's going to email you some song ideas I've had, and she can start working on them. We talked yesterday about tone and tempo. I can't see why I won't be in tomorrow. Joe's already stocked the place with saltine crackers, bananas, and electrolyte drinks. I'll be as good as new in the morning if I rest up all day."

Heather perked up at Savana's instruction. "Sounds like he's good at looking after you."

"He's had so much practice over the years, he should be. Anyway, have a great day, and I'll see you tomorrow."

"Will do. Feel better soon." Heather ended the call, jumped up, and danced a jig around the room, ending at the windows with a double fist pump.

"Celebrating something?"

Oh, crap. Heather turned to the door to see an amused looking Louie leaning against the doorjamb, looking sexy as all hell in a tight gray T-shirt and loose jeans hitched on her hips. A rainbow-striped TomboyX waistband showed above them. Her mouth felt as dry as the heart of a haystack when she realized she was staring and hadn't responded to Louie's question. "Nice T-shirt," she said, floundering for an explanation as to why she was dancing around like the women in pink hats on Louie's shirt.

"Thanks." She pulled it away from her chest and looked down at it. "It's to commemorate the first anniversary of the global Women's March movement."

"That's cool." *And I am not.* "You voted Hilary, then?"

Louie raised an eyebrow, and the corner of her mouth turned up in a half smile. "Didn't you?"

Heather moved away from the window and sat on the arm of the couch, trying to feign a flirtatious confidence she didn't feel. "What do you think?"

Louie pushed off the door and closed it behind her. Three hundred square feet seemed to shrink to the mere few yards of plush carpet between them, and Heather couldn't be sure whether she was glad Louie had shut them in or whether it made her want to bolt faster than a sneeze through a screen door.

"You didn't answer my question."

Louie took a few steps toward her, reducing the space between them and apparently Heather's ability to speak. Unable to think of a valid excuse and with her lack of words becoming far right of embarrassing, Heather simply laughed. "I'm not about to give you answers to everything you ask, Louie Francis."

Louie shrugged, placed her guitar case on the large wooden table, and flopped down into the sofa opposite Heather. "Why not? Do you have secrets to hide?"

Heather bit her lip to stop the conversation disintegrating into total flirtation. "Savana can't make it today, but she wants you to get started anyway." She ignored Louie's head shake at her patent avoidance tactic and walked to the display cabinet that had held golf trophies a few hours ago. She picked up her iPad and tapped in the security code. "Joe's sending me some song ideas Savana's come up with, and she wants you to start working on them yourself." Heather rested her butt on the counter on the cabinet where the previous occupant's liquor stash had been replaced by a tray of small bottles of mineral water. She flicked through to her emails and kept snatching sneaky glances of Louie over her screen. If her current reaction to Louie's presence was an indicator of her ability to resist succumbing to Louie's considerable charms, Heather was screwed. Louie probably wasn't even trying to be so delightful since her response to Emma's text indicated she was happy to stick to Heather's schedule. Shame Heather didn't know what that schedule was.

Louie unclipped her case, pulled out her guitar, and began to fine-tune it. "Will you be staying with me?"

God, I'd love to. Heather wanted to abandon the past five years of celibacy with a flick of the privacy glass from transparent to opaque and let Louie make music with her body instead of a guitar. "I'd be of no help. Songwriting isn't one of my talents."

"Behind every songwriter is a stunning source of inspiration. You could be my muse."

I'd like to be more than your muse. Heather motioned to Louie's Gibson. "That's a beautiful guitar. Is it the one your mom bought for you?" Louie smiled in a way that said, "That's the way this is going to go, is it?" for every tactless change of subject Heather would have to instigate.

"It is." Louie held it up. "Do you want to take a closer look?"

Heather sighed. Why did every sentence have to mean something else? There was no way she was moving any closer to Louie. One whiff of her hot and spicy scent, and Heather was certain she'd be jumping on Louie faster than white on rice. "I don't trust myself—it looks expensive. I'll admire it from afar. What's it made of?" Heather knew little of guitars or their construction. Her knowledge ended at whether or not they were in tune, but she hoped it might be a safer conversation.

Louie looked amused but answered anyway. "The body is maple, the neck's made from mahogany, and the fretboard is rosewood."

Heather pressed on, repeatedly flicking at the refresh button and willing Joe's email to arrive so she could leave Louie to her writing and get back to trying to be a professional. "It's got an old-fashioned look to it. What color is it?"

"I like the traditional styling, and the official color name is 'antique burst.' Do you play?" Louie asked.

Heather shook her head and tried not to focus on the slender strength of Louie's fingers as she turned the tuning knobs at the head of the guitar. "I'd like to, but I never seem to have the time to learn. I don't really get time to do anything much other than work."

"Maybe you'd let me teach you?"

Heather nearly laughed out loud. No matter the topic, it seemed impossible for it not to degenerate into double meaning. "I'd like that." It seemed like an innocent enough reason to spend more time with Louie while they were working together. She looked down at her iPad again and was relieved to see the promised email from Joe. "Here it is," she said with far too much enthusiasm and hoped Louie wouldn't misinterpret it. She turned away rather than try to read Louie's expression and switched on the portable printer she'd situated on the cabinet shelf, as per Joe's requirement. She printed the contents of Joe's email twice, a copy for each of them, and looked back in time to see Louie jerk her head upward, clearly guilty of checking out Heather's ass while her back was turned. They exchanged a knowing look, and Heather was glad no one else was around to witness Louie's visual grope. She smoothed nonexistent lines from her skirt and ventured toward Louie. She handed Louie the papers, careful to ensure there was no accidental-on-purpose touching of fingers or romantic comedy electric sparks.

"Thanks," Louie said and began to flick through them.

Heather sighed, aware she should leave and yet unable to pull herself away now that she was within Louie's magnetic range. She was about to excuse herself when her cell rang, and she saw Savana's ID come up. "Hi, Savana. How're you doing?"

"A little better. Did you get Joe's email?"

Heather smiled at Savana's expectation that her whole working day revolved around her requirements. "I did. Louie is just reading through it now."

"She's there already? That's a good sign. Would you put her on for me?"

"Of course." Heather handed her phone to Louie and sat on the edge of the antique chaise longue she'd had to temporarily steal from Donny's office because Savana had commented on it. Louie looked fully focused on the paperwork she was laying out on top of her guitar case, and Heather took advantage of the moment to simply stare at her with unabashed longing and let the phone conversation fade into the distance. She couldn't attribute her behavior to the fact that she hadn't been with a woman for so long or to the undeniable truth that she found Louie sexually attractive in a visceral, instinctual way that she'd never experienced before. Right now, she didn't care to analyze it much. The time would come when the first flurry of initial fascination would fade and other considerations would have to come into play: did they have anything in common? Were they compatible beyond the bedroom? Did her heart ache to be with her again after they'd parted?

Louie scribbled on the pages with a fountain pen, something Heather liked because it seemed so much more romantic and creative than a boring ballpoint. She pulled out a travel-sized leather journal from her guitar case and made more notes, and Heather took the time to watch the delicate formation of words from Louie's ink. Her hands looked strong and capable, not surprising since the guitar was such a dexterously demanding mistress. She expected that the fingertips of Louie's left hand would be hardened from the constant pressing of steel strings against the fretboard and wondered how her fingers would feel caressing Heather's skin. What Heather could see of the rest of Louie looked damn fine. She wasn't skinny, as Emma had said, but she wasn't particularly muscular either. Heather wished Louie was wearing a V-neck as she had when they'd first met so she could spend some time appraising her skin and the contours of her chest. But she had to satisfy herself with imagination instead, and she was desperate to explore every curve and angle of Louie's body to commit them to memory. She was definitely gathering enough sensory info to fuel tonight's engagement with her silicone companion. She figured she might as well buy some batteries in bulk as her vibrating ally might be the only thing between her and sexual insanity.

"Heather?"

Louie's voice brought her around from her dreamy musings, and she focused on Louie holding out her phone. She accepted it, expecting to continue with Savana, but she'd already gone. "All set?" Heather rose from her chair reluctantly.

"Savana wants you to keep me company." She smiled mischievously and wiggled her eyebrows.

"Really?" Heather failed to contain her surprise. "Why? I'm of no help, surely?"

Louie shrugged and tilted her head slightly. "You should be more confident. Savana values your opinion. She's sure that you know what sound she's looking for, and she said it's the next best thing to her being here."

Heather couldn't resist a self-congratulatory smile, again reminded that Savana had asked for her personally and that it was a condition of her signing with Rocky Top. She still wasn't quite sure *why* Savana placed such trust in her, but it sure felt good to be believed in. But Savana's faith meant a full day in Louie's company with no buffer. How was she supposed to control herself against such temptation? "Tim and Vetti."

"Sorry?" Louie asked, clearly not understanding.

"Tim and Vetti. I'm going to get them. Six ears are better than two. I'll be back in a moment."

Louie grinned, and Heather's gaze fell to Louie's lips.

"You know, I can just about control myself around you. There's no need to fetch yourself a couple of chaperones," Louie said, as she leaned back in the sofa and put her foot on the table.

Heather glanced at Louie's crotch and nodded. "I know." She opened the door and escaped into the corridor. *I'm not sure I can say the same.*

CHAPTER TWENTY-FOUR

Louie's first day writing for Savana had disappeared far faster than she had wanted it to. Savana's absence had created a more relaxed atmosphere, and she'd enjoyed getting to know Tim and Vetti. Spending more time with Heather had been a bonus too. She'd suggested they round the day off with coffee at a place called Anti Bean just around the corner from Rocky Top. Thankfully, Tim had to rush home for a hot date with Emma, and Vetti had to get home to her cat, leaving Louie and Heather on their own.

Louie shifted in her seat, unable to decide whether to tuck a leg under her ass or stretch her legs out under the table. She enjoyed taking up more space than she needed, usually something reserved for men. She hated that women were almost taught to disappear and take up as little space as possible. Heather returned from the restroom looking like she'd refreshed her makeup. It might not have been for Louie's benefit, but she wanted it to be. She resisted the urge to comment on how beautiful Heather looked, conscious they were here under the guise of business colleagues winding down after a big day. She didn't want the day to end abruptly or to push her luck. If Heather needed time to figure out how this was going to work, Louie would have to relax and wait.

"I've ordered your hot milk," Louie said.

Heather laughed. "And your sludge?"

Louie nodded. "Are you happy with how today went?" She wanted Heather's approval on the progress she'd made with Savana's ideas.

"Absolutely. I think Savana will be thrilled."

Heather looked beyond Louie and around the vast space. Louie had chosen a spot away from the stairs and in the far corner of the first floor. It wasn't particularly busy, but Louie felt Heather's discomfort. She couldn't imagine how exhausting it was to be so acutely aware of the need to hide. Again, she withheld a comment.

"I really enjoyed watching you work," Heather said quietly.

Louie ran her hand through her hair and couldn't hold Heather's gaze. Her intensity bore into Louie's soul. "Really? Why?"

"Your hands. Your eyes. Everything about you was just totally absorbed in the art of creation. It was a joy to witness."

Louie saw the waitress come up the stairs and waited until she'd placed their drinks on the table and gone before she responded. "That's the way it's always worked for me. Everything else softens and goes out of focus." She took a sip of her coffee and sighed. "This is really good coffee." She wanted to say that Heather remained sharp in her vision while she was writing but opted for a funny comment instead. "Shame you won't taste it."

"I can't help liking it the way I do…I can't help liking you the way I do," Heather said and averted her eyes.

"That's a good thing, isn't it?" Louie pushed her phone around the table, anything to stop herself from reaching for Heather's hands. "I liked your text last night."

Heather gave a short laugh. "That wasn't me. It was Emma. I don't do text speak. It offends the grammar policewoman in me."

Louie sat back in her chair. The revelation was a sharp gut punch.

"But I would've said the same thing if I'd had the courage," Heather said.

Louie perked up and leaned forward again. "What are we doing?"

Heather pulled her cup closer and inspected the contents as if it were the most interesting thing on earth. "Following our hearts?"

Louie swallowed hard. She wanted this. But she couldn't pull Heather close to her, couldn't move to kiss her. This was more than being discreet. This was restriction on her freedom to express her feelings. "What about being professional?" Louie asked.

"I'm not saying we should start dating yet. But there's nothing to keep us from getting to know each other better, is there? Maybe we'll find out we don't have much in common and shouldn't bother going any further."

Heather laughed, but her eyes were serious and searching. Her vulnerability radiated from her, and Louie's desire to hold her deepened.

"That seems unlikely." Louie picked up her coffee but didn't drink. "I want to see where this might go, Heather, I really do." And she hoped she could handle being in the closet. Heather had all but promised it wouldn't be forever. Why was Louie thinking about forever already anyway? "Okay, quick-fire round: tell me about your family." It seemed like a good place to start.

Heather rolled her eyes. "God, really? I'm a disappointment to my mother. My father's spineless. My younger brother is the family golden child. That's me done. You?"

"That's not nearly enough information. How could your mother not be proud of what you've achieved here?"

Heather shook her head. "You said quick-fire."

"I didn't mean *that* quick."

"Now you're changing the rules?" Heather asked.

"They're my rules. I get to change them as much as I want." Louie winked and took a mouthful of coffee.

"That's the way this is gonna go, is it? Fine. No, Mommy dearest is not proud of me. I came to Nashville to be a singer and I failed. She wanted me to be a teacher like her and Dad and always thought music was a waste of time. I put off speaking to her because she asks when I'm giving all of this up and coming home every single time."

Heather leaned back in her seat and ran her hand through her hair. Her eyes were full of tears, and Louie's heart ached for pressing her for more detail. But it made her even more grateful for her own mom. She wanted to hold Heather tight and tell her that her mom was an ass for not loving everything about her daughter. But there was no way Heather would let her. "I'm sorry. I shouldn't have pushed."

Heather took a Kleenex from her purse and dabbed at the corner of her eyes. "I think you like to see me cry. This is the second time. Distract me and tell me about your family."

Telling Heather about her mom seemed particularly cruel. "My dad left my mom as soon as she became pregnant. My grandparents were assholes and never let Mom forget she failed to keep her man. I'm an only child, and my mom miscarried what would've been my big brother."

"Now you've made it a pity competition."

Heather smiled genuinely, and it lifted Louie's spirit. Could it be possible that she was even more beautiful when she smiled? "You've already won my heart. I can't have you winning everything."

"Your heart? You fall in love that easy?" Heather asked.

Louie wagged her finger. "I didn't say I was in love with you. That would be crazy. You're in my heart, that's all. Like Gabe." Louie should have been able to rattle off a list of friends, but there was no one else. The realization sank heavily in the pit of her stomach, but she pushed it away. "You were the one that said we were following our hearts."

"Whoa there, Miss Blamey Pants. I was teasing. But what was it Shakespeare said about protesting too much?"

"I have no idea," Louie lied. "English was never my favorite subject. I used to skip it and sneak into the music rooms for extra guitar practice. Next question: who was your first TV crush?" Louie watched as Heather looked up to the sky as if searching for the answer. Heather may have been teasing about falling in love, but the more time Louie spent with her, the more she could easily see it happening.

❖

Louie swept open the front door. Gabe sat on the sofa with his guitar playing a song she didn't recognize. "I need a cold shower." She pushed the door closed with her foot, placed her guitar on the floor, and dropped her keys on the table.

"Heather King?" Gabe grinned and nodded, somehow managing to look understanding and jealous at the same time.

"Heather King." Louie wandered past him toward her room. Gabe spun around on his seat and hung over the back of the sofa. "Wait, what? That's all I get? I want details."

"And I told you, I need a cold shower. You'll get details when I'm done." She pulled her bedroom door closed, stripped off her clothes, and padded into the bathroom. The marble tile cooled her feet but did nothing to cool her ardor. She turned on the shower, and without waiting for it to warm fully, she stepped into the bath and pulled the curtain across. She bent her head directly underneath the showerhead and enjoyed the powerfully prodding needles massaging her scalp. Louie closed her eyes and pictured Heather in her graphite-gray power suit. She loved a woman with the quintessential Marilyn Monroe hourglass figure. And the heels Heather wore practically made love to the carpet as they walked across it. They were so sexy and made Louie look at the fetish of having a woman in stilettos walk across your chest in an entirely fresh light.

She rolled her neck, grabbed her shower gel, and foamed up. Heather had relaxed considerably after their last meeting, and their intimate discussion over coffee had Louie tumbling into dangerous, deepening feelings kind of territory. She respected Heather's professionalism and insistence on not doing anything about their attraction until they stopped working together. At least Heather seemed relatively comfortable about them getting to know each other more in the meantime.

Louie recalled her thought process in selecting a seat at Anti Bean. She'd never considered the proximity of other people before, but Heather's need for discretion had already rubbed off on Louie. She wasn't at ease with it yet. She wasn't sure she ever would be. She had as much right to be proud of who she was as the next person. The next straight person. Louie wondered what her mom would make of Heather's need to be in the closet for the sake of her career. She'd be furious, Louie was certain. But she didn't get it. She didn't understand the things you have to think about when you're gay, the places you can't visit in the world because your sexuality is illegal, the places in the states where kissing your girlfriend could get you hospitalized. Her mom only saw the person, not the sexuality. And she'd raised Louie to stick her middle finger up at anyone who thought otherwise.

Being around Heather, wanting to be with Heather, forced Louie into considering another perspective. Louie knew she'd been lucky, having a mom who accepted and encouraged all of her. Heather hadn't had the same experience. Her family saw her as a disappointment. There was little wonder that she seemed to feel guilty about being a lesbian.

Louie switched her thoughts back to the album. A month had never stretched so far into the distance as the one she now faced, but she had no intention of rushing her process. The songs would take as long as they took, and from what she'd managed to glean from Heather and Tim, Savana might be a more difficult taskmistress than she'd initially presented as, and it could take longer than a month. Working with other creatives could often be challenging if visions didn't align, but Savana had seemed pretty certain Louie was the writer for her, so she'd just have to see how things played out.

And though the day had been pure sexual torture—the glimpses of Heather's cleavage and the number of times she'd had to watch Heather's ass swish from side to side like a mesmerizing metronome—just being with her had been wonderful. In between intense bouts of writing, they'd laughed and shared silly stories, and Louie felt like Heather was beginning to let her in. Tim was a nice guy, too, but it had surprised her when it turned out he was seeing Heather's friend Emma who she'd seen perform at the Bluebird on the same night she and Heather first met. She hadn't seemed like a settle-down kind of woman, but the way Tim talked about her, he clearly worshipped her like the goddess she looked like, and he saw the rest of his life with her. More than once, she'd seen Heather make a variety of faces that indicated Tim should slow down, and Louie heard her say as much over a couple of Krispy Kremes. Louie had avoided those doughy balls of heaven—she wanted to lose the little belly she'd become aware of over the past week. Tim had been disarmingly open, and although he wasn't classically good-looking, Louie could see why Emma liked him.

Louie began to sluice off, and as she directed the water between her legs, she rubbed her fingers across her clit and jumped slightly at how sensitive she was feeling. It was no shocker. She hadn't gotten off since leaving Chicago, and given the day of stimulation she'd had in the form of Heather, she kind of expected she might explode if she didn't give herself a release soon. She lay down in the tub so that the water still fell on her body, positioned her left leg over the side, and closed her eyes.

❖

"I thought you'd fallen asleep in there. That was the longest shower in history, buddy."

Louie shrugged. Some things were never for sharing with friends. "Told you I needed it. That and a beer. Do you want one?"

"Sure."

When she got back from the kitchen and handed him a cold one, he clinked her bottle with his.

"Are we celebrating or commiserating?" he asked and took a long swig.

"Both." Louie dropped onto the sofa beside him and ran her hand along the back of her head, glad she'd managed to get in a visit to Gabe's stylist yesterday. She'd gone a grade lower than usual around the back and sides, and it felt satisfyingly prickly to the touch. Heather had commented on how much she liked it, but Louie had held back the offer for her to feel it, fully aware she would've declined for fear of being seen.

Gabe slid his guitar onto the floor and leaned back into the corner of the couch. "How so?"

Louie held her beer to her forehead and enjoyed the chilled droplets against her skin, her blood still running hot with filthy thoughts of Heather. "It was a great writing day. I got one song almost finished and the bare bones of two others pulled together."

"And Savana's happy with them, yeah?"

"That's the other part of my day. Savana wasn't there so I spent the whole time with Heather and two other execs. Ten hours in a room with her, and I couldn't touch or kiss her. It was agony, Gabe, pure agony."

"Aw, poor Louie, having to spend all day with a beautiful woman. What's this? What's this?" Gabe ran his index finger back and forth over his thumb.

"I have no idea what you're doing. What the hell is that?"

"It's the smallest violin in the world...playing just for you," Gabe said.

Louie picked up a cushion and threw it at his face. "You can be such an idiot."

He grinned and puffed out his chest. "But you love me anyway."

Louie couldn't argue with that; he *was* adorable. "I'm just sticking around until you're a big country star with millions of dollars in the bank. Then you can keep me in Twinkies and Pop Tarts, and I'll never have to work again." She motioned toward his laptop on the table. "Speaking of which, how's your video doing?"

Gabe bounced off the sofa and grabbed his computer. "I had about a hundred views and a few shares when I looked this morning before I went to work. I haven't checked since 'cause on the way home, I got this tune in my head, and I've been working on it since I got back." He booted up and opened the web browser.

"That's a great number for less than twelve hours, little bro."

He looked up at her and smiled with a sincerity that tucked up her heart in a winter comforter. In the time she'd spent alone in Chicago, she hadn't realized how lonely she'd felt, even though she was barely ever alone. Now that she lived with Gabe, their easy friendship meant more to her each day.

"Whoa..." Gabe turned the screen toward Louie and pointed at it.

She scanned up to the top right-hand corner and read the stats. "Whoa is right. Sixty-five shares and nineteen hundred views. That's amazing." She grabbed his shoulder and shook him, unable to contain her excitement.

"Look at the likes, Louie, nearly two thousand...people think I'm okay."

Louie smiled at Gabe's open vulnerability. If only he understood how great his talent was. Maybe all his Facebook friends would prove it to him, and their plan really would work out the way they hoped. "They'd have to be deaf not to. You're a fantastic singer."

Gabe placed his laptop on the table and turned back to Louie. "Can we do another video tonight? I've been thinking I could do 'Perfect Storm.' It's one of my favorite love songs ever."

Louie glanced at wall clock. It was just after ten, and Savana didn't want to start until late the next morning. "Do you need to practice or do you think you'll be able to do it in one take?"

"Erm...Oh crap, I almost forgot. Mia came into work today and asked for you to call her on her cell tonight. Crap. Sorry, Lou."

"I have to do that now, Gabe. You practice the song, and we'll do it when I'm done." Louie picked up her phone, dialed Mia's number, and headed to her bedroom for some privacy. She closed the door behind her as Mia answered.

"Hey, Mia."

"Louie Francis. I heard you were in town. I was beginning to think you might never make it on your own."

The sound of Mia's husky tones caught Louie by surprise. She'd expected her to be cold and harsh, but instead she spoke like they were still lovers. "You want to know what I heard?"

"I do. Why don't you come and tell me all about it at Patterson's in Midtown?"

Louie rubbed at the back of her head—hard. Mia's attitude confused the hell out of her. She was acting as though everything was all right between the two of them. "Sure. I'll be there in thirty minutes."

"I'll be waiting," Mia replied and hung up.

"Shit." Louie hastily pulled on a fresh shirt and jeans and styled her hair. She pulled her hair this way and that to get it just right but stopped when she realized she was making too much effort. She went back out to Gabe. "I have to meet Mia." She ignored his raised eyebrow. "If you wait up, we can do the video when I get back, and you can pick up the pieces from whatever mess this is going to leave me in."

Gabe tilted his head to the side and looked less than impressed. "Be careful, Louie."

She picked up her keys and jacket. "I promise."

❖

Despite the bar being packed, Mia wasn't hard to spot. With her blond and bouncy curly hair and her equally bouncy breasts, Louie found her with one quick sweep of the room. Still as beautiful as Louie remembered, Mia was sitting at a booth with a woman who could easily be mistaken as her twin from this distance. Louie watched for a few moments, and the nature of their relationship became clear. They weren't all over each other, which was probably a good idea in Nashville, but it was obvious from the way Mia looked at her. It was the exact same look Louie had thought was reserved just for her. She'd been such a sucker and now Mia had her claws in another one. She took a deep breath and strode over toward them. Louie was only a few steps away when Mia looked her way. She jumped up and threw her arms around Louie with such force, Louie had to steady herself to stop them from tumbling to the floor. The familiar press of Mia's breasts against her chest was blatant, but Louie didn't respond.

"Louie," she exclaimed, sounding for all the world like she'd missed her. She held Louie at arm's length and looked her up and down. "You look fabulous. Love the new hair." She turned to her companion. "Diane, this is the amazing Louie I've been telling you about."

Louie smiled as politely as she could manage. "Hi, Diane. It's nice to meet you."

Diane raised an eyebrow and bit her bottom lip. "You said she was handsome, but you neglected to say *how* handsome." She held out her hand.

Louie shook it gently. "That's very kind of you to say." This wasn't going at all like she'd anticipated.

"Diane, would you get us some drinks?" Mia ushered Louie into the seat and slipped in beside her. Diane stood and looked like she was waiting further instruction. "The cocktails here are the best I've ever tasted. Are mojitos still your favorite poison?"

Louie nodded, slightly stunned Mia had remembered. "But I'm driving, so I'll just have a Coke, thanks."

Mia motioned Diane away. "Maybe you could take us home, then. What're you driving?"

Louie dismissed the flirtatious way Mia delivered her words, the invitation for a threesome blatant. She dropped her keys on the table. "Ford Ranger."

"Ah, nice. There's something about a truck." Mia slid a little closer, and her thigh touched Louie's.

Louie inched away and looked over to the bar. It was three deep, and Diane didn't look like she was making much progress. She decided to get the unpleasantries out in the open while Diane wasn't present. "Have you spent all our money yet?"

Mia smiled and shook her head. "Ah, handsome, you're not still hung up on that, are you?" She put her hand on Louie's neck and stroked her hair.

Louie swallowed and rolled her neck, trying to move Mia's hand without doing it defensively. Mia's nerve really was something. "Does that surprise you?"

Mia sighed theatrically and placed her other hand on Louie's leg. "I'm sorry I did that, baby. I got stupid and blinded by broken promises." She traced small circles on Louie's thigh. "We could make it up to you tonight…if you want."

Louie tensed her legs and removed Mia's hand. "Aren't you forgetting you're with someone?" She glanced over at Diane, who hadn't made much of an inroad toward the front of the bar and wondered how long it would be before Mia discarded her like the wrapping on a pack of smokes.

"We have a very open relationship," Mia said and waved her hand toward Diane. "And I've already told her about how fabulous you are in bed. She wants to find out for herself."

Louie ignored the flattery. "Why did you tell Heather King I was a violent drunk?"

Mia's gaze didn't falter. "I said no such thing."

"You've told people I was aggressive when I got drunk." Louie clenched her jaw, sure that Heather had no reason to make it up. Mia continued to draw light patterns in Louie's hair until Louie took her wrist and pushed her away.

"I may have said you could be after a few drinks," Mia said, then pouted while rubbing her wrist as though Louie had done damage. "Like now."

"No. It was way more specific. Why would you do that?" Louie recognized Mia's old pattern of shifting blame when she knew she'd been caught out.

Mia shrugged. "I don't know what you want me to say. I don't remember saying anything like that, Louie."

Louie sighed. She was here to close this door and get on with her life. "Please don't say anything about me to anyone. I'm trying to start fresh, and I don't need that kind of reputation."

Mia shrugged. "Fine. Do you want me to act like I don't know you at all?"

Louie sank back against the booth. "There's no need for that. Just don't make any trouble for the sake of it. I'm not going to the police about you stealing almost everything I own—and I know about you trying to get my guitar—so I'd appreciate it if you didn't spread any rumors about me."

Diane returned to the table and disturbed the tense interaction. She settled in opposite Louie, pushed a large glass of soda toward her, and smiled. The dark shadowing of eyeliner beneath her light gray eyes made them sparkle. Louie was sure it wouldn't be long before Mia took that sparkle away.

"Here's to new friendships," Diane said, oblivious to the frosty atmosphere she'd returned to.

Diane and Mia clinked their shot glasses together and knocked them back, followed by two more each with no words and only suggestive glances between them. Diane picked up her mojito and pulled the straw into her mouth with her tongue, looking between Louie and Mia as if she wasn't sure who to devour first.

Louie felt the point of Diane's shoe travel up her calf. She leaned over the table, and her breasts swelled over the tightness of her shirt. "I hope a boi like you won't take advantage of two girls like us…"

She didn't say it like she meant it. It sounded more like a dare. Louie reached down and pushed Diane's foot away. "I'm flattered.

But I'm not interested." She and Heather might not be an item just yet, but there was no way she was getting into whatever the hell it was Diane and Mia were offering. Her phone vibrated in her pocket, and she hoped for some psychic link to Heather that had caused her to text Louie at that exact moment. "Thanks for the soda, but I've got to go." Louie motioned for Mia to slide back out of the booth and let her leave.

"Can't you stay? I'd like to catch up," Mia said.

Louie pushed her soda away and picked up her truck keys. "Sorry, no." She had no interest in anything Mia had to say. It would all be self-serving bull crap anyway. Diane looked perplexed, and Mia sighed heavily before slowly doing as Louie had asked.

"Don't forget me, Louie," Mia said, putting her hand on Louie's shoulder as she moved past her.

Louie paused, suddenly aware that she'd successfully negotiated her first encounter with Mia since she'd disappeared with all their money. The work she'd done on letting go had paid off, and her concern that Mia would wheedle her lying way back into Louie's heart had been unfounded. "I won't," she said and walked away, never tempted to glance back. She'd remember the lessons she'd learned from Mia, for sure, but the rest of it she'd push to the dark recesses of her mind where it belonged. Louie pulled out her phone to see the text message was from Heather: *Loved having coffee with you (even though you take it as black as the devil's soul :) Can't wait to see you tomorrow.*

Me 2. Sorry I made u cry again. Promise the next time I do that, it'll be for a way better reason. Louie returned her cell to her pocket and headed back to her truck, thinking about what it would be like to make Heather cry out with pleasure.

CHAPTER TWENTY-FIVE

Heather usually looked forward to Fridays. They meant sleeping in on Saturdays. She still spent the weekend evenings at bars, clubs, and gigs if required, but at least she got to slob around in her sweats the rest of the time. Today was different, and she was willing the time to go more slowly.

It'd been a full-on week with Louie and Savana working on the new album, and they'd been pulling fifteen-hour days. Savana had insisted that Heather be present as much as possible, and Donny had instructed her to delegate all her other responsibilities to other colleagues. That hadn't gone over well with her colleagues, and their level of jealousy remained high. She'd decided to be more Zen about it and let it go. There was nothing she could do about it, and it wasn't her fault that Savana had asked for her and not them. She didn't need them; she had all the help she needed from her team of Vetti and Tim.

And she got to spend more time with Louie. As the week wore on, everybody seemed to become increasingly relaxed, and seeing Louie in professional mode was even more of a turn-on. Savana banished Tim from the writing room because of his constant babbling about Emma, and Heather couldn't blame her. She wasn't aiming for an album of gushy country love songs. She wanted her sound to be harder and edgier, and Louie was delivering precisely that.

"Let's go over 'I Won't Be A Whisper' one more time. I'm still not sure about the key change on the bridge into the final section."

It was Heather's favorite song so far, and she was sure it was already perfect, but Savana wanted nothing less than perfection. Louie smiled graciously and winked at Heather, making her feel like a cheerleader getting attention from the school track captain. She wondered if Louie played sports at school...she would've liked to have worn Louie's letterman jacket.

Savana touched Heather's wrist, and the feather-like caress made her shiver involuntarily. "Is everything okay?" Heather asked.

"Would you record this version for me, please? I want to compare it to the one we did on Wednesday."

"Of course." Heather turned on the portable multitrack recorder and the attached microphones that were set up close to both Savana and Louie. "Check volume." Savana sang a few lines, and Louie played a couple of bars of the song. "The levels look good. Four, three, two, one." She pressed record and motioned with her finger for them to begin. Heather stepped back silently just as she felt her cell vibrate in her pocket. She pulled it out to see a text from Donny wanting a verbal progress report.

Savana stopped singing. "Heather?"

Heather paused the recording. "I'm really sorry. Donny wants to know how things are going. He wants me in his office right now."

Savana's expression softened, and she nodded, smiling. "Tell him he's an asshole."

Heather smiled and shook her head. "I'll let you tell him that in person." Heather offered the remote to her, and she took it, accidentally touching Heather's fingers as she drew it away. "I'll be back as quick as I can."

"We'll miss you," Savana replied, a hint of mischief in her eyes.

Heather closed the door behind her and headed to Donny's office. Savana had become more playful over the past few days, and Heather couldn't figure out whether she was enjoying it or not. On the one hand, it was beginning to feel like she and Savana were becoming friends, but on the other hand, it seemed less than professional, something Heather was determined to be, no matter the situation.

Heather stepped out from the elevator onto Donny's floor, and Mandie smiled at her as she drew closer. "Hello, stranger. How are you doing?"

Heather blew out a long breath. "Does that answer your question?"

Mandie chuckled and nodded. "It sure does. Hang in there." She motioned to Donny's closed door. "Go on in. He's been waiting for you."

"Thanks." Heather waved a good-bye and briefly pondered Mandie's direction to "hang in there." What had she heard? The only people who'd been in the writing room had been Savana, Louie, Tim, and briefly, Vetti. Savana seemed happy with what she was doing; there were radio and magazine interviews lined up, and she'd managed to get the Opry to agree to the album launch being held there on the proviso Savana would preview at least half of the new songs.

"About damn time, girl."

Donny's barked address knotted Heather's insides. His constant reference to her as a girl when she was a woman in her late twenties was irritating at best and sexist at worst. The more meetings she took with him, the faster she wanted out of Rocky Top for good. She closed the door behind her wordlessly and sat down. There was no point responding that she'd come as soon as she'd received his message. He wanted her to keep Savana happy so even if she *had* been held up, he shouldn't be grumbling at her. She tried to relax, knowing it'd be over soon enough.

Donny poured himself two fingers of an amber liquid. "Would you like one?"

He'd never offered before, and Heather almost felt like she couldn't refuse. But it was barely noon.

He chuckled, having obviously caught her attempt at a subtle glance at her watch. "It's five o'clock somewhere." He capped the cut glass decanter and ambled back to his desk. "Tell me how's it going."

"Really well. Savana and Louie are very much playing from the same songbook. Savana was sick on Tuesday, but they've got two songs almost complete and another two started. As you know, Savana wants me in the writing room, but I'm still managing to get things organized around that time." Donny nodded approvingly when she told him about the Opry and the interviews.

"That's good."

His short response surprised her, and there was a heavy feeling in the air that he wanted to talk about something but wasn't sure how to broach the subject. Her stomach tightened, and she leaned back in her chair, fighting to control the irrational fear. Donny was known for his bluntness. She hadn't known an issue yet that he didn't grab by the tail and slam on the floor in short order. Her mind ran to the worst scenario, and she fought the rising panic. Everything was going well. There was no reason for him to fire her. "Is everything okay, Donny?"

He swallowed the rest of his drink and refilled it with three fingers' worth. "Of course it is." He returned to his chair, and it creaked in protest as he pushed his considerable frame farther into it. "Is Savana acting okay?"

It was a weird question. "In what way?" They'd been working together for a week; how was Heather supposed to know what her "acting okay" looked like?

He tapped his ear. "What kind of sound is she coming out with?"

"I guess you'd say it's edgier than her earlier stuff, and there's certainly no 'stand by your man' kind of vibe."

Donny leaned forward in his chair, and Heather noticed his shirt straining to stay buttoned.

"You'd 'guess'? I don't pay you to guess, girlie. I pay you to know."

He took another swig of his bourbon and scratched at his balding head. He seemed more irritable than usual, and Heather was no closer to knowing why. She kept her voice even and calm. Ex-colleagues that had tried to shout back at Donny got them nowhere but on the sidewalk with their office crap in a cardboard box. "They haven't written that much yet, but there's a lot of focus on not being a quiet little woman anymore."

"Explain."

Heather tried to recall the lyrics to "I Won't Be a Whisper" to give him an example, but they evaded her, as if they didn't want Donny to hear them yet. "She's talking about being a powerful woman and not needing a man to be successful. I expect some of that is in reference to her recent breakup. There's also some anger toward her father and his favoring of her brothers. That's about as far as she's gotten." It seemed plenty to Heather, but Donny sounded more concerned with the content than the speed with which they were working. "Are you worried her sound isn't going to suit Rocky Top?"

He wrinkled his nose as if Heather had just wafted a plate of curdled milk under his nose.

"She's split up with Chip Jackson?"

"Uh, yeah. I thought Joe had told you."

He brought his fist down on his desk and snorted. "That creep doesn't tell me shit. He's strutting around with a bug up his ass, and he's avoiding talking to me unless Savana's around." He sipped on his drink and said nothing for a few moments. "I can count on you, can't I, Heather?"

The fact that he used her name told her his request was serious. "Of course you can." Until she'd gotten enough money and investment to start her own label.

"I gave you your first shot in this town, and I promoted you when everyone else advised against it."

She didn't know who was supposed to be the "everyone else" who'd told him not to hire her, and it had been Aaron who'd given her a job when she'd failed to get through the reception of the other top labels in town. "You did, and I'll always appreciate that."

He leaned farther over his desk. "Your loyalty is toward me, yes?"

It was another weird question, but something had gotten him riled in a way she'd never seen before, and his grasping behavior unnerved her. "What are you worried about, Donny? I thought Savana joining Rocky Top was nothing but good for us."

"Are you loyal to me or not?"

"Yes, I am. But I'm confused, Donny. What's concerning you?"

He relaxed back in his chair and dismissed her question with a wave of his hand. "Hopefully nothing. But I need to know I can count on you to come to me if you think anything's happening that could compromise the reputation of this label. Do you understand?"

Not at all. "Absolutely."

"Good." He motioned toward the door to indicate the meeting was over. "Daily reports by email and make an appointment with Mandie if it's something serious. She knows to get you in regardless of my schedule."

Heather rose and retrieved her iPad from Donny's desk. "No problem."

She exited the office as quickly as her heels would allow without fear of an inelegant fall, knowing full well that he'd be leering at her ass despite whatever bizarre concerns he was harboring. She'd been in there less than fifteen minutes and he'd managed to freak her out more than usual. Heather had no idea what he was worried about, and he'd given her no clues. He'd never questioned her loyalty before. Hardly anyone expected loyalty in this town anymore. It was a different world with each person looking after themselves. Everyone used everyone else until they no longer served their purpose, and some were lucky enough to always be useful. It all seemed so Machiavellian, but it also seemed to work just fine.

Donny had been stoked to sign Savana, but his questions hinted at a case of cold feet with her change in direction. And what did he mean by letting him know if anything might "compromise the reputation of the label"? Signing Savana was as good as printing money for Rocky Top, so why was Donny worried? And Savana was her artist now, so she had to balance her happiness and creative expression with the needs of the label. Why did she have the impression they no longer aligned?

CHAPTER TWENTY-SIX

Heather perched her finely shaped ass on the barstool and sipped at her margarita through a tiny straw. Beyond her, Louie could see a couple of hundred people on the ground floor of the Mai Tribe club. If any one of them had looked up, they wouldn't have seen them. Savana had secured them the VIP mezzanine area complete with one-way privacy glass.

"I wasn't expecting this invitation," Louie said, watching Heather's expression carefully. It'd been a great first week working with Savana, but she'd come to suspect that Savana wanted Heather around for a different reason than she'd been letting on. And Heather had seemed quite receptive to the attention.

"I wasn't sure you'd say yes." Heather smiled and placed her drink on the high bar.

"I thought I'd better play along. It would've looked strange if I'd turned Savana down when everyone else jumped at the offer." Louie motioned to Tim and Vetti, dancing on the small stage together. "Why did you think I'd say no?" Savana waved and beckoned them to join her, but Louie shook her head. If she got dance-close to Heather, close enough to smell her light perfume, Louie knew her hand would rest on Heather's hips and she'd draw her nearer still, putting just inches between their lips. It was too much temptation, though she wasn't sure that Heather's attentions weren't elsewhere now that Savana had clearly settled in to make her own play for Heather. Louie guessed it made sense that Heather might be more interested in someone who must've spent a lifetime passing as straight when she was still more or less closeted herself.

"I thought it might be hard for you, for us. A night out dancing is a whole lot different from a quiet coffee." Heather looked a little unsure. "I know it's hard for me."

Louie raised her eyebrows. Maybe she'd misread the situation from Heather's side. "You're right. It *is* hard." She fought the urge to reach out and caress Heather's cheek and picked at the label of her beer instead. "But I've got some other things on my mind."

Heather nodded as if she might have an inkling of what those other things could be. "We haven't had a chance to talk. How did it go with Mia?"

Louie smiled, cheered by the thought that Heather might be slightly bothered by Mia's presence in her life. "She was a lot friendlier than I thought she was going to be." She kept the offer Mia had made of a threesome with her girlfriend to herself.

"Is she going to keep her foul rumors to herself?"

"I hope so."

Heather looked as though she had more questions, but Savana touched her shoulder and she jumped. Vetti and Tim sat on stools beside Louie.

"Are you two okay?" Savana asked, looking only at Heather.

Louie continued picking at her beer label, trying to quell the rising ball of jealousy that saw her imagining dropping Savana with one strike.

"We're fine." Heather raised her glass. "Thanks for this. It's really nice of you to invite us out to celebrate a great first week working together."

Savana held her champagne glass to Heather's and then to everyone else's. "It's absolutely my pleasure. You've all been amazing. I finally feel like I'm getting somewhere with my new direction." She looked at Louie and smiled. "And you were the final piece of the puzzle."

Louie returned her smile and tried to make it genuine. Maybe she was imagining things. Savana was a beautiful, generous woman.

That didn't make her gay, and even if she was, it didn't mean she wanted Heather. Though she'd be crazy *not* to want her. "That's nice of you to say."

Savana turned back to Heather and grabbed her wrist. "Dance time for you."

Heather glanced at Louie, but her expression gave nothing away, and she seemed to let herself be led away willingly.

"Are you coming?" Vetti asked.

Louie shook her head. "You guys go. I'm no dancer."

"Ah, come on. Tim can't dance either, but it doesn't keep him from enjoying it."

Vetti tried Savana's trick and took Louie's wrist, but she held firm and pulled back, gently but firmly. "I'm good drinking my beer and watching."

Tim put his hands on Vetti's waist and tugged her back. "Leave her be."

Vetti shrugged and they headed back to the dance floor, leaving Louie room to breathe again. Despite the size of the room, claustrophobia and the desire to bolt always kicked in when people wouldn't take no as her definitive answer. She went back to her beer and tried to focus on the rest of the club rather than watch Heather. Savana's arms were draped over Heather's shoulders, and Heather looked less than comfortable. She thought about straight female friends she'd had in the past. A lot of them liked to dance that way with her, and maybe that was all Savana was doing now. Heather had said Savana knew her secret, and perhaps this was her way of showing Heather that her sexuality didn't matter to her. Could be that she even wanted a one-time walk on the wild side. Heather was gorgeous and easily in Savana's league. Maybe it was Louie that wasn't in Heather's league.

Louie closed her eyes and shut out the music. Gabe had played her a guitar hook when she'd called him to let him know she was heading straight out after work, and she couldn't stop thinking about it. She needed to sit down with her guitar and write down the lyrics and tune that had come to her before they disappeared.

A light touch on Louie's shoulder disturbed her flow. She opened her eyes to see Heather looking a little worried.

"Is this really not your scene?"

Louie checked behind Heather and saw Savana and the rest of Heather's team still on the dance floor. She nodded to the chair beside her, and Heather hopped up onto it. "It's not that. I'd love to dance, properly dance, with you, but it wouldn't do much for your being in the closet, and I've got a feeling Savana wouldn't like it either."

Heather frowned. "What are you talking about?"

Louie leaned closer and whispered, "I think Savana's got a thing for you."

She laughed. "Don't be silly. She's as straight as they come."

Louie smirked and shook her head. "The only thing straight about her is her hair. You've been wondering why she was so desperate to work with you; maybe this is your answer." The wounded look on Heather's face made Louie regret her words. *Way to charm her, asshole.* She reached over and touched Heather's forearm gently. "Hey, maybe she is straight, and she only wants you because you're so beautiful."

Heather's mouth barely turned up at the corner in the briefest of smiles, and she pulled away from Louie's touch. "I need another drink."

Sure that anything else she said would worsen the situation, Louie pointed toward the bar. "I'll get it."

Louie stood and took Heather's glass from the table. The DJ upped the pace of the music, and the throng on the floor below yelled out in appreciative delight.

Heather watched Louie walk away without a backward glance, and despondency knocked for her attention. The thought that Savana might have chosen her to work with simply because of her sexuality made her stomach clench, and the throwaway manner in which Louie said it bothered her even more. She wanted to dismiss Louie's observation that Savana was obviously a lesbian or bisexual, or whatever the hell it was Louie thought, but she couldn't help but think it made some sense. All the things she'd taken as simple and friendly gestures of affection now took on extra meaning. Heather had been slightly uncomfortable with Savana's closeness in the writing room, and even though she kept inching away, Savana would casually touch her or move away only to return, closer still.

"No. There's no way."

"There's no way what?" Savana asked from behind her.

Heather spun around on her barstool and smiled, slightly unnerved by Savana's stealthy approach. "Nothing. It doesn't matter."

Savana sat on the stool Louie had just vacated. "Louie's crushing hard on you. Is that why she just tore out of here? Did you tell her you weren't interested?"

"She's gone to get us more drinks." Heather wrinkled her brow. Why would Savana assume she wasn't interested? "I think she's got a certain appeal." She held back on her true desire to jump all over Louie but she wasn't sure why. What did it matter what Savana thought anyway?

"I wouldn't have plugged her as your type." She wet her finger before running it around the rim of her glass. It hummed a monotone tune in response.

Heather decided to play along. Louie's assertion had caught her unawares, and this seemed like a good opportunity to test Louie's theory out. "And what kind of woman do you think is my type?" She smiled to give the impression the conversation was lighter than it felt.

"A more traditional woman. Feminine. Long hair, lipstick, and heels."

Savana had just described herself, but running to stereotypes surprised Heather, particularly after she'd shown such sensitivity around pronouns and Louie's potential gender. To be fair, Savana's assessment of Heather's type was to the letter of her previous relationships. But that didn't mean she had a type, because she'd been instantly attracted to Louie. Heather pushed her skirt closer to her knees, suddenly feeling a little vulnerable. She cursed herself for being so egotistical and falling for Louie's misguided allegation. "I like all kinds of women." It sounded all wrong, like she'd had hundreds of bed partners.

Savana smirked and raised her eyebrows. "Are you telling me you're a player, Miss King?"

Heather laughed and shook her head. "I don't think two longish-term relationships qualifies me to take that moniker." She almost smacked herself upside the head. She'd blurted her response without thinking. Damn, she hated playing games. Why couldn't people just be straight with each other?

"Still, with your position and ambition, can you afford to have such an...obvious partner?" Savana sipped on her champagne and held Heather's gaze. "I suppose that's why I thought you might prefer feminine women. Women who can easily pass as straight."

Louie came into view beyond Savana's shoulder, holding two bottles of beer aloft. She seemed unfazed by Savana having taken her stool and dropped onto the one opposite both of them. She held out the bottle and Heather gratefully seized it to take a long drink. It wasn't like she could respond to Savana's words now that Louie had returned, but there was an unrest in the air she didn't want to address. She wondered if Louie could sense it. Was she right about Savana? Is that what she'd been doing her whole career: "passing"? It seemed ludicrous to suggest it but also strangely logical. Savana had been with Chip Jackson for the past decade or so and everyone had wondered why they had never gotten married. Were they both just covering for each other, passing as straight to make sure their careers didn't falter? They'd just broken up, and Savana was determined to take her career in a new direction, one that her agent, Joe, didn't seem to fully support. Heather had interpreted the song "I Won't Be a Whisper" as a rallying cry for stronger-voiced women in an industry where being a girl in a country song meant cut-off jeans, bikini tops, and looking good for the guys. But was it to be Savana's coming out song? And had Donny heard something? That would certainly explain why he'd called her into his office today, being totally vague about the interests of Rocky Top.

"I'm glad you're happy with how the new songs are turning out," Louie said, focusing her attention on Savana. "We're not writing the kind of songs you're famous for."

Savana tipped her glass Louie's way. "And is that a good thing?"

Louie laughed. "That's an impossible question to answer."

"Why is that?" Savana asked.

"Aw, come on, Savana," Heather said. "If she says that it's a good thing, she's essentially trashing your entire career so far. If she says it's not a good thing, she's declaring that the new songs aren't as good as your old stuff. It's a frying pan or fire kind of question." Heather sat back and took another quick drink, not wanting to look Savana in the eye after her little outburst. It wasn't as though Louie couldn't handle the question, but Heather had somehow felt compelled to jump to her rescue. When she put her bottle on the table, both Savana and Louie were looking at her with raised eyebrows and amused smiles.

"Want to take a shot at answering for yourself now, Louie?" Savana asked.

Louie bit her lip and sighed, but Heather saw a hint of a grin at the corner of her mouth. She reprimanded herself for interfering. Louie could take care of herself.

"I love your back catalogue. Your early songs were traditional fare that launched you as a superstar and sealed your place in people's hearts," Louie said. "The music you've produced over the past five years showed a move away from that and into something stronger, more woman-centric, and less 'stand by your man.' The songs we're writing now signify your confidence in your status as a country icon. You're baring your soul. You're keeping yourself relevant, and it's going to introduce you to a whole new audience of country fans ready for something more than God, trucks, and first kisses. You're like the Madonna of country music, only younger and without the multiple husband baggage."

Heather suppressed any facial reaction to the husband quip. If Louie was right about Savana's sexuality, it might be a little too on the nose. Savana didn't respond immediately, adding some suspense to the situation. Savana smiled the way Heather had seen on a thousand magazines and TV interviews.

"I like the way you see my music," Savana said. "It reinforces the gut instinct I had to take a chance on a new writer when Donny was desperate for me to work with someone more established." She stood and took another sip of her champagne. "I need to dance some more. Are you joining me?"

Her question seemed like it was open to both of them, but Savana looked at Heather. "I'm still out of breath from the last song. I'll join you in a little while," Heather said.

"Dancing isn't my forte. Your feet are safer if I stay here." Louie smiled and tipped her beer bottle toward Savana.

Savana raised her eyebrows and smiled. "Your loss."

Heather waited until she was a safe distance away before turning to Louie. She wanted to forget about Savana for now. She was more interested in how things had gone with Louie and Mia. Louie had been a little evasive about it, and Heather needed to know if there was some chance of reconciliation in the air. Mia didn't deserve someone as sweet as Louie, she was sure of that, but she didn't want to be caught in some lesbian lust and love triangle. Lust being the operative word for now. Louie made her buzz in places that for the past five years had only responded to battery operated stimulus. "So. Mia."

Louie laughed. "Subtle. What do you want to know?"

"Are you getting back together?"

Louie stopped midair as she raised her bottle to her lips. "That's very straightforward of you."

Heather shrugged. "I don't see the point in mooching around the subject. You and I are attracted to each other, but we're waiting until we've finished working together to do anything about it. If that's changed, I'd like to know now so we can have a professional relationship." She had no idea where her forthright attitude was coming from, but she maintained momentum. "I like you, Louie, but I won't wait around like a cute—but unwanted—puppy at the pound. Tell me straight, and we'll be good." Heather would be bummed, but at least they could be friends.

"Okay." Louie held up her hands and grinned. "Mia wanted to have sex with me…and her girlfriend. I'm not sure whether or not that meant she wanted to start things back up with me." Louie took another long drink of her beer.

Heather didn't know how to parse Louie's statement out. Had they had a threesome? Did she even want to know if they had? She floundered, a little out of her depth, and tried to change the subject slightly. "Emma said Mia perked up when she told her about your gig with Savana."

Louie dropped her beer onto the bar with such force it made Heather jump.

"What? When did Emma tell her that?"

Heather eased back in her stool. Louie was practically bristling with aggressive energy, and it unnerved her. Louie had been drinking. Was this the violent drunk coming out like Mia had warned? Louie's usually calm demeanor had fallen away like dead leaves in winter. "It was when Emma told her you wanted to get in touch about something. Why?" She reached out tentatively and touched Louie's forearm, glad when she didn't shrug away her gesture.

She ran her hand through her hair and rubbed hard at her scalp. "I should've known she was trying to play me. She just wanted to get close to Savana."

Heather went to hold Louie's hand but held back. "And did you let her play you?" She had to know.

"No. Turns out she no longer has any sort of hold on me." Louie clinked her bottle to Heather's. "And I got a text from you that reminded me I'd moved on."

The storm in Louie's eyes had passed. Considering what Mia had already done to Louie, her reaction to Mia's manipulation was completely natural. She hated that she'd allowed Mia's accusations to settle in her mind. "I've got no right—"

"Sure you do."

There was a promise in Louie's eyes Heather couldn't miss. "And will she stop telling lies about you?" Heather asked, feeling super protective.

"She denies saying anything at all—"

"I didn't make it up, Louie."

"Whoa," Louie said. "I know that. I could tell she was lying."

Heather let the tension in her shoulders go, relieved that Louie didn't think *she* was the one being deceitful. "I'm sorry."

"None of this is your fault. You've got nothing to apologize for," Louie said. "Everyone has a past they have to deal with sometime. I'm sorry you had to get involved in mine."

Louie's phone lit up with a message, and Heather glanced away, not wanting to invade her privacy.

"It's Gabe," Louie said, perhaps reading Heather's thoughts. "He's desperate to get another video out there."

"I watched 'There Goes My Everything.' It's really something." She hoped Donny had seen it too *and* how popular Gabe was. "Was that your idea or his?"

Louie pushed her phone around the table and looked shy. "That depends on whether you're impressed or outraged by the concept of launching a country artist via Facebook."

"I'm impressed." Heather winked.

"Then I'll admit it was me. If a pop star can do it on YouTube, I didn't see why Gabe couldn't do it on Facebook. Next step will be a Kickstarter campaign to record an EP." Louie's enthusiasm practically bounced from her body.

"I love that you're helping him find a different way to launch his career. You're so wonderful." And so sexy.

Louie looked at her, and Heather's stomach flipped. If they'd been in an animated romance film, there would have been sparks and fireworks all over the screen. Heather wanted to run her finger over Louie's lips, kiss her hard and passionate, let their desires take them away from this place.

But Heather didn't move closer, and neither did Louie. The silence stretched out before them like a road disappearing into a horizon unknown.

Louie coughed, drew back slightly, and focused on her phone. She looked up after reading Gabe's text. "I'm gonna go." She waved toward Savana and indicated she was leaving by pointing to the door. Savana nodded and waved back.

Heather stopped herself from touching Louie's hand. "Do you have to go?" she whispered.

Louie sighed and slowly shook her head. "If I don't go, I won't be able to stop myself from giving in and kissing you. Discretion be damned."

Louie's words made Heather swallow hard, and her groin pulse harder. God, she wanted that too. Hiding who she was had never been this difficult to manage before. "I'll miss you."

"I'll text you."

Louie seemed to hesitate as she stood to leave. Was she thinking about leaning in to kiss Heather good-bye? She smiled tightly before she picked up her jacket and headed to the stairs. Once again, Louie didn't look back, and a pang of sadness hit home. She wanted to be the center of Louie's attentions. She didn't want Louie to be able to leave so easily. Heather glanced across at the dance floor and Savana waved her over. Heather wished Louie hadn't mentioned her suspicions about Savana's sexuality or that her affections might be directed toward Heather.

If Louie was right and Savana *had* stayed in the closet all these years to protect her career, that was her prerogative. But Heather was just biding her time until she'd established herself. Then she'd be with whoever she damn well pleased, regardless of their ability to pass. Heather had spent far too much time in enforced reticence about her sexuality, and she had no intention of staying closeted a minute longer than was absolutely necessary. She hoped Louie would stick around in the meantime.

CHAPTER TWENTY-SEVEN

"Night, Gabe." Louie closed Gabe's bedroom door and left him to upload his new music video. She walked lightly through the living room and paused at the kitchen. The blue LED clock display on the microwave lit up a bottle of Jack Daniels, as if luring her to drown the abject loneliness that had seeped into her soul while she was videoing Gabe and thinking only about Heather. Her mom had said her father was a drinker, and there was no way she was following in his missteps or giving truth to Mia's lies. She dismissed it and opted for a bottle of water instead. She headed for her bedroom and closed the door behind her quietly.

Louie flopped onto her bed and tried to relax every muscle in her body one by one. Leaving Heather at the club had been agony. Louie had wanted to grab her by the waist and bring her home. She wasn't interested in delayed gratification. She wanted Heather and she wanted her now. Not after Savana's stupid album was finished. And not in private. If they were going to be together, Louie wanted to shout it from the top of the Nashville Parthenon. She didn't want to keep quiet. She didn't want to stay closeted for fear of ruining Heather's career. Screw Nashville if they were so backward that they couldn't accept same-sex couples.

But that wasn't how Heather wanted it. She'd been the one in the closet for the past five years. She was the one risking everything to have a relationship with Louie, even if it was going to be behind closed doors and "discreet." God, she was beginning to hate that word. But who was Louie to ask Heather to jeopardize her dreams? Louie was being selfish. Heather had said she'd come out eventually. Wasn't that promise enough?

Louie grabbed her phone and texted Heather. *I know I have 2 wait for u, but I need something to look forward 2. Come on a date with me when we've finished the album.* Louie watched the status changed to delivered. Moments later, flashing bubbles indicated Heather was responding.

Heather: *Are you that desperate for me?*

Louie: *Beyond words.*

Heather: *But you're a wordsmith. Use your words.*

Louie laughed gently. She liked the way Heather came over all dominant and demanding in texts. And she hated text speak. Louie thumbed out her message more carefully: *I need to be with you more than the night sky needs the stars to light its darkness.*

Heather: *That's what I'm talking about. Smooth, Louie, smooth x*

Louie: *Smooth enough to let me organize our date?*

Heather: *Yes. But it has to be somewhere private. You understand?*

Louie ran her hand through her hair and dropped her head onto her pillow. She wanted the whole world to see them together. *I understand. Trust me x*

Heather: *I want to do so much more than trust you x Got to go. See you tomorrow x*

Louie guessed Savana was still around. What if Louie was right and she made a play for Heather? How could she compete with her? Louie sat up and punched her pillows into submission until she was propped up comfortably. It was too late to call her mom, so there was only one thing to do when her head was racing like this—write about it or write about something to take her mind away from it. She retrieved her satchel and pulled out her current lyrics journal. She wanted to think about the possibility that she and Heather were destined *not* to be lovers. If it had to be that way, Louie at least wanted to establish a friendship.

"Jesus. Why am I such a sucker for a femme?" She laughed at her clichéd addiction and its contradiction to her dismissal of labels and boxes for herself. If she became a famous songwriter, would she want to be known as a lesbian songwriter or just a songwriter? In all honesty she didn't care what people called her, but didn't young lesbians need to know that they could be gay and successful? She'd always thought that her sexuality wasn't that important and that it was just a part of her, like the food or music she liked. But to people who struggled every day, who were threatened or hurt every moment of their existence because of their sexuality, it was so much more. It held such enormous power that was both positive and negative. What was freedom to some was jail to others. And with the current president rolling back LGBT rights all over the place, strong role models were more important than ever.

Maybe that was why she'd been so hard on Savana. She was such a beloved country star. Didn't she owe it to young lesbians everywhere to come out of the closet and celebrate her sexuality, rather than it being something she was ashamed of? Something she thought could be used against her to destroy her career. *That's what I want to write about.* Louie flipped open her book and began to scribble words and phrases. She didn't think for a second that Savana would have the guts to record it, but if she read it, perhaps it might give her the courage to consider coming out.

"You look terrible." Gabe put a mug of coffee in front of Louie.

"Gee, thanks," Louie said, taking the offering gratefully. She hadn't even tried to sleep until she'd gotten the basics down for her latest song and that wasn't until way past four. Even then, thoughts of Heather as her lover competed with those of her as a friend as she tried to figure out how she was supposed to cope with a closeted relationship. She looked up to see Gabe obviously expecting details. "What do you want to know?"

Gabe shook his head. "I want to know that you haven't changed your mind about Mia."

His protectiveness made her smile. She'd told him all about their relationship and the way Mia had left her in Chicago. He was most disgusted that Mia had tried to steal Louie's precious guitar. When she'd recounted the story of Mia offering a threesome, Gabe had impressed her with his retort of, "You better not have done it." Most men would've been badgering her for details.

"I'm not that much of a pushover. And anyway, I found out she was only trying to get close to me so she could further her career." Louie sipped at her coffee and nodded appreciatively. "You make great coffee." She didn't want to talk about Heather and the troubles she was having with balancing her need to be herself and her desire to be with Heather.

"Thanks, but what do you mean about Mia and her career?"

"Emma told her I was writing with Savana Hayes. Mia was just using me so she could get in with Savana." Louie sighed and ran her hand across the back of her head.

"I knew she had to be up to something like that." He formed a pistol with his hand and fake-fired it. "Bet you're glad that you blew her off."

"I am."

"Good. You deserve better than that, Louie. You deserve better than her."

Louie nodded, but she wasn't sure she agreed. It wasn't as if she was anything special. She hadn't done anything with her life so far, and she'd come from a pretty rough background. Who was to say what she deserved? And Heather seemed way above her level, but she also seemed interested enough to see where it might lead. Louie wasn't about to write any relationship potential off just because of a self-esteem issue. She'd let it play out and see where the chips would fall. "That's nice of you to say, buddy." The album with Savana was going well. Gabe was a great roommate, and if everything went well, she'd soon be able to move her mom down and finally get her away from her grandfather. She had no idea if Heather was "the one." How could she know that after only beginning to get to know her over the past week? What Louie did know was that she wanted to explore the future with Heather and find out.

"Enough of her. You've got that interview with Hawthorne today, haven't you?" Gabe asked.

"Yep. Then I'm back to writing with Savana." Heather had given Louie a list of contacts, and Hawthorne had been the only one interested in her until they all found out Louie was writing the next Savana Hayes album. Suddenly everyone wanted a meeting. But Louie had a thing about loyalty. Hawthorne had shown they had faith in Louie's work just from the songs she'd submitted. The others had read those same songs and just added her to their slush pile until news filtered through about Savana.

"I reckon they'll sign you up right there. They'd be stupid not to."

Louie loved Gabe's enthusiasm and was glad to see it back. He'd recovered pretty well from the Rocky Top knock back. She hoped she could pull this gig with Hawthorne off, but she wasn't counting on it. "I guess we'll see." Louie drank the rest of her coffee, wondering if her luck would hold.

CHAPTER TWENTY-EIGHT

Heather took the last bite of her bagel and put the plate in her sink. It wasn't often Emma was lost for words. "Do you think it's possible?" Heather asked again. "It can't be, can it? She's country's most loved female artist, and her life has been picked over to the nth degree for nearly two decades. Surely she couldn't have kept such a massive secret all that time?"

"I don't know, Feathers," said Emma. "It seems unlikely, but Rock Hudson did it for decades and no one suspected him, did they?"

She had a point. Heather rubbed her forehead as if it might stave off the complications of this situation. "Do you think Chip Jackson has just been a cover boyfriend all these years?"

Emma laughed. "That would make him gay or stupid, wouldn't it? What does it matter anyway? Why are you worried?"

"Because Louie thinks Savana has a thing for me. And I don't want anything getting in the way of what I want with Louie."

"Why would it? Has Louie said it would? Is she worried you'd choose Savana over her?"

"Jeez, Em, one question at a time, please." Heather cradled her phone between her shoulder and ear and tucked her iPad into her bag. It had been too late to call Emma by the time she'd gotten home last night, but she'd wanted to speak to her this morning before she faced both Louie and Savana again. Savana had decided she wanted to work the weekend just as they were parting ways at the club, and Heather was in no position to refuse. But she needed Emma's honest opinion, and she never held back with the truth, no matter how hurtful it might be. Heather treasured that. "I don't know if Louie's the jealous type, but she seems convinced Savana is about to make a move. And I think Louie believes I'd go for it if she did. How am I supposed to handle it if Savana does make a play?"

"How would you handle it if Donny came on to you at work?"

She took a bottle of water from the fridge and tossed it in her bag. "Ew, thanks for that disgusting thought."

"I know. But you'd knock him back, wouldn't you? The principle is the same with Savana…unless you're interested?"

Emma had cut straight through all the protective tissue and got to the heart of the problem. Until Emma posed the question, Heather hadn't actually thought to address whether or not she was interested. She'd only considered the impact of Louie's suspicions from a work perspective, but her answer was instant. "Of course not."

Emma's chuckle sounded disbelieving. "Are you asking me or telling me?"

"I'm telling you. And it wouldn't be very professional of me, would it?"

"Ignore that. If you saw her in a bar and she hit on you, what would you do?"

Heather closed her bag and took her phone in hand again. "I've already said I'm not interested in Savana. It's Louie I want." Heather picked up her bag and keys. "I have to get to work. I'll call you later and you can tell me all about how it's going with Tim."

"Hey, you're not mad at me, are you?"

She opened and closed the door behind her. "Of course not." She got in her car. She didn't want to be late even though Savana had said to be in the writing room by around noon. She knew her well enough to know that meant no later than 11:58 a.m.

"Then you can tell Savana from me that I don't appreciate her pulling Tim into work on a weekend."

"Yeah, I'll be sure to pass that on." Heather ended the call and fixed her phone to the magnet on the dash. She thought about calling Louie, but she'd see her in a couple of hours and it would probably make her look desperate. Heather had texted Louie last night, as per

Savana's instructions, and she'd received an immediate response despite the late hour.

Heather reversed from her driveway, but before she pulled into traffic, she tapped on her favorites and hit Louie's number. *Screw it.* She smiled at the photo she'd surreptitiously snapped while Louie was playing guitar on one of Savana's songs. Louie was gorgeous when she was posing and knew she was being looked at, but Heather had taken to watching her while she was caught up in the music. Natural and unguarded, with no pretense or swagger, Louie was even more attractive. And over the past week, she'd had plenty of opportunity to look at her without getting caught out. It had been bliss.

"Hey, stranger. I'm just heading out to Hawthorne. I'll be with you in a couple of hours."

"Good luck with that. I'm sure you'll be amazing." Heather felt sure Louie and Hawthorne would be a great fit.

"Thanks. Were you calling me to bring you a special weak-ass coffee from Anti Bean?"

Heather bit her lip and smiled. Little things like remembering how she liked her coffee always impressed her. "If you happen to be passing that way, I wouldn't say no. I don't expect Mandie will be in today, and she's the only one that knows how to make it exactly right."

"Oh, I don't know. I'd give it a go. I take instruction well."

The way Louie dropped her voice made her meaning clear, and Heather's body responded in kind as she imagined instructing Louie in the bedroom. "Somehow I don't think you ever need much direction."

"You'll be finding out soon."

Heather let out a disgruntled sigh. "Not soon enough."

Louie laughed gently. "*You're* the one making us wait."

"That doesn't mean I can't be impatient about it. I've waited five years for someone like you to come along. Three weeks shouldn't be so bad."

"Three weeks is the whole lifetime of a drone ant."

Heather shook her head as she slowed for lights. "You're not a drone ant. And that's a weird fact to know."

"I'm full of all sorts of weirdness. Not bad weirdness. All good weirdness."

Heather smiled. She liked when the smooth operator slipped and Louie showed herself as just a little nervous.

"So why did you call?" Louie asked after a few moments of silence had passed. "It can't have been to find out about the life cycle of a lazy male insect."

"I wanted to talk to you without everyone else there."

"About what?"

"Nothing in particular. I just like hearing your voice," said Heather.

"Careful. You'll get me thinking that you really like me, then when someone better comes along, I'll have a broken heart."

"Maybe there is no one better." Heather wondered if that might be too much too soon, but being around Louie made her feel so different, so free. What would it hurt to say it out loud?

Louie laughed. "There's *always* someone better."

Heather stiffened. "Are you always looking for the next best thing?" She had no unrealistic expectations of what they might be together, but she did need Louie to at least commit fully to seeing what might happen. If she was already moving on before they'd even begun, what was the point?

"No. I'm looking for true love. I just think you'll always be able to find someone better than me."

Heather heard no edge or humor in Louie's voice. Nor did it sound like she was throwing in a line for compliments. Her vulnerability hooked into Heather's heart and effortlessly caught more of her attention. "When I'm with someone, I'm not looking anywhere else, Louie."

"Do you want me to get a sandwich with your coffee or do you need a sugar hit doughnut?"

Heather pulled into her parking space and cut the engine. The change of subject clearly wasn't designed to be subtle, but she let it go. For now. Louie's issue wouldn't be addressed in a quick phone call, but Heather knew she would want to at some point. Louie should know how special she was. Their connection had grown with each day, and Heather couldn't wait to explore Louie further. Her mind *and* her body.

❖

"Mom!" Louie was barely seated in her truck before she'd dialed the number and got through.

"Louie!" her mom said, matching her tone.

"I got it. I really got it."

"What, baby?" her mom asked. "What's got you all riled up?"

"The publishing contract with Hawthorne! They want my words, Mom." Louie bounced up and down, unable to contain herself any more. When the team interviewing her offered her a contract, it was all Louie could do to stop herself from running around the table and giving each of them a hug.

"I am *so* proud of you, sweetheart. I knew you'd do it. All of it."

Louie's heart swelled at the pride in her mom's words, and she struggled to hold back the tears. Her mom never stopped encouraging her, when everyone else did the opposite. Her mom struggled to send money when Louie was broke and never once suggested she come home and stop chasing her dreams. She owed her everything. "It won't be long before I can buy you that house, Mom."

Her mom chuckled. "That's my girl, always aiming high."

"It's true. In the long run, the songwriter gets more than the artist. Combine this with Savana's album, and we'll finally be able to stop worrying about money." Louie was already planning to visit the local Jeep dealership. That Wrangler Rubicon Recon would soon be in the driveway of her very own house. The nagging doubt trying to pull her down was hanging on, but where it used to be connected to her consciousness by steel wire, it was now a mere cotton thread. Her life was finally changing. She was really living her dream.

"Slow down, baby girl. Make sure it's in the bank before you start spending it," her mom said.

Her mom's mind-reading skills never failed to impress Louie. "I promise." She checked her watch. "Damn, I have to get to Rocky Top."

"Savana's got you working the weekend?" her mom asked.

Louie started her truck and pulled out of the Hawthorne parking lot, cradling her phone between her neck and cheek. "She sure does. But it's all good. When we've finished the album, I've got a big date with an amazing woman."

"Heather hasn't given in on her professional boundaries yet, then? Good for her. It won't hurt you to wait for a good woman, for a change."

Louie let her mom's veiled stab at Mia go without response. She deserved it anyway. "I'll talk to you later, Mom. I want you to visit soon."

"Are you driving?"

"Yeah, that's why I've got to go!" Louie stopped at a red light and dropped her phone into her lap when she saw a cop on the corner. She looked down and pressed speaker. "Love you, Mom. Talk soon."

"Love you, Noodle. I'm super proud of you."

Louie blinked away the light burning sensation in her eyes. "Thanks, Mom."

Louie made short work of the distance between Hawthorne and Rocky Top. She made a quick stop at Anti Bean for Heather's coffee. She couldn't wait to share her news with her. If Louie's career took off the way it could, maybe Louie could help finance Heather's label and get her out of the closet sooner than either of them had planned.

Chapter Twenty-Nine

avana's kept you so busy over the past three weeks, I've
barely seen you."

Guilt tore at Louie's conscience like piranhas on a steer. She
had neglected Gabe, but she'd had little choice. Savana had insisted
on working eighteen-hour days seven days a week. Her regime had
been brutal but resulted in fourteen tracks, any of which Savana was
convinced could be the next number one on the Billboard country
charts. "Tell me how things are with you." She flopped onto the
couch and enjoyed the way it greeted her like an old friend, giving
way to her weight and hugging her body. It felt like she hadn't sat in
it for months, and she'd missed the comfort. The sofa in the Rocky
Top writing room was nice, but this couch was *hers*, and somehow
that made it better.

"Let me grab us a couple of beers and I'll get you up to speed."

Louie leaned her head back and closed her eyes. This was
how good she'd dreamed life could be. With the way things were
going, it didn't look like she'd be getting a wake-up call any time
soon. Her part in writing Savana's album was almost complete, and
her text flirtations with Heather had kept her going. There was a
certain amount of waiting for the other shoe to drop, but she'd been
visualizing a rainbow-painted future for herself to stave away those
darker thoughts. So far it had been working.

Gabe returned and placed a bottle in her hand. "Mia keeps
coming by work. She seems to think I have some influence over
you."

"What does she want you to do?" Louie asked the question but had no real interest in the answer. She liked the feeling of disinterest, but she didn't care for Mia pestering Gabe.

He dropped into the sofa opposite her and shrugged. "She says she wants you back and she'll do anything to make it up to you."

Louie laughed before taking a long draw on her beer. "Yeah, sure. As long as I get her an audience with Savana Hayes and Donny Taylor."

"I'm glad you've cut her loose. I get a bad feeling every time she walks into the restaurant. It's like she sweeps the good vibes away with every swishy step." He looked at her seriously. "You're not going to change your mind, are you? I'm not sure we could go on living together if you did."

Louie raised her eyebrows. "Wow, why don't you tell me how you really feel?"

"I'm not kidding, Louie. I couldn't be around that kind of bad energy."

"I get it." She hadn't realized Gabe was into "woo-woo," as her mom called it, but it wasn't as if she knew everything about him. "And no, I'm not changing my mind. Mom would kill me and you'd kick me out onto the streets. She's not worth that, for sure." She'd felt her mom's disappointment creep through the phone connection when she'd told her about meeting Mia, but her mom hadn't gone as far as to give verbal judgment. She didn't have to. She'd made her feelings clear in the silences.

"Good. But I've got a great feeling about you and Heather. You can't mess that up."

Louie couldn't help but laugh at Gabe's extreme seriousness. It was a side to him she hadn't experienced until now. "Is this a one-man intervention?"

Gabe stroked his chin and smiled. "Sorry. I just worry about you, and we haven't been connecting much while you've been working with Savana."

Louie took a long drink of her beer, not wanting to waste its chill in the warm evening air coming into the living room through the open patio. She'd gotten used to her mom being the only person who worried about her, and she was hundreds of miles away. It was taking some getting used to having someone so close being concerned for her day-to-day existence. The past year in Chicago had left her emotionally isolated, but Gabe's little brother role was slowly breaking through. And as for Heather, Louie's heart simply wasn't allowing any walls to think about constructing themselves.

"I've got a great feeling about me and Heather, too. It's so easy being around her. I don't feel like I have to try to be anything or anyone else." Not so with Mia. No matter what Louie did, it had never been good enough. She'd always wanted more or different. As she'd spent time getting to know Heather over the past couple of weeks, Louie had really analyzed her relationship with Mia. She'd come to realize that Mia had never truly loved her or who she was. She had only loved what Louie could do or get for her. There was simply no comparison between Heather and Mia. Heather was everything Mia had never been; open, kind, and generous. She was everything Louie had ever hoped she could find.

Gabe grinned. "Is it love?"

"Don't be an asshole," Louie said. "We haven't even kissed or been on a proper date yet. This isn't some beach romance novel. It's my life." Gabe looked away and Louie cursed herself for being so harsh. "Ignore me. I'm just tired and cranky…and desperate to kiss her." *And I want her to do a whole lot more than kiss me.* "I've got one more session with Savana on Friday, and then we're free to see each other. I've got an eight o'clock reservation for a private dining room at the Birdcat Bench for Saturday."

Gabe whistled. "You're going all out. I hear that's the best restaurant in town right now."

Louie tilted her head and nodded, thinking of the prices on the menu and the money she'd paid to have the private dining experience. She wouldn't usually be so extravagant and showy, but she was determined to impress Heather, so she'd used a chunk of her advance on Savana's album to bankroll the date. She might have been a gutter rat, but now she had a promising career as a songwriter, and it was only a matter of time before she was going to have plenty of money. She didn't want Heather ever thinking she'd made a mistake. "That's why I had to book three weeks in advance. I've gone for the whole private dining room."

Gabe looked like he was about to say something but didn't. Instead, he took another drink of his beer.

"What?" Louie asked. It wasn't like Gabe to keep anything to himself, even the stuff he really should.

"I don't know. It's none of my business."

Now Louie was intrigued. He usually thought everything was his business. "Spit it out. No secrets except the dirty ones."

"Okay, you did ask...Have you gone for the private room because you're being romantic or because Heather doesn't want to be seen with you?"

Louie nearly choked on her beer. "Jesus, Gabe. That's harsh."

"I'm sorry, Louie. I didn't know how else to put it."

"It's for both reasons." The blunt way Gabe had phrased his question stabbed at Louie's heart, but she wasn't about to show it. And it wasn't that Heather was *ashamed* to be seen with her...was it? "I promised I'd be okay with being discreet."

"And are you?"

Gabe's question was fair, but it was too early to tell. Louie hadn't even given it a go yet. She had no idea how okay with it she'd be. "I'll be fine."

Gabe straightened up on the sofa and looked even more serious. "Next offensive question—and I ask because it's an important date— do you own any clothes other than jeans and T-shirts? Because that place is seriously upmarket and I've only ever seen you in casual gear."

"Fair question, and if you'd asked that on Monday you would've caught me out." Louie smiled at Gabe's attempt at tact. "But now I have a very elegant suit, shirt, and tie. And I even bought a pair of fancy British brogues."

"She'll be impressed. Where'd you get your suit?"

"Indo something or other at the mall, but I'm having it tailored to fit. Tim recommended a great little alteration shop called Black Butterfly in Green Hills run by a cute straight couple. They rushed it through and I'm picking it all up tomorrow." Louie had spent more on this outfit and its alterations than she'd spent on clothes in two years, but this was for a dream girl.

"I've got a late-night gig on Saturday, and then I'm going to a club with Terri from work so you won't have to worry about me disturbing you."

Louie didn't know whether or not her date would end in the bedroom. She hoped it would, but she didn't want to jinx it by planning anything. Louie didn't know if Heather would rush into sex anyway. She'd had her share of fast and loose women when she was trying to get over Mia. Heather was special and worth the wait.

"Terri, huh? Terri boy or Terri girl?"

Gabe blushed. "Terri's a girl. She's cute. I think you'll like her."

"You want me to meet her?" Gabe nodded. The way he'd said it sounded like he wanted her approval. "If you like her, I'm sure she's perfect," said Louie.

Gabe smiled, and it was easy to see he was in the first flushes of love from the innocent, dreamy look he got in his eyes. Louie had every intention of making sure she was good enough for Gabe. She couldn't help but laugh at her protective instincts kicking in.

"What's funny?"

"Me. You." Louie shrugged. "If you'd said six months ago that I'd be sharing a house with a guy in his twenties and that he'd be my brother from another mother..." She shook her head and smiled. "Fate has a weird sense of humor."

Gabe raised his bottle. "Here's to fate and family."

Louie joined his toast and took a swig of the beer that was already too warm. "I'm honored to call you family." She got the sentence out but felt her chest tighten in the way it always did before she cried. "Tell me how your music's going. How many likes has your Facebook page got now?" She knew the change of subject was far from subtle, but Gabe nodded, seemingly recognizing her discomfort at the emotional exchange. Opening herself up again was proving scary, but it also felt damn good.

CHAPTER THIRTY

W hy is it we only ever have Thai food?" Heather asked between bites of a vegetarian spring roll.

"Because we're hidebound about the food we like. But that's okay. We both need some homogeny in our lives to balance the craziness." Emma raised a forked chicken piece and popped it into her mouth. "Besides, we had Italian last month. And Tim doesn't eat tasty food. He's an American burger boy all the way, which probably explains his struggle to keep trim."

Heather laughed. "I thought he was working hard in the gym trying to get you a six-pack?"

Emma wrinkled her nose and shook her head. "The only six-pack that boy's ever going to bring me comes from a liquor store."

"I'm glad to hear it's going well with you guys." Emma had regaled Heather with tales of the fun they'd been having rebuilding their relationship. She'd only seen Emma this happy when she was with Tim on their first trip around the love train. If Heather had been in a fairy tale, she would've already turned green and wicked. But it felt like she and Louie were finding that same connection. Heather was already feeling like she wanted to keep Louie all to herself for at least the first few months while they explored each other in the bedroom.

"Louie?"

The mention of Louie's name yanked Heather from her musings. "Huh?"

"Were you thinking about Louie?" Emma nudged her and winked. "You went all far away. Were you thinking dirty thoughts?"

Heather shoved her back a little harder. "No! We're not all obsessed with sex, you know."

"Well, you should be. Especially at the beginning of a new relationship. The only difference between you and Louie and you and me will be sex."

"I think that's an over-simplification of intimate relationships, but I get your thinking."

Emma lifted her chin. "So…were you?"

Heather's shoulders sank and she focused her concentration on her plate as if might hold the key to eternal life. "Busted."

"Ha. I knew it. It's been too long since we talked. Spill. How have you kept your hands off each other every day at work for the past two weeks?"

Heather closed her eyes and sighed. "To say it's been hard would be putting it mildly." She thought about all their furtive glances while everyone was around. Heather had spent late nights devouring lesbian fiction books to get some inspiration. She could barely wait to try doing some of the things she'd read about. Taking the lead in bed wasn't something she was used to, but she was damn sure she'd give it a go. "It's a romance 101 cliché, I know, but I really haven't felt this way before. It's like there's an electromagnetic field around her, and I…buzz whenever I'm near her. She makes me feel like a horny teenager, and all I want to do is get my hands on her." Heather ran her hand through her hair and thought of how it might feel to wrap her hand around the back of Louie's neck. She kept her hair nice and short, and Heather imagined it would feel nice to run her hand across it. And there was just enough on top to grab a handful of while they—

"Earth to Feathers. Come in, Feathers."

Heather held up her hands. "See? I'm a hormonal hot mess of a woman."

"You're all but done with the album, aren't you? Doesn't that mean you two can get on with it?"

Heather smiled widely. She could barely wait. "We've got one more session on Friday to finalize it, and Louie's got something special planned for Saturday." She realized she was nibbling at the end of her thumb and wondered if it held any significance. Was she that desperate to get her mouth on Louie?

"Really? An intimate dinner at her place, by any chance?"

Heather shook her head. "I don't think so. All I know is that I've got to dress up." She giggled and touched her hand to her lips, before wondering again about the significance of her current obsession with her mouth. The word "excited" simply didn't encompass the vastness of Heather's emotional and physical state. She couldn't remember ever wanting something or someone this much. The torture of spending so much time in close proximity without being able to do anything about it had ramped her anticipation levels into overdrive. Strangely, there was no niggling feeling that the fire might quickly burn into ash once the liaison was no longer illicit.

"Aren't you worried you might not wear the right outfit? Too casual. Too elegant. Oh, the pitfalls, Feathers."

Heather shoved Emma's leg, and she only just caught her plate before it tumbled off her leg.

"Well, I *wasn't* worried, but now I am. So thanks for that."

Emma tapped Heather's leg and nodded. "Glad to be of assistance. I hope you've bought new lingerie?"

Heather put her fork down and stood, her appetite diminished considerably with talk of Louie. She was hungry for something other than food. "You think I'm that easy?" She headed for the kitchen. "I'm getting another bottle. Red or white?"

"White. And as far as I know you haven't had sex with anyone other than yourself for over five years. I expect that you'll be throwing yourself at Louie at the earliest opportunity," Emma said as she followed Heather into the kitchen and sat at the breakfast bar.

The reminder that she'd been so sexually inactive since hitting Nashville was concerning. What if she was no good at it anymore? Was it possible to *forget* how to have sex? And Louie had made it clear she wanted the sex to be two-way. There was no way she could retreat into being a pillow queen. Not that she wanted to. The combination of the daydreams she'd been having of getting her hands on Louie and the hot lesbian erotica had her reaching into her nightstand on a nightly basis. She couldn't recall being this desperately hot for someone. Ever. "I won't be throwing myself at her," Heather said. Emma raised an eyebrow. "Maybe just a gentle jump."

"In public?"

Heather poured the wine into two fresh glasses and pushed one toward Emma. She smiled tightly. "We won't be making out in my office, if that's what you're getting at."

Emma took a quick sip of her wine. "I see plenty of women walking around the city not getting any hassle from anyone. Don't you think you're overthinking this?"

"And are any of those women trying to make it in the music industry?" Heather didn't wait for a response before continuing. "You only have to look at what happened to Caren White's career to see that country isn't the inclusive utopia we'd all like it to be. Rocky Top couldn't get rid of her fast enough as soon as she came out, and her record sales halved."

"But you're behind the scenes, Feathers. Do you think anyone really cares who you sleep with?"

Heather rubbed her forehead and rolled her shoulders. "Aaron was behind the scenes and that didn't matter to Donny. How many times are we going to have this conversation? As long as I work at Rocky Top, I have to be discreet. I told you what Donny said. 'I don't want any queers under my roof.' Until I can start my own label, I have to pretend to be who they think I am." Having to justify her lifestyle to Emma, someone who'd never had to deal with homophobia, bristled like a rough tag in a T-shirt. It was easy to challenge something having never experienced it. Usually Emma was more sensitive to her need to stay closeted, but maybe the wine had loosened her tongue just a little too much.

"And how's Louie going to cope with that? It's not like she's a retiring wallflower when it comes to wearing her sexuality on her sleeve."

Heather pulled the scrunchie from her wrist and tied her hair back. She needed the time to compose herself, not wanting to blow up. It wasn't Emma's fault she didn't understand her situation fully. She knew how hard it was to be taken seriously as a woman in country music, but being a lesbian too was another layer of complicated Emma didn't have to deal with. "Em, it's not like I actually want to be living my life this way, you know? I can't wait to be with Louie, and I want to show her off and just be with her anywhere and everywhere. But I'm pretty certain Donny would fire me if he even got a sniff of the fact that I'm gay." Heather reached over the counter and took Emma's free hand. "I've spent the last five years building my career, and I'm sure Savana's album is going to enhance my reputation. I'm maybe a couple of years away from being in a position to secure an investment to start my own label. I can't—I *won't* blow it now."

Emma smiled and squeezed Heather's hand. "I'm sorry. I'm being an insensitive asshole. *Is* Louie going to be all right being discreet?"

"I hope so. I guess we haven't discussed it in a lot of detail yet. She knows what Donny's like. Savana kind of delighted in telling her that he wasn't happy about her hiring a 'queer' to write her album. It didn't seem to faze Louie. She's probably used to a lot worse than that." Heather nodded toward the living room and held up the wine. "Let's get comfortable with this next bottle."

Heather led the way and topped up both of their glasses before settling back into the sofa.

Emma kicked off her shoes and tucked her feet beneath her. "And what's going on with Savana? Is Louie right? Is she hot for you?"

Heather drew her own feet underneath her ass and scooched closer to Emma as if the conversation they were about to have could be overheard by the northern mockingbirds outside. "Maybe. I don't know." Heather shrugged. "She's very affectionate with me, but I don't know if that's just her way of being friends with someone."

"Is she like it with any of the others in the room?"

Heather pulled her ponytail to the side and began to fiddle with it. Anything to distract her from addressing this possible problem. "Not really. She's fine with Vetti. She treats her more like a body woman, expecting her to tend to her every whim, which of course she's happy to do because that's part of her job." She rubbed her chin, trying to recall little interactions over the past few weeks. "She sits close to Louie, but I've never seen them touch anything other than accidentally. And that leaves Tim. You'll be pleased to know it doesn't look like she has any designs on him." Heather nudged Emma playfully.

Emma's eyes narrowed. "She would have a hell of a fight on her hands if she went anywhere near my boy."

Heather laughed. "Like Tim has eyes for anyone but you."

A hint of crazy flashed across Emma's face.

"He'd have *no* eyes if he did start eyeballing some other woman," Emma said. "But anyway, back to you. Is she flirting with you?"

Heather nibbled on her lip. Was Savana flirting because she was interested or was it just for her own amusement? "I guess so. You know what I'm like. I don't know if a woman is being friendly or if they're flirting for real. Men are damn near transparent, but women?" Heather shook her head. "I have no idea unless they come straight out with it."

"Like Louie did."

"Exactly like that. Lesbians everywhere should take lessons from Louie about letting women know what they want." Heather drifted again to thoughts of doing filthy things to Louie.

Emma waved a hand in front of Heather's face. "There you go again. Off to Louie Land. Dirty bitch."

Heather giggled, once again struck by the carnal nature of her attraction to Louie. So what if Savana flirted with her? It wouldn't matter if Savana draped her naked self on a piano and begged Heather to make love to her. Just like Tim for Emma, Heather only had eyes for one person, and she couldn't wait to cast her eyes over a naked Louie. But Emma's question itched at the back of her mind. Louie would be okay with them keeping their relationship relatively quiet. Wouldn't she?

CHAPTER THIRTY-ONE

Louie closed her eyes as she played the last chord on the first song she'd written for Savana. She wanted to enjoy the moment, the feeling that she was finally getting somewhere with her long-held dream. She let the intensity of the atmosphere wash over her like a tropical rain shower. When she opened her eyes, she looked up to the booth to see Heather smiling back at her through the booth's glass. Either the song sounded pretty good or Heather was happy to lock gazes with her. Maybe both wasn't too much to ask for. Louie returned the smile with what she hoped was a promise of what was to come tomorrow night.

"That was good. Let's go again from the beginning."

The voice of the producer bellowed into the studio space. Heather jumped, and the moment was shattered.

"Good but not great. What was wrong with it?" asked Savana.

"I'm not feeling you. You're holding back," he said.

Louie didn't seek Heather's eyes again. She knew she wouldn't be able to resist a little grin at how the producer had spoken to Savana. Louie assumed they had a long history because she was certain Savana wasn't a fan of being spoken to so bluntly. Instead she busied herself with fine-tuning her guitar and waited for Savana's reaction.

"You think I'm holding back?" Her voice raised slightly. "When have you ever heard me *hold back?*"

Louie glanced up at the producer to see him holding his hands in the air.

"I'm telling it how I'm hearing it. When have you ever wanted *me* to hold back?" He leaned closer to the mic connecting the booth to the studio. "You told me you wanted this to be a defining record in your career. You're not going to achieve that if you're not prepared to go places you haven't been before vocally."

Louie would've whistled had it not been wildly inappropriate. Who was this guy to speak to Savana like that? She saw Savana's manager, Joe, get up from his seat and put his hand on the guy's back. Louie saw them exchange some words off-mic before he shrugged Joe's hand away.

"Why don't you come in here and listen to it for yourself?" he asked.

Louie turned to the session drummer who raised her eyebrows at Louie. *Everyone* was uncomfortable.

"Fine," said Savana. "Take a break."

The rest of the musicians left the room like they'd been called to collect the winning lottery ticket. Louie placed her guitar on the stand and motioned to Heather to join her outside.

"Heather, I'd like you to stay." Savana strode past Louie and slipped through the adjoining door to the booth.

Heather raised her shoulders almost imperceptibly. Louie offered a smile she hoped came off as both sympathetic and rueful. A few minutes alone with her would've been nice. Louie had already envisioned a little tryst in a closet somewhere. But it wasn't to be. She saw Savana dismiss both her producer and manager, then she glared at Louie.

Savana placed her hands on her hips. "What are you waiting for?"

"Sorry." Louie pushed through the adjoining door and walked out of the booth. Something wasn't right, and she didn't like leaving Heather in there alone to cope with what looked like a potential diva meltdown.

Joe stood in the corridor tapping at his phone like a demented otter with a rock on a snail, and the producer was flat out on a couch with his feet up looking completely unaffected by Savana's behavior. If they had a history, maybe he was used to this kind of tantrum. He looked settled though, so Louie figured this might take a while. She probably had time to hit Anti Bean to get a bottle of vitamin water and a weak coffee for Heather.

Louie felt in her back pocket. No wallet. "Aww, crap."

She turned back, knocked, and pushed open the door.

It took a moment for her to make sense of the scene she walked into. Heather was leaning against the mixing desk, and it would've been impossible to fit a guitar pick between her body and Savana's. And their mouths were pressed together in a steamy-looking kiss.

Savana broke off, looked sideways at Louie, and narrowed her eyes. "Can I help you with something?"

Louie didn't respond. She could only see the look of obvious astonishment on Heather's face. Her arms were drawn into her body as if she were shielding herself from something unpleasant, and she looked to be holding her breath.

"What're you doing?" Louie moved into the booth and let the door close behind her.

Savana sneered. "What you've been wanting to do for a month. Looks like you waited too long, or you just realized you're not in Heather's league and that's why you haven't made a move." She jutted her chin toward Louie. "You should turn around and leave."

Louie ignored the provocation. She had nothing to prove to Savana and had no urge to share the beginnings of her relationship with Heather. She looked around Savana at Heather. "Are you okay?"

Heather pushed away from the desk. "I'm fine, Louie. It's okay."

Heather's voice faltered. She straightened her skirt and seemed anything but fine. Savana had a smile on her face Louie wanted to wash off with sulfuric acid. Louie pushed the desire deep down where it belonged.

"You heard what she said." Savanna waved her hand at Louie. "They say the best woman wins, but it's not clear you're really a woman so maybe this was never a fair fight."

Louie clenched her jaw and concentrated her focus on Heather. She wanted to remain professional and had to be careful. "Do you want to step out for a coffee, Heather?"

Savana shook her head. "She doesn't want to step out with you at all. We're all good here so you can disappear."

Heather ran her hand through her slightly messy hair and smiled, but Louie could see it wasn't genuine.

"Honestly, Louie. I'm okay."

Savana put her arm around Heather, but she recoiled from her touch.

"Do you want to be in here with her?" Louie asked Heather, her patience beginning to run thin.

"Who the hell do you think you are?" Savana ate up the ground between them and stood inches away from Louie. "I'm giving you three seconds to turn around and walk away, or I walk up to Donny's office and have you fired."

Louie held firm and imagined her wrists were bound, immobilizing her hands from wrapping around Savana's scrawny neck. "Go ahead. And I'll tell him how his number one signing just sexually assaulted one of his top employees." Louie swallowed, but it was too late to pull the words back. Blackmailing the talent probably wouldn't earn her any more gigs in this town if it got out.

Savana laughed as she reached past Louie and pulled open the door. "I didn't assault anyone. You may not want to believe it, but she consented." She looked smug. "You're finished."

Louie didn't watch Savana leave. Her concern was with Heather. She rushed over and tried to hold her, but Heather held up her arms to stop her.

"Please. Don't." She shook her head. "I'm sorry, Louie. It'd probably be best if you left for the day. We'll talk later. Let me sort this out."

The knockback pulled on Louie's heart like a snapped guitar string. What was happening? Had she misread the situation and Heather *did* want Savana's attention? "Just because she's a woman doesn't mean you should put up with being assaulted, Heather."

Heather took a step back and leaned against the back of a chair. "Don't you think I know that?" She sighed. "Please. Go home and let me deal with this."

Had Louie just rode in like a misguided white knight to save the damsel who wasn't in distress? "What about the rest of the recording session?" Louie asked just for something to say. She didn't dare ask the question bashing at the back of her throat to be voiced. *Did you kiss her back?*

"We may not even continue recording today."

Heather didn't move toward Louie, and the lack of physical contact hurt. All Louie wanted to do was draw Heather into her arms, hold her gently, and tell her everything would be all right. She'd known all along that Savana had designs on Heather, but she never thought she'd end up being so blatant about it. Her contract was to write the album and she'd done that. Donny couldn't fire her. But he did have the power to blackball her in this town. Would this signal the end of her Nashville career before she'd really even begun? Louie looked hard at Heather for something else. Anything else. She didn't know what. But her features were shut down. She'd withdrawn. Louie knew Heather was right. This was her situation to deal with, and Louie had little right to step in and act as if Heather couldn't stand up for herself.

Louie backed away. Heather needed space to process, and Louie didn't want to crowd her. She pushed away the dark cloud that threatened to rain on her plans and wash away the roots of her fledgling relationship with Heather. "Okay. If that's what you want. I'll leave." She put her hand on the door and partially opened it. "You'll call me later?"

Heather nodded. "Of course. And I'll see you tomorrow night."

Relief swept over Louie like a breaking wave. Heather's words seemed genuine. It was selfish considering the circumstances, but she couldn't bear the thought of losing Heather. Even if she didn't really have her yet, she'd fight Savana all the way if she had to. Savana's words were on repeat: "You're not in Heather's league." Fears she'd worked hard to submerge began to float to the surface. Was she kidding herself that Heather would really be interested in her when someone like Savana was in the picture?

CHAPTER THIRTY-TWO

Heather placed her hands on the mixing desk and stared into the empty, dark space of the studio. She took a deep breath and tried to figure out what the hell had just happened and what she was supposed to do about any of it. Everything had happened so fast. Savana had asked her what *she* thought of the track and she'd been honest. She *did* love it and she *did* think that the producer was on the wrong track. Heather said he'd misunderstood what Savana was trying to achieve with this record. The next thing she knew, Savana pressed against her and kissed her. To say it had taken her by surprise was the understatement of her life.

Christ, she didn't want any of this complication and confusion. And she'd handled Louie's concern all wrong. What was she thinking right now? Their first real date was tomorrow and Louie had walked in on her being kissed by another woman. But Louie had been so heavy-handed, acting like Heather needed rescuing from the evil country queen. It was sweet that Louie was quick to protect her, but it also felt like an overreaction. Or maybe Heather was just too used to being sexually harassed that her tolerance level was far higher than Louie's. Far higher than perhaps it should be.

Someone knocked on the door, and as it opened, Heather was relieved to see a friendly face in Mandie. The expression she bore however told Heather her relief would be short-lived.

"Hey, Heather." She closed the door behind her before she spoke again. "I don't know what's going on, but Donny sounds like he's about to have a heart attack. He wants you up in his office right now."

Heather swallowed against the feel of her heart in her throat. She'd thought Savana was bluffing. She'd been certain that Savana wouldn't walk into Donny's office and expect him to be okay with his golden goose telling him she'd been kissing his female executive and that she wanted the romantic competition fired. Unless she'd been spinning tales of another kind.

"Is Savana up there with him?" Heather knew the answer. There was no other reason to be summoned to the boss's office when he knew she was in the recording studio with his superstar.

Mandie nodded. "And she looked none too happy. You had a difference of artistic opinion?"

"Far from it." The exact opposite was true. Had Heather's support against the producer been the reason Savana had kissed her? She thought back to when Savana had come to Rocky Top for their first meeting. She knew of Heather's work, and that was one of the reasons she said she'd wanted to come to this label. But the way Savana had spoken to Louie seemed to speak of Savana feeling a deeper connection to Heather beyond the music. Had she been unknowingly responsible for cultivating that? Had she been sending out the wrong signals?

"Heather? He wants you now."

"Sorry." Heather motioned to the door. "After you."

Heather had seen Donny angry plenty of times before. His professionalism didn't extend to keeping his emotions in check. His professionalism didn't extend period. But there were veins popping out in places Heather didn't think there should be, and his face and neck were the color of a Hawaiian sunset. He was pacing his office floor fast enough to wear out the thread.

Savana was a study in opposites. She looked relaxed, settled back in a piebald cowhide leather couch with a coffee cup in hand. Her legs were crossed in a demure rather than defensive way. She looked…controlled, though Heather couldn't imagine how she remained so calm in the face of Donny's apoplectic actions. Then the penny dropped. If Louie was right and Savana's kiss meant anything, Savana had been acting throughout her whole career. She was an expert at burying her feelings. She couldn't afford to have emotions erupting volcano-like all over the place.

"What have you got to say to all of this, King?"

His use of her surname instead of his usual demeaning "girl" should've felt like progress, but instead it felt like a slap in the face. It already sounded like Donny had decided *all* of this was *her* fault. And what was "all of this?" She had no idea what Savana had told Donny.

She decided to play it safe. The last thing she wanted to do was blow her own career. "What's bothering you, Donny?" She'd learned in a college psych lesson that using someone's name made them feel important and listened to.

"What's *bothering* me?" He stopped pacing and tucked his fingers inside the belt of his trousers. "It's *bothering* me that someone you brought into the label has managed to upset Savana. It's *bothering* me that I'll have to pay that man-dyke thousands of dollars when this album goes multi-platinum. It's *bothering* me that I went against my better judgment to let a homo work in my business and I've been proven right."

Heather glanced at Savana questioningly. The fact that Donny was throwing around homophobic language meant that Savana couldn't have told him the whole story. What exactly was she laying at Louie's feet? Heather felt trapped.

"None of this is Heather's fault, Donny," said Savana before she took a sip of her coffee. "It's Louie Francis you should be calling in here, not Heather."

"Where is the runty little dyke?" Donny paced back to his desk and sat in his chair.

Heather's nostrils flared at Donny's description. Calling him on it would divert his ire to her. She heard the voice in the back of her mind call her a coward, but she ignored it. She had to choose her battles carefully.

"I sent Louie home so everyone could calm down," said Heather. Though she was thankful for Savana's interjection that this wasn't her fault, it still hadn't given her much in the way of explanation. Treading water wasn't her forte, especially with a boss as temperamental as Donny.

"I'm blackballing her. Him. It. Who does she think she is speaking to Savana like that?"

Heather clenched her teeth at his repeated and ignorant discrimination. "It was a misunderstanding. Louie was just trying to protect me."

"Protect you from what?" asked Donny.

Heather hesitated. Savana stood and stepped in front of her to block her from Donny's questioning glare. As she rose, she half turned to Heather and shook her head almost imperceptibly.

Savana returned her attention to Donny. "That's not really relevant. As you say, it's not for someone like Louie to speak to me so disrespectfully regardless of the circumstances."

Heather's lips may as well have been frozen together. So many things competed in her brain to get out of her mouth, but none won out. If she stood up for Louie and told Donny the truth, she wasn't sure he'd do anything about it anyway and he'd most likely fire her. If she kept quiet, Louie's career was over before it had really started, and that *would be* Heather's fault. Rock and a hard place barely came close to describing what she felt caught between.

"So what would you have me do about this, Savana?" asked Donny. He flipped open his cigar box, yanked one out, and began to chew on it. "I want you to be happy here, and I don't want anything to jeopardize that."

"The album's been written. Louie's usefulness to me has expired. I was just being kind letting her play guitar on a few tracks on her last day here. It's not like I'd want someone like that in my tour band in public." She tossed another glance Heather's way before she continued. "That bit me on the ass. Lesson learned. I want her gone, Donny. I don't want to run into her in this town ever again."

Donny grinned and spat out the end of his cigar into a nearby ashtray. "Done."

Heather stepped around Savana and approached Donny's desk. "Will you at least take the weekend to think about it, Donny? You're talking about ending someone's dreams." Heather could see his mind was already made up about firing Louie. Hell, he seemed pretty much gleeful that his prejudiced misgivings about "queers" had been supported by what Savana had told him of Louie's actions. Play to their egos. "You're a reasonable and fair man, Donny… and I'm sure Louie wasn't acting maliciously." She nodded toward Savana. "Louie has written you what's going to be a career-defining album, and you're both going to profit from that." She turned back to Donny. "She has the talent to write some of the best songs Nashville has ever heard, and you could benefit from that." Donny hadn't interrupted her so she pressed on. "I don't know if you were aware, but Louie's been picked up by Hawthorne. You know they're the biggest provider of songs for the whole of Music Row. She could make millions for both of you." Heather hoped she'd said enough to save Louie's songwriting career without destroying her own.

Donny leaned back in his chair and scratched his neck. "I guess you're right about that."

He lit his cigar and made a poor attempt at blowing smoke rings. Too many moments of silence passed and even Savana didn't fill them. Heather dared to hope that she'd gotten through to both of them. Pandering to egos and talking about financial gain tended to do that.

"What are you going to do, Donny?" asked Heather, conscious she and Louie were supposed to be going out on their first date tomorrow night. If Louie still wanted to date a coward. Louie would want to know what had happened and Heather didn't want to lie. It had already been soul-destroying to face Donny and be economical with the truth. Not standing up to be counted, not fighting for what she really believed in felt as weak as it did justified.

"Get…*Louie* in here eleven a.m. sharp on Monday. Savana, I'd like you to be present, too. That gives you the weekend to think about this situation, just like me." He tipped his head toward Heather. "She's got some smarts in the wisdom department maybe we could both benefit from."

Heather tried not to react to Donny's final statement. It was about as close to a compliment as she'd ever gotten from him.

Savana nodded and turned toward Heather. "I'll take the weekend." She walked to the door before she glanced back at Heather. "But some feelings don't change."

Savana's meaning wasn't subtle, but Heather still found it hard to believe. Savana *did* have the hots for her. She needed her sounding board, but there was no way she could get to speak to Emma until tonight, and Louie would be expecting a phone call. Christ, a month ago she'd been celibate for five years and all but uninterested in women. Now she had two vying for her attention. Under normal circumstances that might be something to be happy about, but Heather was far from that emotion. All this proved was that she really shouldn't mix business with the personal. More than that, this whole situation had rammed home that not being true to herself, while good for her career, was not good for her.

CHAPTER THIRTY-THREE

L ouie adjusted her tie for what felt like the hundredth time in the hour she'd been wearing it. She opened the top button of her shirt to allow herself to breathe more freely and give her neck a little more room. The waitress who'd introduced herself as Chloe and shown Louie to her private dining room caught her eye and smiled. She was cute but the only woman Louie was interested in was late. She checked her watch again. Three minutes past eight. Louie retrieved her phone from the inside of her jacket. No messages.

"Would you like a drink while you're waiting?" asked Chloe.

Louie looked up and nodded. "A bottle of water would be great." Louie didn't miss the note of hope in the girl's voice that her date wouldn't show. Or maybe Louie was just transferring her fear onto her.

Chloe nodded and left her post at the open doors to Louie's dining area. The space was completely separate from other dining pods like it, each hosted by their own waiting staff. At least if Heather didn't turn up, no one but Chloe would witness her humiliation. Louie shoved the unwelcome thought away. Heather didn't seem like she'd be the type to do that...but then Mia hadn't presented as someone who'd just up and leave and take all her savings either. She figured the old saying was right: you never did truly know someone, maybe not even yourself.

Heather had called last night as promised, but she didn't give Louie a straight answer about what had happened with Savana. She said it'd be better discussed in person, but talking about work wasn't where Louie wanted to focus her attention tonight. After nearly a month of flirtation and promise, Louie simply wanted to see where she and Heather might lead. But Savana had stepped in and tried her best to mess things up. Louie had been certain that Heather didn't welcome Savana's attention. She'd looked panicked, even frightened, when Louie entered the studio. That wasn't something that was easily misinterpreted. Unless Louie had seen what she wanted to see and made more of the situation than was actually there.

Either way, she really wanted tonight to be about them spending quality time with each other away from work. Louie was determined not to spend all night talking about work. She'd completed the album as contracted. But Savana had made her intentions toward Heather clear, and she had a lot of power in Nashville. Louie took a deep breath and tried to focus on Heather. The less conversation they shared about Savana, the better. If the night was a success, Louie hoped that any romantic thoughts Heather *did* have toward Savana would disappear.

"I'm so sorry I'm late. There was an accident on Broadway, and I had to detour around it."

Louie didn't care. As soon as she looked up and saw Heather in the doorway dressed in a mid-thigh, ink-blue dress and heels, all concept of time fell away. She looked stunning in a 1950s movie star kind of way that not many women could carry off these days. Demure. Sexy. A hint of naiveté about just how beautiful she was.

Louie stood and pulled Heather's chair from the table. "You look amazing."

Heather nibbled at her bottom lip and smiled. "As do you. That's a beautiful suit," said Heather as she sat.

Louie grinned, glad that the effort and money that had gone into her outfit hadn't gone unnoticed.

Chloe had accompanied Heather and placed a bottle of water on the table.

"Would you like a drink, miss?"

Heather seemed to hesitate. "A glass of your house red would be lovely."

Louie placed one hand over Heather's, sure that her hesitation came from thoughts of how much this whole meal was costing. Louie's stomach fluttered a house of butterflies when Heather didn't pull away. "Would you get us the wine list please, Chloe?"

"I'm sure the house wine is fine," said Heather.

"No. Fine is nowhere near good enough for you." Louie nodded to Chloe to reconfirm her wish and she left with a smile.

"I've heard a lot about this place, but I never thought I'd ever eat here." Heather waved her hand at the room. "Especially in a private dining area."

Louie was glad she stopped short of saying something like *"How the hell can you afford a place like this?"* "I wanted to make our first proper date super special, so you'd remember it always."

"Mission accomplished."

Heather smiled and Louie's breath hitched. Heather's smile was like she switched the light on in Louie's darkened heart. It gave her hope that she could be in Heather's league. Chloe reentered the room and handed them both a wine list.

"Which red wine would you recommend, Chloe?"

"That often depends on what you're going to order. But for a wine that goes with pretty much everything, I'd recommend that one."

Chloe pointed to a name Louie had no chance of pronouncing. She noticed there was no price, either for the bottle or the glass. That's what her credit card was for. She saw Heather raise her eyebrows and wondered if she had an idea that it was expensive or was knocked sideways by the no-prices policy.

"We'll take a bottle of that, please."

Moments later, Chloe returned again, uncorked the bottle at the table, and poured a small amount into Heather's glass. Heather looked slightly shy as she took a sip and nodded.

Chloe topped up the glass. "Let me know when you're ready to order," she said before retreating to just outside the door.

Heather took another taste. "This is the best wine ever." She looked around the small pod and refocused on Louie. "I don't think I've ever seen a place with private dining booths before. I like it."

"I know privacy is important to you. I want you to know I'm okay with that." Being closeted was no great shakes, but Louie understood why Heather needed to be careful, especially in the center of town. She'd never been one to hide, though to be fair, the way she looked meant that she couldn't even if she wanted to. Gabe had helped Louie check out the gay bars in the area, and they'd found some in South Nashville. They weren't quite at the county line, but they were far enough away from the city that Heather might be able to relax and even be a little more open. Louie wondered how difficult this would all be. She'd worked hard to be comfortable with who and what she was. Louie worried that being with Heather might work to undo all that progress. She figured she'd see how she felt when they were actually in the relationship.

Louie flipped the menu and saw again that there were no prices. She glanced up at Heather to see she'd flicked straight through the pages to find salads. Louie took Heather's hand. "Please don't do that." Heather's lack of response indicated that she knew what Louie was talking about. "I wouldn't invite you to a place I couldn't afford."

Heather leaned in, perhaps hoping not to be overheard by Chloe.

"But there are no prices, Louie."

Louie brought Heather's hand to her lips and kissed it gently. She'd been assured that the waiting staff here were beyond reproach in terms of privacy. "It doesn't matter. Please order what you want to eat, not what you think might be the cheapest."

Heather looked unsure but she nodded. It took a few minutes before Louie called Chloe back to the table for their order. When Chloe left them alone again, Louie decided to address the dark shadow of Savana so they could get on with their date.

"Do you want to talk about yesterday afternoon?" Honestly, Louie was most apprehensive about whether or not Heather invited the kiss.

"Sure."

Chloe came in with their appetizers and set them down. Heather waited until she was gone again before she continued.

"Donny wants you to come in for a meeting with him and Savana on Monday at eleven."

Louie raised her eyebrow. Her poker face had never been anything to ride a fortune on. "Really? There needs to be a meeting? I don't see the point since I've finished writing the album."

Heather ran her hand through her hair and sighed. "Savana didn't tell Donny the whole truth. She just told him you'd been disrespectful and spoken to her in a way that was unacceptable."

Louie screwed up her toes then tried to relax them before tackling Heather's explanation, which was all kinds of wrong. "Okay…did you tell him what really happened?"

"I told him it was a misunderstanding and you were trying to protect me."

Louie speared a piece of mango, fighting off the desire to imagine it was Donny's podgy face she was forking. "Did I misunderstand the situation?" Louie tried to keep her tone even. The night had barely warmed up. She didn't want to toss a bucket of ice on it already, but she had to know.

Heather swallowed whatever she was eating and washed it down with another mouthful of wine. Louie busied herself with eating while she waited for a response, wondering if she really wanted to hear it. Her mom always told her, *don't ask a question unless you're prepared to hear the answer.*

"No. But it's complicated."

"You said that yesterday." Louie cursed herself for the harsh retort. Heather didn't really owe her anything. They'd just agreed to see where their attraction led. Maybe it had already led Heather to Savana, to femme familiarity. Maybe she was just too not-a-girly girl for Heather, and Savana had reminded her of that. "I'm sorry. Please, talk to me."

"It happened really fast. One minute I was talking, the next she was kissing me, and then you burst in."

"Did you like it?" The question felt intrusive, and Louie felt she had no right to ask it, but she did anyway. If she and Heather were going to pursue their attraction, Louie wanted total honesty. She'd fight for Heather, no problem, but she had no interest in sharing.

"Of course not. I'm not interested in Savana, Louie, please know that. It's trying to keep my career that's complicated." Heather chased an asparagus tip around her plate with a fork. "This feels like an odd conversation for our first date."

Louie nodded. "Agreed. But sexual harassment is the same whether it's perpetrated by a man or a woman. You didn't invite it. She abused the position of power she has over you." Louie took a breath, aware she sounded like a feminist lecture. She didn't want to push her views on Heather, but women everywhere put up with too much shit because they feared for their job or at worst, their lives.

Heather put her fork down and looked across at Louie. "You really want to talk about this now?"

Louie offered an apologetic smile. "If it's okay with you, I really do."

"Okay, let's do it. But you have to promise you won't get angry."

Louie frowned, unsure why Heather would assume her reaction would run to anger and that she wasn't in control of her emotions. Maybe Heather couldn't fully dismiss Mia's accusations about her temper. "I don't really do angry, Heather."

"Okay. Savana's always been an idol to me. Her music has been in my life for a decade, and she was one of the main reasons I took the chance to come to Nashville in the first place." She moved a stray piece of hair that had fallen across her eye and tilted her head to the side. "Granted, that didn't work out quite as planned, but I'm happy doing what I'm doing now and I have a plan for my own label."

Louie liked the sound of that. She could picture Heather as an indie label head, signing artists like Gabe, artists she believed in. She thought again about the potentially huge royalty checks she would receive from the Savana album. Could they run a label together?

"I was beyond flattered when Savana came to Rocky Top and said that she wanted to work with me," Heather continued. "And she listened to every thought and suggestion I had about each of her songs." She paused and took a long swallow of water. "When she kissed me, I didn't know what to do, and you're right if you thought I looked panicked when you came into the studio. I've looked up to Savana for ten years. I love her music, and yeah, I had a crush on her when I was younger. But when we started working together, I went beyond that. For me, it was purely professional, and I didn't have any sexual thoughts about her." She smiled and looked a little coy. "Those were concentrated fully on you."

Louie smiled back. She didn't want to make this harder than it had to be, and so far she'd heard nothing to suggest there was anything to worry about it. Savana was wrong. She was in Heather's league because Heather wanted her there. "That makes me happier than you could ever know."

"But here's the thing I'm struggling with when you're talking about framing what Savana did as a sexual assault. If I *had* liked it and *had* responded, doesn't that just make it a successful come-on from Savana? Is it only because I didn't respond that people might want to call it an assault?"

Louie nodded. "I see what you're saying, but in this situation, it feels more like an abuse of power. She's used to getting what she wants when she wants it, as if there's no option for anyone to say no. I never saw you give her any signals that you might be interested. It wasn't as if you'd given her the eye across the studio and invited it, y'know?"

"You asked if I liked the kiss." Heather touched her fingers to her lips for a moment as if recalling the feeling.

Louie wanted to gather her in her arms and kiss her with such passion that she'd forget she'd ever been kissed by another woman. "And…"

"I felt nothing. It didn't set my world on fire." She cast her eyes downward. "Not like I think you might."

If Louie's heart could've performed an Olympic gymnastics routine, it would have. All the fears she'd been having, the flashbacks to Mia's betrayal, the thought she wasn't good enough for Heather, softened like an out of focus photograph. Louie pushed her chair away from the table and knelt beside Heather. She reached up, took Heather's face in her hands, and pulled her gently into a soft kiss. Heather's hair fell onto Louie's skin and made her shiver. Heather kissed her back, and just as she'd predicted, her lips lit Louie's internal world. A fire of passions raged through her body from her mouth to the tips of her toes. She felt somehow more solid and yet weightless. The heartbreak of past experience fell away like petals from flowers in a strong wind, and it swept Louie up into a vortex of aching from which she didn't want to escape. All thoughts of Savana and Rocky Top dissipated and lost their importance.

Louie reluctantly broke away, aware they weren't as alone as she felt in that moment. She got back to her feet, retook her seat, and looked at Heather with a smile. "The world I know just went up in smoke."

❖

Louie scooped the last spoon of whatever dessert she'd ended up with into her mouth. If Gabe was going to ask what she had to eat at the fancy-pants restaurant, she'd have no real idea. The night had passed by in a blur since she'd kissed Heather. They could've been in a room filled with a hundred of Nashville's finest, and Louie would have been oblivious to all of them. All she could hear, all she wanted to hear, was Heather. All she wanted to see, touch, and taste was Heather.

Louie paid the bill, leaving Chloe a hefty tip, and offered Heather her hand. "I'm assuming you came by taxi?"

"I did." Heather stumbled a little on her heels. "Which is a good thing since you've gotten me a little buzzed."

Louie raised her eyebrow. "Tell me you can still make sound decisions though, huh?"

"Oh, of course." Heather looked at Louie as if she were her next course. "I never drink that much unless I'm at home. Which is where you're taking me, yes?"

Heather's straightforward attitude appealed greatly to Louie. "Absolutely." Whether or not the offer of a chauffeur service would get her access inside Heather's house was unclear. For now.

As they headed out of the pod, Louie offered her arm for Heather to hook into, but she shook her head. Louie looked around. The corridor was empty and the doors to the other dining pods were closed. They were alone but for Chloe and she was walking away. Yet still Heather couldn't—or wouldn't—simply put her arm through Louie's. Hell, straight friends walked through town like that all the time. But none of those friends looked like Louie in a two-piece suit and tie. Louie clenched her jaw and waved Heather through to the back exit where she'd parked her truck. Another gesture of discretion on Louie's part that didn't sit well.

Heather caught hold of Louie's hand at the exit door and pulled her back into a deep kiss that pushed Louie's irritation to the back of her mind. She opened her eyes to see Heather looking beyond her. Louie broke away. "I should get you home."

Heather held onto Louie's hand as she opened the door onto the steel staircase at the rear of the building. She felt cool but it didn't reduce Louie's rising temperature. Problem was, she was both horny and irked. The alley was dark and the steps came out a few hundred feet from the sidewalk. Louie led the way down with Heather still firm in her grip.

A side door from the restaurant swung open against some trash cans and shattered the silence. Heather loosed her hand from Louie's instantly. She balled her now empty hand into a fist and stuffed it into her pocket. The guy who emerged from beyond the steamy heat barely noticed them and was focused on lighting his cigarette. Louie unlocked her truck. She moved to open Heather's door, but Heather put her hand up.

"I got it," she said.

Louie shrugged and got in the driver's side, gunned the truck, and sped off the moment Heather clicked her seat belt into the lock.

"In a hurry, baby?" Heather asked.

The way Heather drawled the sexy term of endearment almost had Louie pulling over and diving into the back of the truck like a sex-starved teenager. Her mind, preoccupied with the clandestine nature of their date, was battling her body and starting to lose out. She didn't want to think about any of that. She just wanted to hold Heather in her arms and let the heat of their attraction hit the gas and take off.

"Something like that." Louie drove in silence before she pulled into the Capitol Mall State Park and switched off the engine.

"I haven't parked since I was a teenager, and it never went well," said Heather. "But my driver was never a girl, and they weren't a quarter as hot as you are."

Louie released her seat belt and leaned toward Heather, who moved closer and took Louie's face in her hands. Heather caressed Louie's cheek and her eyes focused only on Louie. Not beyond or around her. On her. Louie stopped overthinking and let it be. She kissed Heather hard and deep, the sexual frustration of the past month melting and reforming into an uncontained passion. She put her hand on Heather's thigh and slowly dragged her fingers and the hem of Heather's dress upward. Heather traced her tongue over Louie's before she sucked Louie's upper lip into her mouth. Louie's breath hitched and her pussy tightened in response.

Heather released her own seat belt and slipped her hands around Louie's back. She pulled Louie's shirt out of her pants and ran her nails along the base of Louie's naked back, making Louie moan softly. Louie gripped Heather's thigh harder, kissed her deeper, tried to express all her longing without words.

Louie opened her eyes to see the bright headlights of another car pulling into the lot. She broke away unwillingly and breathless. "I better take you home before we get arrested."

Heather adjusted the hem of her dress and slid down a little in her seat. "That's a good idea."

Louie turned the ignition and drew away. She adjusted the crotch of her trousers to get more comfortable. Heather's handling of her had her throbbing against their seam. "Am I coming in for coffee or hot milk?"

Heather laughed. "You think I'm that easy? The meal and the company were divine, but I don't tend to put out beyond second base on a first date."

"A true lady." Louie placed her hand on Heather's thigh, just about keeping the temptation to push a little higher at bay.

"A lady on the streets..." Heather said, gave Louie a sideways glance, and winked.

Louie swallowed hard. She couldn't wait to put the end of that saying to the test.

CHAPTER THIRTY-FOUR

If the look on Mandie's face was anything to go by, Heather was heading into a storm of epic proportions. She wore a mix of holy hell, pity, and good luck, if the combination of such things could be conveyed in an expression, and she looked even more overwhelmed than she had on Friday. Heather decided she'd ask if Mandie would be interested in joining her label when the time was right. She wouldn't be able to offer her the same pay or company benefits, but she could offer a more stable and pleasant environment to work in. And there'd be no stupid rules about having to wear skirts. Heather smoothed hers down as if it had ruffled in rebellion at the thought of being banished from her work wardrobe. She knocked and waited until she heard Donny's harassed voice call her in.

Predictably, Savana was already there. Heather had been hoping she'd be able to have a private chat with Donny before everyone else descended, but it wasn't to be.

"You're late."

Donny's gruff bark disconcerted her more than usual. He was clearly in no better mood than he'd been before the weekend. She glanced at her watch to see it was ten thirty. The meeting wasn't scheduled until eleven, so she wasn't quite sure why she was being yelled at for being late, but she didn't question it. Savana barely made eye contact, and her smile was brief and unconvincing. Heather guessed she didn't take kindly to her calls and texts going unanswered all weekend.

"Sit."

Donny motioned at the couch Savana occupied and Heather did as she was bid. He went back to a call on his cell phone at the far end of his office, speaking in tones hushed enough that she couldn't hear him. Heather had never heard him whisper, especially on the phone. His logic seemed to be that the louder he was, the more powerful he was.

Heather wished she'd brought her iPad in with her so she could at least pretend to work. Instead she was forced to inspect her nail polish and cuticles as though she were appreciating a priceless work of art. The silence and awkwardness between her and Savana stretched on for minutes.

"Where were you all weekend?"

Heather frowned at Savana's question, more than a little taken aback at her invasive tone. "Busy catching up on some audition possibles." Donny had delegated her regular duties to a seasoned exec, but they hadn't been keeping up. Heather picked up the slack while she thought about the hot Saturday night make-out session with Louie. She didn't feel the need to share that nugget with Savana.

"On your own?" asked Savana.

Heather smiled politely. "Yes." She stopped herself from asking why. Savana's sub-question was clearly, *"Were you with Louie?"*

Savana sighed deeply and leaned forward. "Really? Then Louie didn't rob a bank to take you to the Birdcat Bench?"

Heather fought to keep the immediate rise of panic that constricted her throat. Louie had assured her the waiting staff were discreet, and she'd even arranged for them to use the VIP exit to minimize the possibility of them being seen together. How could she explain it? There was no way dinner at the Birdcat could be construed as a business meeting regardless of the fact they'd just finished Savana's album and were working together. Louie's understanding had been amazing, but for a moment, when Heather pulled her hand from Louie's as they left the Birdcat, Heather was sure she'd seen Louie clench her jaw. It left her with the feeling that maybe Louie wasn't as cool with being quiet about their relationship as she'd said she was.

She brought herself back into the room. The silence after Savana's question had already been too long. And how Savana had gotten the information was largely irrelevant right now. How she might use it could be a problem. So far Savana had neglected to let Donny in on her own secret; surely, she wouldn't out Heather and get her fired.

"What does it matter, Savana?"

Savana gave a short laugh and shook her head. "You can do better than her." She leaned closer to Heather. "I know you felt something when I kissed you," she whispered.

Overwhelmed. Surprised. Stunned. Heather glanced at Donny, still at the farthest point away from them and apparently too intent on his own conversation to hear theirs. "I wouldn't have thought you wanted to talk about that here."

"Where else can I talk about it when you won't answer my calls and texts?"

Heather crossed her legs and leaned back into the sofa, feigning a sense of calm she didn't feel as she tried to make sense of what was happening. The Queen of Country was acting like they were in some sort of romantic relationship. Heather had heard all about lesbian drama from Emma's tales of the city, and she'd been glad she'd managed to avoid it for the most part. Until now. "I needed some thinking time."

Savana raised her eyebrows. "And you can think while you're having a romantic meal in a private area of the most exclusive restaurant in town with a nobody?"

Heather struggled to minimize her physical reaction to Savana's incendiary words. Who the hell did she think she was? Louie wasn't a nobody. She was a wonderful, kind, and gentle woman, and the way Savana spoke about her inflamed Heather. *Defend her then.* Her reticence taunted her, while her ambition grabbed hold of her vocal chords to prevent her from protecting Louie's honor. Heather compensated by giving herself assurances that Louie was perfectly capable of standing up for herself.

"I'm not sure what you want me to say, Savana," said Heather, totally out of her depth with this whole situation and wishing she had Emma speaking into an earpiece to give her some damn clue as to what she should say.

"I want you to say that you'll stop seeing that boi bitch and be with me."

Heather looked at Savana for some sign that she wasn't being completely serious but saw only sincerity. How could Savana have jumped from an unsolicited kiss to a full-on relationship? Was she that used to getting what she wanted and people never saying no that she applied the same logic to her relationships? "Savana, I've always loved your music and I really enjoy working with you, but...be with you?" Heather became aware Donny had ended his conversation when he strode into her periphery. She fell silent and simply shook her head.

Savana's nostrils flared and her eyes narrowed. Heather tried to relax, unsure of what the consequences of saying no to her might be.

"So, what are your thoughts, Savana? Did you consider Heather's logic in how we might handle this?" asked Donny after he sat on the couch opposite them both.

Heather didn't like the obvious inference that this was a joint decision, but she wasn't surprised. His loyalty was to the company's bank balance, and keeping Savana happy was his top priority.

Savana looked sideways at Heather as she moved closer to Donny, and Heather got the impression she was about to discover the consequences of her refusal sooner than she'd expected.

"I haven't changed my mind, Donny. There are plenty of great songwriters out there with a damn sight more professionalism than Louie Francis. Just because she's talented doesn't mean she should be allowed to behave any way she pleases."

How Savana didn't choke on her last sentence, Heather had no idea. Surely she realized that she'd just described herself. If Donny caught the irony, he didn't show it.

"So what are you saying?" asked Donny.

"Exactly what I said to you Friday. I want her out of Rocky Top and I want her out of my city."

The whole meeting began to feel a little like a bear trap, and Heather had done little to prepare Louie for it. After they'd kissed,

Heather had been caught up in the date, forgetting the fact that Donny had threatened to blackball Louie across the city. She ran the conversation over in mind and realized she'd made this meeting sound like a small formality. "You can't do that!"

"What makes you think that?"

Christ, I said that out loud. The knock on the door prevented Heather from responding. Donny commanded the visitor to enter, and Louie walked in dressed in a smart shirt tucked into skinny jeans. She'd finished the outfit with a tie, and she looked amazing. Heather knew it was completely the wrong choice of clothes for a meeting with this homophobic asshole, but she was pretty certain that Louie wouldn't be seen in a skirt or dress for any amount of money. Louie grinned at Heather, and it made her smile, albeit briefly.

Donny didn't offer Louie a seat. Instead, he stood and returned to the chair behind his desk.

"You know why you're here, and I'm not one to beat around the bush. You're done, Francis."

Louie nodded. "I was under the impression I already was. I finished the album. I've only come here today as a professional courtesy."

Louie looked at Heather, and it seemed like she was holding back what she really wanted to say in response. Heather was thankful for that, but she didn't expect it to last if Donny told her what else he was planning.

"So we're done and I should go now." Louie thumbed toward the door.

"We're done, yes," said Donny. "And you're done in this town. You don't disrespect the Queen of Country and expect to work in Nashville again."

Donny pulled out a cigar and bit down on it as if he were signaling the end of the conversation. His nonchalance was outrageous, but Heather felt powerless to do anything about it.

Louie ran her hand across the back of her head. "Exactly what is it I'm supposed to have done that was so wrong?"

Donny's face fell blank, and it became clear that Savana hadn't given him any real details. She didn't need to. As far as he was concerned, it was only a matter of time before Louie did something unprofessional or unacceptable. That's what he expected of anyone who didn't fit into his narrow construct of a decent human being.

"Did she tell you that I walked in on her pinning Heather to the mixing desk and forcing herself on her?" asked Louie, her voice rising with each word.

Donny spat his cigar out onto his desk and pushed out of his chair. "What?"

His sense of absolute disbelief was tangible.

"You heard me," said Louie. She waved her hand in the direction of Savana. "Your Queen of Country was hitting on Heather and Heather wasn't interested," said Louie. "All I did was stop what might have turned into a serious sexual assault, and you're trying to ruin my career for that?"

Oh God. A rush of competing emotions and reactions struck at once. What did she expect Louie to do when threatened with being blackballed? She stood up for herself just like Heather had thought she would. But this made everything worse...for her. Heather tried to stop herself from being so selfish. At least she'd added that Heather wasn't interested and hadn't exactly outed her.

Donny tilted his head and looked at Savana. "Is that true?"

"What does it matter?"

Savana sounded defensive, and for the first time, Heather thought she saw a hint of vulnerability. It was almost enough to elicit her empathy, but Savana had brought all of this to Donny's attention. Heather wished for a device to go back in time and stop any of this from happening, but that was the stuff of sci-fi novels not real life. You got one chance on this ride and there were no reruns or rehearsals, only regrets.

Donny moved around from the back of his desk and closed in on Savana. "It matters because you sold yourself to this label as a normal woman."

Donny's wording, loaded with malice and years of prejudice, stabbed at Heather's sensitivities. This was exactly what she had desperately wanted to avoid.

"What's normal, Donny?" asked Savana. "You think you're normal? You're the gold standard of human being? God help us all if you—"

"Stop. Don't say another word," said Donny.

He looked beyond Savana at Heather. She didn't know what she should do. Mostly she wanted to leave the room, hide in her office, and wait for a resolution, preferably with her career intact.

"Heather."

"Yes, Donny," she said as she stood, no longer wanting to be the only person in the room lounging on a soft sofa.

"Is this album going to make money and what are the fans going to make of it?"

Heather nodded. "Absolutely." At least this was something she could answer honestly. "I think her die-hard fans will love it because, while it's a change in direction, it still stays true to her roots. And I think she'll garner a whole set of new fans because the sound is far more current than Savana's trademark sound."

Donny ran his hand over his mouth. "Okay. You." He pointed toward Louie. "What do you intend to do with your allegation?"

"I had no intentions until you threatened to destroy my career. I'm just defending myself. You're worried about the press," Louie said in a no-nonsense, matter-of-fact way.

"Heather, if this was leaked to the press, would you corroborate the story?"

Oh God, no. Saying the right thing and doing the thing for her career were diametrically opposed. This was a no-win situation. Louie looked at her imploringly. Heather's answer had the power to impact Louie's career. And it would definitely impact her own, one way or another. Donny was looking at her as though he shouldn't even have had to ask the question, and the longer he waited, the more his eyebrow seemed to reach for his hairline. Savana's expression was unreadable. Once again, Heather wished for the spy-like earpiece and Emma to be on the other end of it. But then she wouldn't be taking responsibility for anything that came out of her mouth. This had to be her decision because *she* was going to have to live with it. Nothing that came out of her mouth would make everyone in the room happy. She cast her eyes downward, unwilling to see the impact her words were about to have.

"No," Heather whispered. "No, I wouldn't back that story up."

"Good." Donny didn't miss a beat, almost as if he were expecting that answer. Heather hoped that meant he wasn't questioning her sexuality. "That would give it less credence. But it'd still be coming from inside the camp. People would still think there might be some truth to it." He motioned to Louie. "Get out of my office."

Louie loosened her tie. "What about your threat?"

Donny grunted. "I'll keep my mouth shut if you do, but don't darken my door again."

Louie looked across at Heather as she began to leave the office. "I can promise you won't have to worry about that."

The hurt and betrayal in her eyes was as clear as the bluest ocean. Heather mouthed "Sorry" to Louie as she opened the door, but she closed it just as swiftly and Heather wasn't sure she'd heard or seen her. Heather couldn't blame Louie if she never wanted to see or hear from her again. She'd played roulette with Louie's career for the sake of her own. Would Louie ever forgive her?

CHAPTER THIRTY-FIVE

Louie heard the knock at the front door but ignored it in favor of a slug of Blanton bourbon. It burned and she almost spit it out. She'd picked a bottle of it up from the liquor store on her way back from Rocky Top. Drowning her sorrows seemed like such a rote response to yet another betrayal, but she didn't feel strong enough to eschew the cliché. The server had complimented her choice and regaled her with some tale of how it was originally bottled for VIPs. That almost had her swapping it out for something else. She couldn't be further from feeling like an important person to anyone.

"Louie. Heather's at the door. Are you coming out?" asked Gabe.

The gentle tone of his voice stopped Louie from snapping some retort back. "No. I'm good in here, buddy. And I've got nothing to say she'll want to hear."

"Okay. I'll tell her."

She waited for Gabe's heavy-footed retreat before pouring herself her first full glass. She didn't bother with the pretense of serving a couple of fingers' worth. She wanted to either pass out or empty the bottle. She wasn't close to either and knew she didn't really have the stomach for it.

Her bedroom door swung open and Heather stood in the doorway. Gabe joined her within seconds.

"I'm sorry, Louie. She kind of pushed past me and I didn't want to stop her," he said, looking apologetic.

Louie smiled at him, knowing there was no way he'd ever lay hands on a woman even after the way his mother had treated him.

"Why are you here, Heather?" Louie swirled the bourbon in her glass a little too vigorously, and a dash of it spilled onto her jeans. She slammed the glass onto her desk and brushed it away with a muttered curse, sure the amber liquid would stain the pale denim. Her mom would know how to get it out. The thought made her wish she'd called her mom instead of wasting eighty dollars on something that she'd probably end up pouring down the sink.

"I was hoping you might like to talk." Heather looked over her shoulder at Gabe. "Alone."

Louie half-laughed and shook her head. "What would you like to talk about, Heather? Do you want to talk about how you lied to save your career? Or maybe you'd like to discuss how you threw me under the bus instead of being true to yourself?"

"I think I'll leave you to it." Gabe raised his arms in the air in mock surrender before he disappeared from view.

"What was my alternative?" Heather leaned against the doorjamb. "Tell the truth to save your career and kill mine? I was in an impossible situation, Louie. You must understand that."

"Must I?" Louie didn't bite back the rage at being treated like street trash…again. Her anger overruled her thoughts of how she'd dreamed of Heather on the threshold of her bedroom in far more conducive circumstances. She reclaimed her glass and swirled it around, still not ready to knock it back. "Why are you really here, Heather? Do you want to ease your conscience? Do you want me to forgive you and tell you that I understand? That I know you had no choice and that you wish things could be different…that you could be different?" Louie stood and put her glass on her bedside table. "I don't want to hear it. You pass yourself as straight because you can, because it's easier. You stay in the closet because you're afraid to come out and be yourself. You don't know if you'll like the real you. And if you don't like the real you, how will anyone else?" The words tumbled from Louie's mouth unchecked. She barely knew what she was saying, but she could see it was having the desired effect on Heather. She flinched at every statement like she was being struck with a whip braided with barbed wire. Her reaction spurred Louie to keep spewing. "You want me to tell you the real reason you won't start your indie label? It's not because you're waiting for the right time because there's never a right time to take a chance on building a new business from scratch. It's because you're scared you'll fail." *Here comes the home run.* "Just like you failed with your singing career."

Heather wiped her eyes and sighed. "Have you finished?" she asked, her voice faltering slightly.

"Why? Wasn't that enough?" Louie turned back to her desk. Heather's tears dampened the fire of her anger, but there was no way Louie could forgive her for what she'd done. Heather had done exactly the same as Mia. Her passion for her career outweighed her passion for Louie. It was further proof that Louie wasn't worth a damn to anybody.

"I'm not afraid of failing."

Heather's words were so quiet Louie barely heard her. Still, they made her feel like an evil witch held her heart and was squeezing it so tight she was struggling to breathe. But she tried to ignore it. She couldn't just keep giving in and expecting the result to be different. That was the definition of insanity.

"What would you have done in the same situation, Louie? Tell me that."

Louie flopped back into her chair and shook her head. "I wouldn't have put myself in that situation, Heather, because I'm true to who I am whether people like it or not." She picked up her glass, more carefully this time, and took a small sip. It tasted like warm gasoline. What the hell was the appeal? "I wouldn't have taken a job where I was expected to wear skirts and cosmetics to fit in with the crowd. I wouldn't compromise myself for my ambition. But how far will you go to keep your career on the path you've got all mapped out? Will you sleep with Savana if she threatens your career instead of mine?"

Heather pushed away from the door and stood upright. "That's too far, Louie."

"I told Gabe you wouldn't want to hear anything I had to say. Why don't you just leave and save us both this..." Louie stopped herself from saying heartache. "Trouble. None of this is worth it." *I'm not worth it.*

"No. I'm not going anywhere until we sort this out. I'm not giving up on us."

Louie got out of her chair, grabbed her leather jacket, and maneuvered by Heather. "Then I'll leave." She slammed the door as she left. It felt like she was slamming the door on their relationship too. She couldn't allow herself to go through the same thing again.

❖

The eight ball bounced back out of the pocket as if it'd been rejected. Louie felt the ball's pain. She'd hit it way too hard but didn't care that she'd effectively thrown the game she had fifty bucks riding on.

The hefty butch Louie was playing laughed, picked up the money underneath the chalk, and shoved it in her back pocket. "You better not be hustling me, kid." She took a long slug of her beer then passed it back to the long-haired brunette who was hanging on her every word.

"I've read enough lesbian BDSM stories to know doing that wouldn't end well for me," said Louie. Three beers and she'd slipped into entertainment mode effortlessly. Maybe it was because this kind of place was perfect for who she really was. She should've known her Nashville dream was exactly that—just a dream. Louie still had her job at Hawthorne Publishing House, and Donny had said he wouldn't kill her career. She could probably trust him about as far as she could spit him. She figured it'd only be a matter of time before Hawthorne dumped her. Even though this type of suffering was perfect for a songwriter, Louie wondered if she should simply let it all go and move back home.

Louie pulled at the chain attached to her wallet and produced another fifty. "Go again?"

Hefty butch's eyes sparkled at the chance of more easy money. Brunette bit her lip and squeezed her lover's sizable bicep, which Louie thought was easily the circumference of her own thigh.

"Go on, baby. You can beat her again."

Louie waved the bill in the air. "What's it gonna be, Butch?"

She studied Louie from tip to toe slowly. "Sure, why not? Loser racks 'em," said Butch.

Louie didn't miss the wink Butch threw her, or the sly smile on Brunette's lips, despite the fact that the whole room was in soft focus.

"Having fun?"

Mia. Louie took too long to decide whether or not to turn around, and she felt Mia's hand on her hip as she circled her, bringing them face-to-face. She leaned back a little and wafted her hand in front of her nose.

"Celebrating the end of your album with Savana Hayes?" asked Mia.

Louie shrugged. "Something like that." Mia would kill her own mother for the gossip Louie had. Mia would happily blackmail Savana for a shot at the big time.

Diane came into view and put her arm around Mia. "When are you going to introduce us to Savana?"

Louie grinned. All pretense of politeness had disappeared with the dregs of her fourth bottle. "Err, let's say never."

"Aw," said Mia. "Don't be like that."

She put her hand around Louie's neck, tilted her head, and nibbled on her lip just like she used to when they were together and she wanted her own way. Louie shrugged her away.

"If you don't mind? I'm playing pool." Louie moved around them and chalked her cue. Butch and Brunette looked vaguely amused.

"Catnip to the ladies, huh, kiddo?" asked Butch.

She gave Louie a shove that she figured was supposed to be gentle, but it nearly sent her flying across the pool table.

"I guess so." Louie steadied herself and bent over the table to make the break. Maybe three balls smashed into the pockets and

Butch gave her what looked like an *I warned you* stare. Louie smiled as the white ball, still rolling, dropped into the bottom pocket.

She glanced across the table to see Mia and Diane still loitering with fading intent. Louie shooed them away and turned her attention back to the table. When she looked up again, they were gone.

"Girl trouble?" asked Butch after she'd sunk another two balls.

Louie nodded. "Like you wouldn't believe."

"You know the best way to get over a girl—"

"I know, I know. Get under another one. The old clichés are still the best." Louie shook her head. "That strategy isn't going to work for me this time."

Butch shrugged. "That's a shame. My girl and I would've happily volunteered for the job."

Louie grinned. "And on another occasion, I would've happily employed you both." She swallowed against the creeping ball of sadness in her throat and ran her hand through her hair. "You okay to just play pool instead?"

Butch nodded and slapped Louie across the back hard enough to perform the Heimlich maneuver. "Abso-fucking-lutely, kid."

Louie lost count of the games she lost before she sank into a sofa, defeated, and was sandwiched by them both. She raised her current bottle of beer. "I'll finish this one, then I'm hitting the road." She tapped her phone in her pocket.

Butch shook her head. "No need for an Uber, kiddo. We'll take you home."

CHAPTER THIRTY-SIX

Heather checked her phone again then looked at the email from Mia on her iPad. The subject line read "Told you to be careful with this one." She could see it had an attachment, but she hadn't opened it yet. Something told her it was about Louie, like Mia couldn't wait to gloat or give her some gossip to ruin her day. When Louie had left her last night, she didn't know her well enough to have any kind of guess as to where she might go—by the river, to a park. Her least favorite option was a bar or club. If Mia's email *was* anything to do with Louie, the last choice seemed most likely. Heather had spent the past painful hours at her own house, worried sick about all the possibilities. It wasn't like her to be so much of an Eeyore, and it wasn't like Louie had driven, but she couldn't help thinking that the worst could happen. Gabe's text had come in around three a.m. and simply said, *Home safe.*

It didn't say if she was alone and Heather didn't ask. It wasn't her place to question what Louie was up to…or who she was with. And yet, the thought of her with someone else felt like a spur digging into her side.

She hovered her finger over the email, desperate to know what kind of woman Louie was in the heat of an argument. Louie had shown her anger last night, and Heather certainly didn't begrudge her that. And though Louie's words stung, she deserved everything Louie had said and probably a whole lot more that she didn't stick around to say.

Had she already lost her? Louie wasn't really hers in the first place. They'd only had one date. One amazing and perfect date in a dream location. And though things had gotten hot and heavy fast in Louie's truck, there was no judgment in her eyes when Heather told her she wouldn't be coming in to finish what they'd started. It was a decision Heather found herself regretting now. At least if Louie was really done with her, she would've had the memories of one night to keep her warm in her still-empty bed.

Because ambition was a cold mistress. It didn't wrap protective arms around her, kiss her neck, and tell her she was the most precious thing in the world. And what did success mean if she had no one to share it with, no one to go home to every night? Over the past five years, Heather had told herself so many times that she didn't need anyone and that she was fine by herself. She didn't want to buy into the whole human evolution pair-bonding theory. Why was society so obsessed with finding the "one?" Why couldn't there be more than one? Why did there have to be anyone at all? Heather strove to be self-sufficient and dependent on no one, and yet here she was, wondering why she'd chosen her career over someone she'd felt a deep and natural connection to. And why wasn't it possible to have both?

She touched her finger to the screen and then pulled away as if it had burned her. Mia rambled on about being sorry for sharing, but that she felt like she had to because Heather was her friend. Heather shook her head. They weren't friends. They were barely acquaintances. Heather knew exactly the kind of person Mia was and she wanted none of it. She had no idea why someone as sweet as Louie would fall for such a…Heather sighed. Mia was driven by ambition and overwhelmed by thoughts of success. Just like her. Maybe that's why Louie had pursued Heather. Maybe that was the kind of woman she couldn't help falling for. And maybe that's why Louie had pushed her away so hard. She didn't want to repeat mistakes of the past and get hurt.

Hurting Louie was the last thing Heather had in mind. After their date, Heather had dared to allow herself to think about how being with Louie would be. And all she could imagine were good things. The only stumbling block was Heather's unwillingness to be...herself. Be out. To say, *this is me*, and screw the consequences. Wasn't that kind of personal happiness worth far more than her career?

Heather downloaded and opened both attachments. A lasso caught on her heart and tightened. Louie. Playing pool and looking sexy as all hell with a couple who were obviously together. Louie. Walking out of the bar sandwiched between the same couple, arms all around each other. What was it about lesbians and threesomes?

She thought about calling Emma, but she already knew what she'd say—who could blame Louie for finding herself some action after Heather had left her hanging in the wind? She could hear her saying, "I would have done exactly the same...in fact, I have. Several times." Emma was Heather's very own Jiminy Cricket and little devil combined, but she didn't need her to tell Heather she'd made a mistake. Ice-cold fingers already gripped her conscience.

Heather picked up her phone and quickly thumbed a text.

I hope you had a good time last night. I...

No, that sounds snarky.

I wish you'd stayed to talk last night. I was wrong to expect you to understand why I did what I did. I was wrong to do what I did. I hope you can forgive me. Call me x

She deleted and added the kiss three times before she left it and hit send. She watched it say *delivered*. She was surprised to see it *read* just as quickly. Heather waited for the bubbles she'd enjoyed seeing while they'd played with each other over text in the past couple of weeks.

None came.

She didn't count how many times she revisited the screen while she was getting ready for work, but it was a lot. On no occasion were there any bubbles.

Louie tossed her phone back on the bedside table and rolled over. Her mouth felt like the inside of a birdcage, her head was like someone had used it for a bass drum, and her guts were rumbling louder than a freight train. She hadn't had this kind of hangover in years. But all of it faded into insignificance when she listened to the pain in her heart and head. What was Heather really saying by admitting she was wrong? That now she'd back Louie up if she decided to go to the press? Or did she think that just saying she was wrong would make Louie hit the reset button and start again?

She turned over and checked the time. It was way too early. Louie had only been in bed a few hours. Heather would be on her way to work, business as usual. She wondered if Heather would think of her when she went to get her morning coffee. She smiled at the thought, but it quickly faded when she wondered if Heather would be working with Savana. Louie didn't think that Heather's apology would come with a promise not to work with the Queen of Country anymore, and it wasn't realistic to expect it to. Heather had a career to think about. Her behavior at Rocky Top yesterday showed that it might be all she thought about, and Louie just couldn't handle that.

She saw her phone and remembered Butch and Brunette had driven her home in their car. She looked down to see she was still in a tank and shorts and wondered which one of them had undressed her. Louie wished she'd remembered their names. She was sure they'd told her, but she'd been way too messed up to retain them. She *did* remember that Mia and Diane were at the bar, and she allowed herself a small smile when she recalled that she'd blown them off. As much as she was hurting, that had felt damn good. It was nice to be over Mia…even if she had fallen straight into another heartache.

Louie picked up her phone and dismissed Heather's text message. She had no idea what she wanted to say or if she wanted to say anything at all. Everything that had come out of her mouth last night had been pretty brutal. Louie felt entitled to that outburst, but she had no desire to go at it again. What she needed was her mom.

"Hey, Noodle, you're up early."

Louie was soothed by her mom's voice, but it made her wish she was wrapped up in her arms too. She wanted to hear everything would be okay…one day. "Not by choice, Mom. Heather woke me early with a text."

"And how are you two lovebirds?" her mom asked.

Lovebirds. Parrots that mated for life. Is that what Louie was looking for and might never find? "I'm pretty sure we don't qualify for that title," said Louie, unable to stop the regret in her voice. She didn't know why her mom had jumped to that conclusion in the few conversations they'd had when Louie had mentioned Heather... unless she'd given away some hidden, deeper feelings.

"Talk to me. What's happened?"

Louie gave her mom an honest rundown of the events on Friday and their fabulous date on Saturday. She told her all about Heather throwing her under the bus to protect her own career and then coming around the same day, not to apologize but to seek Louie's understanding. And she rounded off the tale of the bar and Heather's text apology moments ago.

"And how has all that made you feel right now, in this moment?" asked her mom.

Louie closed her eyes and could see herself sitting at the kitchen table, both hands in her mom's and an earnest look in her mom's eyes. A calm settled over her that only her mom could instill. "Angry."

"No. You were angry last night. How do you feel right now?"

Louie dropped her shoulders and sighed. Her mom had a way of cutting through the surface crap. "Faded. Like my life has less color in it because I've pushed her away."

"Did you like this one?"

Louie pushed her head back into the pillow, not wanting to give the answer but not wanting to lie either. "Sure I did. I thought she was special."

"What are you going to do about it?"

"Nothing. I'll get over her...eventually." The words sounded hollow and unconvincing, so her mom was bound to know it was bull.

"Louie, don't you remember the inspiration for your name came from the first lady of NASCAR, Louise Smith? And what did she say?"

Her mom's use of her name instead of her pet name meant she'd brook no nonsense. This was why Louie had called her. She needed objectivity from the person who knew her best of all. Her mom had always helped her navigate the shark-infested waters of her over-emotional brain. "You can't reach for anything new if your hands are full of yesterday's junk." Louie knew the quote word for word. It had been her mom's mantra as Louie was growing up. They needed it with the cards they'd been dealt. "But I can't just forgive her, Mom. If Donny wasn't paranoid about the damage an unsubstantiated claim would make, he could've ended my career with a few carefully placed phone calls."

"I know, Noodle, and that sucks. But talk about a rock and a hard place. If she had backed you up, it sounds like it would've ended *her* career. There was no decision she could've made that would have been right for both of you."

"But, Mom—"

"No, Louie, no buts. There are no guarantees in this life. Who knows what you would've done in the same situation."

"I guess," said Louie, but she wasn't fully convinced. She was sure that with the tables turned, she would've backed Heather.

"You're lucky that you're so comfortable with who you are and don't care what people think—"

"Thanks again for that." Louie had her mom to thank for being so at peace with who she was, and she felt for those who didn't have that. She'd somehow lost sight of that with Heather, but that didn't make it any easier to accept.

"It was a pleasure raising you, baby. But you told me before that people had been fired from Heather's label for being gay, so it's little wonder that she's keeping her sexuality under wraps. I'd love for the world to be an all-inclusive place, but it isn't and it may never be. And Heather's working within the parameters of that at one of the biggest labels in the city. So what are you going to do, Noodle?"

"I'm going to reply to her text and meet up to talk about it?"

"Don't ask me, tell me. Noodle, you don't want regrets. You've got to live like you were dying. You know I've always said that. But…"

Louie laughed. "After all that, there's a but?"

"*But* you deserve someone who treats you right, too. I don't think you can take this incident as any indication of future behavior, but you make sure she doesn't think she can treat you like the other one did."

Louie smiled at the way her mom referred to Mia. The other one. Because there'd only ever been one as far as her mom knew. "Okay. I get it."

"Good. I love you, Noodle. You deserve the world."

Louie ran her hand through her hair. "I love you, Mom. I can't wait to see you for the holiday."

"I'll be there."

Louie hung up the phone and scrolled back to Heather's text.

Okay. Let's talk. Meet u at TJ's, South Nashville Fairground at 9 tonight.

She tossed her phone under her pillow and pulled the comforter over her head. Forgiveness was a wonderful concept until you had to give it.

CHAPTER THIRTY-SEVEN

Tim held the door open for Heather and Emma to enter. Heather hadn't seen Louie's truck in the parking lot and she was fifteen minutes early, making her glad she hadn't come alone. They ordered at the bar, then chose a booth midway through the main bar area. Heather surveyed the room without making eye contact and tried not to look like she was cruising.

"Do you want us to leave you alone now or do you want us to wait until Louie comes?" Emma draped her arm over Tim's shoulder and sipped her wine.

"Would you stay? I'd feel strange sitting here by myself with you guys across the room." Heather didn't want to be by herself. She'd heard nothing from Louie after confirming tonight's... meeting? She guessed it wasn't a date, but at least Louie had agreed to see her again.

Emma winked and squeezed Heather's arm. "Of course, Feathers. We'll stay in case she stands you up."

Heather pulled away and scowled at Emma. "Thanks. I really needed that. Especially when it's a distinct possibility that she will."

Emma lightly tapped Heather's hand. "Don't be so defeatist. Louie's not stupid. She knows she shouldn't let you go."

"Let you go where?" asked Louie when she walked up, her hands shoved deep in her pockets.

Heather had gotten so used to her soft, melodic tones that hearing her speak had become addictive. But there was a harsh edge to her voice tonight that repeated and echoed Heather's betrayal.

"Nothing," said Emma. "It doesn't matter. We were just keeping her company until the main act arrived."

Emma slid out of the booth and gave Louie a hug as if they were friends. Louie looked awkward, and Heather saw her use one arm to half-hug Emma back. Tim did the cool dude nod in Louie's direction, and she returned it with a dyke style that made Heather twitch down south. She'd always admired that kind of outward, screw-you-all confidence that butch women strutted so naturally, like it had been handed out at birth along with their sexuality.

Emma and Tim drifted away, and before Louie had settled in opposite, a server was at their table.

"What can I get you tonight, Louie?" she asked in a heavy Georgia accent.

Heather thumbed the lipstick away from the edge of her glass, trying not to react to the familiarity the server had for Louie. How often did you have to come to a place like this before they knew your name?

"Bud Light Lime please, Ness," said Louie and looked at Heather. "Do you need a top up?" Heather shook her head. "Thanks, Ness."

Louie smiled and it reminded Heather what she'd lost. "You must come here a lot for her to know your name." Heather gave herself a mental shin kick. She sounded all shades of jealous and possessive.

"It's one of the benefits of belonging in a community. People get to know your name and they look out for you."

Heather didn't respond and they sat silently. Louie's words set the tone for the rest of the evening. And whether or not she meant it that way, it felt like a shot at Heather's lack of willingness to engage with the LGBTQ community.

The server returned with a Bud and a glass covered in ice.

"I'd kept a glass on ice ready for you," she said.

Heather's jealousy ramped up a notch, and she enjoyed a mental image of slapping the server six ways to Sunday.

"That's sweet of you, Ness. Thanks." Louie placed a ten on her tray. "Keep the change."

Louie rubbed at the etched glass on her bottle, and it reminded Heather of the old-style paper labels people would pick off because they were bored. Was Louie bored already?

"Thanks for agreeing to meet me, Louie. I was worried about you last night."

Louie took a drink of her beer and set it on the table. "I had to leave because you wouldn't."

That struck Heather like a high heel to her chest. If anything had happened to Louie last night, it would have been her fault because she'd run her out of her own house. "I'm sorry about that. I should never have barged in or expected you to listen to what I wanted to say."

Louie shook her head. "No. You shouldn't."

Heather rubbed imaginary dirt from her glass. Louie was making this tough, but what had she expected? For Louie to forgive everything and pull her into a deep kiss? Heather drifted to the kisses they'd shared in Louie's truck just a few days ago. She wanted to taste Louie's lips again. She *had* to make this right. "I'm sorry for what I did, Louie. I gambled with your career and I had no idea how it would turn out." Heather glanced at Louie to see if her words were making any difference, but she couldn't read her at all. "It was selfish, and I don't expect you to understand or accept why I did it."

Louie's expression appeared to soften, but it might've been wishful thinking. Heather took the small silence as an opportunity to have a drink of much-needed wine. If Louie didn't give her some indication of forgiveness, she'd be wanting a damn sight more than a glass to comfort her.

"I understand why you did it, Heather," said Louie softly. "It's not the way I would've done it, but we're very different people..." She took another long draw on her beer. "You're an amazing woman, and you've got a lot of ambition." Louie held up her hand to stop Heather from interrupting. "And that's great. I've got dreams too. We're just going about them in two very different ways."

Heather waited in case there was more. She wanted there to be more. She wanted to hear Louie say that she didn't care about those differences and that they could give their relationship a try anyway. Hell, maybe it'd work because they were so different.

But Louie said nothing else and just kept sipping on her beer.

"Did you have a good time last night?" asked Heather, barely able to keep her voice from trembling. For some reason she felt confident that Louie hadn't done anything with the women at the bar, but she wanted to hear it from Louie.

Louie raised her eyebrows. "I had a few too many drinks, played some pool, and made some new friends. Nothing more. I was hurt, not horny. Somebody tell you something different?"

"Mia sent pictures, Louie. It's impossible to do anything in this town without someone seeing and misinterpreting it. That's what I'm frightened of." Heather's moat bridge was beginning to rise in reaction to Louie's apparent indifference. Withdrawing had always been her go-to defense. Louie emptied her beer and motioned to the server for another one. She was staying a little longer, at least. Hope fired a spark in the dying embers of Heather's dreams of their relationship. "She was trying to convince me you'd had a threesome."

Louie's laughter seemed out of place, but Heather took it happily. It was a sound she was sure she'd never tire of.

"With a big butch and a sexy little femme?" asked Louie and a playful smirk emerged.

"Yep."

"That's not me, Heather, and it looks like you know that. Mia can't help herself."

Louie sounded hurt, and Heather wished she could just hold her and make all of this go away. "I do know that. You were angry and you had every right to be."

Louie rubbed the back of her head, then rolled her shoulders. "I was hurt."

Knowing she caused the look in Louie's eyes drove a spike through Heather's heart. The neon window sign glistened in them, and she looked on the verge of tears. Heather just wanted to start afresh.

Heather reached over and placed her hand over Louie's. "I'm sorry, Louie…again. Tell me what I need to do to make this right." She'd beg if she had to.

Louie let go of her beer and put her other hand on top of Heather's. "And what about this? Are you going to be okay to do this out on the streets? Or would I only get your affection when we're safely away from spying eyes?"

Heather began to withdraw her hand but stayed put because it felt so good. "I thought you understood."

Louie nodded. "I do. But it doesn't mean I can live like that. I thought I might be able to, but when you pulled away from me at the Birdcat because you thought you might be seen, you may as well have pushed the sharp end of a shovel through my chest." Louie traced light patterns on Heather's hand. "I want to be with you, but I don't think I can compromise myself that much anymore. And I've only just recovered from being betrayed by Mia for her career. I can't keep walking the same path. I have to be who I am…and you have to be who you are."

Heather pulled her hand away and closed her eyes to keep from crying. When she opened them to see Louie's lip trembling slightly, her control slipped away, and she let her tears fall. This was letting go when no one actually wanted to. This was a sacrifice made for a career. Was it worth it?

Louie moved to get out of the booth, and Heather grabbed her arm.

"Please don't go. Neither of us want to say good-bye," said Heather, just managing the sentence before the ball of pain in her chest choked her words.

Louie took Heather's hand and kissed her knuckles. "That may be, Heather, but we both know what we *do* want. Life is a jigsaw, and right now, our pieces don't fit together."

Louie let go and walked away, leaving Heather with unchecked tears ruining her mascara. Makeup was easy to fix. If only the same could be said of her life. Letting Louie go could be the greatest mistake of her life.

CHAPTER THIRTY-EIGHT

Over a week had passed since Louie had seen Heather. Gabe had collected the little bit of gear she had at Rocky Top. He said Heather had asked after Louie and looked "forlorn," whatever the hell that looked like. She'd received a text not long after Gabe returned. *Can we at least be friends? I miss you.* Louie hadn't responded. It still hurt too much to think about. "I Won't Be a Whisper" had soared straight to number one on the Hot Country Billboard within a day of its Friday release and had hit over one hundred thousand downloads. No doubt Donny was happy his cash cow hadn't been ruined by a scandal over her sexuality. It was the fastest selling song of the year, and whenever Louie turned on a radio, got into her truck, or went into any shop or bar, she heard Savana's voice and her lyrics. As much as she loathed Savana, she had to admit it sounded amazing. And her distaste was offset by the mechanical and performance royalties already beyond twenty thousand. She hadn't received a check yet, but she'd already flown her mom over early for the Fourth of July. Gabe's dad was visiting too, and they'd both arrived that morning so it'd been a crazy few hours of airport runs.

Louie had spent the week helping Gabe with a Kickstarter campaign to raise money for studio time and a producer for his EP, and he was halfway to his target. His popularity on his Facebook page had rocketed, and he'd managed to get over half a million views on the music videos they'd made together. It was happening for him, and he was doing it his own way, without the backing of traditional Nashville avenues. Louie wished that Heather could've seen a path to her own journey that way. Maybe then Louie wouldn't be so lonely. And she'd have someone to share *her* first success in Nashville.

"Are you ready?" asked Gabe, knocking on Louie's open bedroom door as he walked through to the living room.

"Sure am." Louie picked up her guitar and joined him. His dad, Daryn, and her mom were on the couch laughing over baby pictures of her and Gabe. "Come on, Daryn. Time to see your son in action."

Daryn rose from his chair and helped Louie's mom emerge from the deep sofa.

"I've been waiting for this moment for a decade." Daryn smiled at Gabe and motioned toward the door. "After you."

The trip to the Head Cayce studio was quick and painless. Louie parked her truck on the street and fed the meter before following Daryn, Gabe, and her mom inside. The receptionist settled them into tracking room three and introduced Gabe's producer for the EP.

"Thank you for flying me out to see this, Noodle. I'm so excited to hear your lyrics and listen to you play."

"Thanks, Mom." Louie lifted her Les Paul from its case by the neck. "None of this would ever have happened without your support."

Her mom shook her head. "You did this by yourself, Noodle. I just helped along the way."

Louie smiled at her mom's humility. She'd probably never grasp just how important she'd been to keeping Louie going through all the hard times, and there'd been a *lot* of hard times. How her mom had kept going herself, let alone be such an awesome mom, amazed her every time Louie thought about it.

"Y'all ready to go?" asked Gabe's producer.

"Sure thing." Gabe clapped Louie on the shoulder. "Wait till you hear this, Dad. This is the first song Louie and I wrote together, and it's for you. It's called 'Bronzed Baby Shoes.'"

Daryn surprised Louie when he pulled them both into a bear hug. "You're like family, Louie. Gabe hasn't shut up about you since you two met. You were there for him at a tough time, and I really appreciate that."

Louie sank into the arms of Daryn and Gabe. So this was what having a real Dad felt like. Not that she felt like she'd missed out. Her mom had given her everything she could and more. Daryn released them, and Louie followed Gabe to the recording zone.

They knocked out three slightly different versions of the song before the producer suggested they take a quick break and listen to some playback. Louie went back into the mixing area and could see both Daryn and her mom were barely holding it together.

"That was beautiful."

Gabe grinned at his dad. "Are you proud of me?"

Daryn pushed up from his seat and hugged Gabe again. "I've always been proud of you, son. I'm just glad everyone else on this planet is going to get to know what a wonderful man you've become."

Louie swallowed past the gigantic lump in her throat and looked up to the ceiling to prevent her own tears from falling. It was such an intimate moment, she felt a little voyeuristic. A quick glance in her mom's direction told her she felt the same.

"Shall we go grab some lunch for everyone?" Louie motioned to the door.

Gabe pulled out of his dad's arms. "Poor Louie. Showing emotions is just too hard for you to cope with, isn't it, buddy?"

Gabe's words were closer to the truth than he realized, maybe more than Louie did too. She'd always been open to experiencing emotion, even when it hurt like it did with Mia. And Heather felt like history repeating itself. But she wondered if she'd actually pulled away when it really mattered, when things didn't run smoothly, so she wasn't completely destroyed. Was that a simple case of self-preservation or was it counterintuitive, resulting in an inability to truly let go?

"Gabe told me about your girl," said Daryn as he sat back on the sofa beside her mom.

Louie clenched her jaw, not sure where the segue was that connected the two. "Unfortunately, she's not my girl anymore."

Louie thought about the wonderful date they'd shared and the hot make-out session in her truck. So much promise and passion. And yet Louie had let it slip through her grasp like wind through silk. For what? Her high-and-mighty beliefs about being true to yourself? Who was she to impose them on anyone else? She stopped herself. She wasn't imposing them on anyone, she just wasn't prepared to stop living them herself. "I guess she never really was."

Her mom poked her in the thigh from her seat on the couch. "I thought you were going to talk to her?"

Louie sighed, not sure she wanted to have this conversation with all of them but not wanting to be rude. "I did. But we want to live our lives different ways, Mom. I won't hide, and Heather is convinced she has to, at least for now." Louie had spent restless hours when she should have been sleeping, hoping that maybe Heather would start her record label sooner than she'd planned. Maybe then they could be together. It was more than a feeling; it was a deep-seated yearning to reclaim the connection she'd felt when she was with Heather. But a little hope was a very dangerous thing. How long would she allow herself to wait and dream and wish for something that might never happen?

"And you think there's no compromise in between?" Daryn looked at her seriously.

"Does there always have to be compromise?" Louie crossed her arms and leaned against the mixing desk.

Daryn and her mom laughed, but Louie didn't get the joke. Why did everyone assume that being older resulted in being wiser? Gabe looked at her and shrugged apologetically. She raised her eyebrow at him. Apology not accepted.

"There's compromise in every relationship, whether you're talking about lovers or brothers," said Daryn. "The best relationships don't even realize or care that they're compromising because the end result is what's important."

What would compromise look like? Was Louie being shortsighted about a potential future with Heather? She'd said that she planned to have her label within the next two years. Was that too long? Wasn't Heather worth the wait? Louie had happily waited a month before they could even have a date. And Louie would've waited six times that long for the kisses they'd shared in her truck that night. Two years wasn't a lifetime. So what if they didn't go out to the bars parading their relationship to everyone else? Would it be so bad to stay home making love, eating home-cooked meals, watching action movies, and getting a little chubby?

But what would Heather be compromising? Or would she get the best of both worlds—her ambitions and her home life fulfilled? Would that be so bad? Still, the fact that Heather had cast her aside in favor of her career was still on her mind. It was like a hole in her mouth after a wisdom tooth had been removed; she couldn't stop tonguing it. The more attention she gave it, the less likely it would be to heal.

She looked up to see all three of them watching her intently. She guessed she'd been off in her head long enough to make it weird. Louie half-turned to the mixing desk and hit play, then looked back at them all. "Didn't the producer want you to listen to your song?"

Gabe smiled and clapped silently behind his dad's back. So it wasn't a masterful change of subject and she'd just proven his point completely. But she didn't want to make a decision this intense by committee. "We'll talk later, Mom." Right now she wanted to immerse herself in Gabe's music and help make his EP a smash. He had everything riding on it, and he had to be her focus, not Heather.

Heather would have to wait…unless she'd accepted they were through and had already moved on to Savana. She was better for Heather's ambitions; they could be closeted career girls together. She pushed that thought away like a catwalk model would discard a decent meal. She had to trust in her destiny, and that just might be the hardest thing she'd ever had to do in her life.

Chapter Thirty-Nine

Heather waited in line for her pre-work wake-up drink. She didn't try to stop her mind from drifting to Louie and how she'd remembered exactly how Heather liked her coffee. Her mind had been drifting to thoughts of Louie every spare moment *and* all the times in between when she really shouldn't let it. "Right now, our pieces don't fit." Louie's soft parting words had become an earworm she couldn't shut down. She'd decided to focus on the "right now" part. It seemed like it was a hint that Louie hadn't kicked Heather out of her heart completely. And as each Louie-less day had passed with her texts unanswered, Heather became more convinced that Louie's heart was exactly where she wanted to be.

Problem was, her work situation hadn't changed and there was little likelihood that it would. She had a plan for her label, and she was further along it than she could've imagined, partly thanks to Savana, but breaking out on her own was scary. Saying good-bye to the security of a monthly paycheck and hello to debts and uncertainty was going to take some preparation.

She came out of the elevator to see Savana and a selection of groupies surrounding her, fawning about her new success. Savana motioned to Heather to wait, and she shooed away her entourage.

"Can we talk?" she asked, but she was already moving toward an empty office.

Heather followed anyway. There was no point denying her. Now that the dust had settled, her album was recorded, and she was number one on the charts and at Rocky Top, Heather had no choice but to play nice. Savana closed the door behind her so Heather pulled up the blinds. She tried not to make it obvious but figured she'd probably failed. At least she wouldn't be giving Savana confusing signals this way. If Savana spotted it, she didn't react.

"You should know that I was thinking about coming out, Heather. This whole album was about preparing the ground. That's why Joe was walking around looking so pissed all the time. He was worried my career would go the same way as Caren White's."

Heather hadn't seen that coming. Louie called it, but Heather had been oblivious. She wanted to call her and tell her she was right, but Louie probably wouldn't pick up. She brought herself back to the present and considered Savana's words. They sounded like she'd changed her mind. "And what about now? Your first single looks like it's heading toward platinum, maybe even diamond at the rate it's going. Would now be a good time?"

Savana tapped the desk with her nails. "I can't do it, Heather. There's never going to be a good time for me. I can't let go of everything I've worked so hard to build."

Heather swallowed hard. The similarities between her and Savana were unpleasant to realize. "So you're going to continue living behind closed doors?" The question was as much to herself as it was to Savana.

Savana frowned and let out a small laugh. "That sounds awfully judgmental, particularly coming from someone in exactly the same position."

Heather smiled tightly. She couldn't argue against Savana's logic. "You're right. I get it."

"Then maybe you'd like to come around to the house soon? I could show you my home studio."

The way Savana had raised her eyebrows and smiled indicated she was talking about making a different kind of music. "Thanks… but I can't." Just because she couldn't have Louie didn't mean she'd changed her mind about Savana and would jump into her bed and hide with her.

Savana stood a little straighter. "Because of Louie?" she asked with an unmissable edge.

The way Savana said Louie's name made her want to pluck out her disrespectful tongue. "Please, Savana. We have to work together."

Savana shook her head. "No. No, we don't, Heather." Savana opened the door. "I'll be asking for another exec as soon as Donny gets in today."

Heather shrugged. "Whatever you need to do, Savana." Heather walked out and headed for her office, her heart pounding. She hated confrontation, and she had no idea what else Savana might be capable of, but she wouldn't be forced into a relationship just because Savana wanted it. It was time someone said no to her.

She heard her desk phone ringing as she approached her office and tried a little jog to get to it before the caller hung up. She tripped on her heels and almost ate it. She managed to catch hold of her door handle and steady herself with one hand. She even managed not to spill her coffee. "Damn you, Donny," she muttered, wishing she could wear slightly smaller heels to work.

She grabbed the phone. "Heather King."

"Heather, it's Mandie. Are you okay? You sound breathless."

"Yeah, just my wardrobe disagreeing with my sense of balance," said Heather. "What can I do for you?"

"Lexi Turner's here. She'd like you to come up to Donny's office immediately."

Lexi Turner owned the company that owned Rocky Top and several other labels on Music Row. Heather had been modeling her own career on Lexi's steady rise to the top. She pursed her lips and took a breath. "Please tell me I'm not walking into another crisis."

"Well...I don't know if you'd use that word for this particular instance."

It was clear from Mandie's phrasing that she couldn't talk properly so Heather guessed that either Donny or Lexi or both were hanging over her. "Not a problem. I'll be there in five minutes."

Heather replaced the receiver and retrieved her coffee. She took a sip, but it was already cold so she left it in her office. She armed herself with her iPad, feeling like she might need a protective barrier between her and Donny. God only knew what this problem could be.

Mandie greeted Heather with a wink and a smile and ushered her into Donny's office. It wasn't what she was expecting. Five years working under Donny Taylor had taught her only bad things came from being summoned to his office.

Lexi, looking as glamorous in a Calvin Klein skirt suit as she did in all the magazine features Heather had seen of her, stood from behind Donny's desk and came around to greet her. Lexi reached out to shake Heather's hand, and when she let her tight grip go, Heather flexed her hand to make sure it was still in one piece.

"Please, sit down." Lexi motioned to the sofa behind Heather.

She did, and Lexi joined her. Donny's absence loomed larger than he would if he were there. "Is Donny in the restroom?"

"I should flush him down the toilet. But no. He's not." Lexi leaned back on the sofa and crossed her legs. "I've fired the idiot."

Her frankness was refreshing but terrifying. Had she been called up here to be the next one to clear out her desk? Although by the looks of his office, Donny hadn't even been given the time to do that. "Oh." It was the only response that seemed professional and appropriate. Jumping up and doing an impromptu dance on the glass coffee table certainly wasn't.

"He was an ass. And he was using my funds to pay for sex workers. I'm not a fan of that."

Lexi spoke in punches. Each sentence was short and sharp, like she almost didn't want to waste her breath speaking at all. Her presence made Heather want to take up as little of her space and time as possible. It was clear how she'd developed such a hard-ass reputation.

"I didn't know anything about that. I'm really sorry." Heather perched on the edge of the couch, ready to bolt as soon as Lexi just got it out and fired her too.

"I know that. I wanted you in here to talk about taking his job."

Heather froze like she'd been stunned by a venomous puffer fish. She'd heard wrong. Hadn't she? She pulled a strand of hair away from her eyes and tucked it behind her ear. "Sorry...what?" She didn't want to sound like a moron, but she was sure she'd misunderstood what Lexi just said.

"It's a shock. I get that. But I've been following your career, Heather." Lexi patted Heather on the knee. "I see myself in you two decades ago. You're ready to head a label. This one."

Heather ran her hand over her face as if to wipe away the shock. "Wow. That's amazing...thank you so much." Heather struggled to believe what was happening. Another big break. This was huge. And she had no one to share it with.

Lexi smiled. "I heard how you handled the Savana Hayes issue. That impressed me."

Heather's sudden high was tempered by the recollection of her betrayal to Louie. If that had contributed to her getting this job, it was like getting a new car home and finding a deep scratch in the bodywork. "Savana's our top artist. I know we have to make sure she's happy."

Lexi tilted her head a little. "She wanted something you didn't want to give though, didn't she?"

Heather looked away, unable to maintain eye contact with Lexi's penetrating stare and responded with a small shrug.

"It's okay. I know where you're coming from. There are more of us in this business than you could ever imagine."

"You're..." Heather began the question for confirmation but stopped herself. It didn't seem like a question she should ever ask of anyone in a professional situation.

But Lexi nodded. "I'm gay and in the closet, just like Savana and you. There's no room in country for us. We have to stick together."

Heather blinked hard as a realization knocked her on her ass. Lexi was a multi-millionaire, with numerous labels and other companies to her name. She'd been at the top of the business for over a decade. And yet, she still hadn't come out. All that money hadn't bought her the freedom she clearly craved. What if Heather never had the courage to come out? She could easily take this job and continue building her reputation. As label head at Rocky Top, she could sign the acts she wanted without personal financial risk. If she was successful, would there even be a need or desire to start her own label? Or would it fade as quickly as her bank balance grew?

Would she settle in to a comfortable closet of her own, amongst other prominent women in the industry who weren't, as Louie would put it, true to themselves? Would that be her version of the LGBTQ community Louie was so proud to be a part of? Would she forget all about her own dream to be an independent label head? And with it, the opportunity to be herself without censorship, without fear, without barriers?

Suddenly, everything Louie said made sense, and the impact of the monumental mistake she'd made threatened to swallow her up like a school of fish in a whale. Regret wrapped around her heart and squeezed without mercy.

"I'm sorry, Lexi. I have to go." Heather stood and offered her hand to the big boss, who looked like a stunned goat. "Thank you for the opportunity, but I can't take it. I have to be..." God, she wished Louie was here for this. "I have to be true to myself."

CHAPTER FORTY

Heather's text arrived just as Louie and her mom had finished talking about regrets and missed opportunities. A life well-worn was made of a patchwork of mistakes, but regrets tugged on your trousers like an irritating child wanting candy. Heather's timing was damn near perfect.

"I'm going to the Bluebird, Mom. Don't wait up."

Louie kissed her smiling mom good-bye, grabbed her keys, and headed out the door. It was Friday night and the line for the Bluebird ran across the strip mall as far as the bank. Louie quickly thumbed a text to let Heather know she was working on getting in and joined the back of the line. Moments later, Heather was striding toward her with a wide grin. She took Louie by the hand, walked her beyond the thirty people before her, and into the Bluebird. She didn't let go until they got to the bar, and Louie felt the loss instantly.

Heather still hadn't said a word to her. "So…hi." Louie tugged at the back of Heather's blouse while she was busy ordering drinks.

Heather turned, took hold of Louie's T-shirt, and pulled her close enough that Louie could see the dark flecks in her eyes.

"Hi, handsome." Heather leaned in even closer and kissed Louie, deep and hard.

Louie reached out for the barstool to steady herself, taken aback by the force of her advance. Heather released her and offered her a bottle. Louie accepted, but she didn't want to wash away the taste of that kiss with beer.

Louie motioned to the vast array of country's movers and shakers dotted around the room. "Not that I'm complaining, but unless you covered us with an invisibility cloak while I wasn't looking, you just outed yourself in Nashville's most classic country bar."

Heather grinned and shrugged. "I've been thinking about what you said, and I don't want to hide anymore. And I definitely don't want to hide *you*...if you can forgive me for being such a selfish ass."

Heather's smile grew wider and Louie's heart swelled in direct proportion. Was this really happening? This wasn't the compromise Louie had come here prepared to accept; this was Heather going all out to meet Louie where she stood. "Just to see you smile...I'd do anything."

"Even forgive such an epic betrayal?" Heather slipped her arms around Louie's waist and kissed her chest.

"You can't ever do that to me again." Louie placed her finger beneath Heather's chin and gently tipped it up so that Heather looked up to her. "Do you understand?"

Heather nodded. "I'm going to take you home and show you exactly how much I want to understand all of you."

Louie's clit twitched at Heather taking control. Strong feminine women had always been Louie's Achilles' heel; they weakened her in the best possible way. Louie wanted to sink into Heather's perfectly-manicured hands and bend to her every will. The room went slightly dark as Louie's eyes half-lidded, a sure-fire giveaway of her arousal.

Louie put her untouched beer back on the bar and wrapped her hand around the back of Heather's neck. Her long, silken hair caressed Louie's skin with passionate promise. "There is nothing I want more."

Heather took Louie's other hand, led her back out of the Bluebird, and across the parking lot to her car.

"I'll bring you back to pick your truck up in the morning." Heather pushed Louie against her car, pressed her body to Louie's, and kissed her again. "Or maybe tomorrow night. I might not let you out of bed until then."

Louie almost laughed. Heather was being everything she'd imagined she would be…everything Louie wanted in a woman.

❖

Louie took the time to watch Heather move as she unlocked her apartment door. Her hand shook slightly as she found the keyhole in the dim light. She turned and smiled, before she pulled Louie in and closed the door behind them. There were lit candles everywhere, leading a runway around the living room and, Louie guessed by how she was being guided, toward the bedroom.

"You really shouldn't leave candles on when you're out," said Louie, only marginally worried and mainly teasing. "You could start a fire."

Heather turned and pressed Louie against the hallway wall. "You've already done that." She took Louie's hand and placed it over her heart. "Right here." She turned away again and pulled Louie into the open doorway and Heather's bedroom. "And besides, Emma did it for me. We only just missed her."

"Perfect timing then." Louie didn't want to run into anyone or anything that could disrupt Heather's flow and whatever it was she'd planned.

Heather pushed Louie into a sitting position on her bed and took a step back. Louie leaned back on her hands, stretched her legs open, and relaxed, ready for the show. Heather began to slowly unbutton her blouse. Louie clenched her sex in response to the sight of Heather's deep cleavage in a black lace bra. She reached the last button and pulled the blouse from the waistband of her skirt, before taking it off and tossing it to the side. Louie swallowed. There was no way she could watch and not touch. She moved to get up but Heather held out her hand.

"Don't move."

Louie frowned and bit her lip. "You can't do *that*," Louie motioned toward Heather's discarded blouse, "and expect me to just sit here."

"Oh, Louie, that's exactly what I expect you to do."

Louie sighed and sank back onto Heather's bed. It was her own fault. Louie had told Heather that her taking control would really turn her on.

"Take off your shirt."

Louie didn't argue. She took the hem of her T-shirt and pulled it over her head slowly. So slowly. She threw it in the same direction as Heather's discarded blouse then leaned back, wanting to make sure her stomach looked as flat as possible.

"No bra?" Heather nodded toward Louie's naked chest.

Louie nibbled the inside of her cheek. Was she disappointed? "I kinda don't need one." Louie nudged her left breast with two fingers. "They don't tend to make minus A cup..."

Heather came closer and knelt between Louie's legs. She gripped Louie's hips tightly and fixed her mouth around the breast Louie had just dismissed. She flicked her tongue over it and nibbled it lightly. The buzz traveled straight to Louie's throbbing center, and she wrapped her hand in Heather's hair, desperate to touch her.

Heather broke away and took Louie's hand. "No, baby. Not yet."

Louie frowned. "This is painful."

"No, baby. This is pleasure."

Heather gently pushed her body against Louie's and pressed her to the bed. Her mouth found Louie's and she felt Heather's tongue searching for hers. She met it and allowed her in, turned on even more by her forcefulness. Heather unbuckled Louie's belt and pulled it from the loops. She lifted herself from Louie and smiled at her wickedly, holding the belt in her hands. Louie's breath caught. Heather's silent question was plain to see, and Louie nodded, eager to release all control to her. Heather grinned and Louie saw desire flame across her eyes as she wrapped the leather around Louie's left wrist, through her metal headboard, and back around Louie's right wrist. Louie swallowed hard and lifted her hips toward Heather's crotch. Heather placed her hand on Louie's stomach and pushed down gently.

"Patience, sweet Louie."

Heather unfastened Louie's jeans and she motioned for Louie to lift her ass off the bed. She pulled them off and they were swiftly followed by Louie's shorts. Heather's hands felt like a hundred flickers of heat across her body as she ran them all over her chest and stomach. She paused when she reached Louie's neat triangle of hair.

"Is this what you want?" asked Heather, her hand barely brushing Louie's body.

Louie ached in places she didn't think possible. "God, yes."

Heather bent down so that Louie could feel her breath on her lower lips. "Should I kiss you here?"

Heather's breath cooled and set her on fire at the same time. She strained at her bindings, grateful for their restriction but wanting to have her hands on Heather. She lifted her hips again and Heather's lips touched her and made her jump.

"You're so sensitive."

Louie drew a shallow breath. "Not usually. This is all you," she whispered. Louie slammed her head back into the pillow when Heather's tongue finally touched her. Heather pressed her mouth around Louie's rock solid clit and circled her tongue gently at first, but she seemed to grow more confident with each stroke, sucking and licking alternately. Louie caught hold of the headboard's bars and gripped hard as Heather's rhythm took hold and pushed her up toward her orgasm. Louie felt it building, like her whole body hummed with electricity. Heather pressed her hands onto Louie's hips, keeping her firmly in place. She wasn't going anywhere. Heather withdrew her hand and Louie felt Heather's fingers softly exploring the wetness she'd created. She barely broke rhythm as she slipped what felt like two fingers inside Louie. The extra stimulation caused Louie to drive her hips toward Heather's face, but Heather simply pushed her back down to the bed with her free hand.

Louie half-closed her eyes. She could feel almost nothing except where Heather's mouth and hands were. That's all she needed to feel. All the teasing, the heavy make-out session in Louie's truck—all of it was leading to this moment. That Louie had to wait another week made her need even more overwhelming. She ground her hips in sync with Heather's mouth and sank back into the bed with her eyes closed. So close. Heather must've felt Louie's desire building. She nibbled a little harder and drove her fingers even deeper. Louie cried out as Heather took her over the edge and she came in her mouth, her body convulsing beneath Heather's control.

Louie's whole body trembled and Heather traced her fingers along the hollow of Louie's hips, making her shudder with little aftershocks. Heather kissed Louie's inner thigh and looked up. There were no words that would do justice to the moment so Louie hoped her smile would convey her emotions.

"You don't think I'm done, do you?" Heather asked and smiled wickedly.

Louie shook her head. "I hope you're never done with me."

Heather pressed little kisses to Louie's stomach before she settled by her side. She reached up and tugged on Louie's hands gently.

"Still okay?"

Louie glanced at her shackled wrists. "As long as you don't leave me here on my own, I'll be fine."

Heather licked her upper lip before leaning down and taking Louie's nipple in her mouth again. She nibbled it just hard enough to make Louie jerk slightly. She worked her way up Louie's body, over her neck, and up to mouth. Heather sucked Louie's lip and kissed her hard. She broke away and Louie strained to follow her. Heather simply pressed her hand to Louie's chest, and she fell back to the bed, helpless...and loving every moment.

"I have no intention of leaving you *anywhere* on your own." Heather moved her hand firmly toward Louie's open legs.

Louie took a short breath when Heather's fingers slid over her clit and into the wetness she'd created. Heather pushed inside her, softly at first, as if unsure. Louie closed her eyes and sank into the pillow, eager for her to continue. "Please..." she murmured. "I want this. I want you."

Heather pressed her fingers deep and hard, and Louie gripped the leather of her belt as she cried out. The feeling of someone inside her was so unfamiliar and yet exactly what she craved. She opened her eyes to see Heather looking at her intently, perhaps needing reassurance, and Louie lifted her head. "Please kiss me."

Heather's steady rhythm continued as she leaned down and did as Louie asked. A hundred birds took flight beneath Louie's body as Heather's intense kiss took her beyond the physical connection of their sex and into something far more tender, far more intimate. She felt Heather's hand around the back of her neck and her body tingled in response as Heather raked her nails along Louie's hairline. The sensation traversed Louie's body into her core, and she lifted her ass toward Heather, wanting her to drive deeper.

Heather briefly separated her lips from Louie's. "What do you want?" she asked, and her eyes seemed to search Louie's expression for approval.

"Harder…" Louie's instruction sounded more like a plea. She was desperate for Heather's touch, for her kiss, for her everything. Heather looked shy as she smiled and complied with Louie's request. Louie lifted her ass off the bed and synched her thrusting hips to Heather's pace. The throbbing and pulsing of her pussy became all consuming. All sense of the rest of her body fell away, and all Louie could feel was Heather's mouth on hers and her fingers deep inside. Heather wrapped her fingers around Louie's hair and held her tight as Louie bucked her hips to meet Heather's force. The sense of freedom in the restriction and lack of control was entrancing, and Louie succumbed to Heather's power willingly. She felt her release nearing and focused on the beautiful woman taking her—all of her. The promise of love, acceptance, and desire swam in Heather's eyes, and Louie tumbled over the precipice of her orgasm into a warmth of love.

Louie shuddered and shook. The intensity of everything had taken her by surprise. Heather slowly withdrew before she reached up and released Louie's wrists. Louie enfolded Heather in her arms and kissed her.

"You're amazing," she whispered, still out of breath from her orgasms.

Heather smiled and looked up at her. "You are."

She held Heather tightly and they lay quietly. Louie didn't want to let go just yet. She felt the burn of tears well behind her eyes and blinked them away. Heather would think she was a total softie if she let her tears fall as well as her walls.

Louie kissed the top of Heather's head. "You want to fill me in on what's going on with you now that you've had your wicked way with me?"

Heather shifted so that she could see Louie's face. "The short version, sure. They offered me Donny's job, and all I could see was me getting too comfortable in the corporate closet. All I could hear was you saying that I should be true to myself." Heather traced her fingers over Louie's nipples. "I told her I couldn't take the job and I left."

Louie laughed gently. "Wow. So what happens now?"

Heather kissed Louie's shoulder. "I find investors and I start my label earlier than planned, with Gabe as my first signing if he'll come to me."

"I'm sure he would." Louie ran her hand across Heather's cheek. She wanted to share Heather's dream. An independent label focused on the artists traditional Nashville simply wasn't interested in. The "others." And with the royalties that would pour in from Savana's album, Louie's life was looking pretty much perfect.

"What if I invested and got you started? I could write songs for you as well as for Hawthorne." Louie looked up at the ceiling, glad that Heather couldn't see her face right now. "Would you share your dream with me?"

Heather bounced up and straddled Louie's stomach. The heat from her pussy almost drove her to forget what they were talking about.

"I would love that, Louie."

Louie scratched her head and tried to cover her face with her hand. The intense vulnerability of baring her heart was far more courageous than she'd ever had to be baring her body. She took a breath and decided to put it all out there. *Rip off the Band-Aid.* "And what happens with us?"

"I want to make our pieces fit, Louie. I want to put my life jigsaw together with you in it. What about you? What do *you* want?"

Louie smiled at Heather's play on the words Louie had used just over a week ago when she thought there was little hope of them ever being together.

"I want to fade into you. I want us to come alive in each other's lives, to be better together than we could ever be alone." Louie slipped her hand into Heather's hair and gently ran her fingers through it. "I want to be your world because I think you're going to be my everything."

Heather snuggled in a little tighter. "I want that too."

Louie smiled. "Our song will be the greatest love song I could ever write." She tracked her fingers over Heather's hips and tentatively parted Heather's legs. "*Now* can I touch you?"

THE END

About the Author

Robyn Nyx is an avid shutterbug and lover of all things fast and physical. Her writing often reflects both of those passions. She writes lesbian fiction when she isn't busy being the chief executive of a UK charity. She lives with her soul mate and fellow scribe, Brey Willows. They have no kids or kittens, which allows them to travel to exotic places at the drop of a hat for research. Robyn and Brey also run a community interest company helping marginalized groups to write and get their stories heard. She works hard to find writing time, when she's not being distracted by blue skies and motorbike rides. Get in touch and find out more at robynnyx.com.

Books Available from Bold Strokes Books

Emily's Art and Soul by Joy Argento. When Emily meets Andi Marino she thinks she's found a new best friend but Emily doesn't know that Andi is fast falling in love with her. Caught up in exploring her sexuality, will Emily see the only woman she needs is right in front of her? (978-1-63555-355-0)

Escape to Pleasure: Lesbian Travel Erotica edited by Sandy Lowe and Victoria Villasenor. Join these award-winning authors as they explore the sensual side of erotic lesbian travel. (978-1-63555-339-0)

Music City Dreamers by Robyn Nyx. Music can bring lovers together. In Music City, it can tear them apart. (978-1-63555-207-2)

Ordinary is Perfect by D. Jackson Leigh. Atlanta marketing superstar Autumn Swan's life derails when she inherits a country home, a child, and a very interesting neighbor. (978-1-63555-280-5)

Royal Court by Jenny Frame. When royal dresser Holly Weaver's passionate personality begins to melt Royal Marine Captain Quincy's icy heart, will Holly be ready for what she exposes beneath? (978-1-63555-290-4)

Strings Attached by Holly Stratimore. Success. Riches. Music. Passion. It's a life most can only dream of, but stardom comes at a cost. (978-1-63555-347-5)

The Ashford Place by Jean Copeland. When Isabelle Ashford inherits an old house in small-town Connecticut, family secrets, a shocking discovery, and an unexpected romance complicate her plan for a fast profit and a temporary stay. (978-1-63555-316-1)

Treason by Gun Brooke. Zoem Malderyn's existence is a deadly threat to everyone on Gemocon and Commander Neenja KahSandra must find a way to save the woman she loves from having to commit the ultimate sacrifice. (978-1-63555-244-7)

A Wish Upon a Star by Jeannie Levig. Erica Cooper has learned to depend on only herself, but when her new neighbor, Leslie Raymond, befriends Erica's special needs daughter, the walls protecting her heart threaten to crumble. (978-1-63555-274-4)

Answering the Call by Ali Vali. Detective Sept Savoie returns to the streets of New Orleans, as do the dead bodies from ritualistic killings, and she does everything in her power to bring them to justice while trying to keep her partner, Keegan Blanchard, safe. (978-1-63555-050-4)

Breaking Down Her Walls by Erin Zak. Could a love worth staying for be the key to breaking down Julia Finch's walls? (978-1-63555-369-7)

Exit Plans for Teenage Freaks by 'Nathan Burgoine. Cole always has a plan—especially for escaping his small-town reputation as "that kid who was kidnapped when he was four"—but when he teleports to a museum, it's time to face facts: it's possible he's a total freak after all. (978-1-63555-098-6)

Friends Without Benefits by Dena Blake. When Dex Putman gets the woman she thought she always wanted, she soon wonders if it's really love after all. (978-1-63555-349-9)

Invalid Evidence by Stevie Mikayne. Private Investigator Jil Kidd is called away to investigate a possible killer whale, just when her partner Jess needs her most. (978-1-63555-307-9)

Pursuit of Happiness by Carsen Taite. When attorney Stevie Palmer's client reveals a scandal that could derail Senator Meredith

Mitchell's presidential bid, their chance at love may be collateral damage. (978-1-63555-044-3)

Seascape by Karis Walsh. Marine biologist Tess Hansen returns to Washington's isolated northern coast where she struggles to adjust to small-town living while courting an endowment for her orca research center from Brittany James. (978-1-63555-079-5)

Second in Command by VK Powell. Jazz Perry's life is disrupted and her career jeopardized when she becomes personally involved with the case of an abandoned child and the child's competent but strict social worker, Emory Blake. (978-1-63555-185-3)

Taking Chances by Erin McKenzie. When Valerie Cruz and Paige Wellington clash over what's in the best interest of the children in Valerie's care, the children may be the ones who teach them it's worth taking chances for love. (978-1-63555-209-6)

All of Me by Emily Smith. When chief surgical resident Galen Burgess meets her new intern, Rowan Duncan, she may finally discover that doing what you've always done will only give you what you've always had. (978-1-63555-321-5)

As the Crow Flies by Karen F. Williams. Romance seems to be blooming all around, but problems arise when a restless ghost emerges from the ether to roam the dark corners of this haunting tale. (978-1-63555-285-0)

Both Ways by Ileandra Young. SPEAR agent Danika Karson races to protect the city from a supernatural threat and must rely on the woman she's trained to despise: Rayne, an achingly beautiful vampire. (978-1-63555-298-0)

Calendar Girl by Georgia Beers. Forced to work together, Addison Fairchild and Kate Cooper discover that opposites really do attract. (978-1-63555-333-8)

Lovebirds by Lisa Moreau. Two women from different worlds collide in a small California mountain town, each with a mission that doesn't include falling in love. (978-1-63555-213-3)

Media Darling by Fiona Riley. Can Hollywood bad girl Emerson and reluctant celebrity gossip reporter Hayley work together to make each other's dreams come true? Or will Emerson's secrets ruin not one career, but two? (978-1-63555-278-2)

Stroke of Fate by Renee Roman. Can Sean Moore live up to her reputation and save Jade Rivers from the stalker determined to end Jade's career and, ultimately, her life? (978-1-63555-62-4)

The Rise of the Resistance by Jackie D. The soul of America has been lost for almost a century. A few people may be the difference between a phoenix rising to save the masses or permanent destruction. (978-1-63555-259-1)

The Sex Therapist Next Door by Meghan O'Brien. At the intersection of sex and intimacy, anything is possible. Even love. (978-1-63555-296-6)

Unexpected Lightning by Cass Sellars. Lightning strikes once more when Sydney and Parker fight a dangerous stranger who threatens the peace they both desperately want. (978-1-63555-276-8)

Unforgettable by Elle Spencer. When one night changes a lifetime… Two romance novellas from best-selling author Elle Spencer. (978-1-63555-429-8)

Against All Odds by Kris Bryant, Maggie Cummings, M. Ullrich. Peyton and Tory escaped death once, but will they survive when Bradley's determined to make his kill rate one hundred percent? (978-1-63555-193-8)

Autumn's Light by Aurora Rey. Casual hookups aren't supposed to include romantic dinners and meeting the family. Can Mat Pero see beyond the heartbreak that led her to keep her worlds so separate, and will Graham Connor be waiting if she does? (978-1-63555-272-0)

Breaking the Rules by Larkin Rose. When Virginia and Carmen are thrown together by an embarrassing mistake they find out their stubborn determination isn't so heroic after all. (978-1-63555-261-4)

Broad Awakening by Mickey Brent. In the sequel to *Underwater Vibes*, Hélène and Sylvie find ruts in their road to eternal bliss. (978-1-63555-270-6)

Broken Vows by MJ Williamz. Sister Mary Margaret must reconcile her divided heart or risk losing a love that just might be heaven sent. (978-1-63555-022-1)

Flesh and Gold by Ann Aptaker. Havana, 1952, where art thief and smuggler Cantor Gold dodges gangland bullets and mobsters' schemes while she searches Havana's steamy Red Light district for her kidnapped love. (978-1-63555-153-2)

Isle of Broken Years by Jane Fletcher. Spanish noblewoman Catalina de Valasco is in peril, even before the pirates holding her for ransom sail into seas destined to become known as the Bermuda Triangle. (978-1-63555-175-4)

Love Like This by Melissa Brayden. Hadley Cooper and Spencer Adair set out to take the fashion world by storm. If only they knew their hearts were about to be taken. (978-1-63555-018-4)

Secrets On the Clock by Nicole Disney. Jenna and Danielle love their jobs helping endangered children, but that might not be enough to stop them from breaking the rules by falling in love. (978-1-63555-292-8)

Unexpected Partners by Michelle Larkin. Dr. Chloe Maddox tries desperately to deny her attraction for Detective Dana Blake as they flee from a serial killer who's hunting them both. (978-1-63555-203-4)

A Fighting Chance by T. L. Hayes. Will Lou be able to come to terms with her past to give love a fighting chance? (978-1-63555-257-7)

Chosen by Brey Willows. When the choice is adapt or die, can love save us all? (978-1-63555-110-5)

Death Checks In by David S. Pederson. Despite Heath's promises to Alan to not get involved, Heath can't resist investigating a shopkeeper's murder in Chicago, which dashes their plans for a romantic weekend getaway. (978-1-63555-329-1)

Gnarled Hollow by Charlotte Greene. After they are invited to study a secluded nineteenth-century estate, a former English professor and a group of historians discover that they will have to fight against the unknown if they have any hope of staying alive. (978-1-63555-235-5)

Jacob's Grace by C.P. Rowlands. Captain Tag Becket wants to keep her head down and her past behind her, but her feelings for AJ's second-in-command, Grace Fields, makes keeping secrets next to impossible. (978-1-63555-187-7)

On the Fly by PJ Trebelhorn. Hockey player Courtney Abbott is content with her solitary life until visiting concert violinist Lana Caruso makes her second-guess everything she always thought she wanted. (978-1-63555-255-3)

Passionate Rivals by Radclyffe. Professional rivalry and long-simmering passions create a combustible combination when Emmett McCabe and Sydney Stevens are forced to work together, especially when past attractions won't stay buried. (978-1-63555-231-7)

Proxima Five by Missouri Vaun. When geologist Leah Warren crash-lands on a preindustrial planet and is claimed by its tyrant, Tiago, will clan warrior Keegan's love for Leah give her the strength to defeat him? (978-1-63555-122-8)

Racing Hearts by Dena Blake. When you cross a hot-tempered race car mechanic with a reckless cop, the result can only be spontaneous combustion. (978-1-63555-251-5)

Shadowboxer by Jessica L. Webb. Jordan McAddie is prepared to keep her street kids safe from a dangerous underground protest group, but she isn't prepared for her first love to walk back into her life. (978-1-63555-267-6)

The Tattered Lands by Barbara Ann Wright. As Vandra and Lilani strive to make peace, they slowly fall in love. With mistrust and murder surrounding them, only their faith in each other can keep their plan to save the world from falling apart. (978-1-63555-108-2)